The Chronicles of Etheria:
Book 1

A LEGEND OF LIGHT & SHADOW

Jillian A Wiley

To those who hide their demons behind a wall—who conceal their
pain with a smile.
I see the flames burning in your eyes.

Act I

The Fates have sung their song.

CHAPTER 1

" **J** *en...e..vieve.."* the chilling whisper caressed her mind as a tendril of darkness reached for her. *"We've been looking for you."*

Jenevieve shot up with a tremendous gasp, her skin covered in a thin layer of cold sweat.

She clutched her heaving chest and tried to slow her erratic heartbeat, her eyes darting around her bedroom as the rasping voice vanished.

Jen groaned and rubbed her temples.

She was safe in her home; the dark cave and menacing figures only existed in the fading recesses of the nightmare. She pulled back her soft, burgundy blanket and flung her legs over the bedside just as morning light peeked through her window.

She ran her hand over her long, golden hair as she walked to the wash bowl in the corner.

Maybe the cold water would clear her head.

She dabbed her face with a soft towel and glanced into the mirror above the bowl.

"Now, my faithful Knight of Eseer, the realm is shifting towards darkness, and light will make itself known—it cannot help itself..."

Jen dropped the towel and spun around, searching her room for the source of the voice.

Still nothing.

She snatched the towel from the floor and tossed it in the washbowl before yanking off her nightdress. She grabbed a deep green dress from the rack by her bedroom door and coaxed it over her head, smoothing it out as her eye momentarily snagged on the ivory linen gown still hanging—the one she'll have to don later that day.

She looked at herself in the mirror, pinching her cheeks to return some color to her face. Her fingers deftly braided two plaits and pinned them together at the back of her head, the rest of her hair flowing down her back.

The wooden floors creaked beneath her feet as she padded towards the window, the golden halo surrounding her hazel eyes sparkling in the morning sun.

Jen had always appreciated the unique color of her eyes; ripples of green and brown merging together in a striking hazel hue, a ring of scorched earth circling her pupil.

"Soon you will be consumed by darkness, the light will disappear. It's only a matter of time."

Jen whirled around.

"Durche yahvak."

She stumbled into the corner of her wooden dresser, the harsh, foreign words scraping against her skull. She winced and rubbed her hip.

I'm hearing voices. Great.

Jen jolted at the sudden scuffing of chairs and exasperating groans coming from outside her door.

Get a hold of yourself.

She shook the tension from her arms and exhaled sharply, then forced a smile and entered the kitchen.

Her youngest sister, Darya, sat at the kitchen table frantically sewing a gown the color of the spring sky. Beads of sweat formed at her hairline where strands of bright blonde hair had fallen from her braided bun.

Their younger brother, Jamie, sat beside her, gnawing on a piece of bread, watching with amusement as the panic took over Darya's entire body.

Jen's mother, Maelia, stood at the sink washing dishes. She turned and her emerald-green eyes sparkled with her warm smile.

"Morning, Mama," Jen said, attempting to keep her voice even as she approached. Maelia glanced at her out of the corner of her eye and passed her a bowl to dry.

"Did you sleep well, darling?" she asked. Jen nodded, although it sounded like her mother sensed her lie.

"Is Rhea—?" Jen asked.

The sound of her name summoned her other sister into the room, sauntering about in her nightdress. Jen smirked and moved to embrace her, receiving an awkward squeeze in return.

Rhea had never been one for physical affection, even when they were children. They were practically raised as twins, born two years apart. Their mother would dress them up in matching outfits and braid their hair before they took off into the meadows to chase butterflies.

Whilst Jen grew into music and gardening and teaching, Rhea found any excuse to roughhouse with the boys in the village—the brown-haired, tough antithesis to her golden hair and soft heart.

"Are you ready?" Jen asked, slumping into a chair at the table. Rhea sat down beside her and grabbed a piece of bread, mindlessly spreading jam on it.

"Ready for what?" she answered, her eyes darting to their mother for a reaction.

Maelia didn't disappoint—dropping a plate into the sink with a *splash*. She spun around, the front of her jade, cotton dress now soaked.

"Rhea! Can you at least *pretend* today is important?" their mother scolded, snatching a towel to pat herself dry. The girls laughed at the burst of outrage.

"Mama, relax, I'm kidding—sort of," Rhea teased as she punched Jamie in the shoulder. "I don't particularly care for proclaiming my love in front of a huge crowd of people." She leaned her head on Jen's shoulder and sighed. "But the time for objecting has passed and has also been *ignored*."

Darya stopped sewing and narrowed her baby blue eyes.

"You bet it's too late; I've been working on your dress all night. You just *had* to practice dancing in it." She lifted the dress off the table. "Look at this, you put so many holes in it. How did you even manage that?" she huffed.

Finding things to stress out about was Darya's specialty, as was their mother's. Five years younger than Jen and with a flair for the dramatic, the running joke between the two older sisters was that they didn't remember much of Darya as a child, but the memory of her banshee screams still made their ears want to bleed.

Luckily, as she grew older, she traded in the screaming for grumpy mutterings and pointed scowls.

"Long dresses are hard to move in; you're lucky a few holes are the only issue with it," Rhea retorted.

Jen smirked as she stood and grabbed her worn brown boots from the growing pile by the front door. She bent down to lace them up and was greeted with a second pair of feet in front of her own.

She glanced up to find her brother towering over her, his sandy-blonde hair hanging over blue eyes that matched Darya's.

Jen was eleven when he was born, and from the start he was always too kind for this world, too gentle. Her sweet Jamie.

None of them knew how he turned out that way, living in a house full of women and having no male role model to speak of. He could have turned out a complete jackass and Jen would have given him a pass.

"Where are *you* going?" Jamie asked, playfully tousling her hair before walking back towards the sink.

Jen scowled and attempted to fix it. "I have wedding errands to take care of; *someone* has to be excited about today," she jabbed at Rhea.

"Everyone is aware that I love him, right?" she said, throwing up her hands in defeat. "I feel like that's getting lost under all the pomp."

"And here I thought you'd been with him for so long because you *hated* him." Jen rolled her eyes. "Thanks for clearing that up."

Rhea snorted a laugh as Jen walked out the door and hurried down the stone walkway to the front gate.

"Jen?"

She turned to find Maelia following her down the path. Her mother had always moved with effortless grace, often keeping to herself and her family, but her quiet beauty made it impossible not to notice her.

"Are you alright?" she asked, caressing her daughter's cheek. "You seem…troubled."

My mother's way of saying I look rough.

"Just a bad dream Mama, that's all," she said.

"You were pale when you came into the kitchen," Maelia pried.

Probably because I'm hearing voices.

"It's nothing," Jen sighed, waving her hand at nothing.

But then her mother lifted a brow—a sign that she was deciding whether Jen was lying, something she'd done since her childhood.

And she was always, annoyingly, accurate.

Jen sighed; she knew she was not going to let this go.

There were two voices." She looked down at her feet. "One of them— well—he knew my name." Something flickered over Maelia's expression, but it was gone in an instant.

"One wore a crown, and there were some kind of tattoos on the other—but I couldn't make them out…vines, maybe? And then there was this… snake…" she finished in a whisper, the memory of a serpent made of thick shadows coiling its way up her body rendering her silent.

Jen glanced at her mother and forced a small smile.

"It was just—not like any dream I've had before," she said, trying to force a reassuring tone.

Maelia tucked a strand of hair behind Jen's ear.

"I'm sorry, darling."

 Something in the way her mother looked at her gave Jen pause.

Why is she apologizing for a bad dream?

She stepped back towards the gate. "I should go," she said awkwardly. "I still have to stop by the school before I meet Emelie." Jen glanced back at Maelia. "Do we need anything else?"

The odd look in her mother's eyes had disappeared. "Nothing else. Just enough flowers for the crowns, and that *arch*." She looked past Jenevieve to the meadow across from their cottage. "Tell Damien it doesn't have to be so...*elaborate*," she said, walking back towards the house.

Jen turned around to an extravagant archway out in the middle of the pasture. The corner of her lip pulled up and she wandered over to it.

The sun showed overhead, a few clouds dotted the sky, and a gentle breeze blew through her wavy hair as she closed in on the man next to the arch. She came up behind him and sauntered past to lean on the opposing side.

"My mother thinks this thing is *ridiculous*," she said.

"I think you're a liar; this is a work of art," he said as he fastened a metal supporting rod between the two vertical arched pieces.

"Is that what you've been telling yourself all morning?"

He chuckled. "Amongst other things, *Bug*."

Damien stood a foot taller than her, with the strong shoulders and rough hands of a blacksmith. His piercing blue eyes held the crystal-clear hue of a winter sky, and his cheekbones lifted so high that when he smiled it consumed his entire face.

Ten years ago, Jen had fallen hopelessly and irrevocably in love with him after a chance meeting beneath the two oak trees further out in the meadow.

They were only twenty at the time, but the devotion they felt towards each other had utterly consumed them both.

As soon as he met her family, Damien took it upon himself to look after them; a family of traumatized women and a sad little boy. He didn't even think twice about it, already protector of his own fatherless family; a sweet-natured mother and a beautiful older sister.

And so, Damien built a wedding arch for Rhea as if she were his own sister—he wouldn't let anyone else near it.

He stepped away from the arch to examine his work.

"Wait, does Maelia really think it's too much?" Damien said uncomfortably, running a hand through his raven locks. He had always kept the sides shorter, with a slightly longer mess on top.

Jen smiled kindly and stepped beside him.

"It's incredible, Sparky, thank you. Rhea will love it too, if we can get her out here," Jen said as she squeezed his arm. Her gaze shifted down to the sheathed sword leaning against the arch.

She quirked a brow. "Why do you insist on lugging that thing around everywhere?"

Damien followed her gaze. He stopped what he was doing and picked up the sword, unsheathing it halfway.

As the village blacksmith, he forged all sorts of things in his shop; hinges, horseshoes, tools. But what Damien truly loved creating were swords.

Jen would argue he was borderline obsessed.

There were dozens upon dozens of stunning blades lining the back wall of his shop with elaborate pommels so pristine they formed a long, lethal mirror of sleek metal.

Of course, they all went unused. There wasn't any use for them in their village—or any of the surrounding ones either.

The sword he was currently holding was the first one he ever made—a razor-sharp, silver blade with a black hilt and a pommel engraved with a small ladybug.

"It's here to defend my precious arch," he chuckled as the metal gleamed in the sunlight.

"From what? A brazen squirrel?"

Damien slid the blade back into its leather sheath and looked at her very seriously. "They grow bold this time of year."

Jen stifled a laugh as Damien returned the sword to its spot on the ground.

"I feel much safer, thank you." She glanced up at the arch, but then her gaze drifted to a pair of large oak trees atop a hill further in the meadow.

The lover's trees.

A small, nostalgic smile tugged at Jen's lips.

"Jen…Jenevieve…hello?" Damien said, waving his hand in front of her face. She scoffed and smacked his hand away.

"What? Were you imagining *us* under the arch?" Damien teased, nudging her with his shoulder. Jen shook her head. At one point in their complicated history, she actually *did* imagine that. But life had made other plans for them.

Over the years, the weight of their own inner demons had led to some truly excruciating moments of heartache and pain. At times, love and hate became almost interchangeable; two sides of a very thin coin.

But, somehow, they had always managed to find their way back to one another, whether that was as friends, lovers, or some variation of the two.

And no matter what, Damien never faltered in showing up for Jen when she needed him most.

Never.

"You see *right* through me, don't you?" she said sarcastically. She took a few steps towards the dirt road that led to the village.

"One day, huh, Bug?" Damien said as he resumed working on the arch.

"Sure, Sparky, one day," Jen answered. She glanced back at him, but her eyes were drawn past the hill with the lover's trees to the Forest of Bri that loomed at the edge of the village.

She squinted.

Something was moving.

Jen took a cautious step towards it, her eyes straining as she tried to make out what she was seeing.

She sucked in a breath.

A serpentine shadow slithered along the forest edge.

"It's too late, Jenevieve. Welcome to the darkness."

Jen's heart shuddered as the shadow disappeared into the trees.

Annnnd now I'm hallucinating. Fantastic.

"You okay?" Damien asked, his thick brows furrowed.

Jen squeezed her eyes shut, and when she opened them, the shadow had disappeared. She glanced back at Damien, concealing her apprehension behind a smile. "I'm fine," she said.

"Alright..." he said slowly. She continued onto the dirt road leading to the center of town.

"Tell William I say hello," he called after her. Jen tossed a hand up in acknowledgment before turning back towards the road.

She walked on, passing by endless pastures dotted with small herds of cattle and sheep and an array of small but charming cottages, an occasional neighbor appearing on the front porch to say hello. Most of them had known her since she was small.

Her hand brushed against the tall grass that collected at the fence posts lining the path. The still and solitary moment calmed her.

It was just a dream.

The fields made way for store fronts as Jen entered the village. The dirt road that led her from the countryside turned to cobblestone where Damien's empty blacksmith shop stood, alongside the carpenter's workshop brimming with wooden planks of varied shapes and sizes. She waved to the proprietor's wife—their young son one of her students.

The weekend market was buzzing as shop owners and patrons filed in for the day. The smell of salted caramels and fresh baked bread enveloped her as she crossed through the center of the square towards the school.

A family gathered around the baker's stand nestled by the dressmaker in the corner of the square. One of the children, not yet three, spotted Jen and came running over. The little girl beamed up at her and opened her hand to reveal a small pastry.

"Miss, I got this for you," she said proudly. A smile spread across Jenevieve's face, and she gratefully took the pastry.

"Lucy." Jen knelt in front of the little girl. "I adore these, how did you know?" She leaned in close. "Are you magic?" she whispered, looking at Lucy with wonder.

Lucy clapped her hands over her mouth and giggled through her fingers. "You're so silly, Miss," she squeaked. "There's no such thing!"

Jen stood just as Lucy's father approached. He gave Jen an apologetic smile, picking up his daughter and placing her on his shoulders.

"Let's not bother Miss Jenevieve on her day off, sweetheart," he said.

Jen grinned at the young father, and then up at Lucy. "You could never be a bother, Lucy." She gave her a conspiratorial wink and lifted the pastry in her hand. "Especially when you're sharing your treats with me."

Lucy shrieked with laughter, causing her father to stumble beneath her as he turned back towards the rest of their family. Jen pressed her lips together, suppressing her own laugh before she walked away, nibbling on the pastry and hopping over small puddles that accumulated in the sunken cobblestones.

She turned up the street and a few paces later the gated school yard came into view, mostly empty on the weekend.

Two buildings lined the yard; both painted in a shade of misty gray to hide their age. Atop the walls sat a weathered, black thatched roof that served as a perch for the occasional wayward bird.

Jen walked across the yard and up the two small steps that led to her classroom. She stepped inside to an embrace of warmth from the sunny yellow walls she and Damien painted four years ago.

A pile of hand strung banners, small crowns of ivy, and a more intricate ivy crown laced with blue ribbon to match Rhea's gown awaited on her wooden desk across the room. Finger paintings and colorful handprints of her tiny learners adorned the walls and a simple blackboard stood in front of a colorful woven rug.

In the back corner of the room was her piano, gifted to her by Missus Baelle, the owner of the flower shop in town.

Although it was nothing fancy, just a simple upright piano of dark oak that was chipped in a few places, it was one of Jen's most prized possessions.

She had always been drawn to music, even as a small child, yet no one else in her family had ever shown any interest in it.

If anything, her mother had tried to steer her away from it—which is why the piano lived at the school, where she could lose herself in the cathartic release of a beautiful melody when her mind became too noisy.

She retrieved a satchel from the coatrack and began packing up the banners and crowns. Her mind wandered aimlessly for a moment, but then, as if being pulled by a river's current, her unfocused thoughts morphed into a clear vision.

The side of a limestone mountain... a hidden path—and the low whisper of a woman's voice:

"The time will come when the hubris of good and the shadow of evil will bring forth a power long thought lost."

The voice was cut short by a serpentine shadow slithering across her mind.

She gasped and fell to the floor, closing her eyes tight, clutching her head as if to squeeze the image from her thoughts.

In a flash, it faded. She peered up and her eyes darted around the room; no shadows, no whispering voices.

This is getting ridiculous.

Nightmares were, unfortunately, a regular occurrence, but they *never* haunted her the entirety of the next day. She stood up and pressed her hands against the desk, her body trembling, unable to process the visions and the voices.

Jen took a few deep breaths through her nose, forcing her lungs to fill to capacity before exhaling slowly.

Her attempt to quiet her mind was interrupted by a thunderous voice coming from the other room. She immediately knew who it was and let out a heavy sigh before picking up her satchel and setting off through the archways connecting to the main school building.

The voice grew louder as she turned into the room and leaned in the doorway to watch. She'd forgotten this was happening today, as it wasn't a usual occurrence to hold a class on the weekend, but his students had all but demanded it.

William paced excitedly at the front of the room, his hands sweeping through the air, punctuating his words with a contagious energy that had his students leaning forward in their seats.

His kind brown eyes sparkled with intrigue as he continued his lesson in his favorite subject; myths and legends.

"You see, a thousand years ago, legend says that Heltior committed a crime so dark, so evil that it shattered the laws of nature. To restore balance, he was cast out by the Council of Suran."

A small hand raised tentatively.

"Gregory?" William asked.

"Sir, what is the Council of Suran?"

"Excellent question! It was comprised of powerful men, women, and magical beings, whose purpose was to maintain peace and balance throughout the realm," he answered. William looked up and locked eyes with Jenevieve, who gave a small wave and gestured for him to continue.

"The council exiled him to a distant land where he could do no more harm."

There was a moment of silence, and then Gregory spoke again. "Was that it? Was he gone *forever*?"

William rubbed his beard.

"No, Gregory, he was not. Heltior returned, and upon discovering the Forest of Bri, he became enraged" he explained. A hush fell over the room. "In a fit of insanity, he tracked down and slaughtered every member of the council. One. By. One. Plunging the realm into utter chaos." He crouched low for effect.

"After the destruction of the council, he disappeared. It is believed he spent five hundred years learning every manner of dark magic, and from that, amassed an army of creatures more terrifying than you can imagine."

His class sat stunned for a moment before erupting into a frenzy of questions and commentary.

"What creatures?" "What was the crime?" "He tracked them all down?" "He SLAUGHTERED them?"

"That's all for today!" William shouted over the excitement. "We will plan our next class in the coming weeks, where we will discuss the differences between mages and druids!"

Groans of disappointment filled the room while the students gathered their belongings and filed out. Jen walked down the center aisle as William packed up his books and packets of parchment.

"Jen!" he exclaimed, dropping his books on the desk. He bounded over to her and wrapped her in a crushing embrace.

"Great class, William—" she grunted, tapping his arm to signal her lack of oxygen. He released her quickly.

"You seemed pretty entranced as well, *Miss Jenevieve*," he mused, running his hand through his short brown hair.

"It almost sounded like you *believed* those legends," Jen said as she looked around the room.

The legends and myths he taught were stories passed down for centuries, all Nimeans had grown up hearing them, but no one knew how to tell them quite like William.

"It's all in the delivery—" William trailed off.

Jen looked over and found him staring out the window that faced the street behind the school. She snuck behind him to peer over his shoulder and saw what, or rather, *who* he was looking at.

"Of course," Jen teased. William was staring at a girl with a curly mane of wild crimson hair, and blue eyes the hue of a clear lake. She carried a small white puppy in her arms, laughing in the company of her mother and sister.

"You know, she'll be at the wedding," Jen said, nudging William with her shoulder. He cleared his throat and turned back to his desk.

"That's good. I'm sure she'll have a good time…you know…um…because she's so…you know…um…" William sputtered while he rustled through his pile of parchment.

Jen arched a brow.

"Just ask her to dance, what's the harm?" she said.

"It depends on how much wine I've had, and if that wine makes me brave or makes me an *idiot*," he shrugged.

Jen patted him on the back.

"Don't worry, I'll keep an eye on you," she said.

She walked towards the door to the school yard, but she stopped when her hand clasped the doorknob. Jen bit her lip, something from her nightmare nagged at her.

So much for pretending it didn't happen.

"William?" she asked nervously.

"Hmm?" he grunted while he finished packing up his bag. Jen hesitated, but before she could stop herself, it came tumbling out of her.

"Have you read anything about… a Knight of Eseer?" she asked.

William dropped his books on the ground and fumbled after them.

That reaction was reassuring.

"Where—where did you hear that?" he asked nervously. His jumpy reaction made her immediately regret bringing it up. Now she would have to explain.

"I had a dream last night…well more like a nightmare," she started. William's eyes flickered to one of the books on the ground. He picked it up and began flipping through the pages.

"Someone was addressed by that name," she said quietly. Jen had been actively trying to keep it from her thoughts but explaining it to William brought back the terrifying images and made her sick to her stomach.

"That's some dark stuff, Jen," William said slowly. He stopped on a page of his book and turned it towards Jen. "According to legend, the Knights of Eseer were once people, but Heltior consumed their souls for power and left only darkness within them," he explained.

So, nothing too terrifying—just devoured souls.

"The Knight had tattoos on his arms…with some kind of symbol…I don't know. It was just a *dream*," Jen reassured her friend.

There had not been any magic in Nimea for over a thousand years, and even the legends and lore that surrounded that time were approached as mere rumors—there was never any proof.

William's eyes widened as he turned a few pages back. He stared straight at her and pointed down at the symbol.

"Was it *this*?" he asked firmly. Jen's eyes flickered down, and to her horror, saw the symbol from her dream: a rounded trident, with a large eye where the three prongs met the haft. When her eyes widened in recognition, William quickly closed the book.

"You…you probably overheard one of my lessons from last week," he said, putting the remaining books in his satchel. Jenevieve could see the look on his face—he was nervous.

The urge to leave had her crawling out of her skin. She had no desire to think about this anymore, and so she strode to the door.

"I'll see you this evening?" she asked.

He nodded.

She walked out into the schoolyard, unaware of William watching her go, his face contorted with concern.

CHAPTER 2

The weekend market emptied out as the afternoon wore on. The shopkeepers packed up what goods they didn't sell, and families huddled together on benches in the middle of the square taking inventory of their purchases.

Jen looked to the southern corner of the square at an enchanting assemblage of the flower shop's colorful blooms. Rows of large pots full of daisies and sunflowers, hanging wicker baskets of lobelias and petunias, and bouquets of white roses gave off a sweet aroma.

As she approached the shop, a dark-blue dress flurried across her line of sight, speeding around the various crates of flowers and plants.

Emelie bumped her head on one of the hanging baskets and wildly gestured behind Missus Baelle, whose face held a perpetual scowl, as she wove through the tiered aisles of flowers toward the counter at the back of the store.

Jen chuckled to herself and hastened to the entryway of the open-air shop. She waved her hand, but Emelie was laser focused.

"Em—Em—Emelie," Jen said, attempting to follow her. Emelie was moving so erratically that when she turned around in a rush she knocked into Jen and dropped her flowers on the ground.

"Jen! I'm so sorry," Emelie giggled, stooping down to pick up the flowers. Emelie's dark brown hair draped over her face, covering her chocolate brown eyes.

She was one of the oldest children in a large family, and usually possessed a patient and kind nature, but, at the moment, that patience was nowhere to be found.

"I got here a while ago and picked out some flowers for those ivy crowns you made and look!" she said as she picked up the remaining flowers from the ground. "I found these big sunflowers and daisies for the arch." Emelie shoved a massive blossom into Jen's hand.

"I've been trying to haggle a good price out of Missus Baelle, but she's a stubborn old mule if I've ever seen one," she said, side-eyeing the old woman.

Missus Baelle released an exasperated sigh and continued pruning, rather aggressively, a bouquet of hydrangeas.

"Ah, so that's why you were accosting the poor thing," Jen teased. She examined the giant sunflower in her hand—beautiful, but not too sensational, which would work favorably with her sister.

"These are perfect Em," Jen said gratefully. She walked over to Missus Baelle, and when the old woman saw her approach, her expression softened.

Missus Baelle was cross with everyone else in the village but, for some reason, had seemed to take a liking to Jen. Not only had she gifted the piano to Jen's classroom, but she regularly saw to it that it was properly tuned.

The kind woman placed her hand on Jen's wrist and gave her an affectionate squeeze. "The tuner will be there tomorrow to fix that pesky D."

"You're too kind." Jen squeezed her hand in return.

Missus Baelle glanced behind her, and her brows knitted together. "Just with you, dear." She jutted her chin, and when Jen turned around, Emelie had traipsed over to the herbs, scouring over the aromatic greenery.

Jen walked up beside her friend. "What are you looking for?" She idly twirled the flower in her hand.

"I'm just looking for—aha!" Emelie exclaimed as she plucked a large handful of some kind of plant.

"What do you need that for?" Jenevieve asked, eyeing the odd flora.

"This is milk thistle, it's a useful remedy after a night of…*merriment*," Emelie bemused.

She means the whole village will likely be drunk in a field later.

Emelie was a skilled healer in Nimea, and she was saving up to open an apothecary of her own. For now, she worked from her medicinal bag, filled with homemade ointments and herbal treatments, and made home visits to those who called on her.

She paid Missus Baelle and tossed the bundle of purple flowers in her bag, linking arms with Jen as they left the shop.

"You'll be visiting lots of homes tomorrow, mine most likely included," Jen whispered. Emelie snorted a laugh.

The pair headed back down the road towards the countryside. As they neared the end of the cobblestone, they passed by the kennel; a long wooden building with a thatched roof resembling a stable, but instead of horses, it housed dozens of dogs.

A young woman with a mane of crimson curls emerged through a gate leading to the large, fenced-in yard, a little white dog nestled in her arms.

Jen pulled Emelie closer.

"That's Leeyna," she whispered. They slowed their pace for a better look. "William is *completely* enamored," she continued.

Leeyna placed the tiny dog in the grass, and it took off to join the others playing nearby. She glanced up at Jen and gave her a friendly wave.

"Will we see you at the wedding later?" Jen called out as she waved back.

"I'm just about to get ready!" Leeyna answered as she started walking back towards the main building.

"Save a dance for William!" Emelie blurted out. Jen smacked her arm and she let out a small yelp. Leeyna turned a deep shade of rouge.

"Don't mind her, she's been sniffing flowers for the last hour," Jen said, shooting Emelie a pointed look as they hurried down the road.

The quiet charm of the countryside shimmered with new energy as the excitement of the upcoming wedding danced through the air. Jen's neighbors changed into festive garb, and some of them sat on their front porches pinning flowers in each other's hair.

Jen looked out at the pasture across from her cottage. Damien was all but finished with the arch, but her gaze went beyond him and passed the lover's trees to the Forest of Bri.

The never-ending wood had always existed, but Jen never paid much attention to it. The first league into the forest was flushed with the golden light from the sun streaming through the trees, with deer and rabbits for hunting and a lush river for drinking water.

Beyond that, the forest grew dark and gnarled, making it completely impassable. Those who tried to venture into the entanglement always returned fruitless—or not at all.

It was deemed dangerous, and so none of the inhabitants in any of the Nimean villages attempted to journey past the first league.

Jen squinted at said tree line, and for a moment, she could have sworn she saw something moving within the trees.

Probably just a deer—or a shadowy demon.

Emelie noticed Jen's gaze, but instead of looking towards the forest, she saw Damien in the distance. She raised one of her eyebrows.

"So, you want to tell me what's going on there this time?" she asked, jutting her chin toward Damien. Jen's head snapped back.

"What are you talking about?"

Emelie rolled her eyes so dramatically Jen thought they may get stuck in the back of her head.

"Don't play coy with me, *Jenevieve*," she said sarcastically as they reached the front gate. "He's out there in a field building a freaking arch for your sister's wedding."

"I'm aware," Jen said as she walked through the gate toward the front door. Emelie trailed behind her. "Nothing is going on," she said with a serious tone.

And that was how it needed to stay.

Jen and Damien had finally found a solid footing. They were friends, best friends—though she would never admit that part to Emelie.

He had become an irreplaceable tenet in her life, and the idea of upsetting that delicate balance made her stomach twist into knots.

That could also be the nightmare currently haunting me.

Emelie looked at her, completely unconvinced.

"For now," she responded, opening the front door and sauntering into the house.

Jen groaned and turned back to find Damien staring at her.

It wasn't that she didn't still find him attractive. She wasn't blind after all; piercing blue eyes, sculpted arms from years tending the forge, and hands that intimately knew every inch of her—

Jen shook her head.

I will NOT add Damien's hands to the list of things swirling around in my mind right now. There's only room for weddings and scary shadow snakes in there.

She glanced back at him. He smiled and gave a little wave. Jen waved back but realized she was swinging a giant flower at him.

Gods. I'm an idiot.

His laughter followed her as she shuffled inside the cottage.

Jen and Emelie walked into the kitchen where her family continued preparing for the nuptials.

"Oh, good! You've brought reinforcements," Maelia said as she walked from the hearth to give Emelie a warm embrace.

"What can I do to help?" Emelie asked.

Jen's eyes widened at the kitchen table crammed, almost comically so, with jugs upon jugs of wine and Meade. She walked over and attempted to unload her bag of decorations beside them.

"Good thing you got that milk thistle," she murmured to Emelie.

Darya grunted from where she laced Rhea into her light blue gown, clearly growing flustered while Rhea leaned into her palms against the wall as if she were going to be sick.

Jen came around and quietly shooed Darya back to the table. She gently turned Rhea around and revealed a simple bracelet from her dress pocket.

Rhea beamed, returning some of the color to her face while Jen fastened the bracelet to her wrist.

"Are you thinking about him?" Jen asked quietly as she kept her gaze on the bracelet.

"Troi? Of course," Rhea said with slight humor in her voice. Jen gave her a weak smile.

"You know who I mean," she said cautiously.

Their father abandoned them eight years ago, and in the time leading up to it, he had become so volatile and unpredictable that Jen ultimately turned herself into a living shield in an attempt to protect her younger siblings from the horrible mayhem that rocked their home.

Unfortunately, it still reached them.

"He made his choice, and I have made mine," Rhea said.

Jen had always been envious of her sister's ability to cut off anyone she no longer deemed worthy of her; their father was at the top of that list.

"If you felt a little sad, that would be… understandable," Jen said, pushing her sister's long brown hair over her shoulder to lace up the rest of the dress. Rhea stiffened.

"Jen, I'm fine I swear. Would it be nice to have a father who stayed around." She shrugged. "Sure. But we have Mama. I wouldn't want it any other way." They both glanced back at Maelia, who chatted with Emelie a few feet away.

Jen tied the ends of the ribbon and tucked them inside the wedding dress. Rhea turned, and to Jen's surprise, pulled her in for a tight hug.

"Thank Damien for me; the arch is beautiful," she whispered before letting go. She squeezed Jen's hands and headed into her room.

Maelia approached her. "I sent Emelie and Darya outside with the decorations and Jamie is helping some of the neighbors with tables and chairs."

She slumped into a chair and poured herself a small goblet of wine, slinging it back in one gulp. Jen snorted a laugh.

"What can I do, Mama?" she asked. Maelia looked around the room and out the back door of the cottage.

"Oh!" she snapped her fingers. "We need a few more flowers from the garden for Rhea's bouquet,"

Jen nodded, grabbing a basket from the shelf beside the back door before stepping outside.

The grass seemed especially green, so verdant it almost strained her eyes, but her gaze shifted to the dilapidated old shed in the corner of their property, having peeled and faded with time and no longer the vibrant crimson it had been when she was a child.

A tall, light oak tree stood in the middle of the lawn, with a family of birds perched near the top, calling to each other as she strolled towards the garden.

She'd spent the last few years taking diligent care of the flowers and vegetables that resided there. Her mind was always able to find some temporary solace when her hands worked through the damp earth.

Jen knelt before one of the flower beds and pulled a few unruly weeds from the soil, leaning in closer to breathe in the fragrant purple blooms of her favorite herb in the garden.

Lavender.

She released a long, soothing exhale and began plucking flowers and placing them in her small wicker basket.

After collecting a respectable variety, she stood and dusted off her dress. She bent down to retrieve her basket when something in the corner of the garden caught her eye.

A lily.

Not just a lily, a dying lily.

The once pure, white bloom was wilting, brown decay beginning to distort the petals. Jen sat on her heels and stared blankly at it, and then glanced around the yard as if someone would appear and claim the rogue blossom.

She peered closer; and her confusion only grew.

Those don't grow here.

Jen extended her hand toward the flower, and an unfamiliar warmth bloomed in her chest. Her outstretched fingers reached the browning pedals and gently danced with curiosity over the decay.

The warm bloom in her chest traveled down through her arm like an invisible trail of silken threads leading down to her hand. It gained momentum, her wrist curving into her hand like an ocean wave as the feeling surged through her palm and extended into her fingertips.

A faint, white light emanated from them.

She watched in shock as the decay receded, and, slowly, the flower arched upward and straightened as if touched by the morning sun.

She sucked in a harsh breath and ripped her hand away. Her eyes darted around the empty yard as the warmth disappeared as quickly as it came.

Don't panic. Don't panic.

Jen closed her eyes and tried to calm her breathing. After a moment, she slowly regained control of her body. She tilted her head at the healed lily. She felt drawn to it, like someone was gently nudging her from behind.

She reached down and plucked the flower from the earth. When she brought it closer, a familiar voice entered her mind.

"Only when a child of light and a child of dark become one in tandem shall those who were lost be found," the voice echoed as Jen's vision flashed with white light, *"and the legend of light and shadow shall be known."*

The blinding light was suddenly disrupted by a dark funnel cloud that took the form of a snake and consumed the light. The ground trembled beneath her as immense pressure built inside her mind.

It became so unbearable she dropped the lily and fell to the ground, holding her head in her hands. Pain wrung a groan from deep inside her. Through the battle raging in her head, a voice beyond called out to her.

"Jen!" the voice yelled. Jen didn't dare move or look up, but she heard footsteps. Then someone dropped in front of her and grabbed her shoulders.

Damien lifted her face to meet his rattled gaze. Jen looked around frantically. The ground was no longer trembling, and the war of bright light and dark serpent clouds had disappeared.

Damien gently shook her.

"Jen, hey, what happened?" his voice laced with concern. Jen pressed her lips together. She couldn't tell him about healing the flower or hearing prophetic voices; it would make it too real.

"I—I almost passed out," Jen explained. It wasn't technically a lie but was also not the most accurate truth. Damien's eyes narrowed.

"Where did you come from anyway?" she deflected quickly. "Were you just sneaking around my house?"

He raised a brow.

"I came over to tell your mother the arch was finished, *if you must know.* She told me you were out here," he said as he stood up. He offered his hand and helped her to her feet.

She walked over to retrieve her basket, and when she turned back around, Damien was bent over, his hand reaching for the lily. Jen gasped and rushed over, snatching it from him.

"What the—"

"I'm sorry." She threw the flower in her basket. "I picked that for Mama," she lied again. Damien looked at her like she was insane. He scratched the back of his head as they walked back toward the house.

"Weddings bring out an interesting color in you," he said warily, opening the back door for her.

Maelia was sitting at the table cutting ribbon when they entered the kitchen. Jen placed the basket of flowers in front of her before grabbing a piece of bread from the cutting board on the counter. She tossed a second piece across the room to Damien.

Jen gestured to the basket. "Do you think that's enough?" she asked as she leaned on the counter.

Maelia glanced over. "Oh, they're beautiful darling, I—" she trailed off as her eyes settled on the lily. Maelia slowly picked it up, her eyes widening slightly.

"What's this…"

Damien walked over to the table.

"Jen picked it for you before she almost passed out in the yard," he said, pushing against one of the kitchen chairs. Jenevieve glared at him.

"When I came around the house looking for her, she was on the ground with that lily in front of her," he said. He looked at her sternly. Damien knew when she was lying to him, and his way of retribution was selling her out to her mother.

Jen looked back at Maelia and spotted the same odd flicker she'd seen in her eyes earlier that day.

"I'm okay Mama, I swear. I just felt a little faint," she reassured her, but Maelia was still looking at the lily in her hand. She blinked a few times, as if coming out of deep thought, and gingerly placed the flower on the table.

"Where did you find it?" she asked, her tone making Jen feel uneasy.

"The edge of the garden…I didn't think lilies could grow here," Jen said, walking around the table to face her mother.

"Yes. That—that's very curious indeed," Maelia said in almost a whisper. Her hand rose to the small, green gem hanging from the gold necklace she wore.

After a long pause, she smiled up at Damien and stood. "Damien, you should go home and get ready. Jen, put on your dress while I finish the bouquet," she said.

She gathered the rest of the flowers from the basket. Jen and Damien gave each other a *what in hells was that* look, before ultimately shrugging it off. He walked toward the front door.

"I'll see you ladies in a bit," he said, winking at Jen before marching out the door.

She started down the hall, but when Jen looked over her shoulder, her mother was staring down at the lily, worry etched into her expression as she held tightly to the little green gem around her neck.

A question burned the tip of her tongue.

"Mama," Jen started, looking to press the matter further. Her mother was usually very calm and level-headed. Her reaction to a lily—a lily Jen had just healed somehow…

Maelia, now aware that Jen was looking at her, immediately tucked away any sign of worry. "Yes, darling?"

"You looked at that lily like it was—"

"Jen!" Darya called from the front gate, her voice straining like she was carrying something heavy. "Come out here! We need an extra hand!"

She was jolted back to the present moment.

Shadow snakes and prophetic voices and rogue lilies would have to wait. Today was about her sister.

And Jen would make sure it was a day her family would never forget.

CHAPTER 3

"**M**ay you jump into your married life with both feet and loving hearts!" the priest proclaimed joyfully.

Jamie placed a small broom on the ground in front of Rhea and her new husband, Troi. They grabbed hands and hopped over it, receiving an exuberant eruption of cheers and applause.

As the family and guests began to stand and mingle, Jen attempted to weave her way through the joyous crowd, but, as the older sister of the bride, she was consistently stopped and pulled into circles of small talk.

She finally spotted Emelie next to Maelia, who stood at a long oak table near the food. Behind them sat an obscene number of ale barrels, and with the large number of jugs situated in front of them, it was beginning to smell like a tavern.

They arranged the goblets in rows, along with ornate silver pitchers already filled and ready to pour, chatting happily while they worked. Jen leapt towards Emelie and wrapped her arms around her shoulders.

No shadows. No voices. Just my sister's wedding.

"What's gotten into you?" Emelie asked as Jen spun her in circles. She twirled herself around and let her hair blow in the breeze, her ivory gown billowing around her.

"Rhea is married, and the joy is infectious!" she exclaimed, skipping over to Maelia who smiled and kissed her daughter's cheek before resuming her task.

"The joy is *infectious?*" Emelie gave Jen a pointed look. "Why are you talking like that?"

Jen grabbed two goblets and filled them to the brim. "Because if one more person asks me how I feel about my *little sister* getting married, I'm going to throw my goblet at them," she said through gritted teeth.

Emelie snorted as they walked past another long table laden with roast chicken and all the trimmings for an immaculate wedding feast.

The center of the gathering was lined with tall wooden poles in the loose shape of a diamond; each connected to the other with the strung banners Jen and her students made.

They sat at a table close to the bonfire blazing in the center of the party. Nearby, a small company of musicians tuned their instruments, preparing to accompany a series of country dances.

She tapped her goblet to Emelie's in cheers and took a long sip. The tart liquid laced with oak and elderberry quenched her thirst and put her mind at ease.

She looked up from her cup to see Damien across the meadow at another table around the fire, chatting with his mother and sister.

He was lounging back in his chair, his foot resting on his knee and one of his arms draped along the back of his mother's chair beside him.

Jen loved seeing him like that.

There was a specific tenderness he reserved solely for his mother, such an easy affection that radiated from him when she was around. It was one of the things that had made Jen fall so quickly for him, the fierce love he held for his family.

Emelie nudged her.

"What are you staring at?" she asked, already knowing the answer.

Jen looked down at the table.

"I'm not staring at anything," she said firmly, taking another sip from her cup. "Don't let me drink too much of this," she joked. Emelie looked at her suggestively.

"Why? Afraid it may loosen you up?" she winked. Jen let out a small laugh as the bonfire roared in front of her, the light bouncing off the tables and wagons. Within a few minutes, music filled the meadow.

Rhea and Troi emerged from their private moment away from the chaos and walked to the space in front of the fire meant for dancing. A hush fell over the guests, and they began their first dance as a married couple.

They moved as if they were the only ones there, their gaze fixed on each other. Jen rested her head on Emelie's shoulder and released a contented sigh.

Her sister was happy, *loved.* Troi would protect her and cherish her, and that's all Jen could ever want for her sister. That's what she wanted for Darya, for Jamie; protection, love. Things that were stolen from them when they were so young.

No matter how hard she tried to prevent it, the scars had still found a way to brand their hearts; the only proof that their father had ever been there.

Witnessing him morph from a loving father to an unhinged monster and being helpless to stop it—it broke something in her that never fully healed.

It broke them all, and Jen carried that around as her own failure.

Gods, my mind is insufferable today.

Emelie shrugged her off, tipping her head to their left and jolting Jen out of her thought spiral.

Her eyes trailed over to where William sat a table away, alone, staring off with a dreamy twinkle in his eye. The ladies tracked his gaze and, to no one's surprise—Leeyna. She stood a few tables over with a goblet of wine in her hand watching the newlyweds, also alone, shifting from foot to foot.

Emelie and Jen looked at each other, back at William, and then nodded at each other. They approached on either side of him.

He jumped and almost spilled his drink.

"Jeez! Why'd you have to sneak up on me like that?" he asked, checking his shirt for a spill. The ladies took quiet sips of their wine and stared at the bonfire.

"We didn't," Jen said.

"You were just lost in a trance," Emilie continued.

William looked between them with his mouth agape, but they kept looking forward with humor dancing in their eyes.

"I...uh...I...no...I—" he stuttered.

"William, you've been looking at her like that for *months,*" she said.

His cheeks flushed. "But look at her. She's so beautiful. How could someone like her possibly go for someone like me?" William said as he looked back at Leeyna. Emelie placed her hand on his back.

"Come on, you're a catch; have a little confidence," Emelie said kindly. Jen placed her hand on his back as well.

"Look, she's alone now, but I can't guarantee that a beautiful girl at a wedding is going to remain that way," she said.

She snuck a glance at Emelie, and with a nod between them, they pushed William forward in Leeyna's direction. He fumbled for a moment, but quickly regained his composure before looking back at them with a shy smile.

Emelie gave him a reassuring thumbs up while Jen took another slug of her wine.

He turned back around and took a breath so deep, his shoulders moved with it. With a resolved courage in his step, he marched over to Leeyna. Her eyes lit up when William approached her.

They were out of earshot, but it must have gone well, as Leeyna laughed so hard she spilled some of her drink. Her face turned bright red as she nervously tucked her hair behind her ears.

Emelie squealed.

William had, rather smoothly, taken Leeyna's cup from her hand and placed it, along with his own, on the table beside them before offering his hand to her. Leeyna smiled bashfully and accepted, following William towards the other couples who'd already joined the dance.

Emelie shook Jen's arm so fervently she spilt her wine.

"Okay, okay, calm down. It worked," Jen said.

They watched intently as William and Leeyna laughed, realizing neither of them was a particularly gifted dancer. They took turns gazing at the other, each trying to figure out the steps.

Darya and Jamie plopped down at a table. Darya's back was stiff as a board, her eyes darting around as she watched the guests closely. Jamie didn't seem to be aware he was at a wedding, pulling his hand through his hair until it looked like he had just rolled out of bed. Jen glanced over at them and gestured for Emelie to follow her.

"Hello, siblings," Jen said with an air of sarcasm as she sat next to Darya. Emelie sat across from them and quickly turned back around so she could continue gawking at William and Leeyna.

Darya looked at the tables and scattered decor with a sour look on her face.

"What's wrong with *you*?" Jen asked while she tried to figure out what exactly her sister was looking at. Darya let out an exasperated sigh.

"I'm just thinking about how much cleaning I'm going to be saddled with tomorrow," she said, putting her head in her hands. Jen looked over to Jamie, who just shrugged nonchalantly.

"Has she had any wine?" she asked him. He shook his head and looked at Darya with a small eye roll. Jen slid her cup over to her sister.

"You need this more than I do," she joked, sliding her cup to her sister. She slid it back.

"No thanks, I don't need to feel awful tomorrow *and* have to clean all of this up at the same time," she said, standing up to join their mother at the food table. Jen tilted her head to Jamie.

"Well, *she's* a bundle of joy today, isn't she?" she said, lifting the goblet to her mouth. Jamie snatched it out of her hand with a sardonic grin.

"If she doesn't want it, I'll take it," he said before Jen snatched it back.

"Absolutely not; you're *ten*," she said, taking a huge gulp. Jamie's mouth dropped open in shock.

"I'm *twenty*," he said, trying to reach over her for the cup while she took another long sip.

"Nope, I don't accept that. You are a child," she teased as he continued to wrestle her for the cup. She finished the last of it and flipped the cup upside down to show him.

Jamie stood in a huff. Jen peered up at her baby brother and wrapped her arms around his waist.

He froze, and when Jen didn't let go, he awkwardly patted her on the head before releasing himself from her embrace. He headed off to find himself a drink that wasn't held hostage by his sister.

Jen smiled after him, but when she looked back towards the fire, two piercing blue eyes met hers across the flames. Damien watched her over the rim of his cup with an expression that sent a wave of heat up the back of her neck.

No, I'm just too close to the fire.

He put his cup down and cut through the couples dancing to reach her. Emelie stopped watching William and Leeyna, tracking Damien as he passed her and stood in front of Jenevieve. She looked between them, anxiously awaiting who would break first.

Damien silently offered his hand. Jen's eyes flickered down to it, and then back up at him. He subtly arched a brow. She swallowed the lump in her throat and tentatively placed her hand in his, and as he pulled her to her feet and led her towards the musicians, she threw a glance over her shoulder—Emelie was fanning herself dramatically.

He twirled her around to face him, his hand finding her waist. He pulled her close, and an involuntary gasp escaped her lips.

Okay, no more wine.

He smirked as the music began underneath them. Their bodies responded instinctually to a dance they'd known for years. The slow beat moved them across the ground.

Jen wouldn't meet his eyes; instead, she looked around at the people gawking. She could feel their eyes on her, hear the murmurs all around them. She felt as though she were on display, and it made her stomach churn.

For the last ten years, everyone in the village had watched on in veiled judgement as Damien and Jen took turns loving and hurting each other. Most of the time, they themselves couldn't even explain what they were.

"Everyone is staring at us," she said nervously as Damien spun her in a circle.

"What else is new?" he said as a smile tugged at his lips, seemingly unbothered by it.

"Damien, we're being very *distracting*," Jen warned. She finally met his gaze. His thick eyebrows softened, and he pulled her a bit closer.

"Hey, just look at me," he said gently. "It's just you and me. Two people enjoying a dance. Let them stare," he joked as he dramatically spun her and dipped her so low, she almost met the ground. Laughter escaped her as her shoulders pulled away from her ears, her feet spinning more freely.

Slowly, the onlookers paid less attention to them as the dancing continued. It was nearing sunset, and the yellow-orange orb sat just above the tree line of the forest, casting a magenta hue over the surrounding meadow.

Damien moved closer to Jen with every step, maybe it was nostalgia; perhaps it was the wine. But she felt safe and happy in this moment, moving in tandem with him.

She wondered why this never worked, why they took turns not being ready for one another, why they continued to hurt each other. Simple, sweet moments like this made everything seem clear, and yet, it always grew murky.

As if Damien could hear her thoughts, he tugged on her hand. Jen hesitated, but when he looked back at her and tilted his head in silent question, she allowed herself to be led away from the festivities.

He brought them behind a small barn just out of earshot from the celebration. He nudged her against the wall of the barn and placed his hand on her waist.

"Hi," he breathed as his hand trailed around to her back, his other hand on the wall next to her head.

"Hi," she murmured. Damien slowly rubbed her back and lowered his head towards hers. Jen pushed against his chest, keeping a safe distance between them.

"We shouldn't," she said. Her rational mind knew it was not a good idea. They had finally found a good rhythm. They were friends.

And yet, everything in her wanted to let him run his hands down her—

"Why not," he said, his voice low and husky. His head slowly traveled down her neck, his lips brushing her skin and moving behind her ear. Jen swallowed hard and pushed on his chest once more.

"Because it's you and me, Damien," she said a bit more firmly. Maybe if she spoke with more conviction, her body would stop responding to him.

"What's wrong with that?" he asked, pulling his head up to look into her eyes.

"We've tried this, and it never works," she said. Jen thought her new, no-nonsense tone would deter him, but his hand traveled from the wall to her neck, his thumb caressing her jaw.

"What if this time was different?" he asked as his lips moved closer to hers. Her breath hitched in her throat. "What if after all this time, we finally…figure…"

He moved within an inch of her lips.

"Damien…I…" she muttered breathlessly. Her hand relaxed on his chest as he grazed her lips with his own.

She stopped abruptly just before the moment could consume her. Damien froze, noticeably caught off guard.

She raised her ear to listen harder. Maybe it was just in her head; it wouldn't be the first time that happened today.

"What—" Damien started.

"Shh." Jen clapped her hand over his mouth. She listened intently with Damien reluctantly doing the same. A high-pitched shriek faintly entered her ear.

"What *is* that?" she whispered to herself. Damien lifted his ear a bit higher, but his eyebrows were stitched together, perplexed.

"I don't hear any—" he began but cut himself off as the sound of three slightly louder shrieks entered their ears one right after the other. His wide eyes fell to her.

They rushed out from behind the barn to see the celebration in full swing with laughter, dancing, and children playing all through the meadow.

Damien looked at Jen, bewildered. Had they both imagined those sounds? Jen searched the crowd and spotted Emelie chatting excitedly with William and Leeyna at a table close to the bonfire. She grabbed Damien's hand and dragged him over.

"Did any of you hear that sound?" she asked, abruptly interrupting the group's conversation. They all looked at her like she was crazy, and Jen was beginning to feel like maybe she was.

"There are a lot of sounds out here Jen; it's a party," Emelie said in confusion, placing her hand on Jen's arm.

"No, there was shrieking, coming from behind the forest. It sounded like some kind of animal," Damien explained.

Jen was grateful someone else heard the sound, otherwise she would've truly seemed deranged. She looked around the field of oblivious villagers— everything seemed fine.

"Maybe there wasn't anything to worry about," Jen said, but the sentiment changed immediately when she met her mother's gaze across the bonfire.

She looked terrified, but something else flickered in Maelia's eyes. Jen took a step forward, but like a startled deer, her mother bolted across the field into their cottage.

"Mama!" Jen called after her, but to no avail. She took a few more steps towards the cottage before being yanked back.

"*Ouch!* Damien, what in hells?" she scowled at him, but he wasn't looking at her, and neither were her friends. They were staring past her, above the tree line of the forest. Jen slowly turned at the harrowing sound of a shrieking animal. The wedding guests were starting to notice as well.

"That can't be what I think it is," William said quietly.

It looked as though a swarm of birds was coming up over the trees to block the setting sun. Dread pooled in the pit of Jen's stomach when the drove of amassed wings grew larger, forming a horrendous wave of darkness as they jolted and jittered towards the reception. The wave's jerking movement was accompanied by a terrifying motif of overlapping, high-pitched shrieks.

Jenevieve's heartbeat wildly in her chest. She grabbed hold of Damien's hand to find it slick with sweat.

Those aren't birds.

The creatures swarmed like a tempest as they closed in on the meadow, and with a loud *BOOM,* they hurled balls of fire at the barn she had just come from. When it burst into flames three of the dark figures broke from the swarm and dove towards the villagers below.

Four more broke away, and more fire rained down, hitting the ground by Troi and Rhea near the bonfire. Those frozen in fear regained sensation in their bodies and ran as fast as they could, the party shifting fast into frenzy.

Rhea screamed in terror.

"Rhea!" Jen cried through the wall of flames, but her sister couldn't hear her. Troi pulled her up from the ground and ran with her across the dirt road to their home.

Jen spun around, frantically searching for Jamie and Darya, but her line of sight was bombarded by flashes of terrified people running for cover. The creatures were starting to target the nearby cottages, their flames dancing menacingly on the rooftops.

She finally found her other siblings hiding under the long table used for the feast. Jen locked eyes with Jamie and mouthed, *run.*

He nodded and yanked Darya out from the table. Using his arm as a shield over his sister, Jamie guided her back to their cottage.

Jen exhaled heavily and her eyes caught sight of her friends hiding under the table behind her, save for Damien, who darted toward his mother and sister.

She dropped down beside them.

"What in *hells* are those things," she asked urgently. The group flinched as the ground shook from another firebomb. William was trembling.

"If they are…what I…what I think they are…" he stuttered, attempting to keep calm. "They're—the *morai*." Jen blinked. They had no idea what he was talking about.

"But they aren't *real!* I don't know how they're here. They come from a legend. I don't understand what's happening," he said, clapping his hands to his head.

"It doesn't matter if they're from legend or fairy tales. They're here *now*. We need to get out of here," Emelie said sternly as she tucked her fear away.

Jen nodded to the rest of the group, and they filed out from under the table as fast as they could. They ran together across the meadow to the table of goblets.

"Hide behind the barrels!" Jenevieve barked at them just as a harsh gust of wind hit her back. She spun around and her heart leapt into her throat at the sight of a morai standing a few feet from her.

It was black as oblivion, with the legs and arms of a human, but the head of a bat. Massive membranous wings extended out from its back—a horrifying distortion of human and monster.

It stalked up to her. Jen stumbled back and found herself flushed against the barrels her friends were hiding behind.

The creature opened its mouth and its long black tongue and razor-sharp canines leered at her, the threat of flames forming in the back of its throat. Tears pricked the corners of her eyes as she turned away and braced herself.

But the flames didn't come, only the sound of metal crashing through flesh and a pointed cry.

Her eyes widened, her mouth dropping open.

There was a blade sticking out of the morai's chest. A black tongue hung out of its mouth as it collapsed off the blade onto the ground with a *thud.*

Damien stood with his bloodied sword, his chest heaving as he stared down at the demonic creature.

A flood of relief whooshed through her, and she pried her hands from the barrels behind her. Damien dropped his sword and marched over to her. He cupped her face and kissed her forehead, his lips trembled on her skin.

"Are you okay?" his eyes searched hers.

Jen nodded. "That was bigger than a squirrel."

Damien huffed a laugh as he retrieved his sword and wiped the blood from the blade.

"Your mother and sister?" she asked quickly.

"They're alright, they ran for the shop," he said as the others emerged from behind the barrel. Emelie lunged at Jen and hugged her tight. "Holy crap, are you alright?"

Jen shook the near-death experience from her mind and grabbed her friend's hand.

"I'm fine. I–" she started but was rendered silent by the sound of a crying child.

A fireball slammed into the bonfire with a loud *BANG* and sent heaps of flaming kindling into the air and onto the dry grass surrounding it, causing walls of chaotic fire to erupt and spread in every direction.

The rippling flames reflected in Jen's eyes as warmth bloomed in her chest. She looked across from the fire and saw a little girl crying out for her papa.

Lucy

Jen darted toward her.

"Jen, stop!" Damien yelled after her.

She dropped to her knees and held Lucy close.

"You're okay, you're okay. Let's find your papa," Jen crooned. She spotted him nearby, running around in a craze, and waved her hand to get his attention.

Lucy's cries grew shrill. Jen felt a rush of air and heard massive wings behind her. She stood up quickly to shield Lucy, who clung to her legs. Another morai stood before her, a sick smile curled on its beastly face.

"Stay away!" she screamed, but that only seemed to provoke it.

It stormed up to her and struck her across the face. Lucy screamed as they fell back onto the ground. Damien dashed towards her, sword in hand. She could barely hear him calling her name, Lucy's cries consuming her.

In a moment of suspended time, she felt the warmth from her chest travel down through her arms and into her hands through her palms and fingertips. She looked up at the beast towering over her, ready to attack with its fiery breath.

Jen raised her hands in front of her.

"ARGHHHH!" she cried out as two wild beams of light expelled from her hands and joined together to make one powerful blast that incinerated the morai, the force of it knocking Damien to the ground just before he reached her.

The light receded and Jen collapsed to her knees. She stared down at her hands in shock, not even looking up as Damien grabbed Lucy and placed her in her father's arms.

"Go now. Run as fast as you can," he said firmly. Lucy's father nodded and glanced nervously at Jen. Damien pushed him.

"Go, *NOW!*"

They ran off. Damien crouched next to Jen.

"Hey. *Hey,* what was *that?*" Damien said cautiously. Jen looked down at her hands again, then up to the scene in front of her; black dust and bone fragments were all that was left of the creature.

"I—I don't—" she started to mumble but was cut off by a hand yanking her to her feet.

"Mama!" Jenevieve winced as Maelia dragged her behind the wagon next to them. Damien whistled and the others sprinted over and hid behind the flipped table beside it.

Her mother pulled her to the ground, the sound of screams and raging flames echoing in their ears.

"Mama, what's happening?" Jenevieve asked desperately. Maelia looked at her sharply.

"We don't have much time. The morai are here for *you*," she said in a hushed tone.

Jen's eyes widened. "Me? Why?" Her head was spinning.

"They felt your magic, darling," Maelia continued.

"What are you talking about— "

"The *lily*," her mother breathed. Damien darted over to them.

"Maelia, what in *hells* is going on? We need to *go*," he urged, his composure slipping. They ducked as the morai flew over them.

"My name isn't Maelia." she said.

Jen blinked at her, utterly lost.

"My name is Fjora, and I'm not your mother. I'm your protector."

CHAPTER 4

"My wha—" Jen sputtered.

"Jenevieve, we don't have time. I must get you to the forest. *Now*." Fjora said, pulling Jen up and dashing into the chaos.

Damien and her friends followed suit as they ducked and dodged the flames, hoping to reach some semblance of safety. The morai flew in small groups, erratically shifting directions like they were searching for something.

Jen ran closely behind Fjora.

"You'll use the same path I did to get through the forest thirty years ago; it's marked by a trail of trees carved with an X," Fjora yelled over her shoulder. She stopped the group when they reached a cottage closer to the forest. They hid in the shadows as the morai hunted above them.

"Where are we supposed to go?" Jenevieve panted.

"The Arc of Zaniya."

William made a sputtering sound. "The—*THE ARC OF ZANIYA?*" he choked. He looked like his mind was going to evaporate out of his head. "It's real?"

"It's *very* real. When you make your way out, head there as fast as you can. There should be the remnants of a road that leads to the city. You can see the Arc from the forest's edge."

"*Mama.* Tell me what's going on," Jenevieve whispered. Fjora pulled her away from the group and crouched down to disclose a large burlap sack from within her cloak, and Jen noticed a second necklace hanging beside the gold one her mother usually wore.

Silver, but whatever hung from it was hidden beneath her dress.

Fjora opened the burlap sack and handed Jenevieve a black cloak."Here, put this on. Quickly," she ordered. Jenevieve draped the cloak around her shoulders and tied it in front of her neck. "Your dream, from this morning. He called your name, didn't he?" Fjora asked, rummaging through the sack.

"I—I didn't tell you that." Jenevieve looked back at her friends. The sound of firebombs and screams were muffled; they were a fair distance from most of the violence now.

Fjora found what she was looking for. She removed her hand from the bag to reveal a dagger.

Jen sucked in a breath.

"Your mother, your *real* mother. She had the same dream the night she gave birth to you," Fjora said with nostalgic sadness, running her thumbs along the hilt of the dagger. "The morai came a few hours after. I knew when you mentioned the tattoos, and then the lily…" Fjora offered the dagger to Jen. "This was hers. She wanted you to have it when the time came."

Jen's hands trembled as she took the dagger and turned it over in her palm. She ran her finger down the silver blade and felt the sleek stone of the hilt before she noticed something carved into it.

A lily.

Her eyes shot up to Fjora.

"Listen to me." Fjora cupped Jen's face, her hands trembling. "The fates have sung their song." Her eyes lined with tears. "You must reconvene the Council of Suran—"

But before she could say anything else, the cottage caught fire.

They'd been found.

The horde of morai circled and screeched overhead before they converged on the cottage below.

"RUN!" Fjora yelled. Jenevieve and the others ran as fast as they could to the tree line.

"GO DOWN THE HILL! STICK TO THE TREES!" Fjora ordered, running right behind them.

Jenevieve led them down a steep hill, her feet almost giving out under the erratic tempo of her frantic strides. They could hear the morai growing louder, and when she chanced a glance over her shoulder, she saw that half of the swarm had broken off and was closing in on them.

Fire rained down, igniting the trees of the forest and swallowing them in thick billows of smoke.

"DON'T LOOK BACK!" Fjora choked. Jenevieve had no idea where they were going, all she could do was force her legs to keep moving. Up ahead sat a large tree with a long, crooked branch extending from its trunk, as though it was waving.

"THAT'S IT! TURN AT THE X!"

"I DON'T SEE IT!" Emelie exclaimed.

But as they neared the tree, Jenevieve saw it; a roughly carved X glowing in the worn bark.

"THERE!"

She veered her friends to the right and under the canopy of the forest. Damien went to follow but Fjora yanked him back.

"You have to protect her, Damien," Fjora implored. She shook his arm. "Promise me. She's too important."

Damien blinked rapidly but quickly placed his hand on hers.

"You have my word."

Fjora nodded. "Now go. I'll hold them off as long as I can."

Before Damien could intervene, Fjora ran out from the tree line in the path of the morai. She released her cloak from her shoulders and ripped the silver chain from her neck, revealing a pendant the shape of a white flame. She whispered something to it and thrust her hand into the air.

A blast of white light erupted from it, engulfing the meadow around them and blinding the horde. The force of it careened through the tree line, knocking Jen and others to the ground before they could shield themselves.

The morai released rageful screams, their unison movements dissolving into erratic chaos.

Fjora sprinted into the meadow towards the village with her pendant, drawing the horde away from the tree line. Damien sprinted into the forest and rammed into Jen.

"Where's my mother?" Her eyes darted around.

Her wild gaze met Damien's just as he glanced towards the meadow. He looked back at Jenevieve, his mouth agape. Her eyes widened before she lunged towards the meadow, but Damien held her back.

"No. NO! Let me go! Mama!" Jenevieve thrashed against him. Damien shook her shoulders and forced her to look at him.

"Jen, we have to keep moving. They aren't after her, it's *you* they want," he implored.

Her eyes welled with tears.

"She'll be okay," Damien pulled her into a tight embrace. "They'll all be okay."

Jen blew out a shuddered breath against his chest. She had to believe he was right, she had to hang onto the hope that her family was okay, it was the only way she could convince her feet to move.

Damien placed his sword in the leather sheath strapped to his back and laced his fingers with hers, leading them to the front of the group.

She pointed towards the X on the next tree and continued into the forest. "We need to follow the marked trees," she said.

A crease formed between Damien's brows. "There isn't an X on that tree, Jen."

"I don't see an X on any trees," Emelie said, her eyes searching the forest around them.

We don't have time for this.

She marched up to the tree and tapped the carved X. "It's right here." She glanced further down the path. "And there's the next one."

"We—We don't see them," Leeyna said quietly.

Jen looked at each of them, and then back to the tree. She whirled around to Damien, pointing at the X. "You can't see that?"

He shook his head.

Am I the only one who can see them? They're fucking glowing.

She clapped her hand to her head. "Okay—I—just—just follow me then," she stammered.

Before anyone could object, Jen started walking.

It's not enough that a horde of demon bats are after me, I'm also the only one who can find the way out of this forest. Terrific.

After a moment, she heard the group following quietly behind her. They headed deeper into the forest, only the sound of heavy breathing and exhausted limbs coexisted with the snapping and crunching of the dark forest around them.

They were almost a full league in when they heard a distant sound coming from the direction of Nimea.

"Is it them?" Leeyna whispered. "Did they find us?"

Jenevieve paused and lifted her ear to listen. "That's not the morai," she murmured.

What is that?

It sounded like a low-pitched horn that ascended the longer it was held, and was further joined by many others, all calling out one on top of the other. The sound rose higher until it reached a visceral cacophony of dissonant harmony that made them all clap their hands to their ears.

Where is that coming from?

Jenevieve looked around, wondering who, or rather what else was in the wood with them. Damien peered up through the trees.

"Everyone, get down!" he ordered in a hushed tone. They dropped to the ground, camouflaging themselves within the large trees as well as they could. They craned their necks to see the horde of morai flying above them. The creatures were shrieking, but they sounded pained, like something was torturing them.

The horns.

"The horns. The horns are driving them away," Emelie said, wonder and fear floating in the timbre of her voice.

William stared up at the retreating swarm. "The call of Zethyna." he whispered in awe, seemingly unaware of his friends staring at him. "An ancient interlude of horns fashioned from the remains of a fallen star of the same name. Said to have been enchanted by the Goddess of Light herself." He broke his gaze to look at the group.

"What? I read a lot."

"William, who... or what... blows those horns?" Jenevieve asked nervously. She was not up for fighting another race of creatures that weren't supposed to exist. William put his head between his knees and laced his fingers behind his neck. He was clearly overwhelmed.

"The Warriors of Kiara," he mumbled at the ground.

Leeyna took a small step towards him. "Who?"

William took a deep breath and sat back up. "The Warriors of Kiara. I don't—how is this—"

"Take some deep breaths. It's going to be a long night," Jenevieve said as she fumbled to her feet. She looked up and saw no sign of the morai, the shrieking sounds fading into the distance.

"We should keep moving," she said. She picked up her burlap sack and walked over to the nearest tree with the carved X, slowly running her hand over the glowing mark in the weathered trunk.

The forest beyond was shrouded in an ominous gloom of formidable darkness. But staring into that abyss was not what gave Jen pause. Her skin prickled with fear at the unknown awaiting on the other side of Bri, and where the task she was charged with would lead her.

She closed her eyes and exhaled, her fingers curling against the bark. *Alright Mama, lead the way.*

No one had ever been this deep in the forest before. Everyone was on high alert, each insignificant sound becoming a possible threat. Emelie quickened her pace and fell in step with Jen at the front.

"Hey," she started, twisting her body to avoid a mess of thorny shrubs. Jen gave her a distracted smile. "Did—did your mother—Fjora, ever mention any of this to you?"

Jen shook her head sadly.

"Not a thing."

"Did you ever suspect anything?"

"If I did, I would've left Nimea and taken the danger with me," Jen snapped. Emelie shrunk away from her. She sighed as she ducked under a low branch.

"I'm sorry. I'm just—" she started. "I'm just taking this one step at a time."

Emelie walked alongside her for a few quiet moments.

"Do we have any kind of plan?"

Jen kept her eyes out for the X trees.

"Follow the trees in hopes they lead out of the woods," she said. "You really can't see the X's?"

Emelie shook her head.

Jen looked back at the rest of the group to make sure everyone was still with them.

"What's beyond the woods?" Emelie asked apprehensively. Jen glanced down at her feet as she walked.

"I don't know," she said, disheartened. "I didn't know there was anything beyond the Forest of Bri."

"Zaniya… the Arc of Zaniya… what is it?" Emelie asked.

William cleared his throat.

"It's a library," he said. "The largest in existence. It's supposed to house the world's memory."

"What wor—" Emelie started, but a rustle in the brush a few leaps away halted the group.

"Shh." Jenevieve signaled at them to duck behind the tall, thick trees a few steps away. The fear was palpable. It radiated off of them like heat from a hearth.

She very cautiously looked around the tree towards the rustling. Something—someone—was running through the forest at a great speed.

Not just one, but almost a dozen of them.

It was difficult to see much of their attire in the dark, but under the light of their torches, she could just make out black, hooded cloaks.

She released a breath.

They weren't in danger. It was clear the cloaked figures weren't looking for them; they came from several directions, meeting up in a group to continue moving swiftly through the forest.

Jen crept closer, careful to remain hidden. Ivory colored armor peeked out from their cloaks as they leapt between the trees and deeper into the thicket. She came out onto the path, and as they moved further away, something caught her eye.

Is that—

On the back of each of the flowing garments was an embroidered lily.

"Come on," Jenevieve whispered to her friends. Everyone cautiously came out from their hiding spots to meet her in the small clearing.

"Jen, we can't follow them. We don't know who they are..." Leeyna said anxiously.

Jen glanced at Damien.

"Their cloaks," she said to him, to which he turned and squinted towards them. His gaze snapped to Jen.

"Lily..." he said, trying to work out the significance of it.

She took off in the direction of the mysterious group. Damien was by her side in an instant, followed quickly by the other three.

"What if we get lost?" Emelie asked through heavy breathing. Jen spotted a nearby tree holding another glowing X.

"They're following the same path as us," Jen said, attempting to keep a decent distance from them.

They followed the faint light of the torches. Jen's eyes darted around and noticed the forest growing thicker, more gnarled.

Before, the moon showed brightly through the canopy, giving them a luminous path through the forest. But now, the canopy blocked any light; the darkness of night came and swept through the woods. The trees grew closer together, the branches more tightly intertwined the deeper they went.

They were forced to move into single file as the trees made an almost impassable labyrinth for them to climb through. Jen turned to check on her friends, all of whom were struggling to climb over and around the mangled branches and expelled roots. When she turned back to face forward, she stopped.

Where are the torches?

William hadn't noticed her sudden stop and knocked into her.

"Oof."

Jenevieve tried to look through the thicket, but the combination of darkness and claustrophobic trees obstructed her sight.

For a moment, she panicked, her gaze shifting to the trees around them. She released a sigh of relief; there was an X on a tree a few feet ahead. Without the help of the torches, there was no way they would be able to keep moving.

Jen turned towards her friends.

"We've lost them, and there's no way we'll be able to find our way without the torches. We should stop here and build a fire," Jen said as if this was the plan the entire time.

Damien peered at her through the dark. "There's a small clearing through these two trees over here; we'll have our backs protected," he said.

He helped each of them climb between the two trees to the clearing. Jen followed, keeping track of where the next marked tree was in relation to their camp.

Damien offered his hand to her, and when she took it, he squeezed it gently. She held his gaze for a moment, but the intensity of the understanding and compassion in his eyes was too much for her to bear.

He must have noticed the shift because he quickly cleared his throat. "I'm going to grab firewood," he murmured.

Jenevieve let go of his hand and came into the small clearing. She started gathering a small pile of dry leaves and twigs, using two stones to light a spark in the kindling. She blew gently on the small flame to coax it to ignite the rest of the brush.

Walls of flame. Fire-breathing demons. Terrified screams.

She jerked up, clenching her fists open and closed.

Magic. My magic.

William paced in front of a large tree a few feet away, pulling Jen's focus back to the present.

"William?" she asked.

"I'm sorry—I'm just—I don't understand what happened tonight." He jerked to a stop. "Did I hear your mother say those things were looking for you?"

You mean my protector.

Jen rose to her feet, glancing first at Emelie and Leeyna who sat against a tree, before returning to William. "Yes."

William sputtered. "But—I don't—why?"

Jen wrapped her arms around herself. "I don't know."

William's eyes grew wide. "You don't know why a horde of morai came after you?

Jen threw her hands up. "Maybe it was the fucking magic I didn't know I had?" She jabbed her finger in the direction of Nimea. "I didn't even know what those things were until you told me, William!"

"D—Do you know kn—know what's on the other s—side of Bri?" Leeyna asked through chattering teeth. She and Emelie were still in their linen gowns from the wedding, and it was no longer a warm spring day, but rather a cold, unpredictable night.

Jen untied her cloak and tossed it over to them. It was her fault they were out here; she could at least attempt to keep them from freezing.

"No, I don't."

William groaned. "So, we followed you out here and you can't tell us anything?"

You must reconvene the Council of Suran.

Anger surged and Jen took a charged step toward the fire. "Do I look like I have any idea what's going on?" She pointed her finger at him. "And I didn't ask any of you to follow me—"

"Hey! What's going on here?" Damien appeared beside her with a pile of wood in his arms.

William shifted his gaze to Damien. "Our village was attacked and now we're following a path that only Jen can see through a forest no one has ever made it through alive." His eyes turned pleading. "All to cross into a land that we all know to be MYTHS AND LEGENDS."

"Well, they aren't just legends anymore!" Jen shouted.

William released a harsh laugh. "I knew something was going on when you asked about the Knight—"

Damien dropped a log on the fire. "Wait, what Knight?"

Jen threw a scathing look at William, but he crossed his arms and threw an equally scalding look in return.

She turned to Damien. "I had a nightmare last night—and someone in it was referred to as a Knight of Eseer," she explained. "I asked William about it when I went to the school this morning."

Damien looked at her like he knew she wasn't finished. She squeezed her eyes shut. "And I may have been hearing voices all day."

"Wasn't aware of the voices—that's just great," William said.

Jen snapped her head towards him. "The nightmare wasn't real."

William threw his arms out towards the woods. "We're well past assuming what's real or fiction."

"Trust me, William," Jen seethed. "You want that nightmare to remain fiction."

"When I found you by the garden," Damien narrowed his eyes. "Were you hearing—"

"And seeing things. Yes."

Damien blew out a breath. "And the lily?"

A sad laugh scraped against her throat. "Let's just say my hands have glowed more than once today."

A tense silence stretched over the group, the crackling of the fire serving as the only sound.

"I can take you all back," Jen said quietly. She looked around the fire. "We were under attack, and everyone was caught up in the chaos."

Damien opened his mouth to argue, but Jen placed her hand on his arm. "None of you agreed to this."

To be fair, neither did I.

Emelie, having been a quiet observer, pushed herself up from the tree. "Jen, we would never leave you here, alone."

But Jen lifted her hand. "I will not rip you away from your lives."

"There may not even be lives to go back to," Leeyna breathed.

My sisters. My brother. Fjora.

Jen pressed her lips together, running her hand over her hair. She wouldn't let herself think about them. Not now. "We wait until morning, and then if you want to go back, I will take you."

Damien grabbed her wrist. "I can take them—"

"I'm the only one who can see the path." She sighed. "I don't have a choice here." Her eyes bounced between all of them. "But you do."

She looked into the fire.

"We're headed for a land we thought was a myth, on our way to a library to find information on more things we never knew were real." She glanced at William. "I have to reconvene the Council of Suran."

The blood drained from his face. "But—why?"

She laughed sadly at the lunacy of what she just said. "I didn't get many details, you know." She pointed towards the sky. "Demon bats."

"And I realize that's nothing to go on." Jen clenched her jaw. "But I have to do just that, go on."

Jen felt it as soon as she walked into the clearing; a subtle pull from the center of her chest, urging her towards the other side of the forest.

She gave William an apologetic smile. "You probably know more than I do right now."

Damien stepped between them.

"Look, nothing is going to be resolved right now," he said. "We're exhausted. We're in shock." He glanced back towards the path. "We can talk in the morning after we've gotten some rest."

He unhooked his sheath from his chest and placed it at the foot of the tree nearest to the path. "I'll take the first watch."

Some of the tension eased from the group as they all tried to find a comfortable place to sleep.

Emelie returned to Leeyna's side and snuggled in Jen's cloak. William settled into the tree beside them, hugging himself for warmth.

Jen knelt down and rummaged through her bag, finding a small blanket. She put it to her face and inhaled deeply, it smelled like her cottage—aged wood and the floral scented oils her mother always used. Her eyes burned, but she blinked it away.

She tossed the blanket to William. His eyes trailed from the blanket to her, but she gave him a look that said you can't be mad at me if you freeze to death.

He gave her a curt nod and wrapped it around himself before leaning his head against the trunk of the tree.

Jen walked over to Damien and lowered herself to the ground beside him. He gave her a sidelong glance and took a deep breath.

"Why didn't you tell me?"

Jen's head dropped between her knees.

I thought if I ignored it, it would just go away.

"There wasn't a good time."

Damien's hand rose to her cheek, his head tilted. "'I picked that flower for my mother?'"

She chuckled softly. "I panicked. I thought it might be dangerous—my head was still spinning from the visions."

He arched a brow. "Death by flower." He placed his hand on his chest. "What a disappointing way to go."

Jen gave him a weak smile and turned her gaze to the fire. "My mother." Her head dropped. "My protector. What if she—"

"I have no doubt she's okay. You have to believe that, Bug," Damien said with conviction in his voice.

Jenevieve shuddered a breath, turning her face away from him.

She's not my mother.

"You don't have to hide that from me," Damien said gently. He reached up and wiped away a rogue tear from her cheek.

"I know," she said.

"I'm not going to let anything happen to you." He ran his thumb along her cheekbone.

Jen put her hand on top of his. "You sound so sure."

He shrugged. "That's what we do. When we aren't screwing things up." Damien dropped his gaze, but Jen lowered her head to catch it.

"We protect each other."

Jen placed her other hand on his cheek, the fire dancing in his eyes. She pressed her forehead against his.

He turned his head, and his lips softly brushed her cheek.

"You should get some sleep."

Jen pulled away slightly and searched his eyes, finding nothing but compassion looking back at her. She reluctantly nodded.

She positioned herself on the ground, using Damien's lap as a pillow. He looked down at her as he ran his hand softly through her hair, trying his best to comfort her.

After a moment, he spoke.

"I love your eyes."

Jenevieve gave him a small smile.

"I love *your* eyes."

They fluttered closed and she breathed deeply, attempting to empty her mind. Damien's gentle caresses lulled her into a deep sleep.

50

CHAPTER 5

D*arkness wove itself between the trees surrounding the camp. The fire had dissipated into a soft glowing ember, and when Jen's eyes blinked the bleariness of sleep away, she found her friends slept soundly around it, their bodies relaxed, and their faces no longer contorted with fear.*

Her chest released a small sigh of relief against the cool ground beneath her. She raised her head slightly and realized it no longer rested on Damien's lap, but rather his arm, his other one wrapped around her waist as he slept soundly behind her.

Odd. He was supposed to be on watch.

She gently lifted his hand and sat up, rubbing her head and squinting up into the gnarled canopy. The moon was nowhere to be found, and the warped trees that surrounded her were closing in. Jen shook her head; it was only the darkness playing tricks on her mind. But, when she slowly stood, she became aware of something strange about her surroundings.

Everything had a subtle shimmer, like it had been covered in a thin layer of stardust, and the air around the trees seemed to shiver like steam after water hits a scalding stone.

Her heart skittered against her chest.

What is this?

She glanced into the forest behind the clearing. Her brows furrowed at a sudden movement in the distance.

Following the mysterious movement into the ominously dark forest was, rationally, not the best idea, but it seemed that the decision-making portion of her mind was still sleeping beside Damien.

Jen found a small branch and held it against the glowing fire to form a torch. She carefully maneuvered through the two trees leading back to the marked path and squinted to see further into the darkness.

Someone was walking toward her, a flaming torch in their hand.

A Warrior of Kiara?

The hair on her arms rose and her breathing quickened. She stood still as the figure came onto the path and stopped a few leaps away. Not a warrior— a man. His cloak was dark-brown like the trees that hugged the path, and there was no sign of an embroidered lily anywhere on his person. His hood was drawn over his head, dousing his face in shadow, but still, she could feel his gaze searing into her.

Her eyes were drawn down to the amulet around his neck. Connected to a leather cord rope, delicate threads of silver wrapped an amulet of black stone.

The air became thick with a feeling Jen couldn't place.

The corner of the man's mouth twitched, and a voice that came from everywhere and nowhere spoke within her mind.

"Come find me."

She jolted awake.

Dawn whispered at the edges of night, pressing gently against the gloom that lingered like an oppressive shroud. The sun still hadn't pierced the dense canopy, but Jen could finally see more than a few feet in front of her.

William glanced over from where he stood beside Leeyna.

"Oh good, we all survived the night. That's promising."

"Very astute," Leeyna teased, playfully hitting his shoulder.

"Bad dream?" Damien asked, watching her as he fastened his sheath to his chest. Jen sat up and took in the camp. Nothing was shimmering and the air no longer shivered around the trees.

"Just an…odd one," she said, rubbing her head.

The others were already up, and by the look of it, they had been for a while.

Emelie walked over and offered her hand, pulling Jen to her feet as Damien snuffed out the remaining embers of the fire.

"We should go," he said.

"Alright," Jen said, peering towards the path. "Hopefully we can get back to Nimea by mid-morning—"

"We're not going back to Nimea, silly," Emelie said, draping the borrowed cloak over Jen's shoulders with a knowing smile.

"What?" Jen breathed, hope quietly blooming in her chest.

Emelie secured the cloak around Jen's neck.

"We're going with you," she said, looking back at the others.

"All of us."

"But—"

"I know that look," Damien said, leaning against the tree closest to the path. "We talked it over before you woke up." He looked down his nose at her. "You won't change our minds, Bug."

She was at a loss for words. Jen was resolved to wake up and escort them back to the remains of their village. She was prepared to emerge on the other side of Bri alone.

Jen grabbed Emelie's hands. "But you're family—"

"They will take care of each other." Emelie brought their hands to her chest. "And *you* are my family too."

Jen fought the stinging in the corners of her eyes. Emelie had always been her family—the sister she *chose*. But to hear her say it out loud, to acknowledge their importance to each other—it was overwhelming to say the least.

Don't cry. Don't cry. Don't cry.

"I'm with you," Emelie said firmly, heading towards the path. "Besides, you'll need a healer." Her eyes twinkled with humor. "William is bound to injure himself at some point."

She disappeared through the trees.

Before Jen could comprehend what was happening, Leeyna was in front of her, gently taking her hands.

"I'm with you, too," she said.

"But your mother? The animals?"

Leeyna looked in the direction of their village, an unreadable expression on her face. "Let them think I'm dead," she said, a hint of resentment in her voice. "It's better that way."

She let go and followed after Emelie.

A little dark, but I'll take it.

She glanced over at William. A heavy sigh wrung from him as he looked down at his feet, scuffing over the already extinguished fire.

He took a few steps towards her and slowly lifted his eyes to meet hers. "About last night—"

"You had every right to be upset," Jen said.

Willam nodded. "I'm sorry, Jen. If I made anything worse—"

Jen huffed a laugh. "If things had gotten worse, it would *not* have been because of you, William."

He laughed with her, and the awkwardness between them slowly fading into the embers of the fire behind them.

William stepped closer and placed his hand on her shoulder, his kind eyes filled with conviction. "I'm with you."

"Are you sure?"

He smiled at her. "I've spent my life reading about the adventures of courageous men." He squeezed her shoulder. "It's time I became one."

His hand fell to his side, and he stepped towards the path, clapping Damien on the back as he passed by.

Jen bent down to grab her bag, and as she swung it over her shoulder, her gaze snagged on the wisps of smoke that rose from the ashes of the fire. A tingling sensation prickled along her fingertips, but as soon as she glanced down, it ceased.

She clenched her hand a few times and turned around to find Damien still leaning against the tree, his hands resting over the buckle of his sheath.

"What?" He pointed at his chest. "Am I supposed to say, 'I'm with you,' too?"

Jen snorted as she made to join the others, but Damien grabbed her hand, pulling her close. She peered up, and, for a moment, felt as though she were flying through the winter-sky of his piercing blue eyes.

"I am with you," he whispered. "Always."

Jen smiled softly.

She had never doubted that. Not for a single moment.

Jen walked out onto the path with Damien right behind her. She glanced towards the next marked tree, and an unexpected chill ran down her spine.

Come find me.

The low voice caressed along her mind; delicate, but unwavering.

"What are you looking at?"

She practically jumped out of her skin when Emelie appeared behind her. "Nothing." She willed her heart to stop racing and looked over her shoulder. "Is everyone ready?"

They started down the path, sunlight fighting against the labyrinth of trees, the forest stuck within a perpetual state of twilight. Through the dim light, Jen now had a clear view of just how condensed and mangled the forest was.

The trees were practically on top of one another, branches growing in twisted ropes that connected with the surrounding wood.

Jen searched for the next X, and as the foliage grew more entangled, the marks became more frequent, as if whoever carved them was aware of just how convoluted this forest was.

William stared down at his feet as he walked behind Leeyna.

"So, you like animals?" he broke the tense silence to ask the back of her head. Emelie and Jen looked at each other.

"Well, my family ran the kennel," Leeyna said, grabbing a branch to step over an exposed root.

"Oh, right—that—that makes sense," William said, following her stride and hoisting himself over the same root. He looked back at Damien with pleading eyes. Damien opened and closed his mouth, clearly having not expected to be part of this conversation.

"Favorite animals?" He shrugged.

William cleared his throat. "Do you have a favorite animal?"

Emelie stifled a laugh.

"I've always been partial to wolves, actually," Leeyna said.

William made a sound that made it clear that he was not expecting that as her answer.

"I've never seen you with a…wolf," he said as he ducked under a low hanging branch.

Leeyna arched a brow.

"You've been watching me?" she asked.

"I—uh—no—just in passing. I don't watch you," he fumbled, embarrassment returning to his voice.

Emelie rolled her eyes. "Oh, William."

Jenevieve stopped. She looked ahead at the forest where the treetops became progressively lower. The trunks and branches crammed closer together to form a makeshift tunnel.

Her eyes caught sight of an X on a warped tree where the descent began.

"It looks like we have to go *that* way," she said, pointing towards the next marked tree.

Damien peered over her shoulder. "Are we going to fit?"

"We can only hope," Jen said with a sigh. Emelie and Leeyna looked on anxiously.

Damien stepped in front of William and placed a reassuring hand on Leeyna's shoulder.

"We'll be alright, just go slowly when we get there, careful not to get caught by any wayward branches."

Jen gave him a tentative smile and turned back toward the marked tree. She took a deep breath and walked briskly over a few fallen trunks, and as she came upon the X, the canopy sank towards her, the branches bending down as if trying to reach for her.

Her hands rose to guide her, carefully maneuvering through the increasingly demented forest. She tracked the others by the occasional whimper or small curse after catching themselves on a broken branch.

"Everyone okay back there?" Jen asked. There was a general grumble from the group.

"Shit!" William shouted, catching himself on a rotting root.

"William?" Jen called.

"I didn't hurt myself!"

"We're doing *fantastic*," Emelie grunted as she pulled a twig from her hair.

Jen clapped a hand to her chest.

What is that?

Something tugged on her. An invisible thread wrapped around her sternum and pulled gently in the direction they were headed like the coaxing caress of a lover.

It guided her through the tunnel, and suddenly she instinctively knew where to put her feet. She broke away from the group and sped down the winding path.

"Jen, hang on!" Damien called, but she didn't let up.

"Wait for us!" Emelie yelled.

Her pulse raced, the trees grew thicker around her, but her anxiety had evaporated. Up ahead, the tunnel began to expand, permitting her to stand up straight as she pushed forward.

She followed it down a slope, letting momentum propel her, and when she found even ground, she looked a few feet ahead of her.

Light.

Unencumbered light poured into the last vestiges of the tunnel. Her friends called her name, but it sounded muffled, like they were underwater.

Jen took a few steps forward, and the light touched her shoes. She reached her hands out as the warmth of the sun traveled up her body and kissed her face.

Her friends came running down the hill.

"Jen—" Damien began, but Emelie held her arm out in front of him.

She faced the light and walked slowly out of the forest, and with every step, her skin warmed—her body shuddering as a breath of new life winged through her like a bird experiencing its first flight.

She emerged into a long grassy pasture, the same verdant green as the countryside of Nimea. A few leaps away, the ground ascended towards a ridge.

That gentle thread pulled once again, and so Jen followed it towards the slope. She broke into a sprint, running as if the answers to all her questions awaited at the top. Her legs burned but the pull in her chest drew her up the hill as the wind whipped through her hair until she reached the top, stopping on a plateau.

She gasped.

Emelie and Damien followed quickly behind her, rendered silent by the sight before them. Leeyna and William followed and came to Damien's side. William fell to his knees and Leeyna clapped her hands to her face.

"William," Jen said. "Where are we?"

William released a breath of amazement.

"Etheria."

Jen and the others looked out over the extraordinary landscape. The plateau on which they stood sloped down towards a lush valley that seemed to reach endlessly towards the horizon, only interrupted by a tranquil lake that reflected the blue sky.

Beyond the lake and further towards the horizon began the outline of a long and arduous mountain range rising up to the heavens. The continent seemed to go on forever, an unbelievable thought for someone who spent her entire life in one place.

How could a world so vast and beautiful exist so close to Nimea without any of us knowing? It wasn't even a particularly far distance to travel.

She added those thoughts to her growing list of questions, but until she found someone who could answer even a single one…she glanced over at Damien, a mischievous grin pulled at her lips.

His eyes narrowed. "Don't even think—"

"TAG!" she yelled as she swatted him on the shoulder and took off down the hill into the valley.

Damien bolted after her, hollering as the tension from the last twenty-four hours left his body.

The others looked at each other, and then released their own fears down the descending hill, carrying their exhausted bodies into the valley.

Damien caught up to her and wrapped his hands around her hips, lifting her into the air. She squealed with laughter as they fell in a heap on the ground.

Emelie grabbed Leeyna by the hands and spun in circles, basking in the glorious light of the sun. They all collapsed in a mess of weak laughter and shallow pants.

Jen stretched her hand into the grass, caressing the blades with her fingertips.

She paused.

Jen could have sworn the grass just tugged on her.

She gently pulled her hand away and turned it over in front of her face. No warmth traveling to her fingertips, no glowing, no deadly horde of morai.

She rose to her feet and looked towards the mangled woodland. Jen's mind hurled toward her family. To Darya cowering under a table with Jamie, Rhea's screams slicing through the walls of flames, the look of terror on her mother's face.

Gods, Fjora wasn't her *real mother.*

That is a whole other thought spiral waiting to happen.

Zaniya was the first stop on a mission to reconvene a council she knew nothing about. She scoffed at herself. She didn't understand the significance of any of it, and one thing that Jen detested was being left in the dark.

Why hadn't Fjora told her *anything?* Why did it fall to her to do this? She didn't even know Etheria existed until last night, why would she risk the people she loved for a land she had no connection to?

Her village, her home, endured a brutal attack because of *her.* Were any of them left alive? Did the Warriors arrive in time to save them? What about her family? If they were still alive, would this council help them? Would the morai leave them alone now that she had fled?

Damien gently pried her clenched fist open and intertwined his fingers in hers. He squeezed it, pulling her out of her guilt spiral and back to the present.

Her eyes lifted to his, and they held a deep tenderness—as if he'd heard every thought. His thumb methodically ran over her knuckles.

Jen blinked the burn from her eyes and turned back to Etheria. She pushed the shame and fear away from her mind and looked to William.

"Assuming everything you've ever read is *real*, where would Zaniya be?" she asked.

William's gaze was fixed behind her. He pointed; Jen and the others followed his finger to the western most horizon.

"What is that?" Leeyna asked as she came a little closer to William. He perched his hand on the back of his head.

"The Arc."

It looked to be some kind of tower on a cliff, although it was hard to tell from such a far distance. Damien squinted towards it.

"I think we can get to the city by tonight if we leave now," he said confidently, like he knew exactly what he was talking about. Jen appreciated the feigned confidence; hers was hanging on by a thread.

Emelie surveyed their surroundings.

"Didn't Mael—I mean, Fjora, say there should be a road?"

Jenevieve thought for a moment. Her gaze drew down and she took a few steps forward, kneeling on the ground.

I wonder.

She placed both her hands in the grass and stretched out her fingers as she did before. She felt the gentle tug of the blades, and a wave beneath the ground rippled into the pasture before them. The grass swayed in an unseen wind, and Jen felt the valley pull her forward.

Her head jerked up.

She stood and walked parallel with the forest and the plateau as it began to descend to meet the valley. She stopped where the descent merged with flat ground.

The grass began to thin, and an abandoned, overgrown road revealed itself at her feet.

Jen turned back to her friends and pointed down at her feet.

"I found it," she announced.

They just stood there, gawking.

"Did you just—talk to grass?" William asked.

Jen shrugged. "That's probably the least traumatic thing that's happened in the last twenty-four hours."

She glanced back at the forest one last time. Nothing would ever be the same from this moment on.

"Last chance to turn back," she said.

But without any hesitation, her friends walked towards her.

Jen's heart swelled as they passed by her and continued onto the road ahead. She watched the resolve come over each of them with every step they took into the unknown.

Damien looked over his shoulder and raised a brow.

"Well, are you coming?"

CHAPTER 6

The sun was setting over the tiled rooftops as Jen and the others reached the city gate of Zaniya, a vibrant and crowded port on the shores of the Opaelian Sea along the western coast of Etheria.

Two guards stood on either side of the arched stone entrance, tracking the group out of the corner of their eyes. Jen could have sworn she saw a bit of apprehension flicker over one of the guard's faces.

You're just sleep deprived.

She led her friends down the weather-worn cobblestone streets lined with inns and merchants selling anything from fresh fish to rare gemstones from distant lands.

There was an air of chaos, and yet, everyone seemed to know exactly where they were going.

The labyrinth of streets led to the port itself, the scent of salty sea air pulling Jen's attention towards one of the smaller side streets, where she could just make out dozens of vessels from impressive ships to small dinghies floating beside the docks.

To the northern side of the port, a sandy beach stretched up the coast, turning into hilly dunes that shifted to a mix of sea grass and sand. They ascended higher and higher until they merged with the grass, creating a tract of evergreen cliffs that looked over to the sea.

Jen stopped, her gaze trailing up towards the cliffs.

The Arc.

Atop the highest cliff sat the grand and imposing sandstone tower with impressive windows that stretched towards the sky, the hue of the sunset casting shades of magenta and orange over the massive panes of glass.

The main tower was surrounded by four smaller adjoining ones all lined with the same paned-glass windows, the roof of each a stunning glass dome trimmed with gold.

It was one thing to see it at a distance, but another thing entirely to feel its looming presence waiting at the edge of the city.

Jen forced herself to keep moving down the street, and as the sun descended, she noticed several workers scampering about, lighting lanterns to illuminate the walkways. She glanced over her shoulder to check in on her friends.

William walked between Leeyna and Emelie who showed little interest in their new surroundings; both women looked as though they were about to collapse on the ground.

Damien was behind them, but if he was as exhausted as everyone else, he didn't show it. His eyes darted around, and his body wound so tight Jen thought he might spring at anyone who even breathed in their direction.

She pulled them under an awning away from the main street and knelt, rummaging through her burlap sack.

"Aha!" Jen said triumphantly. She held up an emerald-green velvet bag. Damien looked at it, dumbfounded.

"Is that—"

"I heard it tumbling around in here all day. Fjora gave us some coin," Jenevieve said, astonished that her mother—well—protector, had thought to provide it.

That's going to take some getting used to.

She stood up and looked at her friends.

"We need to find a place to sleep tonight. We can start fresh in the morning and head for the Arc," she said.

Jen walked out from under the walkway into the street and marched further into the heart of the city, her friends trudging behind her. She came to an intersection, and on the far corner, she spotted a sign hanging over the door of a tavern.

The Lion and Lily.

It looked worn, but inviting as she crossed the street to peer through the muntin windows, where she found dozens of people gathered inside. In the corner of the window beside her hung a sign that read:

Rooms for Rent.

Her friends appeared behind her. Damien squinted up at the tavern sign and raised a brow.

"Lily?" he said sardonically. "Seems a bit on the nose."

Jen scoffed.

"Do you have a better idea?"

Damien threw his hands in the air.

"Nope, none. This is great," he amended quickly.

Jen rolled her eyes and opened the door, a rush of comforting warmth greeting them as they stepped inside. Iron sconces flickered against the walls, casting warm pools of amber light along the dark oak tables that filled the room, each lit with their own candle.

Patrons erupted into vivacious laughter at one of the longer tables while the barkeep chatted up a few men at the bar, cheersing their pints and shaking hands with each other.

They stood in the entryway, unsure of where to go when William's stomach rumbled like a roll of thunder. Leeyna clapped a hand to her mouth but ended up cackling through her fingers.

Damien chuckled. "There's a table in the corner there." He pointed. "Let's get some food in our bodies and then maybe we'll have enough brain power to figure out the rooms."

Jen wove through the room to claim it, and everyone filed into either side. They let out a collective sigh of relief; it felt incredible to sit down. Every muscle in her legs and feet ached as she stretched them under the table.

A barmaid emerged from the kitchen carrying a tray of hot steak and kidney pies, and the smell made Emelie groan. Jen's brows shot up before they all burst into loud, cathartic laughter. She placed her hand on Emelie's arm and squeezed before she stood to grab the barmaid.

"Excuse me, can we get a few of those, and a round of ale please?" she asked the young woman.

The barmaid glanced between Jen and their table, with the same look that the guards had given her earlier. She nodded curtly before continuing across the room.

Jen looked around the tavern, and through all the merriment, she realized more than a few patrons sent subtle glances in their direction.

What are they looking at?

She rejoined the others, and when she sat down, the laughter had decreased to delirious chuckles. William sat with his head propped up on one of his hands.

"You okay?" Jen asked.

William straightened. "Oh, you know, just a typical day of questioning reality. What's a legend? What's real? Oh look, an entire continent on the other side of Bri." He waved his hands in the air.

"So, easy questions?" Leeyna said, reaching out to grab one of his hands.

The barmaid came over to drop off the ale, and when the hoppy brew touched their lips, they instantly sank lower into their seats.

Damien continued to take stock of their surroundings, but when his eyes found Jen, they softened before he lifted his mug to his lips, clearly struggling to relax.

At that moment, a rich, savory aroma wafted from the kitchen as the same barmaid emerged with a tray of pies for their table. They practically salivated at the sight of the steaming, buttery crusts sitting in front of them.

By the time they finished eating, the tavern wasn't as lively as when they first arrived. The crowd had thinned, making it easier for Jen to see the people that were left, instead of everyone blending into a boisterous mob.

Her eyes wandered from the bar to a table in the corner.

A man with broad shoulders taking up most of the booth sat with his back to her. He lounged comfortably in his seat, taking idle sips from a rounded glass filled with an amber liquid.

Jen watched him carefully, her gaze magnetic, unable to look away.

He placed his arm on the table, revealing the beginnings of a tattoo that Jen could only just make out. The sleeve of his deep green shirt pulled up as he lifted his arm to sip from his glass.

Is that a lion?

He turned his head and glanced down his shoulder, as if he could feel her stare.

The hair raised on her arms.

A chill ran down her spine.

She broke her gaze to look down at the mug in her hand and noticed the design etched into it. A lion holding a lily.

Jen's eyes flickered back to the man, but he was gone.

She blinked a few times; she was so exhausted she must have been hallucinating.

Great, more hallucinations, what else is new?

She eyed the table of cleared plates and empty mugs. Her friends were slumped over in their seats.

"I'll be right back," she said as she stood, her body protesting her movements. She concealed a wince as she weaved around a few tables and slid between a few men sitting at the bar.

The barkeep spotted her and came over, his bald head gleaming under the soft lantern light.

"Hi," she said, her voice pitched a little too high. "Can we get two rooms please?"

"How many beds ya' need," he said, his tone indifferent as he continued pouring drinks for others seated nearby.

"Five."

The barkeep considered her, wiping his hands on the brown apron hanging over his dark blue shirt. He scratched his full beard and glanced over at Jen's table.

"Ten dakras," he said.

She opened her mouth and then shut it.

Dakras?

He quirked a brow and then rubbed his fingers together. Jen's eyes widened in realization.

Oh, right.

"Sorry," she said as she fumbled with her velvet pouch. She tried her best to hide the amount of money she was carrying around, but she had no idea what she was looking for.

Jen grabbed a small handful and gently placed the coins on the bar top. She looked at the barkeep sheepishly.

Please don't steal all my money. It's been a very long day.

The indifference melted from the man's face, and he reached over the bar to collect the copper coins from the pile before helping her collect the remainder.

"You'll want ta be careful with that." He jutted his chin at the velvet pouch. "This pub is safe, but yer in a port city. We get all sorts 'o riff raff here."

"Thank you…" Jen started. His eyes twinkled with a warm smile.

"Marcos," he said, extending his hand.

She returned his smile with one of her own and took his hand gratefully, relief swelling in her chest. "Jenevieve."

"Well, Miss Jenevieve. Yer rooms are numbers three and four, just up the stairs 'round the corner there," Marcos said as he pointed towards a flight of stairs by the front door. "Room four 'as three beds."

"Thank you," Jen said. "Can I pay you for the…?" She gestured to the table of empty mugs and plates. Marcos glimpsed between the table and Jen. He placed a rough hand on the bartop in front of her and tapped the dark oak.

"You can pay in the mornin', ye'? Yer friends look like they might fall asleep in ma' bar," he said with an air of humor.

Jen perched her elbow beside his hand. "You know, I think they might," she said.

Marcos slid her the room keys and gave her a wink.

Jen returned to her friends, flashing the keys at them. With a colorful collection of groans, they lugged themselves out of the booth and up the steps on the inn side of the building, clutching onto the railing as if it was the only thing keeping them from passing out.

Jen led them down the hallway and unlocked room four to let Leeyna and Emelie in. They dragged their feet over the threshold.

She gestured across the hall to room three. "Alright, boys, this is your room," she said, handing William the key.

Jen stepped into her room, but when she turned to close the door, Damien was standing in his doorway. Her brows raised.

He took two steps into the hall, putting himself almost nose to nose with her.

Jen thought he might try to kiss her, and if she was being honest, that wouldn't be the *worst* ending to an otherwise horrific twenty-four hours. But what would it mean? Did he just want a distraction from the situation they were in? Was it something more? Gods. They never had a chance to finish that conversation in the barn.

Too many fireballs.

She chanced a glance up at him and found him already watching her, his head tilted like he could see all the questions churning inside her head. That's what happened when someone knew another person as long as Damien had known her. They were laid bare to one another, unable to hide.

Before she realized what was happening, he was wrapping his arms around her—holding her. Jen pressed her face against his strong chest as her arms instinctively fell around his waist and interlocked at his back.

She inhaled him. He smelled like unkempt pastures and smoke from his forge; the familiar scent anchored her in the center of a new unknown.

He stroked her hair, his cheek resting on the top of her head. He had held her like this hundreds of times, but this one, this one was sorely needed, and she hadn't realized how much.

Damien always knew when and how to hold her together when she was on the brink of falling apart.

He stood there with her for several minutes, seemingly in no hurry to let go—he would probably stand there all night if she wanted him to. But she needed to let him sleep, and so she, reluctantly, released him.

Damien placed a soft brush of his lips on her forehead.

"Goodnight," he whispered. She gave him a weak smile and turned away before she could think better of it.

She closed the door behind her and found Emelie and Leeyna already asleep on top of their beds, not even bothering to get under the quilts.

Jen crept over to the remaining bed in the corner and lit the candle sitting on the nightstand beside it, the dim light casting shadows along the walls.

She placed the burlap sack on top of the soft quilt and began going through it. There was the velvet pouch of coins, which she gingerly placed on the bed.

And then the dagger.

She unsheathed it halfway, examining the silver blade. Her fingers felt the carved lily, and she was overcome with a wave of emotion.

It belonged to your mother.

Jenevieve sheathed it and dropped it on the quilt. She raised her hands to her cheeks, the comfort of Damien's embrace evaporating as the gravity of her circumstances grew heavier.

A completely different life laid on the bed before her. A life she knew nothing about.

She grabbed the bag and flipped it upside down to shake any remaining items out of it. The cloak and blanket came tumbling out, but something else fell to the floor.

She bent over to retrieve a folded piece of parchment. It was sealed with wax—a symbol she did not recognize. Jen flipped it over and froze.

Jenevieve.

Tears pricked at her eyes as she ripped the seal open. She sank down on the bed, her hand clasped over her mouth.

My Darling Jenevieve,

I don't have much time. I'm sure you must have so many questions. I am so sorry that this burden has been put on your shoulders. This was never supposed to happen this way; we were supposed to have more time.

You, and your safety, are the most important things now.

Yes, you are in Etheria. It is very real. It was my home before I was charged with your protection, and it is where you were born.

Firstly, find your way to the Arc, there you will find the history of the continent in its many volumes. Seek out anything associated with the descendants of the Council of Suran. If things transpire the way I dread they will, then I have told you why.

I wish I could tell you more, but this guidance alone is dangerous.

Then, you must head to Sachandes, the realm to the north of Zaniya. The kingdom dwells beside the Waelyn Valley in the heart of the Kalli Mountains. You will find King Haythem and Queen Eliana. They are good people. You should be welcomed with grace. If you should run into any discord, give them a message from me.

Tell them, Fjora lives.

I love you my darling,

Mama

Jenevieve sat with the letter in her hand, staring at the words. She pressed the paper to her chest and attempted to push away the onslaught of emotions churning beneath her skin.

She didn't know if her mother—Fjora—was even alive, and that unknown felt like a hot iron was pressing down on her heart.

Jen stood up and tossed the letter on the nightstand. She didn't want to chance that Emelie, or anyone else, would see the state she was in, so she carefully opened the door and closed it quietly behind her.

She stepped across the hall and lifted her hand to knock on the door, but she paused. Damien would want to help—but there was nothing he could do to make this better, there was nothing *anyone* could do.

Jen walked down the stairs back to the pub. It was all but cleared out, only a few stray patrons left at the bar top. She sank onto one of the stools, a desolate ache radiating in her chest.

Marcos was wiping down glasses and noticed her sitting down.

"You're back!" he said enthusiastically.

He tilted his head, concern crinkling in the corners of his rich-brown eyes as he took in her expression.

Like a father looking at his child.

That only made the ache in her chest worse.

"Can I get you something?" he pressed, his voice painfully kind.

Jen nodded. "Maybe something stronger than ale?"

"She'll have what I'm having, Marcos," a low voice rumbled. Marcos nodded and grabbed a rounded glass. He poured an amber liquid from a glass bottle sitting on the back shelf behind him.

A looming presence approached from behind her, and, for a moment, her breathing grew shallow. They leaned against the bar top beside her, elbows propped up on the lip.

Her eyes traveled from the dark oak of the bar to the tattooed arm of the stranger from earlier that evening.

The lion.

Her gaze slowly flicked up and met the deep, vivid green eyes of a tall, beautiful man. His dark chestnut brown hair hung around his face, framing a sharp jawline shadowed by a slight stubble.

Jen forgot for a moment why she was in this tavern to begin with. All sense of the world around them fell away and into the verdant pools looking back at her.

He was studying her.

She dragged her eyes away from the man as Marcos placed the glass in front of her. She swirled the liquid within it, examining the golden amber color. The man continued to watch her as she took a small sip.

Jen let out a harsh cough as it burned the back of her throat.

He ran a hand through his hair.

"Ardovian rum. Absolute shit people, but they do have their talents," he said, taking a languid sip from his own glass.

They sat in silence for a moment.

"Ronan," he said simply.

"What?" Jen asked.

"My name," he said with an arrogant smirk.

"I didn't ask for it," Jen retorted.

Ronan looked out into the near empty pub.

"Really? I could have sworn you did," he drawled.

Jen took another sip and released an exasperated sigh.

"Look. I'm not in the mood for…whatever this is you're doing," Jen said with a wave of her hand.

Ronan sat down on the stool beside her. She scoffed when he scooted brazenly close. He dipped his head towards her. "Do you want to talk about it?"

"No. Thanks."

"I'm a good listener."

"Somehow I find that hard to believe."

He ran his thumb around the edge of his glass.

"You and your friends aren't from here, are you?" Ronan asked, less of a question and more of a statement. Jen couldn't help but let out a harsh laugh.

"Is it that obvious?"

He chuckled. It was low and visceral.

"Inbetween'ers?" he asked as he raised his eyebrow in curiosity.

"Am I supposed to know what that is?" she asked, her eyes darting over to Marcos, who was absentmindedly cleaning the bar and very clearly eavesdropping.

"From the Inbetween?" Ronan explained without actually explaining anything. Jen looked at him like he was speaking in another language.

His eyes narrowed.

"Where are you from…?" he asked, now in a much softer voice. Suddenly Jen's hands grew clammy around her glass. She drank the rest of her rum and took a deep breath.

"Nimea."

Ronan sputtered his drink over the bar. Marcos came running to clean it up. "I'm—ehem—I'm fine Marcos. I got it," he coughed as he took the rag from him and quickly cleaned the mess. "I'll take another one; she will, too," he said with no hint of a question in his voice.

"Did you say you're from Nimea?" he asked in a hushed tone. Jen didn't understand why this was so shocking. But then again, she realized very quickly that she knew very little, and everything was in fact—shocking.

"No…I said…Nim…pala…" Jen said, her eyes wandering as Marcos poured her another drink. Ronan's brows formed a hard line. "That's not a place."

"It could be."

"It's not."

Jen sighed.

"Fine. Yes, Nimea. Why is that a big deal? Do you even know where that is?"

Ronan took a long sip of his rum.

"I do. But it's not supposed to exist. It was destroyed a thousand years ago."

Jen was dumbfounded. It seems that the people on this side of Bri were also told falsehoods. For some reason, that made her feel a little better.

We can all be confused together.

"Is that why people have been gawking at me and my friends?" she asked.

"Most people on this continent don't think your people exist. They wouldn't know what they were looking at," Ronan replied.

Jen threw her hands up in defeat. "Then, what?"

"You all were…well *are*, wearing ivory."

"So?"

Ronan seemed rather stupefied by their conversation.

"Regals of the Inbetween—their colors are bronze and ivory."

Regals? Great. More words I don't know.

But then Jen thought back to the woods the night before. The cloaked figures running through the trees. The flicker of ivory at their feet.

Ronan stroked the stubble under his chin.

"You should get some different clothes if you don't want to be stared at," he said looking at her ivory linen dress. "People here are weary of magic, living in a port city exposes them to the best and worst of it."

Her body tensed, a prickling sensation nipping at her fingers.

Okay, so there's magic on this side of Bri. Act casual. It's not like blinding beams of light exploded from your hands last night. Maybe that's normal here?

"Thanks for the advice," Jen said as she finished off her drink. Her mind lurched back to the forest, and to her mother, her family. Lilies. Fire. Destruction. Screaming.

Ronan tilted his head. "Something is weighing on you."

Jen opened her mouth to say something quip, but she was too exhausted to deny it.

"That's very presumptuous…"

Ronan looked down at his glass.

"It's all over your face."

Jen hesitated.

"I've just. It's just…" she struggled.

Ronan reached for her. His fingertips met the top of her hand, and the touch sent a tingle through her skin. She pulled away instinctively. Her gaze flickered back to him.

His calloused fingers thrummed on the bar.

"Who *are* you," he asked, his voice lower now.

"I—"

"You don't know, *do you?*" he said, rubbing his hand.

Jen looked back at him for a moment that felt like an eternity.

"I intend to find out," she said unconvincingly.

"As do I."

Jenevieve scoffed at the arrogance of this man.

"How do you carry that ego around?"

Marcos barked a laugh from the opposite corner of the bar. Ronan glared at him.

"That rum is making you bold." He jutted his chin at her glass.

"You prefer a docile doe?"

He slid even closer to her.

"Absolutely not."

Jen's mouth stood agape.

Who in hells is this guy?

After a moment, she blinked and shook her head. She turned around on the stool and realized instantly that she stood up too fast. Black spots invaded her vision as the combination of rum, exhaustion, and overwhelming trauma sent her legs crumbling beneath her.

"Whoa!" Ronan said, catching her before she could hit the ground. Jen felt his muscles tense around her.

"You alright?" he asked, searching her eyes.

"Yes. *Oof.* That's embarrassing," she said, laughing it off as she found her footing. She wiggled out of his arms and pulled at her sleeve.

"Okay. New clothes, then the Arc," she said, dusting off her dress.

"The Arc?" Ronan asked.

Whoops.

"That's why we came here," she said.

Shut the fuck up, Jen.

"Fair enough," Ronan said as he leaned back on the bar. Jen wrung her hands awkwardly and turned to leave.

"Well, have a good night, Marcos," she said as she gave the barkeep a small wave. He returned her wave with a kind smile. "Night, dear."

She looked at Ronan, who watched her curiously.

"Goodnight, Ronan."

She walked a few steps before she stopped by the stairs.

He raised a brow.

"Jenevieve."

"What's that?"

"My name."

His lips twitched.

"Goodnight, Jenevieve."

As she walked around the corner to the stairs, she heard the *wap* of a bar towel.

"What?" Ronan scowled.

Jen smirked. She was no longer thinking about the letter from Fjora or the terrifying unknown ahead of her, but rather the mysterious man— his voice, his green eyes, and the lion etched into his forearm.

CHAPTER 7

"Jen…wake up, sleepy head."

Jen groaned as gentle hands rocked her back and forth, coaxing her awake. She'd slept a dreamless sleep, something she was acutely grateful for.

She cracked one eye open, finding Emelie kneeling beside her.

"Leeyna and the boys are already downstairs," Emelie said, rising to her feet.

Jen stretched as she sat up, noticing the cloak, velvet pouch, and the dagger lying on the bed beside her. The letter was still on the nightstand, opened just enough to see the beginnings of her mother's writing. She snatched it up and shoved it into the bag before Emelie turned around.

Jen looked down at her clothes, her mind wandering briefly to the mysterious man from last night.

I wonder if he's still downstair, lurking.

She pushed the image from her mind.

"We need to get out of these clothes," Jen said, throwing her belongings in her bag before heaving it over her shoulder. Emelie looked down at her own dress with a puzzled look on her face.

"What's wrong with our clothes?" she asked.

Jen didn't have the mental capacity to explain *him* and their late-night drinks, and, honestly, she hadn't understood half of their conversation anyway.

"We just need new clothes, okay?"

"Whatever you say," Emelie muttered as they made their way down to the pub.

The others were seated at a table by the window. Emelie joined them while Jen continued to the bar, but instead of Marcos, there was a woman with caramel-brown hair streaked with gray.

She was placing clean mugs on the shelves when Jen cleared her throat. Her kind, chestnut eyes met Jenevieve's and she smiled warmly.

"Good morning, darlin'. What'll ya 'ave?" the woman asked with a slight lilt.

"Good morning, I need to pay for the meal and ale from last night," Jen began to explain. "Marcos told me I could pay in the morning…" she continued self-consciously. Recognition came over the woman's face.

"Oh, yes. My husban' told me to be expectin' ye," she said, moving over to a collection of glasses that also needed loading on the shelves. "Ma' name's Daphne."

"Your husband was very kind yesterday, Daphne," Jen said appreciatively. "How much do I owe you?"

Daphne stopped her task for a moment and wiped her hands with the rag laced through the straps of her apron. "Three crescents all around, dear," she said.

Jen rummaged for the velvet pouch and retrieved three silver coins. She placed them in Daphne's open hand. Jen leaned forward on the bar towards Daphne.

"Would we be able to rent the same rooms tonight?"

Daphne's face lit up. "Of course, dear! I'll make sure the rooms are cleaned and we'll have your keys ready when ye' return," she said warmly. Jen returned it in kind, relieved that there were genuine, good-hearted people on this side of Bri.

"Can you tell me the best way to the Arc?" she asked.

Daphne waved a hand towards the door. "Just turn left out the pub and go straight up the main road there. You'll see the Arc from the street, the colossal thing is hard ta' miss."

"How far of a walk is it?"

"Abou' an hour if ye' walk fas'," Daphne chirped.

"And if we wanted to get out of these clothes and into something…less, well… less?" Jen asked, displaying her gown to Daphne.

"Ah, yes." She examined the dress. "There's a merchant's market a few streets down in the square. You'll pass t'rough it on the way to the Arc."

Jenevieve reached for Daphne's hand and squeezed.

"Thank you, Daphne, we'll be back later," Jen said as she turned to walk to her friends still seated by the window.

"Wait a moment, darlin'," Daphne called after her. "You'll be needin' something easier ta' carry then that burlap ya' got there," she said, nodding to the now tattered burlap sack.

Daphne walked back behind the bar shelves and returned a moment later with a rucksack in her hands; brown wool lined with dark leather. "It's a bit warn, but I reckon it'll do better than that mangy ol' thing ya got there," she said.

Jen accepted it, grinning in appreciation.

"Off ya' go then," Daphne said, and turned back to her glasses.

Jen rejoined her friends at the table, where she started transferring her belongings to the new bag. "Alright, Daphne said—"

"Daphne?" Emelie arched a brow. Jen pointed her chin towards the woman behind the bar.

"Daphne said it's about an hour to the Arc if we're quick about it." She folded up the old burlap and placed it inside the rucksack. "We'll be looking for anything on the descendants of the Council of Suran."

Damien rose to his feet. "Do we know what that means?"

Jen couldn't help the snort that came out of her. "Nope."

"Do we know where to look once we're in there?"

She gave him a look that said *quit with the questions I don't have the answers to.*

He pressed his lips together, but the laughter found its way to his eyes. "Great. Everyone ready?" He strapped his sword to his back.

They left the tavern and stepped into the morning light, the town already bustling with early shoppers and merchants on their way to the market.

They were, again, met with an occasional apprehensive look as they walked up the main cobblestone street. The air had the faint smell of sea water and fish, occasionally interrupted by freshly baked morning confections being set out for sale.

A few minutes later they found themselves in the merchant's market. Jen looked at her friends and knew that they were all thinking the same thing.

The weekend markets in Nimea, though quainter and more welcoming than this one, held a strikingly similar energy. Bitter-sweet nostalgia lingered around them as they kept walking.

Stands of seafood, meat, fruits and vegetables lined one side of the market, while fabrics and gemstones lined the other side of the square. Jen shepherded her friends over to that side of the market, where they found a few places that sold simple linen shirts, skirts, and pants.

She grabbed a pair of brown tweed pants, a belt that could hold her dagger, and a leather pouch that could be threaded through the belt to hold some of her coin—she didn't want to make a scene every time she rummaged through her rucksack.

They changed in a nearby alley and threw their Nimean clothing in the rubbish bin, bidding farewell to their life on the other side of the forest.

No going back, now.

Emelie took hold of Jen's hand, and they together led the group towards the towering Arc in the distance.

The street began to ascend, and the shops became scarce where the evergreen cliffs began to form, the rippling surface of the sea glimmering just beyond them.

The Arc grew majestically as they approached, the cobblestone giving way to a dirt path as the city fell away behind them. The daunting sandstone tower was even more imposing than it seemed back in the city.

They arrived at the front of the Arc and gazed at the massive doors that joined with one of the immense windows embedded within the stone.

Well, this is intimidating.

Her brows drew together. Her hand lifted to her chest.

An invisible thread wrapped itself around her and gently pulled her towards the door, and with it, a faint, melodious hum shimmered over the surface of her skin and into her ears. It was everywhere and nowhere, enveloping her mind and thrumming with her heartbeat, calling to her.

She stepped forward, following it.

"Jen?" Emelie asked, trying to get her attention.

Jen placed her hand on the door, and like the blades of grass in the valley, the fibers of the wood seemed to grasp her skin in some kind of familiar embrace. A small smile pulled at her lips as she pushed open the door.

The others filed in behind her, and their jaws dropped at the sight before them.

The tower walls were filled to the brim with endless shelves of volumes and parchment scrolls. Dark wooden walkways appeared every few stories, along with enchanting ladders that could be moved across the infinite shelves. Stairwells jutted out into the main area, each housing a spiral staircase that led to the four smaller adjoining towers.

Warm light from the windows spilled onto shards of sea-glass hewn within the limestone floors; hues of green and blue reflecting like soothing waves lulled by an invisible current.

Jen's attention wasn't held by the current trapped in the floor, the immeasurable number of books or the radiant glass dome of the ceiling, but by what stood straight ahead.

A magnificent oak tree that took root in the middle of the Arc, a seemingly endless cacophony of branches extending out at all heights. They were so immense they had intertwined with the building itself, reaching into the walkways like vines. Delicate lanterns lined the lush greenery of the tree, giving it an enchanted and mythical air.

Damien cleared his throat.

"So…?"

She pulled her eyes away from the tree, beckoning everyone closer. Fjora's voice hung over her as a grave reminder of the dangerous information they were about to search for.

"Right," she said in a hushed tone. "The Council of Suran. William, you know what that is, right?"

William nodded, although he looked hesitant.

"Okay, good. We should split up to cover more ground."

"I think we should explore the Arc and figure out where everything is," Damien suggested as his eyes trailed up the cavernous tower.

"Yes!" William yelled. Leeyna shushed him. "Yes. Yes. Yes," he whispered, bouncing from one foot to the other. They turned their sights to him as he all but leapt with excitement, clamoring for the chance to be let loose.

Jen raised a brow.

"Let's get started," she said.

William grabbed Leeyna's hand and yanked her away into the Arc, eliciting a combination of laughter and visceral sounds of being wrenched by a schoolmaster-turned-child by the discovery of the largest library on the continent.

Emelie skipped away in the opposite direction, taking in the splendor of it all. Damien came up beside Jen.

"So, where to?" he asked. Jen leaned against his shoulder. All morning she'd been watching for the subtle signs he unconsciously gave when he was feeling anxious, and the rigidity of his shoulders was the most obvious one.

"I know why *I'm* feeling anxious," she said quietly, pushing against his shoulder. His eyes flicked to her and then back to the open space of the Arc, his mouth settling into an uncharacteristically serious line.

"We're in a realm that's not supposed to exist," he murmured. "I'm assuming those morai are not the only things to worry about here." He slipped his hand into hers. "I'm just being cautious."

"I don't see any hordes of demon bats at the moment, do you?" She squeezed his hand, earning a tight smile he wouldn't allow to spread.

"At the moment," he retorted.

"Why don't you explore the smaller towers?" she asked, jutting her chin towards a nearby stairwell. He glanced at it, but when his gaze returned to her, a spark of unease lit up behind his eyes.

"You aren't coming with me?"

"I just—I need to do a little exploring on my own first," she stuttered. A concerned crease formed between his brows.

"I'm fine," she said, placing her chin on his shoulder for a moment before letting go of him.

He looked at her, and Jen knew he was searching her face for nerves, but she had carefully tucked them away out of sight. Damien sighed and nodded, turning towards the stairwell. She watched him until he started up the stairs and then turned back to the massive oak tree.

The mystical hum hadn't left her since they arrived at the front doors, even when she was devising a plan with her friends, and now it was clear—it was the tree that called to her.

The hum branched into several melodies blending in both harmony and dissonance. The invisible thread wrapped itself around her and coaxed her forward, and she cautiously followed.

There were few other people in the Arc, and they were either reading at large oak tables or wandering about the many floors—none looked up from their own tasks.

As Jenevieve approached, she noticed the branches were not only adorned with strung lanterns, but with ivory ribbons. Hundreds of them. They were delicately tied, and in the warm light of the sun, they produced an effervescent glow.

She'd never seen anything so beautiful. The humming grew louder, beckoning her closer. The pull tightened, grew more insistent as if a being of its own, until she was before the massive trunk of the great oak. Jen looked up—every branch and every leaf, multiplying like a kaleidoscope around her, stemmed from this point. The never-ending entanglement of a mystical arboretum held her entire being.

Jen's gaze raked over the tree trunk, where several markings marred the bark. Her eyes lowered just above her head, snagging on one of them.

She squinted, then her eyes widened.

The worn carving of…a lily.

Jen took an instinctive step back. The humming in her ear was still beckoning her forward, the thread pulled as if it originated from the tree itself. She slowly reapproached and reached out her hand. Her fingertips danced over the carving, and then her palm flattened against it.

Once again, the fibers of the oak grasped the cells of her skin, but this time they did not let go. The humming stopped abruptly as Jen's palm warmed, and a bright light came soaring through her mind.

"The time will come when the hubris of good and the shadow of evil will bring forth a power long thought lost. Only when a child of light and a child of dark become one in tandem shall those who were lost be found, and the legend of light and shadow shall be known."

The voice.

From her school room.

From her garden.

But this time accompanied by a flood of images. A woman…screaming…

"Breathe mo nuri, Breathe."

"Naedyra! AGH! Naedyra the Book! Please…ARGHHH," the young woman cried out.

A woman, younger than Jen, was in bed giving birth. A dark-haired man sat beside her, holding her hand, and two women surrounded her, a midwife on the ground aiding in the birth, and another who was frantically searching for something in the massive bedroom. She must have been Naedyra.

On the opposite side of the room, a set of double doors opened onto a small terrace where two men stood anxiously pacing while their eyes darted in every direction.

"Close the door! We can't risk anyone hearing!" the man beside the laboring woman barked. The double doors were shut with haste. The young woman was straining to keep quiet, but it was nearly impossible to do so.

"AHHH!" she cried out in pain. The man held her hand tightly and used the other to blot her forehead with a damp rag, pushing her white-blonde hair from her face.

"You're almost there! Come now, PUSH!"

"I can't...I can't..." she whimpered. Naedyra came running across the room with a book in her arms. It was faded white, with ornate silver and gold flames weaving around the entirety of the cover and binding. She placed the book on the ground beside her and grabbed the woman's other hand.

"Please don't forsake me now," the woman pleaded to Naedyra.

"I'm not leaving you, I swear it," Naedyra said as she kissed the woman's hand.

"PUSH, child!" the midwife ordered. The woman leaned forward and pushed with all her might, holding on desperately to her supporters on either side.

"That's it! Here it comes!" The midwife encouraged the woman to keep pushing. The young woman yelled out and then...the cries of a newborn filled the room. She let out a combination of laugh and groan. The man beside her kissed her forehead while Naedyra held the other hand to her cheek.

The midwife wrapped the child in a clean sheet and handed the baby to the new mother.

"It's a beautiful girl, sweetling," she crooned.

The young woman held her baby girl and cried desolate tears.

"No matter how you came to be. You are loved. You are cherished."

The woman's breathing grew shallow, and her eyes began to lose focus. The midwife checked the birthing bed. She was losing too much blood.

Naedyra saw the look of somber defeat on the nurse's face.

"No, please, you have to hang on. We're going to fix you up, alright?" she implored. The young woman gave her a weak smile.

"The Book, Naedyra..."

The young woman lowered her forehead to her child.

"You are the hope of this world, Ainsley."

She kissed Ainsley's head and handed her to the man sitting next to her. He took her and looked back at the young woman with desperate questioning in his eyes. She managed a small smile.

"It's okay, Theo," she said weakly. She turned to Naedyra, who was crying into the young woman's hand.

"I've done my part, now you must do yours," she said as she gestured to the book. "Protect my child. She is...the hope of this world," she continued through fractured breaths.

Naedyra held the book open as the young woman placed her hand on top of the exposed pages. She closed her eyes, and a warm, white light came from her hand and expelled into the parchment. The book began to glow, and wind swirling around the birthing bed as the others looked on.

"Ufriejaa nuri," she whispered.

The light surged and was absorbed by the pages of the Book and the wind snapped it shut before it dissipated. The young woman was fading fast.

"Naedyra..."

"I'm here..."

"He can't find out about her. Hide her away...please," the woman pleaded softly. Naedyra held her hand.

"I swear on my life, she will be safe."

"You have to go now..." the young woman said, going in and out of consciousness.

"I won't leave you," Naedyra said desperately.

"You must...take her...go..."

Her breathing slowed.

"No. Please, Kiara," Naedyra pleaded.

Theo walked around with the child and handed her to Naedyra.

"She's right. You have to go. It's only a matter of time. I'll stay with her," he said as he sat down beside Kiara. "Until the end."

"I love you my sweet child," Kiara whispered. Theo laced his fingers with hers and looked to Naedyra and the midwife.

The double doors flew open, and the two men ran inside.

"The serpent clouds are approaching—he's found us!" they said in a panic.

"Go. Go now!" Theo yelled to the women. Naedyra stood up and looked to the midwife, and then to Kiara, almost gone now. The wind from the dark clouds burst into the birthing room.

"Now!"

Naedyra grabbed the midwife's arm and sprinted with Ainsley in hand out the hidden door in the back of the room and down the steps.

She looked back, tears welling in her eyes as Kiara's chest rose, and then fell, for the final time.

"Those who were lost shall be found, and the legend of light and shadow shall be known."

CHAPTER 8

The bright light returned and engulfed the vision until there was nothing but blinding luminescence. Jen gasped as if she was coming up for air, stumbling back to look at the tree, and then her hand. She clasped it to her chest to calm herself down.

"The Tree of Whispers."

Jen's breath hitched at the voice.

Ronan.

"What the—"

"The Tree of Whispers."

Jen raked her hand through her golden hair.

"What in *hells* are you doing here? Are you following me?"

"Yes."

He kept his gaze on the tree, his face fixing in a neutral expression. Jen followed his gaze warily as she rubbed her hand.

"Why did you sneak up on me?"

"I didn't."

"Yes, you did.'

"Nope."

She pinched the bridge of her nose.

"If I gasped, I was startled. That's sneaking up on me."

"You were witnessing an Echo."

Jen was taken aback. "I was what?"

Ronan lifted his hand to one of the ivory ribbons. He rubbed it between his index finger and thumb, pondering something.

"Who *are* you?" he murmured, almost to himself.

"You think I figured that out overnight?"

The corner of his mouth twitched.

"I've certainly been doing *my* due diligence."

Jen scoffed before remembering what he said before.

"Back up, what's an Echo?"

"You tell me, you're the one who witnessed one."

"You haven't?"

"Don't sound so smug."

Jen scrubbed her hands over her face—this was getting tedious.

"Are you going to tell me what an Echo is or not?"

Ronan let go of the ribbon and faced her.

"It's a memory, and it's a rare ability to be able to access them."

"I wasn't trying to *access* anything," Jen said with offense.

"Okay, calm down. You asked, I'm answering," Ronan said, his emotionless demeanor cracking.

Jen crossed her arms, partly out of annoyance, and partly to keep her hands from trembling.

Ronan glanced at the tree.

"Echoes are memories that are infused with the histories of Etheria. There are several of these trees with different—" He thought for a moment. "*Gifts* scattered about the continent. It's said they took root when the first star fell. And the magic that came from that star nourished the trees, so they grew to be colossal things like this," Ronan explained as he turned to walk away.

Jen scurried after him.

"What are the ribbons for?"

"They're prayers to the Goddess of Light."

"Who?"

"What do they *teach* you in Nimea?"

"That you're not real."

Ronan clasped his face and took a step away from her to examine himself dramatically. "Oh, Goddess. Why did no one *tell me*?!" he exclaimed, spinning in a circle.

Jenevieve groaned at the ridiculous disintegration of their conversation.

"Jen?"

Damien appeared a short distance away, looking rather disgruntled. He looked between her and the man he didn't know.

"Who's this?"

Jen opened her mouth to answer, but she was interrupted.

"Ronan."

Her head fell.

Great. This is great.

Damien's gaze darted to Ronan, and for a second, Jen thought he might lunge at him, but he drew his now *very* tense shoulders back and approached them.

He offered his hand.

"Damien."

Ronan looked down at the hand extended towards him for a moment before reluctantly taking it.

Jen blew out a silent breath.

"Ronan was in the tavern last night, he's the one who suggested changing our clothes."

Damien looked at her.

"Right. You never actually told me why."

Jen had conveniently neglected to tell him about her alone time with the mysterious stranger after he'd gone to bed.

"You looked like Regals," Ronan said flatly, his eyes shifting to the side of Damien's head. "But now I realize you couldn't be."

"Am I supposed to know what that means?"

Jen took a few steps towards him, putting a more substantial distance between her and Ronan. Damien gave her a sidelong glance as she approached, and when she gave him a weak smile that said *we have bigger things to worry about*, he released a loaded sigh and jutted his chin towards the stairwell behind them.

"The others met me at that staircase a few minutes ago. I was just coming to get you."

"Did you find anything?" Jen asked, her gaze followed his chin.

"Not yet, but William said he might know where to go."

"What are you looking for?" Ronan directed at Jen.

Damien rolled his eyes. "No offense. But we don't know you. We'll be fine. *Thanks*," he said curtly.

Jen lifted her hand.

"Damien. He's *from* here. He might be able to help."

Ronan chuckled, his thumb running the length of his stubble lined jaw. "I didn't offer my assistance."

Jen whirled around.

"What was the point of you following me here, then?"

Damien's eyes widened with a flash of disdain. He took several charged steps towards Ronan.

"You *followed* her?"

Ronan picked at his nails, unphased by Damien's power strides.

"She told me you were coming here."

Damien looked at Jen, but this time a flash of hurt came over his face. "Do you *know* this guy?"

A blush crawled up her neck.

"We talked last night in the pub after you went to bed. I found a letter from my mother and I…" Jen started. Damien was trying to keep himself calm, but he was clearly rattled. He ran his hand down his face.

"A letter? *Shit*. Jen—"

Ronan backed up a few steps.

"Clearly I've walked into something so I'm going to…"

Jen scowled and jabbed her finger at him.

"*No*. You are not going *anywhere*," she said sternly. Ronan threw up his hands and then crossed them over his chest.

Her gaze returned to Damien.

"I found the letter last night, and it told me next to nothing. I just—I needed out of that room, so I went downstairs and the barkeep…"

"Marcos."

Jen closed her eyes and took a breath.

Don't hit him, you need his help.

"Marcos and Ronan were already down there. I didn't know he would be *here*. But it's a good thing he was. I just witnessed an Echo."

"A what?" Damien asked, his body relaxing a bit.

"It's a memory, a recalling of the past. I've never seen anyone do it," Ronan clarified.

"If he wasn't there to explain what it was, I would have been terrified," Jen said.

Damien's expression softened.

Ronan stepped forward. "What exactly are you all hoping to find here?"

Jen looked at Damien. He reluctantly nodded.

"We need information on the Council of Su—"

Ronan surged forward and shushed her. Damien pounced, but Jen raised her hand to stop him from following through.

"Do you know how *dangerous* that is?" Ronan gritted out.

Jen's brows cinched together. "Well *now* I do."

Ronan studied her face. "Who the fuck told you to look for that stuff?"

"My mother."

Damien grinned smugly at the floor. Ronan stopped talking, his eyes narrowing on Jen, she could practically see the wheels turning in his mind. Finally, he let out an exasperated breath and glanced around the Arc before returning to her.

"The information you're looking for isn't up here," he whispered, his eyes alluding to the building around them. Jen blinked.

"Not up—"

"Not *up* here."

Ronan's eyes flicked down to the floor, and when realization dawned on her, he nodded to confirm what she was thinking.

"Wait by the stairs with the others."

Damien didn't hesitate to wrap his arm around Jen's waist, guiding her back to their friends, who were all sitting on the bottom of the stairs pretending they hadn't been blatantly eavesdropping.

Jen put her hands on her hips and looked down at them.

"What do you think you're doing?" she chided as if speaking to her school children. Emelie tucked her hair behind her ear.

"We have no idea what you're talking about Miss Jenevieve."

Jen released a stiff chuckle.

William looked at her from his perch a few steps above Emelie. "Who's the other guy?"

Jen's eyes darted to Damien, who gripped her waist a bit tighter. "He knows where to find the information we need," she explained vaguely.

William looked relieved.

"Oh, good. I know I said I knew where to go, but, honestly, I was just guessing."

Leeyna playfully kicked his leg from across the same stair.

"You seemed so confident!"

"I've had a lot of practice in *faking it* over the last few days," William said with a small shrug. "I've just decided not to be *shocked* by anything anymore."

"Keep thinking that," Jen murmured as Ronan sauntered up to the group. Emelie and Leeyna slowly took in every inch of the new mystery man, bottom to top.

Emelie braced her hand on the stairwell wall and hoisted herself up. She locked eyes with him, her voice abnormally firm. "I'm Emelie, Jen's best friend."

Ronan didn't hesitate to extend his hand to her.

"Ronan. Nice to meet you, best friend."

William and Leeyna stood and introduced themselves quickly.

"We don't have much time, maybe an hour at the most, there's always a chance that we're being watched," Ronan said quietly.

"What do you mean watched?" Damien asked.

Ronan looked impatiently at him. "Dark forces have been lurking in Etheria for many years, spies come with the territory."

He looked over to Jen, his eyes dropping to Damien's hand still on her waist. His mouth twitched, and then he motioned for everyone to follow him.

They crossed over the limestone floor towards the stairwell of another adjoining tower in the back of the Arc. They came around the backside of the stairs, where they were greeted by a wall of dark wooden planks.

William scratched his head and looked around.

"Um."

Ronan stepped forward and placed his palms along the wall, looking around to ensure no one else was nearby. He pushed hard against the planks until they made a soft click.

A hidden door.

It cracked open to reveal a sliver of dark space. He pulled it open slowly, where a set of dilapidated stairs descended into the dark abyss below the Arc.

William held his face with his hand. "Sure. Secret ominous door. That sounds about right."

Ronan stepped into the doorway and retrieved two torches. He handed one to Damien and lit them with a fire steel before beginning his descent.

They carefully followed him, disappearing into the dark stairwell.

"Watch your step, there are exposed nails in some of the boards," Ronan warned. Everyone immediately looked to their feet and closely examined where their next steps landed.

"How did you know this was here?" Jen asked in a hushed tone.

"I asked."

"Someone just came out and told you about a secret passage in an ancient building that leads to dangerous books?"

Ronan's head turned slightly.

"I asked politely."

"Who did you ask?"

"A laebhar."

Jen hopped over an exposed nail.

"What's that?"

"They are the watchers of the Arc."

"Don't you mean protectors?"

"No. I mean watchers. They're not the fighting type."

"Oh."

Ronan's voice dropped.

"They mainly exist to make sure no one touches their *tree.*"

Jen blanched.

"Relax, I'm kidding," he said. "Although I'm sure that was an exciting moment for them in an otherwise mundane occupation."

"When I witnessed the Echo, did I look—"

Insane. Asinine. Possessed.

"You looked like you were touching a very large tree—stop overthinking."

"Because I'm so great at that." Jen scowled. "Relax. Stop overthinking," she grumbled under her breath.

Ronan looked over his shoulder, and in the firelight, Jen could see the ghost of a smirk appear on his face.

They came to the bottom of the stairs. He offered his hand to her, and when she came beside him, she found herself in a severely dark room. Ronan helped Emelie and Leeyna as well before walking directly across the room where he lit several sconces on the opposing wall.

"There are a few more sconces near you, if you wouldn't mind."

Damien grumbled something under his breath before lighting the other sconces.

The room filled with flickering amber light, and with that, collections of dusty bookshelves appeared, along with a long, weather-warped table of dark wood in the middle of the small room.

"Well, this is cozy," Damien said as he hung his torch in a holder mounted by the stairs.

Jen wandered over to one of the bookshelves and ran her fingers over the bindings of the dusty volumes. She clapped the dust from her hands and turned to Ronan, who stood before the long table.

"You've been here before?"

He kept his focus on pushing parchment and books to the corners of the table.

"I have."

She went to stand on the opposing side of the table.

"What were you looking for?"

"Nothing of importance."

Damien and Emelie came up to either side of her.

"So, we're looking for council members?" Emelie asked.

Ronan pointed to one side of the large room. "You'll find annuls and family histories over there."

"William and I can begin there," Leeyna volunteered.

"Well, wait. We don't know *who* we're looking for," Damien said with slight exasperation.

Jen hadn't thought about that. She hadn't thought about how to do *any* of this. She was relying on a vague letter and a man she met in a pub the night before.

Wow.

Ronan spoke. "The Council of Suran is an ancient assemblage of Etherians from all races and kingdoms of the continent, magic and non-magic alike," he began. William and Leeyna joined the others around the table to listen. "When Heltior came to power, he tracked them all down and murdered them, but they each had a successor—a *descendant*, and therefore, a traceable lineage."

"But how do we know who they were to begin with?" Jen asked.

Ronan walked to one of the bookshelves on the far side of the room. He retrieved an aged scroll and brought it back to the table. He unrolled it and placed it under the weight of a few candlesticks. Everyone leaned in.

We, the Council of Suran, are charged with the safety and protection of every soul in Etheria. We represent all beings that inhabit this continent, and vow to maintain peace and prosperity until we draw our last breath. This we so solemnly swear.

Underneath the oath were the faded signatures of ten Etherians. William touched the scroll, his eyes filling with reverent disbelief.

"The Council was real..." he whispered.

Ronan nodded.

"Very much so, and for a time, there was peace and prosperity throughout the realms. The Council worked. Until Heltior, and the decimation of life as they knew it."

"That's cheery," Damien murmured. Jen shot him a pointed look. He returned it with his own.

"Is the tragic history of my homeland an *inconvenience* to you?" Ronan said coldly.

"Look, we're still accepting that Etheria is a real place." Damien snapped, doing nothing to hide his lingering indignation "Now, we're in a secret basement being told about its dark history and somehow, we're now involved in its future—it's a lot."

Jen looked between them. He was right, but there was no point in dwelling on that. She splayed her hand over the parchment.

"So, these are the names of the…murdered members?" she asked carefully.

"Yes. This scroll is from a thousand years ago."

"Were there other scrolls like this?"

Ronan pointed to the shelf behind them, there sat dozens more like it.

"Every time a descendant of an original council member came into service, a new oath was sworn by all the existing members to ensure the continuity of the council's purpose," he looked down. "This is the last one."

Jen glanced at the aged scroll and let her fingertips touch the faded ink. "Did the lines of succession continue after the deaths of the Council?"

"The descendants knew Heltior would someday return and so kept the succession a secret. The people of Etheria have no idea that it, technically, still exists."

"It became legend," William said quietly.

Ronan lowered his chin.

"So, we need to take the names that are on this scroll and look for their annuls?" Emelie asked.

"Yes. Some of them are easier to find. These three—" He pointed to three signatures. "They were rulers of the three larger kingdoms of Etheria at that time. Their succession should be the royal bloodlines, meaning the current rulers would be the descendants, but we should find the annuls to be sure. A thousand years of history can make things…complicated."

Ronan pointed to William and Leeyna.

"You two look for Theodoric of House Hoebyn, he was the King of Senya."

He looked at Emelie and Damien.

"You look for Dorian of House Vendari, he was King of Ardovia."
Ronan then turned to Jenevieve.
"You'll look for Soryn I of House Allyn, he was King of Sachandes."
Jenevieve arched a brow. "What will you do?"
"Try to decipher the other names."

They combed through scrolls and tomes. Page after page they searched for the name they were assigned until their eyes strained under the piles of aged parchment.

Jen approached the table with a stack of dusty scrolls in her hand. She clumsily dropped them next to Ronan and fell into a coughing fit as the dust filled her lungs. Engrossed in his new mission and staring closely at the signatures, he didn't seem to notice her.

She collected herself and unrolled one of the scrolls.

"Do all Etherians know as much as you do?"

Ronan didn't look up. "I wouldn't think so. People like to live in ignorant bliss."

"That's a rather cynical view of the world."

"How long have you been in this world?"

Jenevieve went silent.

He wasn't wrong. She grew up in Nimea and had stumbled through only a small fraction of Etheria. She glanced up and found Damien staring at her from across the room, his eyes flashing with a territorial glimmer.

That'll be fun to deal with.

Jen continued reading quietly until something caught her eye. She brought the scroll closer.

"What is this?" she asked. She handed it to Ronan as the others joined them at the table.

"It looks like a treaty between King Soryn and…wait—" He handed the scroll back to Jen and looked down at the oath. He pointed to one of the names.

"Talya of Sayllana. Her name is on this. What's that treaty for?"

Jen skimmed the first few lines of the document, her heart booming loudly in her chest.

"It's a peace treaty between the royalty of Sachandes and the Sachi people."

"Oh, *that*," Ronan said, suddenly not as interested.

"Is peace not something to strive for?" Jen said as Emelie came up beside her. Ronan gave her a look that said *that was a very stupid question.*

"Are the Sachi people from Sachandes?" Emelie asked.

"Does it sound like they are?" Ronan asked.

"Hey, watch it," Jen snapped.

Ronan frowned at her, but his gaze shifted back to Emelie. "Sorry, best friend." He gave her a nod. "Yes, the Sachi are from the realm of Sachandes.

"Are they all paired off like that?" Damien asked. "Two descendants to every kingdom?" He waved his hand. "Realm?"

"Yes." Ronan pointed to another name at the bottom of the oath scroll.

"This is the Ardovian king's signature," he explained. He then pointed to a signature close to it. "This name is Ardovian as well. Mara of Naerinix, that's a city in the mountain province."

He lifted the page containing the Sachi treaty. "You found this over there?" He gestured to the shelves in the corner where Jen had been searching for the Sachandan kings annuls.

She nodded.

"Would Mara's annul be near the Ardovian kings, then?" William chimed in.

Ronan nodded hesitantly.

"What about Theodoric?" Leeyna piped quietly.

Jen looked down to find that name, but another caught her eye.

Naedyra of Saebynn.

"I know this name…"

Ronan leaned over and read the name. His eyebrows raised.

"How?"

"The Echo. She was in it," she said, glancing at Leeyna. "I think Theodoric was in it too, she called him Theo."

"Who?" Damien asked, a line etched between his brows.

Jen looked up to a room of eyes staring at her. Her hands started to sweat. "Kiara."

No one seemed to understand what meant, save for Ronan, who pressed his clenched fists on the table.

"Jenevieve," he said quietly. "What Echo did you witness?"

She paused.

"I saw her giving birth."

Ronan's eyes widened.

"The child lives…"

Jen's brow formed a hard line.

"What?"

His face quickly shifted into neutral indifference, but Jen had already registered his first reaction.

"Jen, what exactly did your mother ask you to do?" Emelie asked fervently.

"I told you," she said, trying to conceal the tremble in her voice. "Reconvene the council…"

"Why would we need to do that?" Leeyna asked, the energy of the room growing tense. "What does that mean?"

Ronan fixed his gaze on Jen.

"It means something dark is stirring in Vondur," Ronan said, his finger tracing over the council scroll.

William's mouth dropped open.

"V-V-V-VONDUR?" he stammered, terror plaguing his eyes.

"Someone please tell me what the heck Vondur is?" Emelie said, her voice heightened with anxiety.

William began to pace. "Holy shit. Heltior is real. Vondur is real. Jen, what are we *doing?*"

Leeyna placed her hand on his arm. "Calm down—"

Damien leaned on the table, his apologetic eyes lifting to Jen. "Walk us through what happened the day of the wedding," he said.

"You already know what—" she said, not wishing to dwell on the horrors of the last twenty-four hours.

"Again," Damien said. "Please."

Guilt fell like a wave crashing into her chest, they had all blindly followed her into the forest and had traveled with her to Zaniya with little to no insight as to what exactly they were doing. But Jen didn't know much more than they did. They were all looking to her for answers, but she didn't have any.

The only thing she could give them was the terrifyingly small amount of knowledge she *did* have.

"The night before the wedding, I had a nightmare. I saw Heltior and a Knight of Eseer…but I didn't know what it was…what it meant."

She blew out a breath.

"It haunted me…followed me, through the day, and then…a dying lily appeared in my garden," she said. "I touched it—*healed* it, and it triggered a vision," her voice grew quiet. "The horde came a few hours later."

Ronan rubbed his chin, his gaze training on the table as she continued. "The morai attacked Nimea because they felt my…magic," she said, still having trouble believing that part.

"They were called by the *pulse*," Ronan said, his voice low.

Jen stilled. "The what?"

He exhaled, his focus dragging up to Jen, considering her as if deciding whether to trust her with what he was about to say.

"There is an ancient bloodline," he said slowly. "It was held as a carefully guarded secret, with very few people on the continent knowing of its existence. For five hundred years, even Heltior remained ignorant of it."

Jen's chest tightened. "Why the secrecy?"

"They were rumored to possess a magic so powerful it had the means to *rival* that of Heltior's."

Jen bit the inside of her cheek, trying—and failing, to keep her expression, and her heartbeat, calm.

Disdain flickered behind Ronan's verdant eyes. "But they were betrayed, and once Heltior learned of the bloodline's existence—of their power, he attacked the realms, determined to find and destroy them all." His hands clenched into fists. "It was known as the Blood War, but with no working council to protect them, it wasn't so much a war as it was a massacre."

The light of the sconces flickered around them. "Afterwards, Heltior became obsessed with hunting down the survivors. He created—"

"The morai," Jen whispered, her face growing pale.

Ronan nodded. "He put out a pulse every fifty years to draw out those of the blood who remained." He looked at her. "It took the form of a *dream*."

Before Jen could react, he shook his head. "But it doesn't make sense. The pulse isn't due for another twenty years."

"Well, I can say with certainty that it happened two days ago," Jen said, fighting away the haunting images that pushed towards the front of her mind.

Damien crossed his arms. "What does this *bloodline* have to do with any of this?" he asked defensively.

"It has everything to do with it," Ronan said, his voice so low it came out as a growl. His gaze shifted back to Jen. "*Doesn't* it?"

The little that was in her stomach churned like a tempest as the thundering realization struck her.

It was the only way these horrendous things made any sense.

The dream. The hallucinations. The lily. The morai. The Echo.

My magic.

She couldn't look at Damien, nor her friends, not when she suddenly knew just how much danger she had put them in by allowing them to come here.

"I—I'm," she stuttered. She placed her hands on her cheeks and let out a shuddering breath through her teeth.

Jen looked up, her eyes settling on Damien.

"I'm in the bloodline."

CHAPTER 9

The air grew heavy as pure shock radiated over the room. Jen paced away from the table; she couldn't stand everyone looking at her. Her eyes darted to Ronan.

"What does it mean, that the pulse came twenty years early?"

Ronan watched her, clearly not as shocked as the rest of them.

"It means Heltior must be planning something catastrophic. Vondur has been a mystery to Etheria for a thousand years. It's out on a peninsula in the furthest corner of our world. It's so heavily warded it's nearly impossible to get through."

"That's why my mother—" she shook her head. "Fjora, told me to reconvene the council. When the pulse came early, she must have known something bigger was happening."

"Fjora?" Ronan asked, his forehead crinkling at the name.

"Yes, she was my protector."

"Interesting." He rubbed the stubble on his chin. "It seems you were right, though, she knew something."

Jenevieve paced back to the table and pressed her palms on its worn surface. "We need to find the other annuls. *Now.*"

The room turned into a flurry of manic searching. They scoured through the scrolls they'd already taken from the shelves. William sat on the ground with several books open in front of him. Emelie and Leeyna moved between the table and the bookshelves, bringing new scrolls with them every time. They found the royal annuls easily enough, but the secondary signatures from the three realms were harder to track.

"I have the royal annul of King Theodoric," Leeyna said as she waved the scroll around enthusiastically. William smiled warmly at her from where he sat on the ground.

"Senya is a reclusive part of the realm. It will be harder to figure out who we're looking for, process of elimination with the other names is our only tactic," Ronan explained.

Jen walked over to Damien who stood at one of the bookshelves. She grabbed hold of his arm, and as if on instinct, he placed his hand over hers and squeezed her fingers.

"This is good. We're making progress," she said as she looked over his shoulder to the scroll he was reading. His shoulders were so rigid that the tension radiated off him.

"But not enough. What does any of this mean for us?" His eyes flicked to the others. "For *you?*" Damien avoided her gaze as he flipped the scroll over and continued reading.

Jen pressed her lips together and stepped away from him, reluctantly walking back to the table where Ronan stood. He was looking closely at the remaining names.

"This name is from the Inbetween—wait," he said as Jen drew closer to the scroll.

Elloryan of Saebynn.

Jen traced the name with her finger.

"He's from the same house as Naedyra?"

Ronan straightened to his full height and rubbed his chin. "They're either related or—" His eyes flashed. "Married."

"If Naedyra and Elloryan were married, their succession would have gone to their children, right?"

"Maybe, but we don't have a way of confirming that yet."

Damien and the others joined them at the table. He glanced down at the council scroll.

"Alright. It seems that we have two Council members from each realm. Sachandes, Ardovia, and Senya..."

"And then we have two from the Inbetween," Ronan said.

"Where do the two remaining names come from?" Leeyna asked, leaning over the table.

Ronan shook his head in frustration.

"I honestly don't know."

"But we have a good start, right?" Emelie asked hopefully.

Ronan stopped for a moment.

"Gaiana is the current leader of the Sachi people in Sachandes," he said. They all looked at him as though he wasn't finished speaking. He realized they had no idea what he was talking about.

"She's the current treaty holder with King Haythem. If she isn't the descendant, I would bet anything she knows who is."

Jen looked up from the oath scroll.

"That's where Fjora told us to go next."

"Maybe there was a reason for that."

Ronan walked around the table with his arms crossed before turning back towards the others, deep in thought.

"We know who we need to talk to in Sachandes, and we have an idea of who most of the signatures are—" he began.

He froze.

The stairs creaked.

He put his finger to his lips, and Damien reached behind him to draw his sword.

There was a sequence of thudding as someone rushed down the stairs. Out of the shadows came a laebhar, who stood out of breath on the bottom step. She looked at Ronan, her eyes wide.

"They think you're being watched. You must go."

Ronan peered at the others who were still frozen.

"Grab as much as you can," he barked. He grabbed the rucksack from the corner and tossed it onto the table. They shoved as many scrolls as they could into the bag before Jen tied it shut.

"What gave us away?" Ronan asked as they blew out the sconces.

The laebhar's eyes darted to Jenevieve.

"She witnessed an Echo, and someone witnessed *her*."

Guilt and fear flooded her body as everyone looked from the laebhar to her. She once again realized that everyone around her was in danger because of her: her destiny which she knew nothing about, her powers which she had no control over. Tears pricked at the corner of her eyes, but she blinked them away.

The laebhar turned and hastened back up the stairs, careful to remain as quiet as possible. Ronan snatched the bag from the table and ran behind her with Emelie, Leeyna, and William on his heels.

Jenevieve remained at the table, attempting to breathe through the threat of tears, when she felt a hand gently grab hold of hers. She glanced over.

Damien stood beside her.

He slid his hand within hers, bringing her fingers up to his lips before pressing a kiss to it. They looked at each other for a moment, and then with a sharp nod of Damien's head, she ran in front of him and darted, carefully, up the stairs. He grabbed the torch from the holder and followed closely behind her.

They all filed out of the hidden door before Ronan quietly sealed it shut. The laebhar looked out into the Arc and came back a moment later.

"They think it's a dhoksha, but we can't be certain," she said in a hushed tone.

William gawked at her.

Ronan turned to the group. "We'll have to split up."

"What's a dhoksha—" Leeyna started.

"Shapeshifter," William finished.

"Vondur has eyes everywhere. Dhokshas can take the shape of anyone, which is why they're used as spies," Ronan explained quietly. "We'll go in pairs and meet back at the Lion and Lily."

Ronan walked towards Jen, but Damien stepped in front of her.

"She's staying with *me*," he said firmly. They glared at each other for a moment before Ronan shifted to Emelie.

"Feel like being a decoy?" He wiggled his brows.

Fear flickered over her eyes. "Okay," she said quietly.

Jen embraced her tightly, her gaze searing into Ronan.

"Relax. She'll be safe with me," he said as he swung the rucksack over his shoulder. He pointed his chin above them. "Go up these stairs and split up onto different floors." He looked at Emelie with a casual smirk. "You'll stick with me, alright best friend?"

Emelie nodded and stepped towards him.

The laebhar looked out once more. "You must go *now*."

Ronan bowed to her. "Thank you Leysa."

She lowered her chin before returning to the main room. Ronan glanced back at Jen, raising a brow slightly before gently nudging Emelie forward, ducking out after Leysa. Damien and Jen led the other two up the stairs to the second floor.

"Cross over to the other side and down the other tower stairs. Jen and I will go up to the next floor." Damien jabbed a finger at William. "Don't run and try not to look *too* panicked."

William looked down at the finger pointing at him. "Oh, no, we're not panicking. We're just running from a mythical shape—" his voice was cut off as Leeyna grabbed his hand and yanked him towards the entry of their floor.

"Not the time William," she scolded as they slowed their pace across the long row of bookshelves.

Damien and Jen ascended two more flights before stopping in the stairwell. She reached out and grasped the railing, squeezing her eyes shut and forcing a deep breath as blood pounded in her ears.

Stay calm. Stay calm. Stay calm.

Damien jerked to a stop beside her. "Bug?" He strode over to her. "We have to go—"

"I can't—" she said through clenched teeth.

He placed his sweat slicked hand on her back and held her other hand for support.

"Yes, you can," he whispered.

He gently coaxed her through the door leading out to the fourth floor and walked inconspicuously towards the adjoining tower at the front of the building. Jen fought the temptation to search for their mysterious voyeur and kept her gaze fixed forward.

They bolted down the stairs as soon as they were out of sight. When they came to the bottom, Damien halted and glanced out into the Arc, squeezing Jen's hand gently before pulling her out into the open space.

Iridescent light spilled into the Arc from the tall windows as they crossed over the limestone floors. Damien yanked open the front door, and as Jen followed behind him, she glanced back one final time.

Her blood turned to ice.

Someone stood in front of the Tree of Whispers.

Deathly still.

The hair rose on the back of her neck and a deep shudder crawled through her bones. The figure wore the same sunset orange robes as the other laebhars, but she knew it was an imposter.

The dhoksha.

Shock cursed through her.

Jen didn't know what she expected, but it certainly wasn't to see a perfect likeness to the peaceful watchers of the Arc, tracking her with unblinking eyes. She expected it to take off after her, but it did not move.

Instead, it slowly lifted its hand and bent its pale fingers.

It was *waving.*

Jen's eyes grew wide, and she darted through the open door into the light of the late afternoon sun. She let the rays warm her face before glimpsing back at the Arc.

"Jen! We have to keep moving!"

Her mind snapped back to the present when she heard Damien calling from the dirt path. She hurried to join him and together they ran towards the city.

The dirt road returned to the familiar cobblestone streets as Jen led them down the main street, vaguely recognizing their surroundings. She stopped where the two roads intersected, and relief flooded her body at the sight of The Lion and Lily.

They crossed over to the corner and darted inside, a wave of warmth crashing over them when they entered the pub.

"We must be the first ones back…" Damien said as he scanned the room. Jen glanced at the bar and saw Daphne wiping down the counter.

"Hello, dear!" she said brightly.

Jen tried to keep her voice steady.

"Have any of my friends returned yet?"

Daphne's smile faded.

"Not that I've seen, dear," she chirped.

The door to the tavern swung open and William and Leeyna bolted in. They spotted Jen and Damien and ran to them, their chests heaving as they tried to catch their breath.

Jen threw her arms around William. "Are you two okay?" She let go and wrapped her arms around Leeyna.

"We waited until we saw the two of you leave," William said. "Did you see something? You stopped at the door before you left—"

The door of the tavern swung open once again. Emelie barreled through the door, her eyes wild. An audible gasp fell from Jen's lips, and they launched themselves at each other, holding each other tightly.

Jen glanced up from Emelie's shoulder to find Ronan leaning against a small pillar by the tables just inside the doorway.

Thank you, she mouthed to him.

He lowered his chin.

Jen blinked away the burning behind her eyes and turned towards the bar. Daphne was looking at them like they had all lost their minds.

Oof. I need a drink.

"Can we get a round, Daphne?" Jen asked as she used her thumb to wipe away a rogue tear streaming down Emelie's cheek.

"I'll send 'em right over, dearie," Daphne said, her expression still fixed in a state of confusion.

They dropped into the chairs around a long table nearby, fear and relief weighing on their limbs. Jen grabbed Emelie's hand. "What took you so long? I would have thought you'd be the first ones back."

Emelie beamed up at Ronan.

"Ronan took us by the port! We saw so many boats bound for distant lands; it was incredible!"

Ronan sank into the chair across from Emelie and leaned back. "We went the long way around."

William cleared his throat. "Did you see something…back at the Arc?"

Jen looked around the table before settling on the tabletop in front of her. "I think I saw the dhoksha."

Ronan quirked a brow.

"How would you know? They're shapeshifters."

"It was just a feeling—"

A barmaid appeared at the table with the ale and passed them out at an unnaturally slow pace, one by one. When she finally left, Ronan spoke up.

"If a dhoshka spotted us, well—*you*, then it won't be long before something worse comes to investigate."

Oh good. There's a 'something worse.' Fantastic.

Jen rubbed her temples. "But what was so significant about me witnessing the Echo?"

"I told you, it's not a common ability," Ronan drawled.

Jen groaned in exasperation.

"But what about it is so *uncommon?*"

"The ability to witness an Echo is connected to a very specific, very powerful type of magic—"

"The bloodline…?"

Ronan shook his head. "No, but regardless, that dhoshka will more than likely send a message up their chain of command."

Jen covered her face and spoke through her hands.

"So, what does that mean for us?"

"It means we can't stay here. We leave for Sachandes at first light." Ronan grabbed his mug of ale and his lip curled in revulsion. "We'll meet with the king, and hope he agrees to uphold the descendancy." He took a sip and scowled at it. "He's always been a noble man, infuriatingly so, at times."

"*We?*" Damien challenged.

Ronan eyed him wearily.

"Yes, *we*. None of you know the way to Sachandes. And how were you planning to get there? Are you going to walk?"

Damien clenched his mug tightly. Ronan chugged the remainder of his ale, picked up the rucksack, and strode towards the door.

"I'll retrieve you at dawn."

He reached for the doorknob, but Jen rose quickly and trailed after him. She grabbed his arm. He paused to look down at her hand firmly around his tattoo.

"Thank you for keeping Emelie safe."

"You don't have to thank me for that."

"Yes, I do."

Ronan freed his arm from her grasp and faced her.

"Anything else?"

Jen's brows snapped together. She pointed at the bag slung around his shoulder. "Why are you taking that?"

"Do you remember when I told you how dangerous this information was?"

"Yes, but if we're all leaving together—"

"Look. I've chosen to help you; I don't appreciate you doubting my integrity."

Jen opened and closed her mouth, taken aback by the abrasive accusation. Ronan's eyes widened slightly, and then he dipped his head, bringing her gaze back up to him.

"Do you trust me?" he asked.

Jen tilted her head, examining him. "Should I?"

The corner of his lips twitched.

"Good answer," he said. "Be down here at first light. I'll secure some transportation."

He bolted out the door, leaving Jen in a stupor.

She shook the odd interaction from her mind and walked over to Daphne, who retrieved their room keys from her apron.

"Where's Marcos tonight?" Jen asked as she reached into the pouch on her belt to pay.

"Oh, he'll be along shortly, just doin' a few errands is all—" She was cut off by the boisterous entrance of her husband through the front door.

"WHERE IS MA' GORGEOUS WIFE?" he bellowed into the pub. He spotted Daphne and charged through the room and around the countertop. He picked her up and laid a sloppy kiss on her cheek.

Daphne feigned disgust but chuckled under her breath. "Oh, get off 'uh me 'ye old coot." She gave his cheek a loving tap and nudged him away. He kissed her forehead.

"Hello, Jenevieve!" His kind eyes sparkled.

"Hi, Marcos," she chuckled. She tapped the bartop and walked back towards the table. Her eyes landed on Damien, who sat at the corner of the table mindlessly swirling the remaining contents of his mug.

The sudden shift in his mood left her in a lurch. She tried to meet his unfocused eyes, but he seemed determined to avoid her.

Emelie glanced between them.

"Jen," she rose from her seat. "Will you introduce me to Marcos?"

Jen's brows cinched together, confused.

"I would love to meet him and his wife *over there*," Emelie said through gritted teeth. Jen's brows rose.

"Oh—*oh!* Sure."

Emelie led them over to the furthest corner of the bartop, out of earshot of the others. When they sat down, she immediately turned to Jen.

"Alright. You need to talk to someone who isn't obviously attracted to you," she said. Jen captured an explosive cackle with her hands.

"*What* are you talking about?"

Emily gave her a pointed look that said *don't be dumb.*

"Let's just take a minute away from everyone to wrap our heads around everything as best as we can, okay?"

Jen blew out a breath and nodded.

"Okay, so. You had a nightmare that was actually a pulse that triggered you to use magic you didn't know you had."

Jen held up one finger.

"Maelia is really Fjora, and she's not your birth mother, she's your protector and came from Etheria."

Jen held up two fingers.

"You were given vague instructions to reconvene a council that was disbanded a thousand years ago and told to travel here and aimlessly wander in a massive library finding anything and everything about said disbanded council."

Jen held up three fingers.

"You are actually part of a secret ancient bloodline."

Jen held up four fingers.

"An absurdly attractive man has appeared out of nowhere as our brooding guide which has royally peeved our equally attractive traveling companion with whom we have a complicated on-again off-again relationship."

Jen put up five fingers and dropped her head into her open palm. She looked up and flagged down Marcos.

"Marcos, this is Emelie." She waved her hand. "Can we please get two glasses of that Ardovian rum?"

Marcos nodded with a chuckle and walked towards the liquor shelf. "Maybe the bottle, actually," she called after him and went back to resting her head in her hand.

Emelie leaned her elbows on the bartop.

"Now, with all of that said out loud, how are we feeling?"

Jen gave her a sidelong glance.

"I *feel* like I need that rum."

"No seriously. What's going through your head?"

Marcos came back with two glasses—and the bottle.

Bless that man.

Jen gave him a weary smile which he returned with a wink. She poured them each a generous amount and swirled the amber liquid around in the glass.

Ardovian rum. Absolute shit people, but they do have their talents.

Emelie took a sip and immediately choked. Jen exhaled a laugh.

"Careful."

Emelie looked down suspiciously at her rum, and then pointedly at Jen. "Answer the question."

Jen closed her eyes and held the glass against her forehead; the coolness of it soothed the headache that was forming behind her brows.

"I should have come here alone," she murmured.

"That was never going to happen."

Jen ran her fingers over the edge of her glass.

"You would be safe."

"Would we?"

Jen glanced over at her best friend.

"Emelie."

"Jen, stop," Emelie said in a loving, but exasperated tone. "This is just misplaced guilt."

Jen took a languid sip of rum.

"I wish my mother—" She laughed sadly. "*Fjora*, had prepared me for this." She waved her hand at nothing. "Any of it."

She currently found herself wishing for several things. She wished her mother had told her something—*anything*, but Fjora allowed her to grow up without a shred of knowledge, intentionally leaving her in the dark, and not knowing *why* was eating away at her.

She wished she knew about the dormant magic that had been weaving itself inside her over the course of her life. She wished she knew what the morai *were* before they attacked; maybe she could have used said dormant magic to better protect her village—her family. *Gods*. She wished she knew if her family was alive. Every time she closed her eyes, the last terror-stricken expression on her siblings' faces seared the backs of her eyelids.

She wished her friends hadn't been dragged into this. They had lives back in Nimea, and now, who knew if, or when, they would ever return to them.

And then there was the obvious pissing contest between Damien and Ronan. Were men always like this? Or was she just wildly unlucky.

It's me. It's absolutely me.

She could feel Damien's mood shifting at the Arc; his shoulders grew rigid, and his jawline grew sharper the more he clenched his teeth. She couldn't help but wonder if the shift was all about their circumstance, or if more than a small part of it stemmed from Ronan's presence. It wasn't like she was outwardly flirting with their new arrogant addition.

And it's not like Damien has any claim to me.

Speaking of that obscenely attractive addition. Although there was no shared history with him, there was something uncomfortably familiar about Ronan, like opening a book she had already read to find the words were now blurred by stains of obsidian ink.

Do you trust me?

Her gut wanted to say yes, but how could she be so naive? She couldn't just throw her trust at anyone who held even a kernel of the knowledge she yearned for. And it was questionable at best that he was suddenly so keen on helping them, dropping everything to guide their journey. But foregoing his help seemed more dangerous, and frankly, more *stupid*, than aimlessly wandering around Etheria.

"Does Damien need a pep talk too?

Jen snapped out of her thought spiral and peered back at their table. She blew out a breath. "Probably."

They rejoined the others and drank, occasionally cracking a joke or recounting something from the last three days, attempting to find some humor within the never-ending fever dream they found themselves in.

Damien stayed quiet for most of it. No matter how much Jen tried to pull his attention, something felt unresolved.

When their mugs and glasses ran dry, they dragged their feet through the pub and up the stairs to their rooms. Emelie and Leeyna walked right into the girls' room and William marched into the boys', eager to sleep the stressful day away.

Damien slowed when he reached the threshold of his room, his eyes fixed on the doorframe. Jen bit her lip and fidgeted with her hands.

"Okay, well…goodnight," she said quietly. He grumbled something under his breath.

Alright, that's enough.

Jen leapt in front of him and closed his door before swiftly turning to close hers as well, trapping them alone in the hallway.

She crossed her arms and narrowed her eyes at him.

"Do you want to tell me what's going on?"

He leaned back against the door, his eyes trailing to the ceiling.

"I don't know what you're talking about."

"Don't do that," she stepped towards him. "Tell me what's wrong."

"Everything is fine."

"Oh, yes." She looked him up and down. "You certainly give the impression that everything is indeed, *fine.*"

His gaze dropped to her, revealing several emotions warring behind the striking blue of his stare. Before she could say anything else, though, he turned on his heels and stalked down the hall away from the stairs—away from her.

She darted after him.

"We're not done talking."

"I've said all I needed to," he spat over his shoulder.

Jen thrust her hand behind her. "You mean, the *nothing* that just happened?" She grabbed his wrist. "Damien, hang on—"

They came to a small sitting room with a few upholstered armchairs in two of the corners and a window between them looking out into the alley between the pub and the building beside it.

Damien jerked to a stop and spun around.

"What do you want from me?!"

Jen let go of him, her mouth opening and closing like she didn't know what to say. "What?"

"Why am I here? What is my *purpose*?"

Jen shook her head.

What in hells is he talking about?

"I don't understand—"

She searched his face and found it contorting with anger—no, hurt, no, wait—Jen had seen this look before, when Damien felt he had no control over the world around him, like a dingy being thrashed about in a raging sea.

Her heart cracked. It was *despair*.

He threw his hands up. "I don't know how to protect you here!"

"Protect me—"

"I know *nothing* about this place." He started pacing back and forth between the armchairs. "Demonic creatures and bloodlines and shape shifters and gods know what else."

"At least now we have help—"

Damien scoffed and his eyes turned to slits, the despair giving way to something else.

Annnnd that was the wrong thing to say.

"Yes. Our *gracious guide*. An all-knowing arrogant *prick* who has come to give you every answer you're seeking."

Jen recoiled. Her chest twisted as her empathy began to wear thin. Damien was now attempting to hide his despair behind insufferable masculinity, another healthy habit of his.

"Jealousy doesn't look good on you, Sparky," she said, balling her hands into fists.

He released a harsh laugh.

"Don't insult me, Bug."

"Because you were doing such a fantastic job at hiding it." She took a charged step forward and jabbed her finger at him. "You all but fucking peed on me to mark your territory, Damien."

The tension in his shoulders seeped into the rest of his body, forming an invisible suit of unbreakable armor around him.

"Oh sure, reduce me to a pathetic, jealous jackass."

"Then stop acting like one." She shoved past him and stomped towards the window. "What would you have me do, huh?" She rounded on him. "Look around. We aren't exactly in a position to turn away help."

"You don't think I know we need him?"

Jen groaned and rubbed her hands over her face.

"Damien, stop." She knew his pride was hurt. She knew he was feeling out of control, but she was having enough trouble keeping her own fears and emotions at bay. "Enough about Ronan," she said through another groan.

"Don't you see?" Damien took a step towards her, his eyes falling to her feet. "I'm useless here."

Jen dropped her hands. "What?"

A sad chuckle came from his chest. "I am laughably unprepared for any of this. How am I supposed to keep you safe?" He ran his hand through his raven locks.

Jen leaned back against the window. "You left everything behind to come with me. I should be keeping you safe."

"No, you don't understand." His eyes met hers, the waves of despair returning to the depths of his eyes. "I promised."

"You promised…"

"I promised your mother I would keep you safe."

"My mother—"

"And I am terrified that I will somehow break that promise."

Jen took a tentative step toward him, but he countered backwards. "Damien."

"I can't let anything happen to you," his voice broke.

She stopped short. How had she overlooked it? She'd been so consumed with her own inner battle that she hadn't noticed the one clashing in the person that mattered most to her.

Her voice drew quiet.

"I didn't realize—you still carry that with you?"

Damien froze.

When he was fifteen, his father had died suddenly—tragically, and Damien had been the one to find him. And that panicked young boy had dropped by his father's body and tried desperately to resuscitate him, to no avail.

It shattered him.

She knew every detail of the harrowing experience because, years ago, it was one of the first moments Damien let her into his heart, his eyes glistening with tears as he recounted it to her while they sat in his bed.

His mind warped a tragic act of the gods into his own personal failure. He carried that burden with him every day. Safeguarding his mother, looking after his sister, defending Jenevieve, it all came from that one horrible moment.

It was one of the things they had in common. One of the things that bonded them—the dire need to protect.

The silence that followed grew heavy with the things Damien could not bring himself to say. Jen pressed her lips together.

He looked at the floor. "You're one to talk."

Jen fought the memories of her own father, stepping around his response. "It's not your responsibility to save everyone," she said.

Damien glanced up at her, his gaze piercing her own.

"Not everyone." A moment passed, and then he released a sigh, the rigidity of his invisible armor melting away as a sad smile tugged on his lips.

"I would do anything for you," he whispered.

His words struck her. In some deep part of herself, she always knew that, but hearing him say it out loud created a chink in her own armor.

She turned towards the window, her eyes burning as she looked down into the alley outside. "Things are growing more dangerous by the moment, and we've barely just begun." She turned back to him. "I am holding on by a thread, and right now, that thread is you. I can pretend that everything will be okay if I can hang on to that."

"Bug—"

"I wish, more than anything, that I didn't need you," she croaked. "That I didn't rely on your presence to keep me anchored, but that is what you've always been for me. So many times, no matter what part of our complicated history we were in, knowing you were there kept me upright, kept me moving forward."

Jen ran her hands through her hair and let out a shaking breath. Damien stood there, his lips parted, a moment passing between them.

"It's just you and me," he murmured.

Their dance at her sister's wedding flooded into Jen's mind, and the barn before the attack, and suddenly the room they were in seemed smaller, the scent of a blacksmith forge laced and unkempt pastures pervading the air.

Damien stared at her, his eyes now steeped with something else, something that made her swallow the lump that formed in her throat. He stepped towards her.

The words fumbled out of her. "What are you doing—"

"I'm not doing anything."

He took another step, his nose brushing against hers. The terror and burdens of the last few days combined with the look in Damien's eye was making Jen's head spin.

"We shouldn't…"

He lifted his hand to her cheek, his eyes softening as his thumbs caressed her cheeks.

"Is that what you think?"

She put her hand on his chest, his heart thumping wildly under her palm. He looked down at her hand, and then back to her, the corner of his mouth raised into a small smile.

He leaned down and paused, his warm breath caressing her as he waited for silent permission. Jen tilted her head.

His lips found hers.

Gentle, patient. She melted into him, parting for him as a sigh sung through her body.

Heat blossomed as his tongue swept in. Her arms wrapped around his neck, everything except his scent fading away into a heady fog.

He coaxed her against the window, his movements growing hungry. Jen turned her head as he grazed her neck with his teeth, stifling the smallest sound of pleasure that escaped her lips as her skin grew hot under his touch.

He pulled away to meet her gaze, his eyes boring into hers. This man, she knew. This man, she trusted. This man, she held onto as an anchor in an unpredictable tempest.

She brought his lips to hers and soon he was consuming her. She welcomed it. Needed it. Needed him. Jen moaned into it and a low growl ripped from his throat.

He pushed himself flush to her and rolled his hips. She could feel him rubbing against her and with it came a friction that fed her body. Damien moved his hand lower—

CRASH.

"Marcos ye' big 'oaf. There's glass bloody everywhere now!" Daphne shouted from downstairs.

Jen yanked her lips away from, her breath coming in short pants. Her hand fell against his chest, and she released a quiet laugh.

What was the plan? Do it in the armchair?

Damien lifted her head. He ran his knuckles along her cheek, his eyes telling her he was, begrudgingly, thinking the same thing. He touched his forehead to hers, gently rubbing their noses together.

He kissed her again.

Softer. Sweeter.

She could have sworn she saw a flutter of smugness float across his face.

"Get some sleep."

He turned on his heels and strode back down the hall, leaving Jenevieve standing against the wall, still attempting to catch her breath.

CHAPTER 10

"I won't leave you!" a desolate voice of a woman echoed through Jen's mind.

"You must take her, go!" a male voice ordered.

The young woman held a small bundle in her arms. The young man held her closely, kissing her amidst shattering heartbreak. He pulled himself away and raised his hands to part the trees which formed a narrow path leading into the forest.

"My love, please. You must go, now!"

"Nel, I can't—I can't do this."

"You must. There is no choice here, for either of us."

"I don't know how to do this. This wasn't supposed to—"

"Naezara can't hold them off any longer, Fjora!"

Fjora heard his sister shouting orders in the distance. She turned back to him.

"Come with me, please."

"I have to hold the path open!" Nelysar shouted over the roar of his power.

"I don't want to live without you. I can't—"

"You are strong. You have everything you need within you."

A sob choked her.

"Don't make me say goodbye to you," she begged.

"This is not the end of our journey, mo nuri. I swear it," Nelysar declared as he struggled to keep his hands raised.

The young woman ran to her love and kissed him one last time.

"I love you."

Nelysar pressed his head against hers, his voice breaking.

"I love you. Go!"

Fjora ripped herself away and made a break into the forest, desperately fighting the urge to look back at the man she loved. She ran under the cover of the trees and stopped in her tracks.

She turned around to see Nelysar standing at the forest edge, tears pooling in his eyes. He weaved his hands in a circle, and the trees began to return to their place, closing the line of sight between them. She watched helplessly as he disappeared on the other side of the trees, the morai flying behind him.

She could feel her breath catching as she fought the feeling of panic and desolation. She looked the other direction into the wood, and all at once, some of the trees began to glow with the mark of an X. The bundle stirred in her arms.

A baby.

It began to let out sad, desolate cries.

"Shh.Shh.Shh..." Fjora cooed.

She rocked the baby as she began following the soft glow of the path, attempting to find a full breath against the shuddering in her chest. When the infant continued to cry out, Fjora fell to her knees, lowering her head to the child as wracking sobs took hold of her.

Together, they cried beneath the canopy of Bri.

Mama!

Jen was jolted awake by harsh pounding at her door. Emelie and Leeyna sat up nervously in their beds as Jenevieve tore off her blanket and walked towards the door.

"Jenevieve! We need to go NOW."

She yanked it open to find Ronan banging on the other door with equal urgency.

"What is it?" she asked. "You said first light—"

"A kashyak was spotted at the Arc."

"A what?" Damien asked, pulling on a shirt as he stepped into the hallway.

"A scout from Vondur," Ronan said, his eyes settling on Damien. "We need to get her out of the city. We leave for Sachandes now."

Damien nodded, turning to the group. "Grab your things and meet downstairs."

Jen darted into her room and grabbed her belt and sheathed her dagger while Emelie and Leeyna dressed quickly, fear radiating from them.

Her own fear was not for herself, but for those who had the misfortune of being her friends. She fought the impulse to surrender herself over to this scout to keep her friends out of more danger.

She tied her cloak around her shoulders and followed everyone down the stairs where Ronan, and to their surprise, Marcos and Daphne, were waiting.

Daphne handed Leeyna and Emelie warm cloaks for their journey. Marcos passed extra provisions to William and Damien.

"How did you know we were leaving? It's the middle of the night," Jenevieve asked.

"Someone in the tavern by the farms was going on 'bout seein' a kashyak while Ronan an' I was havin' a few rounds," Marcos said in an uncharacteristically serious voice. "He spilled his rum gettin' me up to scramble over here."

Daphne approached her. "We know who ye' are dear." She took Jen's hand and patted it. "But don' worry, yer secret is safe wee us."

Jen's eyes grew wide. "Wh—who I am?"

"Ufreijaa nuri."

Jenevieve blinked.

The words from the Echo. Kiara's words.

"I don't understand." She glanced at Marcos as he stepped beside his wife. "How—"

 Marcos took her other hand. "Now is not the time, my dear," his eyes sparkled. "But I'm sure our paths will cross again."

Jen opened her mouth to speak, but Marcos spoke again.

"Ufreijaa nuri," he said as he and Daphne squeezed her hands and brought her in for an unexpected embrace.

"You are the hope of this world," Daphne whispered in her ear.

A flash of Kiara in her birthing bed, pressing her head against her child's, uttering those same words, soared across her mind.

What does that mean?

Ronan cleared his throat.

"We have to go. The horses are waiting at the edge of the city."

Jen looked at Daphne and Marcos, a flurry of questions ricocheted inside her head, but there was not enough time, so instead she said, "Thank you."

"On yer way now," Marcos said as he shooed them to the door.

Ronan led them through a labyrinth of back streets in the pitch dark. The moon was the only light to guide them as they weaved their way to the outskirts of the city.

They approached a small farm where six horses stood tied to a long, wooden fence. Ronan vaulted himself over the fence and quickly untied the reins.

"Everyone know how to handle one of these?" Ronan looked to the others as they climbed over the fence. He was gesturing to the horses.

William coughed. "If I say no?"

"Then it's trial by fire for you, friend," Ronan said as he walked over to help Emelie onto her chestnut mare. William put his foot in the stirrup and launched himself over the saddle, nearly toppling over the other side. He managed to catch himself and clunkily settled into the saddle.

Damien went to help Jen, but she'd already mounted her dapple-gray.

Ronan scoffed from atop his Friesian.

"She's not fragile."

Jen shot him a look. This was absolutely *not* the time for that. Damien took a deep breath and let the comment go before mounting his own horse.

Ronan pointed away from the city. "We make for the Waelyn Valley, just over that ridge there in the distance. We'll be out of view from the Arc by sunrise, but we must move quickly." He steered his horse towards the ridge.

"Everybody, hang on tight."

He took off and the horses picked up speed as they raced out of the paddock and into the surrounding farmland behind him. The moon glowed off the roofs of a few scattered cottages along the stretch of land they traveled through.

Jen felt a rush of freedom as her horse galloped beneath her. If this wasn't a terrifying ordeal, she might have enjoyed it.

To their left, Zaniya grew smaller as they rode further out into the moon kissed valley, the sandstone tower of the Arc rose from the cliff beyond the city. She drove her heels into the sides of her horse and rode up beside Ronan. His eyes darted around for any sign that they'd been spotted.

They rode all through the night, attempting to arrive at the ridge before dawn broke over the horizon. As they neared their destination, Ronan slowed them down.

He guided them in single file up a series of switchbacks, warning them to be careful in their ascent.

Jen glanced over her shoulder and was greeted with the all too recognizable look of exhaustion and fear on her friends' faces. Her chest constricted, knowing there was nothing she could do.

They ascended higher towards the ridge. Aside from the clomping sounds of the horses' hooves, it was quiet—still. Over the horizon, the first flecks of magenta and soft orange painted the sky.

Ronan tensed.

"What's wrong?" Jen asked nervously.

"We're completely exposed here."

Jen looked out towards the speck that she knew was the Arc.

"Would they even see us from here?"

Ronan followed her gaze. "It's not the kashyak I'm worried about."

"What are you worried about—"

But Ronan had already coaxed his horse to move faster up the switchbacks. The soft hues of sunrise were beginning to brighten and bolden as Jen and the others continued behind him.

What's worse than the kashyak? What in hells even IS it?

Ronan arrived at the top of the ridge and moved aside to allow the others to ride in front of him. Jen stopped next to him for a moment. Her jaw dropped at the view.

Out past the vast valley, a grand mountain range of impervious brown peaks speckled with snow loomed as a guardian standing watch over the Etherian landscape.

"Is that—"

"The realm of Sachandes," Ronan said.

Jen opened her mouth to speak, but Ronan went still. His verdant eyes darted behind him where the sky was coming out of its dark slumber. He sucked in a breath and smacked the backside of Jen's mount.

"Go!"

He galloped down the hill and into the Waelyn Valley after her, speeding to the front of the group.

"Follow me!"

He veered sharply to the right over a cascade of rolling hills until the beginning of a rural village began to appear in the distance.

They came barreling to the edge of the settlement, where he leapt from his horse and tied the reins to a nearby fence post. Jen and the others did the same and followed quickly behind him.

The villagers took notice of the wayward strangers as Ronan ducked through the simple wooden houses and stalls draped with vibrant cloth.

At the apex of the mud and stone path stood a warped-wood meeting hall. Ronan motioned for them to stop in front of the steps when several men and women came out from the front entrance.

Leading them was a woman with striking features and an olive complexion and long hair, black as a starless night. She wore a simple emerald blouse with a brown leather fighting vest that held two daggers, the hilts gleaming in the morning sun. Her dark tweed pants were tucked into dull boots that laced up the front of her shins.

She stared at Ronan for a long moment. She lifted one of her thick eyebrows, to which he gave an apologetic shrug.

Her cold stare faded, replaced by a wide smile as she bolted down a few steps and launched herself into his arms. A surprised laugh jaunted from his chest as he squeezed her tight.

The sound was a low, melodious song that shimmered through Jen's veins; a reaction she didn't care for. She shoved her hands in her pockets and glanced away.

Ronan put the woman down. "What are you doing here, Ro?" she asked.

Ro?

"We need your help—" he began.

A chilling screech from the direction of Zaniya filled the air. Ronan rubbed his temples and groaned. Horror filled his friend's eyes.

"Ronan."

The screech came again—louder. His friend looked in the direction of the sound before returning her livid sights to him.

"Why is there a kashyak TRACKING YOU?"

Ronan rubbed the back of his head and pointed his chin in Jenevieve's direction. "She may have witnessed an Echo."

"WHAT?" the woman yelled. "Ronan, who the *fuck* did you bring to my village? What's wrong with you?"

"I know, I know. You can yell at me later, but we have a more pressing issue."

"YOU THINK?"

"I got them to the ridge but the salyaat must have spotted us from the dome—"

Jen stepped towards them. "Salyaat?"

"The thing with wings," Ronan barked as he pointed to the ridge, making Jen flinch.

His friend shoved past him.

The villagers cried out in fear as the screech was no longer a distant sound, but a tangible threat coming over the ridge. It took the shape of a winged reptilian creature and moved as if unhindered by bones and joints. Instead of scales it was covered in thick black feathers—a massive, demonic bird.

Atop it sat a hooded figure—the kashyak.

Ronan's friend leapt onto the nearest wooden table.

"Everyone! Get inside!" She pointed to three boys no older than Jamie. "You three, turn their horses out into the field!" The boys nodded and ran for the fence where they untacked the horses and coaxed them into the open valley. She marched back toward the meeting house, the others following closely behind her.

"Maybe the scent of her is still on the horse. You all need to split up. Two of you go in there." She pointed to a small hut to their left.

William yanked Leeyna towards it and disappeared behind the door.

She pointed to a small blacksmith stall to the right. "Two of you duck in here; there's a room in the back."

Jen threw an imploring look at Damien and Emelie.

"Please go together, keep each other safe. I'll be alright," she said. Damien briefly glanced at Ronan, but then he took her chin and kissed her quickly.

"I'll see you soon," he said before leading Emelie into the shop.

Jenevieve followed Ronan and his friend to the steps of the meeting house.

"You two go in there and find a place to keep hidden. I'll handle the kashyak."

She grabbed his elbow before he could move.

"Ronan, *hide her.*"

"You know I can't—"

"Try."

He nodded and pushed Jen up the steps.

"I got it. I got it." She slapped his hand away.

"Then move *faster.*"

They entered the meeting house, a large room with rows of long wooden tables lining the planked floors. Jen ran over to the front window to try to get a look at the kashyak.

Ronan cursed.

"Get away from the damn window!"

Jen scowled at him, but he wasn't even looking at her. His eyes stopped on a door in the corner beside them.

"There, come on," he ordered. He strode over and opened the door to reveal a small broom closet. Jen crossed her arms.

"You have *got* to be kidding me."

"After you."

"We'll never fit."

"Jenevieve, get in the *fucking* closet."

She stepped in, careful not to trip over the brooms and buckets that sat on the floor. Thin streams of light carried into the cramped space as Ronan followed behind her and closed the door.

Jen pressed herself against the wall while Ronan maneuvered his broad shoulders within the confined space. He stood far too close, the scent of leather from his black vest, and through that, the faintest whisper of wildflowers and soil before a storm pervaded her nose.

Earthy, floral.

She attempted not to breathe him in too deeply; it was doing something unsettling to her nerves.

A wry grin creeped into the corner of his lips.

"Well, this is cozy."

"I'm sure you're *loving* this."

He raised a brow and folded his arms, the lion on his forearm dancing with the movement. "Trust me, Jenevieve, I envisioned being close to you much differently than this."

Jen was prepared to retort when Ronan's head snapped towards the planked wall behind her head. Her body froze.

"It's in the village," he breathed.

He closed the space between them and placed his hands on the wall at either side of her head, his body flushing against hers. Her eyes narrowed.

"What the hell are you—"

He shushed her.

"It can smell you. Keep your mouth shut."

It can smell me?

Jen opened her mouth to speak but felt something fall over them. It was as though a sheer curtain had been gently draped around their still bodies—the air seemed to vibrate…shimmer.

She barely had time to register her relief when her heart plummeted at the sound of massive wings *whooshing* to the ground outside the building. She peeked through a sliver in the wall as fear rattled through her.

The salyaat landed at the edge of the village, its size so immense it casted a shadow over the main path. Its hooded rider, the kashyak, slowly slithered off and moved up the main path with a slow and serpentine gait, like a human with no spine.

The kashyak stopped a few feet from where Ronan's friend stood at the foot of the meeting house. It removed its hood to reveal gray scaled skin covering the entirety of its body, with black fogged eyes and two holes for ears. It inhaled deeply through the slits that served as a nose and turned its head slowly to face her.

"Why have you come here," Ronan's friend seethed. The kashyak jeered at her, its pointed teeth showing from beneath thin lips. It clicked its forked tongue as it spoke.

"I…*click click*…am tracking…*click click*…a most exquisite scent of…enchanted memory," it lingered on each syllable.

The woman crossed her arms over her chest.

"There are no such enchantments here."

The kashyak rolled its neck as if the words tickled its scaly skin.

"I tracked them…*click click*…here…you wouldn't be…*click click*…hiding them…*click*…that would be…a grave…*click click*…mistake."

The woman squared her shoulders.

"We have no reason to hide anyone."

"Then…why…*click*…do I still…*click*…smell her…"

She pointed her chin towards the valley.

"They passed through soon before you arrived on your *foul creature*."

It smiled languidly, baring razor-sharp teeth.

"You had…better…*click click*…proceed cautiously…human…for it won't be long…*click click*…before *they* make their presence known…*click click.*"

She smirked at the revolting creature.

"It is *you* that should be cautious, *my friend*. These are protected lands, and *she* is always watching."

The creature released a ragged breath "Darkness...*click click*...is looming...darkness...*click click*...is coming to devour the light."

The woman looked to the horizon. "Dawn is breaking," she said. "The light will *always* pervade the darkness—and will stand against the vile *depravity* of your wretched realm." She pointed to an ivory flag atop a pole beside her.

It bore the emblem of a lily.

The salyaat screeched and stretched its enormous wings. The kashyak chuckled. "This is a warning, girl...*click click*...Next time it will not be me...*click click*...And...it will not be so...*click click*...cordial."

It leered at each of the village leaders, taking long, languid inhales before slinking towards the salyaat. It turned back before mounting.

"Durche yahvak."

The salyaat released one last terrifying cry before it flew off into the dawn-soaked sky.

CHAPTER 11

*D*urche yahvak. Those insidious words rang a dissonant chord inside Jen's mind. She clenched her teeth as it vibrated through her body, memories of the pulse—of the morai—her siblings' faces frozen in fear, it all came barreling through her.

Jenevieve stood perfectly still, afraid if she moved even an inch the protection over them would falter. That thing had sensed her. Smelled her. It tracked her here.

She glanced up and sucked in a quiet breath, Ronan was almost nose to nose with her—a straight, refined nose accompanied by full lips pursed in concentration, both framed by a chiseled jawline that hosted a well-trimmed stumble, and dark brown hair that curved around his ears in thick strokes of mahogany.

No man has any business being that attractive.

"You like what you see?" he asked, his eyes still closed.

She sputtered, failing to find something quippy to say.

"Keep looking if you like."

She gaped. But before she could manage to string a fucking sentence together, his body relaxed against hers.

"It's gone," he murmured.

She peered up at him, his eyes boring into hers. The protection had lifted a moment ago, but still he stood flushed against her, his head having dipped closer during the ordeal with the kashyak.

Too. Fucking. Close.

Jen swallowed hard as Ronan just stood there, perfectly still. They were so close the ghost of his stubble warmed her cheek. He leaned in towards the wall beside her head, leaving her lips far too close to his neck. He breathed deeply.

"Who are you?" he asked on an exhale, and before she could turn to look at him, he was out of the closet like a gust of wind.

Jen let out a ragged breath.

What in hells was that?

She stepped out of the closet to find herself alone in the meeting house. She ran out the door and down the steps where everyone was emerging from their own hiding spots.

Damien spotted her and marched over, wrapping his arms around her tightly. His brows cinched together. "You're trembling."

A harsh laugh escaped her. "Being tracked and hunted has that kind of effect."

Damien kissed her forehead as Ronan returned in the company of his mystery friend.

"As I was saying, before I was rudely interrupted," he drawled. "This is an old friend, Samara."

Samara waved like she couldn't be less interested.

"Now that that's done," Samara said, right before she rounded on Ronan and punched him in the shoulder, hard. So hard that it knocked him back a few steps. Damien stifled a laugh, as did everyone else.

"What the FUCK were you thinking?" she scolded as he straightened back up. He couldn't help but chuckle at her as he rubbed his aching shoulder.

"I'm sorry, alright? I got them to the ridge just as the sun was rising and I knew the kashyak had her scent already. I saw your settlement and raced here; she would have been caught in the valley."

Samara's eyes darted to Jenevieve.

"Who are you?"

That question is getting very old, very quickly.

Her eyes flickered nervously to Ronan, and he stepped towards Samara.

"I told you, she witnessed an Echo—"

Samara raised her hand to silence him. She studied Jenevieve carefully. "Is that the only reason why that thing was hunting you?"

Ronan subtly nodded at Jen.

"Yes," she said. "A dhoksha saw me witness the Echo and must have sent for it."

Ronan squeezed his eyes shut, and Jenevieve realized she'd said too much.

Samara whipped around to Ronan with daggers in her eyes.

"We need to talk. Now."

She grabbed his arm and wretched him away from the group and back into the meeting house. Jen turned to her friends once they were gone.

"She seems like a bundle of joy," William said.

"I'm sure it's very taxing being friends with that man," Jen said, rubbing her temples.

Leeyna wrapped her arms around herself. "Is it bad that I'm getting used to being in constant danger?"

William nudged her with his shoulder. "I don't think my heart has had a consistent rhythm since the wedding."

Damien quietly placed his arm around Jen's waist, and she laced her fingers with his. She shook the encounter with Ronan from her mind and settled, if only briefly, into a moment of fragile repose.

She glanced over Damien's shoulder, and her brows drew together.

A hooded figure peeked out from the shadows around the side of the meeting house. She glimpsed back at her friends—no one seemed to notice.

There was something familiar about them.

It beckoned Jen to follow. Her gaze shifted to the stream, gently flowing just outside the village.

"I'll be right back," she said shimmying out of Damien's grip.

He tilted his head. "Where are you going?"

"I'll be right over there." Jen pointed to the babbling brook. "I just need a moment to myself."

Damien briefly searched her face but then conceded with a nod. He watched her walk away, and when he turned back to the others, Jen veered sharply behind the meeting house.

The figure travelled away from the village, climbing up a slight hill into a nearby glen where the stream threaded through a vast conclave of high hilltops and jutting boulders.

Jen followed cautiously behind; the familiarity of its movements drawing her closer. It approached the water's edge and slowly removed its hood.

Her heart stopped.

"Mama?" she gasped.

Fjora stood by the water, still as could be; ash-blonde hair in a thick plait, kind emerald-green eyes, a small smile poised on her lips.

"Mama, how did you get here?"

Relief bubbled around her heart. Her mother had survived the attack and had ventured out of Nimea to help her, everything was going to be okay.

Fjora extended her arms out and Jen sprinted towards her. "I've missed you so much, I—"

A whistle of wind flew past her ear.

Fjora's back arched in an unnatural angle, and she fell to the ground, blood pouring from her mouth—and an arrow protruding from her chest.

"MAMA! NO!"

Jen's chest cleaved in two as she fell to her knees before her mother, her eyes filling with horror, unable to comprehend what lay in front of her.

Fjora's once beautiful face began to shrivel and shift into murky green skin, with bulging eyes and thin lips. The rest of the creature's body followed suit, morphing into leathery green with rough bumps scattered about, taking the shape of a human with amphibian features.

Jen clapped her hands to her mouth to keep from vomiting. Her eyes settled at the arrow sticking out of its chest.

Where did that…

She looked over her shoulder, her gaze rising to the hill she had just come from. Ronan and Samara stood watching, the latter with a slack bow in her hand.

Their faces held somber expressions. Samara turned back to the village, but Ronan remained a moment longer, their gaze lingering before she heard someone calling her name.

"*Jen!* Shit, what happened?" Damien came running along with the others.

Jen looked back at the dead thing in front of her. Damien inched toward her, eyeing the creature laying on the ground.

"Bug…"

"It looked like—like my mother. It was so real," she murmured. Damien knelt beside her. "I was stupid enough to think she was here."

Anger roiled beneath her skin.

Anger at Fjora. Anger at herself.

"What is it…" Emelie asked hesitantly.

"A dhoksha."

Samara and Ronan appeared behind them.

"In its *true form*," Samara continued. "I had to kill it, you were getting too close."

"What happens when you get close?" Leeyna asked. She peered over William's shoulder, the sight of the dhoksha draining her face of color.

Ronan stepped towards the corpse.

"A dhoksha can take the form of anyone once they've laid eyes on them. But it can also pull from someone's mind and take the form of a person that holds meaning to their prey."

"Prey?" Damien asked, clearly hoping he had misheard.

Ronan nodded and continued. "They are the silent sirens that lure people to madness, and ultimately, death. If she'd gotten too close to it, it would have first driven her to insanity, and then she would have begged it for death."

The ache in Jen's heart stilled. The constant terror and fear that festered within her was winding its way around her veins, and her mind instinctively intervened to protect her. It shrouded her in a misty fog and coaxed her towards a quiet void, the pain disappearing to give way to a cool numbness.

She rose to her feet, her unfocused eyes drifting over the dhoksha one last time before turning away.

"We should head back to the village."

Jen left the others in a wake of confusion and concern as she made her way towards the meeting house, feeling nothing but the breeze on her skin.

CHAPTER 12

Heat from the crackling fire failed to warm her aching limbs as Jen sat in the grass beside it, a plate of food in her hand. The warmth of the flames simply refused to penetrate her skin, but Jen hardly noticed. She floated in the cover of numbing fog that wrapped around her and kept away the ragged exhaustion that was beginning to seep into her body.

She should be hungry, but she had no appetite. She idly pushed the food around her plate until she felt someone crouch beside her.

"I know what you're doing," Damien said, his eyes fixed on the fire.

Jen stared at her food. "I'm not doing anything."

He crossed his arms, his thick brows forming a hard line.

"You shut down. I saw it happen." He jutted his chin to the other side of the fire. "Emelie did too. We *know* you, Bug."

Jen's eyes flicked over to Emelie who was trying very hard to avoid looking up at her. Of course, they noticed. They always did, and if Jen wasn't already floating in a fog, she would have been annoyed that they'd been watching her so closely.

She put her plate down and rubbed her hands over her face.

"I'm fine."

He lowered himself to the grass, his presence doing more to warm her than the flames in front of her, a ray of sun slicing through the fog.

She knew, as well as Damien and Emelie, that this was a typical reaction when she faced any kind of danger, physical or emotional.

It started years ago to defend herself against her father. During a particularly horrible altercation, her mind had erected a wall of solid, white stone to protect her—and now, whenever something similar attempted to break through, she shoved it behind that protective barrier and down into a dark abyss where it couldn't harm her. But it took its toll. The strength it took to fortify the wall, to keep those terrifying things trapped behind it and away from not only those around her, but from herself as well, often left her feeling numb, cold.

But Jen knew it was easier to feel nothing at all, than to feel everything all at once.

Damien had always been the first to notice when that fog remained around her, and he made it a habit to call her on it before gallantly pulling her out of it—or at least attempting to.

But now, he just leaned into her, choosing to let his presence slowly guide her out from behind the wall and back to the world around her.

He wound his fingers with hers and squeezed them gently, an unsaid conversation floating between them; *I'm right here, and so are you.*

The crunch of boots turned her head towards the meeting house. Ronan approached with a scowl etched into his face. He had gone off with Samara after the incident with the dhoksha, and clearly that had not gone well for him.

His looming presence cast a shadow over Jen and Damien, his eyes flicking over their intertwined fingers. She could practically feel his eyes rolling as he crossed his arms, his gaze falling to her.

"Come with me," he grumbled.

"Why?"

His nostrils flared. "Must you be difficult?"

She raised a brow at him. "With you, absolutely."

Ronan blew out a breath, collected himself, and extended his hand to her. Jen looked at it, and then back at him, her brow arched in confusion.

"I'll go with you," Damien said.

Ronan *actually* rolled his eyes that time. "No."

Damien's body grew tense behind her. Jen gave his hand a reassuring squeeze. "It's okay."

She gave Ronan a pointed look before she let his calloused hand pull her to her feet. Jen turned back to Damien. "Just look after the others, alright?"

He glared at Ronan, but when his gaze shifted to Jen, he softened with a nod.

She followed Ronan through the village, a more expansive maze of paths than she noticed when they first arrived. Although, she hadn't had much time to explore, given she was the object of an unceremonious *hunt.*

They wove around a few vendor stalls and came to a small cabin on the outskirts of the settlement. Her eyes narrowed.

"Ronan, what is this?"

But he ignored her as they walked up two steps to a small porch, and he simply opened the door and stood aside. She took a few tentative steps inside and found herself in a small, lived-in cabin.

Planked floors were covered intermittently with plush rugs, and a small couch of worn leather sat in front of the hearth. The kitchen had a small table with a few chairs, and an empty counter with a minuscule sink. Soft afternoon light passed through the windows and streamed onto the floor where tiny particles of dust floated in the air. The place felt warm—welcoming.

She ventured further and passed by a small washroom, and a room that housed a simple bed with feather pillows and a few soft quilts.

I would love to fall into those blankets and sleep forever.

Ronan cleared his throat behind her. "This is my place, when they migrate to this settlement."

He watched her as she took in the space around them.

"Migrate?"

Ronan slumped onto the couch.

"The nomadic villages of the Waelyn Valley," he started. Jen came around to the hearth and held her hands in front of it, her silence indicating she had no idea what he was talking about.

Again.

He chuckled.

"I forgot, it's like explaining things to a child."

She gave him a pointed look and mustered the remaining strength she had to march towards the door.

He raised a hand. "Easy, I can see we're too tired for *jokes.*"

Jen turned around with a scoff, crossing her arms as she reluctantly waited for him to continue.

"The nomadic villages follow the natural pull of the magic embedded in the earth," he explained; he hadn't bothered to get up. "Any Etherian can tell which way the magical forces are leaning based on which settlements the nomads are at."

Jen slowly walked back to the hearth, struggling to wrap her head around an entire valley of villages moving around like a herd of animals based on some magical pull. But she'd felt it, as soon as she entered Etheria.

The pull of magic.

The draw to light, the seductive whisper of darkness.

"There's another valley in the north, Lutteala, that follows the same pull."

"Why?"

Ronan lifted a shoulder in a small shrug. "No one knows. They've had a similar migration pattern for thousands of years. I'm told it's a visceral feeling that guides them from one settlement to another."

That sounds familiar.

Jen tucked the unsettling similarity between her and the nomads in the back of her mind to obsess over later.

"Why are you telling me this?"

He laced his fingers behind his head and stretched lazily.

"Because I know who the two unidentified signatures are."

She whipped her head up to meet his awaiting stare.

"Wait, there are two valleys?"

"Mhm."

He observed her as the wheels spun inside her head. Realization came over her face. "There's a descendant from Lutteala, and Waelyn."

He smirked.

"I also know—" he continued as he stood gracefully, straightening his broad shoulders. "Samara and I arranged for the village elders to meet us at this cabin."

Jen whirled around, her eyes wide.

"Wha—here? *Now?*"

Ronan picked at his nails. "Why did you think I brought you here?" He gave her a rakish grin. "To show you my bed?"

Jen let out a frustrated groan before her gaze darted towards the front window. "But what about the others? Damien would want to be here."

"You can stand on your own two feet, Jenevieve."

Her eyes narrowed. "I know that."

Ronan crossed his arms.

"Do you? Because all I've seen is Damien coddling you."

"I don't need him to do that."

"Exactly. You don't. Stop putting yourself in a position where he feels he needs to. You're not helpless."

A flash of contempt flickered over Jen's eyes. She practically spat at him. "You're an arrogant bastard."

Ronan released a deep chuckle. "There she is."

A soft knock fell on the front door. Jen's skin grew clammy as her heart slammed against her chest. How in hells was she supposed to do this? There were too many unknowns; she didn't have enough information to give them. She barely understood the purpose of what she was trying to do. She didn't even know who she was or what she meant to this damn continent. They would never agree to reconvene the council with her.

Ronan watched her, as if he could see her panic spiral.

He stepped towards the hearth, glancing down at her knuckles clinging to the mantle like a vice.

"Look," he sighed. "I didn't bring Damien or the others because I wasn't sure if the elders would speak to you if they were all here. What you're trying to do is dangerous. Necessary, but dangerous. I anticipate a lot of push back; the descendant may choose not to step forward."

Jen dug her fingers deeper. "You don't know who it is?"

"Ancient secrets and what not," Ronan shrugged.

She let go of the mantle and lifted a hand to her cheek.

"Why are you even doing this?"

He cocked his head. "Doing what?"

The knock came again, a bit more insistent this time.

"Helping me."

Ronan smirked, but it didn't quite reach his eyes.

"We'll talk about that later—*come in,*" he called to the door.

Samara popped her head inside, her eyes shifting to Ronan. He gave her a curt nod, and she opened the door, walking inside along with four older villagers trailing behind her—the elders.

Ronan held their gaze, waiting, but not desperate. After a moment of tense silence, the elders crossed over to the small table, passing by Jenevieve without a single glance. One of them, a dark-skinned woman, lowered herself into one of the chairs at the table and leaned forward, her stoic gaze finally settling on Jen.

"Who are you?" she asked, but it sounded less like a question and more like a thinly cloaked accusation.

The elders waited, looking utterly unimpressed by the exhausted blonde woman standing before them.

Samara cleared her throat, breaking the awkward, one-sided standoff and gestured to the dark-skinned woman still staring at Jen. "This is Vaelja." Her hand shifted to the olive-complected woman seated beside her. "And Eyva."

She pointed to one of the men, with ivory skin and eyes of wild autumn hues, leaning against the back window of the house. "Einar," Samara continued, before glancing at the dark-skinned man grasping the back of Vaelja's chair. "And Viktor."

Jen folded her hands to conceal the anxiety coursing through her and took a step forward. "I'm Jenevieve."

Eyva lifted a brow. "That is not what she asked." Her expression was stern. "Who *are* you?"

Yes, because the change of inflection imposed on the question is going to magically conjure a more acceptable answer.

"I—I don't know," Jen answered honestly.

Eyva darted her gaze at Samara.

"And yet, you wished to meet with us? To ask something of us?"

Samara glanced at Ronan perched on the edge of the couch, arms folded, observing. He clicked his tongue and stood, retrieving a scroll from inside his leather vest.

He strolled to the table and spread it out, Samara joining him with two candles to weigh it down and silently pointed to the two unidentified signatures on the oath of the Council of Suran.

Vaelja and Eyva gasped.

"Goddess, save us."

"The descendant is bound by the oath of their ancestor." Ronan tapped his finger on the two names.

"Is that why the kashyak was here?" Viktor asked.

"No," Jenevieve heard herself say. Ronan peered up at her, curious as to where she was going next.

"We were tracked because of me. I witnessed an Echo."

She could feel the energy of the room shift drastically, like someone had sucked half of the air from the cabin.

Eyva examined Jen closely. "That is a very rare, very *powerful* ability, child."

So, I've been told.

"What Echo did you witness?" Einar asked, running his hand absentmindedly down the windowpane.

She looked at Ronan out of the corner of her eye. If she hoped to enlist their help, Jen was going to have to give them *something*—something valuable to gain their trust.

Ronan nodded like he heard her thoughts and agreed with her.

"I witnessed Kiara giving birth," she said.

Vaelja's eyes grew into round dinner plates. "The child lives…" she whispered, almost to herself.

The stern look on Eyva's face shifted rapidly to shock.

"Was anyone with her?" Viktor asked. "In the Echo?" He placed his hands on Vaelja's shoulders.

Jen took in their bewildered expressions. "A woman called Naedyra."

Einar's hand halted its nonchalant path along the windowpane—clearly that name had gotten his attention.

"It seemed she and Kiara were friends," she explained further.

Eyva leaned into the table, searching Jen's face as if the Echo were etched into her skin. "Where did you come from, child?"

Samara's eyes narrowed from where she sat on the kitchen counter; Ronan had clearly not told her the next tidbit.

Oh, this will be fun.

"I escaped from Nimea when a horde of morai attacked my—"

Samara's eyes widened. The quartet of elders scoffed.

"Nimea doesn't exist, it was wiped off the map a thousand years ago," Vaelja said, now with more unwavering suspicion in her voice.

Samara hopped off the counter just as Jen took a charged step forward. "I assure you. Nimea is *very real*." There was a ferocity in her voice that she didn't recognize. "My village was attacked by the morai, and *very real* people were killed."

Frightened screams and flashes of flame careened across her mind. She dug her nails into her palms to keep from crumbling around the memories.

"If what you say is true." Einar stepped away from the window. "How did you manage to get through Bri?"

"A path of marked trees, shown to me by my protector."

"And who was that?"

Jenevieve unclenched her fists, leaving half-moon indents across the inside of her hands. She wasn't sure if giving them Fjora's name would help or endanger her odds of convincing them to reconvene. She was unsure if it would mean anything at all

Aside from the tragic vision she'd witnessed, Jen didn't know much else about her protector—well, at least, not much about her identity.

"Her name is Fjora."

The elders froze.

"That's not possible."

Chairs scraped against the floor as the women rose from their seats, the stoic facade cracking as disbelief and an inkling of fear flickered behind their eyes.

"Do you know her?" Jen asked, trying to understand what could warrant this kind of reaction.

"We are asking the questions here, child," Vaelja seethed.

Child. The condescension dripped from the word. She was a fully grown woman, not some naive girl. Although her lack of knowledge about, well, everything, made that argument a bit thin.

Samara whipped her head towards Ronan.

"Did you know about this?"

Ronan simply folded his arms over his chest. "Of course, I did."

"The princess was lost during the last pulse," Eyva insisted.

The color drained from Jen's face.

Um. Excuse me?

"The—the princess?" she stammered.

"The heir to the Sachandan throne, yes," Vaelja barked.

I know what a fucking princess is. I just had no idea I'd been living with one for THIRTY YEARS.

Einar approached the table. "Why would the princess of Sachandes be charged with your protection?"

Fjora is a princess. Fjora is a princess. Fjora is a princess.

"And why did the morai attack?"

Ronan shifted behind her, pulling her away from her revelation as she could practically feel the lethal stare he was shooting at the elder.

Focus Jen. You can freak out later.

She swallowed the lump in her throat, forcing her face into a neutral expression. "They came for me."

A heavy silence found its way over the room as realization dawned over the room.

"You're the reason the pulse came early," Einar said.

"Yes."

The palms of her hands grew warm beneath her skin, but this time it was not from light, but from anger. Ronan stepped closer to her.

"Why?" Viktor asked.

They already knew the answer, they just wanted her to say it. She lifted her chin, a simple gesture, but one that forced her not to break her stare.

"I'm in the bloodline."

There was a scuffle of footsteps as the four elders marched towards the door. Jen's mouth dropped open. Samara leapt in front of them and held up her hands.

Vaelja raised a finger. "You did not tell us that she was in the bloodline. This just became a very dangerous conversation."

"The danger has been growing for years, and you know it, Vaelja," Samara said. Ronan strode over and stood beside her.

"We have all felt it. Your village migrated earlier in the year than it's supposed to, didn't you find that strange? Vondur is preparing for something on a larger scale. This is different from the pulse, they are gearing up for an invasion, and we all know it deep down," he said as he gestured to Jen.

"And what a coincidence that someone from the bloodline comes hurdling out of Bri and witnesses an Echo within three days of being in our realm. Goddess knows this is a sign that the ancient oaths must be upheld. The Council of Suran must reconvene," he proclaimed.

"You are asking us to put our people at risk," Vaelja said.

"It is a necessary risk, Vaelja."

"Heltior wouldn't just murder the council members if he found out," she said, her voice dead calm. "He would slaughter their people and lay waste to their lands. That is the kind of monster we speak of."

Vaelja turned to Jen. "Have you asked any of the other descendants?"

The color drained from her face, her request fading into a pale joke. "No, you're the first."

"You want us to be the first to sign our death warrants," Viktor stated coldly.

"I want you to be the first to fight," Jen heard herself say.

"You don't even understand the gravity of what we would be fighting," Viktor spoke again. "Evil incarnate."

"Until you can get another descendant to answer the call, we cannot help you. We will not risk our people on the hopes of a girl who's been in our realm for three days," Vaelja said.

The elders marched out of the cabin, leaving Jen reeling by the kitchen table.

Well, that was fucking awful.

She felt like an utter failure, their rebuttals ringing true. She couldn't expect them to risk their peoples' lives just because Ronan showed them a piece of paper with an ancestor's name scribbled on it.

Can I shrink up into a ball and disappear now?

She pressed both hands on the table, the weight of the failed meeting and the exhaustion that she had kept at bay came crashing down on her.

Don't pass out. Don't pass out.

Samara bounded to the door. "Let me try to reason with them."

She started leaving when Jen said, "Why? You don't know me, and they're right." She waved her hand at the door. "Why would they risk their people on the word of a woman who doesn't even know what her role is in all of this?"

Samara gave her a small, weary smile.

"Because Ronan is also right. Something dark is headed our way, and I won't let those cowards cost me the lives of my people." With that, she disappeared.

CHAPTER 13

Ronan quietly approached the table, where Jen was using the last of her energy to stay upright.

"We'll get them on board," he said. "They're just afraid. They have every right to be."

"I know."

He watched her, but she continued staring down at her hands.

"Why did you make me do that?" she asked quietly.

He sighed. "Because you are a stronger force than you think you are, Jenevieve."

She risked a glance at him. "You don't know me."

He leaned in. "I know strength when I see it."

"I don't feel strong," Jen whispered, looking away.

I feel like a fucking idiot.

Ronan rolled the scroll back up and placed it within his vest. "That's because you're overwhelmed and exhausted. But you pushed through that and still did very well."

"Who cares about that, I failed."

And, apparently, I was raised by a lost princess that everyone else knew—except me. Big surprise there.

"You think they would agree after one meeting with someone they don't know, raised by someone they thought was dead, in a realm that was supposedly wiped off the map?"

"No," Jen grumbled.

If she were in their position, she would think they were insane. But Jen was also raised with the naive understanding that tales of magic and the world beyond Bri were just that—stories, legends.

Her thoughts grew thick like wet clay as waves of exhaustion crashed through her. Ronan chuckled softly at her drooping eyelids and gently coaxed her away from the table and towards the small bedroom.

She eyed him warily, but he raised his hands.

"As much as I would enjoy watching you sleep, I'm going to join Samara and try again with the elders."

Jen dragged her feet to the bed and plopped down on the soft mattress, her body immediately relaxing into it. Ronan leaned in the doorway and pointed to the small dresser in the corner.

"Samara left you a nightgown, more comfortable than constantly sleeping in your clothes."

Jen stood up clumsily and retrieved the simple white nightgown from the top of the dresser, the soft material felt like a lullaby.

"So," he said, adjusting his vest. "Fjora, huh?"

Jen turned at the familiarity in his voice.

Princess Fjora, actually.

"She…um…went by Maelia… in Nimea."

He scratched his eyebrow. "Interesting."

Pick a different word.

"She couldn't exactly go around introducing herself as the princess of Sachandes."

His mouth twitched. "I suppose not." He jutted his chin to the bed. "Sleep here as long as you want. I'll tell the others to leave you be." He pushed off the doorframe.

Fear seized her lungs. "Will the kashyak come back?" she blurted out.

He stopped in his tracks, not bothering to turn back to her.

"No, the village has been warded."

"Warded?"

"A protective barrier." He turned, finding her anxious gaze staring back at him. "You're safe, Jenevieve."

Her body slumped, as if she needed to hear those words to allow herself to sink into a deep sleep. He paused for a moment, watching the relief bloom over her skin, and then walked towards the front door.

Jen came to the doorway of the bedroom.

"Ronan?"

"Hmm?"

"You didn't answer my question." She bit her bottom lip. "From before."

He arched a brow.

"Why are you helping me?"

A small, sly smile formed in the corner of his mouth. "Maybe I enjoy pissing off your man."

Jen blushed. "He's not my *man*. And that isn't an answer."

"The answer to that question is—complicated," he said. She opened her mouth to argue, but he raised his hand. "And now is not the time."

If she wasn't so exhausted, she would have absolutely made it *the time*. But her body was demanding that this conversation cease so it could shut down.

Ronan crossed to the door, and as he turned the handle, Jen spoke one more time.

"Ronan?"

He glanced over her shoulder.

"Thank you."

"Don't be nice to me, it feels—*wrong*."

Jen folded her arms over her chest and scoffed. "My mistake." A whisper of a smirk appeared on her lips. "You arrogant bastard."

He winked. "There she is."

And he slipped through the door.

Jen appreciated the comforting silence of the cabin as she undressed and slipped on the soft nightgown. She couldn't place the material, but it rubbed against her skin like a soft breeze.

It was only midafternoon, but Jen slipped into the bed, and she pushed away any thought that may keep her from sleeping as her head sunk into the inviting feather pillows.

Jenevieve's eyes fluttered open, and for a moment, she couldn't remember where she was. She rubbed the sleep from her eyes and looked through the doorway of the bedroom to see the small kitchen table.

Ronan's cabin. The meeting. Fjora.

She groaned at the memories.

The failure of a meeting. And princess Fjora.

She sat up and swung her legs onto the floor, the wooden planks cooling her very warm feet.

The cabin was quiet. The sun had still been out when she'd fallen asleep, and now the sky was dark. She had no idea if it was evening, the middle of the night, or early morning.

How long was I asleep?

She wrapped a small blanket around her shoulders and wandered out into the kitchen; the only sounds were of her feet creaking along the boards. The hearth burned low as Jen walked to the window in the back of the cabin.

The Waelyn Valley stretched out beyond the cloudy glass. Shrouded in darkness, she couldn't tell where the sky ended and the valley began, which should have filled her with existential dread, but Jen felt oddly safe within the cabin—a sensation she hadn't experienced since leaving Nimea.

Her hand rose to her chest.

An unseen thread wrapped itself around her and tugged gently, beckoning her into the darkness living on the other side of the windowpane. And then, the same sensation that called her to the Tree of Whispers—a faint, melodious humming that branched into cascading harmony and dissonance, graced her ear.

Something out there was calling to her.

Jen left the cabin and walked down the steps. She realized it was close to dawn, for there was a faint hue of magenta sitting upon the horizon, the gentle pull and the humming guiding her steps in that direction. She tightened the blanket around her and followed the pull into the open valley, glancing back at the village where not a soul stirred.

The strength of the thread grew stronger, and the humming reached a crescendo in her ears. The gentle magenta began to blend with the warm embrace of deep orange as morning twilight faded. She continued on, coaxed by a friend made of wind and spirit.

Then, all at once, the humming and the thread disappeared.

Jen stood in the valley as the first kiss of the sun danced on the edge of the endless vista, scanning her surroundings for the source of the pull. Her gaze snagged on something in the distance, her eyes squinting as she tried to make it out.

Further out, galloping towards her over the nearby hilltop, was the purest white mare she had ever seen. It whinnied as it came towards her, like it'd been searching for her. She stood still as it approached, its long, vibrantly white mane shimmering like millions of tiny stars threaded together.

Jen tentatively lifted her hand; afraid she may spook the mare if she moved too quickly. But it didn't retreat—instead, it stepped closer. Her fingertips met its pearl-white coat as a quiet exhale left her body.

The breeze picked up, whipping and churning in every direction. It blew through her golden hair, dancing the length of her arms and encircling her waist. The blanket flew from her shoulders, carried towards the village by a swathe of woven zephyr.

The ground began to tremble beneath her bare feet. Jen looked back to the horizon, to the hill where the mare first appeared. There came three more horses of the same, pure white, galloping down the slope.

Then two more.

Four more.

And then the ground was no longer trembling, but thundering, as all at once, hundreds of them crested over the hillside and crashed down into the valley as an overwhelming wave, glimmering and gleaming as they raced towards her.

They surrounded her, forming an infinite circle of ancient magic and galloping hooves that glowed as the sun fully broke and dawn rose behind them.

Jen's breath caught in her throat.

This is—What is this?

The mare nudged her shoulder, drawing Jen's gaze back to her. When she turned, she found the horse bowing her head—waiting.

Jen placed her palm on the bridge of its nose, and her lips parted in surprise as her entire body warmed at the touch. It spread through every inch of her until settling in her hand, and a faint, radiant light emanated from it, like a butterfly wing cast in morning light.

The herd slowed their pace and gathered behind her, and when she turned back towards the settlement, hundreds of villagers stood in awe, not at Jen, but the herd—made even more astounding by the soft rays of the morning sun reflecting off them, creating a shimmering expanse of blinding light across the muted green of the valley.

Damien, Emelie, William and Leenya stood at the front beside Samara— stunned.

The elders wove through the crowd and cautiously approached her, their eyes darting from the herd to Jen. She stepped away from the mare, the glow fading from her hand.

Vaelja came forward, shock filling her deep, brown eyes.

She nodded towards the sea of white. "The Rhionnen have not been seen like this since the age of the Aylaenor."

Jen looked at her, confusion crinkling her brow.

Viktor and Einar approached on either side of Vaelja.

"I don't understand," Jen said, her eyes bouncing between them.

"Do you know who Kiara was?" Einar asked. "*What* she was?"

Jen's lips parted, and she shook her head.

"She was *of* the Aylaenor," Vaelja explained. "A people of extraordinary power, lost to us—fated to forever exist within the legends we tell."

"And the bloodline, *your* bloodline," Einar said. "—was *hers*."

The child lives...

Jen stuttered a breath.

Vaelja took her hand, as if sensing her rapid heartbeat. "The Rhionnen were called to you because her blood flows through your veins," she said, her gaze far warmer than the day before.

A thousand questions leapt to the tip of her tongue. But the only one she was able to articulate was, "What does it mean?"

"It means we must move past our fear," Viktor said.

Einar looked out at the herd. "It means the time has come for the council to reconvene."

The air left her lungs. She glanced behind them, where Ronan appeared beside Samara.

Vaelja stepped back. This time, authority pitched her voice low as she spoke.

"I am Vaelja of Eadrym, descendant of Haeleena of Eadrym," she said with her head bowed. "I will stand with you at the Council of Suran."

Jenevieve blinked.

"Ufreijaa nuri," Vaelja said, and she fell to one knee.

"Ufreijaa nuri," Viktor said, following Vaelja to the ground.

"Ufreijaa nuri," Einar whispered, as he, too, lowered to one knee.

The words floated through the crowd of villagers as a whispered prayer, and one by one they fell to the ground, until every single person was on one knee in the dew-covered grass, looking at her as if she were a divine being.

She found Damien kneeling amongst her friends next to Samara and Ronan, each of them with their own expression of disbelief—except for Ronan, whose lips had turned into the beginnings of a shit-eating grin.

Her gaze shot back toward the Rhionnen and the blazing sun beyond them. The hair on her arms raised, every inch of her skin tingled as something stirred deep within her.

Perhaps it was the mark of destiny sealing her on this path. Perhaps it was the flow of magic churning in her veins. Or, maybe, it was the imminence of doom that hid in the shadows.

Act 2

No matter how strong the wall may be, pain will evolve into whisps of darkness and inevitably find its way through. It demands to be seen.

It demands to be felt.

CHAPTER 14

Jenevieve bathed and dressed quickly before she left the cabin, working her way back through the dirt paths of the village.

She nodded awkwardly to the villagers who bowed as she passed and made her way to the fire where Damien and Emelie were sitting; the former cleaning his sword, the latter reading a book.

She sat down in the grass and nudged Damien with her shoulder. He gave her a tight-lipped smile and returned to the blade in his hand.

William and Leeyna leaned against the porch of a small dwelling beside the fire.

"So—you can talk to horses now?" William asked.

Jen huffed a laugh. "I didn't actually *speak* to them."

Leeyna groaned. "I wish I could speak to the horses in Nimea," she said. "Calling them into the barn was impossible sometimes." Her wild crimson curls blew across her face.

Jen gave her an appreciative smile. She eyed Damien beside her, then draped herself over his lap.

He stiffened. "Sure," he grumbled, maneuvering the blade away from Jen's body. "Lay on top of the pointy sword, that's smart."

She patted his arm from where she laid and glanced over at Emelie, where an open, leather-bound book riddled with drawings and lists of ingredients sat perched between her knees.

"What's that?"

Emelie beamed at her.

"A healer gave it to me yesterday." She lifted the book proudly. A wave of affection flooded over Jen as she watched her best friend flip through the pages, her eyes darting around to the painted flowers and the corresponding writings that described their medicinal properties.

Damien grunted; she was still laying on him. She pushed herself up and wove her arm through his, leaning her chin on his shoulder.

He tensed, but after a moment, his body relaxed, and he put his sword beside him. Damien placed his hand on her arm and kissed her hair, breathing her in.

"Do I have to kneel every time you pass by now?" he murmured into her ear. The corner of her mouth lifted slightly.

"Yes."

He chuckled softly. He lowered his head to her ear and whispered, "I can think of much better reasons to kneel—"

Jen elbowed him in the ribs as a flush crept up her neck. She removed her arm and clamored to her feet, smoothing out her pants and tucking her hair behind her ears.

Damien's shoulders shook with laughter.

She kicked his leg. "You think you're so funny—"

"We leave for Sachandes in an hour," Samara interrupted.

She appeared beside them with a bag over her shoulder. She threw it by Jen's feet, forcing her to hop back. The tension rose suddenly as Samara crouched down and unloaded a collection of daggers and blades. Emelie pressed her book against her chest.

"Pick your poison, my friends," Samara said, gesturing to the pile in front of her like it wasn't a heap of shiny death.

Jen bent over and took a blade of aged steel with an onyx hilt adorned with small slivers of silver that danced and threaded around the dark handle.

She lifted it, the weight was substantial, but not impossible to wield. She looked down at her leather belt, which still held the dagger Fjora gave her.

She glanced over at Damien, and he gave her a reassuring smile.

William, Leeyna and Emelie claimed there's as well. William caught sight of an ax of dark smooth wood and a head of dense iron; Leenya—a lightweight blade of shining silver; and Emelie—an anelace dagger with a limestone hilt.

Samara stood and stretched her arms over her head, unaware of the tension floating around her.

"Meet at the edge of the village, we'll call your horses in." She looked at Jenevieve. "I don't believe your horse will answer my call, so I leave that to you."

An hour later, they stood on the outskirts of the village. The jutting peaks of the Kalli Mountains pierced through the white clouds that dotted the far-off horizon to the north.

She fiddled nervously with her fingers.

Okay. Call for a magical horse. Easy.

Taking a few steps into the valley, she inhaled the morning air and forced her mind to focus on the sounds of the earth. The babbling of water in the river nearby, a cricket singing by her feet, the screech of a falcon flying overhead.

A warm breeze caressed her skin and whipped her hair around her face, and within the song of the wind, a name came to her, like a distant whisper.

"Zarah," she breathed.

The stunning mare came galloping back over the hill. When it approached, Jen, once again, placed her hand upon the bridge of Zarah's nose. Warmth radiated under her skin and released a gentle glow from the palm of her hand.

Samara and Vaelja walked up beside her.

"When it is time to reconvene, send a white raven," Vaelja said. "I will be awaiting the call." She took Jen's hand in hers. "Goddess protect you," she said with reverence. She let go and headed back toward the village.

Samara remained, something clenched in her fist.

"I have something for you," she said quietly. She opened her hand to reveal a small object—a white, almost translucent stone that gleamed in the sun's rays.

A buzzing sound zinged through her ears—there was something odd about the small stone. Jen peered up, a question in her eyes.

"The kashyak still has your scent," Samara said.

Jen tried to conceal her fear behind a terse nod, but Samara wasn't fooled.

"This stone has been enchanted to veil you." She dropped the stone into Jen's hand, and as soon as it touched her skin, the buzzing stopped.

Jen cinched her brows, rolling the stone between her fingers.

"Veil?"

But as soon as she said it, an invisible force draped itself around her, like a sheer, weightless curtain—like the one in the closet of the meeting house. But this one was more intimate, like a whisper of security only Jen could hear.

"An enchantment that will conceal you," Samara explained. "It should keep the kashyaks, as well as other dark-wielding creatures, from sensing you."

Should?

"What about everyone else?" Jen glanced over at her friends mounted on their horses.

"*You* witnessed the Echo, the kashyak got your scent from the Tree. If it can't sense you, everyone else will be fine."

Jen pressed her lips together. Her friends had already endured so much, and now they were wielding weapons they were not trained to use and traveling with a walking target.

Samara observed her reaction. "Everyone will be safe, Jenevieve. No one will get to them."

But there was something strange in Samara's voice, like she didn't fully believe it. The flash of uncertainty that sparked behind her eyes didn't do much to assuage Jen's growing unease.

Samara closed Jen's fingers around the stone, the uncertainty disappearing from her gaze. "Keep it near you, Goddess will protect you."

She walked away towards a tacked up dapple-gray.

Jen quirked a brow. "You're coming?"

Samara swung her leg over and settled in the saddle. She lifted her shoulder in a small shrug.

"Someone needs to keep Ronan in line," she winked.

Jen snorted a laugh and placed the stone in the leather purse on her belt.

Ronan needs a wrangler.

She grabbed hold of Zarah's mane and swung her leg up and over. Jen glanced back at the village where Vaelja stood in front of her people, the ones she would protect with her life, a sentiment Jen shared deeply as she looked to her friends.

She nodded at Samara and gently coaxed Zarah forward, the rest falling in step behind. A large Friesian cantered over to from behind the meeting house.

"That was quite the performance this morning," Ronan drawled as he guided his horse towards the dirt road that led through the valley.

"I aim to entertain the masses," she said, eyeing the huge horse beside her. "Does that thing have a name?"

Ronan recoiled. "Thing?" He leaned over and pat the stallion's neck. "His name is Bear, and you've greatly offended him."

"Bear? You're joking."

"I am the most serious." His lips twitched, but his gaze remained focused ahead.

Her laugh was cut off, her hand flying to her chest. Her heart suddenly felt like a damp washcloth being violently wrung out, and then an invisible weight bored down on her shoulders like the hands of a deity pressing her into the ground. She clenched her teeth against the foreign sensations.

Fucking, ow.

After a moment, the painful sensation disappeared, leaving a subtle ache in her chest, and her mind in a stupor.

What in flying hells was that?

But the ache was gone before she could register what happened. She glimpsed over at Ronan, but he didn't seem to notice. Instead, he turned in his saddle and whistled at Samara.

"Off we go," he said curtly as his horse broke into a cantor and took off. Samara passed by a moment later, joining him at the front of the party.

Together, they all ventured into the valley, the daunting peaks of Sachandes stretching out in the distance.

CHAPTER 15

"We'll make camp here," Samara called.

The late afternoon sun painted the sky with strokes of amber and honey as she veered her horse to flat ground next to a winding river, dotted with jutting stones.

Jen dismounted and looked between two nearby hills where a small grove of elm trees swayed in the wind.

"I'll gather firewood," she said, pointing to the grove. Samara followed her finger. "I'll come with you."

Jen caught a glimpse of Ronan as he finished untacking his horse. Tension rippled off him in waves as he placed the saddle on the ground and then abruptly made his way to another hilltop in the opposite direction.

Where's he going?

Samara appeared beside her with a bow and quiver wrapped around her chest. Without realizing what she was doing, Jen opened the pouch on her belt and pulled out the white stone, turning it over in her hand.

Samara smirked.

"That stone is spelled with powerful magic," she said as she made her way towards the grove, "but I appreciate the vigilance."

Sunlight streamed through the canopy of evergreen leaves as Jen and Samara entered the grove. The bark of the trees drank in the light, casting a warm, golden splendor all around them.

The grove stretched into a large forest that wrapped itself around the surrounding hills. The trees there grew wild. Darker. Entangled. Gnarled.

Jen stopped.

Samara narrowed her eyes at the sudden shift.

"You alright?"

Sweat formed at her brow and the small of her back. She fought the bile that rose in her throat as the blood in her veins seemed to wrap itself around her lungs and rob her of air.

Membranous wings. Raining fire. Desperate screams.

The wind picked up in gusts and the trees swayed a taunting dance around her. Her breathing grew shallow as pressure built in her chest. She pressed her hand upon the tree beside her and tried to control the rising panic that threatened to constrict her airway.

Samara tracked the flow of the wind as it howled through the branches. Her eyes settled back on Jen, and she wrapped her hand around her arm with a firm grip.

"Jenevieve."

All at once, the blustering wind died, and the air stilled.

Jen caught her breath like she had broken through the sea's surface after nearly drowning. She sucked in deep gulps of air, using the tree to steady herself.

Her head jerked up, suddenly aware that Samara was watching her. She wiped the sweat from her brow as her mouth opened and closed with sputtering sounds that resembled an apology.

Samara squeezed her arm.

"It's alright."

Jen blew out a breath and pushed herself off the tree. "I'm fine."

Samara raised a brow, her arms gesturing around them.

"So, the wind dance was for… me?"

Jen was at a loss for words. She had always kept careful restraint on her— darker—emotions, they dwelled within that deep abyss behind the stone wall, hidden from view. This sort of suffocating episode hadn't happened in a long time.

There were too many dangers and unknowns coming for her. She couldn't afford to lose control of herself. So, she took a deep breath and shoved the lingering tendrils of inner turmoil back into the abyss they crawled out of.

She lifted her gaze. "Where did the wind come from?"

Samara let go of her arm.

"The magic of Etheria is responding to you."

Because a herd of magic horses wasn't enough.

Jen stepped away from the tree and traipsed further into the grove, careful to keep her gaze away from the panic-inducing thicket in the distance.

"Do you have…magic?" She wasn't sure how to ask that question, her heart was still trying to find a normal rhythm.

Samara smiled as they came upon a small pond. The blue-green water held lily pads the size of platters and reeds that shot from the shallow depths.

"I am a wielder of Taejja."

Jen gave her a look that said *I have no idea what that means.*

Samara laughed. "Taejja is magic rooted in the elements," she said as she knelt by the water.

She raised her palm over the calm surface and closed her eyes, releasing a deep breath. Jen quietly lowered beside her as the water began to ripple and churn, reaching up and forming into a small column beneath Samara's hand.

She drew her fingertips toward the pond's surface and willed the column into her palm where she caressed it into a swirling sphere that floated just above her hand.

Samara opened her eyes, and in one motion, she snapped her fingers into a claw. The sphere broke apart into a small universe of floating droplets.

Jen gasped.

The corner of Samara's mouth quirked up and she released a breath of air, the droplets transforming into vapor before blowing away.

Jen sat stunned for a moment.

"That was—"

Samara wiped her hands on her pants before standing up.

"My party trick," she said.

Jen fumbled to her feet, looking at the calm surface of the pond in disbelief. Samara steered them back towards the grove.

"It seems you have a connection to Taejja, as well."

"Not like *that.*"

Twigs snapped beneath their boots.

Samara winked. "Well, not everyone can be me."

Jen paused. "Wait," she said. "How can I have a connection to something if I don't even know what it is?"

Samara continued walking over to a few fallen trees and started piling up logs from the forest floor.

"You were probably born with it—"

Jen grabbed a small log beside her feet, trying not to think too hard about who, or what, her birth parents were as Samara kept talking.

"—like Regals and others like them—elves, nymphs," Samara explained.

Elves and nymphs?

"Will we come across any of them?"

"Not likely. They usually keep to themselves, and most reside in or around the Inbetween."

Jen retrieved another log from the foot of a wide tree trunk. "Is that where *you're* from?"

Samara smiled mischievously. "No, I'm not from the Inbetween."

Jen dropped her logs and turned to her.

"Waelyn?"

Samara chuckled and pointed up. "I'm from the north."

That's…kind of an answer.

A grim expression came over her as if she was reliving a painful memory. "I've seen some truly stunning magic in my life. But I have also seen insidious things that hail from the ominous pits of dark magic, things I wish I could forget."

Jen crouched by the growing pile. She pressed her lips together before she said quietly. "I'm sorry."

"Corrupt men aimed for power and glory instead of peace and prosperity. Lust for power and control is what created the biggest evil of them all out on that *damned* peninsula, the embodiment of darkness continuously trying to snuff out any whisper of light."

Jen shivered at the thought.

"So, the root of Etheria's magic is whether it's light or dark?"

Samara crossed her arms and leaned on the tree behind her.

"Etheria *should* be striving for *balance*, as it once did thousands of years ago, but darkness is seductive, and light is self-righteous, neither lending itself to a particularly well-balanced world. One is constantly trying to topple the other, it trickles down into the kingdoms and seeks out devastating conflict."

"Wars?"

"Yes, one brutal clash after another, and who wins in a battle when both sides believe they are the righteous ones?"

Jen stood. "No one."

Samara lowered her chin. "Fortunately, the Regals have intervened in most conflicts before they could really gain momentum."

She chucked a log into the growing pile.

"Many of them fought in the Blood War, and they were *not* going to let any civil wars lay waste to what little remained in the aftermath."

"You said Regals are from the Inbetween?"

Samara threw another log onto their growing pile.

"Mhm. The Inbetween is where most Etheria's magic comes from—it's embedded within Mount Naajin. The Regals reside in the capital city sitting at the foot of the mountain."

"I was mistaken for one when I first arrived," Jen said. Samara's gaze shifted to the side of Jen's head.

"How?"

"I was wearing an ivory dress." Before Samara could react, Jen shrugged a shoulder. "Ronan."

Samara chuckled. "He can be an insufferable *idiot*."

"Especially when he's *accosting* me with rum," Jen said sarcastically as Samara snorted. They started gathering some of the logs in their arms.

"I assume you knew about the descendants before the meeting, since, well, you brought one to the cabin," Jen said quietly.

"I did. But to be fair, I didn't know which of them it was."

"Do you know who we are looking for in Sachandes?"

Samara rose with her stack of logs.

"King Haythem and Gaiana, their ancestors' signatures are on that scroll."
The king—Fjora's father.

Jenevieve rolled her neck and secured her arms around her pile of kindling as they began walking back.

No wonder her letter pointed towards Sachandes. Fjora had been pushing Jen towards her home, her parents—the life she had left behind.

"Keep your eyes sharp, Sparky!" Jen squealed as she attempted to spear a small trout. They were shin-deep in the river next to their camp, ready to pounce on anything that moved.

The smile that Damien gave her was the rare kind that spread into his cheek bones and consumed his entire face; her heart leapt at the sight. It was a balm to her overwhelmed heart.

Damien refocused on the task at hand, and speared a trout he trapped between his feet.

"YAY!" Jen yelled, splashing her way over to throw her arms around him. He threw the fish and spear onto the grass, and ran his thumb along her jaw, her hair in tangles and her smile wide and unabashed. He kissed her, and as soon as she leaned into it, he released her.

She tilted her head, and with a mischievous grin, he splashed her. She squealed. Jen kicked the water back at him, soaking them both, before he charged at her, flung her over his shoulder and carried her out of the river, giving her bottom a playful *smack* as he walked.

"Damien!" she scolded.

He plopped her onto the grass by the fire and settled himself beside her. She feigned annoyance as she jabbed him in the ribs.

The sky bled in saturated hues as the sun whispered farewell to the valley, so lovely and serene it could have been a painting. Jenevieve leaned towards the fire and noticed Samara peering up at the sky.

"How early do we start tomorrow?" she asked.

Samara's gaze remained fixed on the faint stars above them.

"Dawn."

Her eyes dropped down to the sheathed sword sitting on the ground next to Damien. "Did you make that?"

"Yes," he reached over to retrieve it. He unsheathed it from its leather holder, examined it, and then slid it back into its home. "I was the blacksmith in Nimea."

Samara gave him a wary, albeit approving look.

"Alright, you get those two" Her chin jerked to William and Leeyna sitting across from her.

"Get us for what?" William asked.

"The group sacrifice," Damien said, not missing a beat.

Jen snorted a laugh as William scowled, grumbling something under his breath.

Damien placed a gentle hand on her knee and spoke through a grin. "*Training*, William—I know Emelie is a great healer, but you plus an axe will test even *her* skills."

Samara chuckled, glancing over at Emelie. "Speaking of which," she said. "Ronan will work with you."

"You'll be with me," she said to Jen with a sardonic smile.

Jen glanced around at the camp, and then the surrounding hills. "Where is Ronan? He's been gone for hours."

Samara folded her hands behind her head and laid back on the blanket beneath her.

"Brooding in the wilderness."

Damien wrapped his arm around Jen's shoulder, and she leaned into his warmth. He kissed her brow as they sat in comfortable silence.

Her eyes wandered to the hills, their stone peaks jutting like sentinels at their backs, wondering where their mysterious guide had disappeared to.

"Wait, we aren't using our weapons?" William asked.

The sun had just barely peaked over the hills, and a sheen of morning dew coated the ground around them. They had gathered between their camp and the grove, having begrudgingly rolled out of their tents only a few moments ago.

Samara and Damien stood with their arms crossed, the latter throwing a wink at Jenevieve as the former spoke.

"Have you ever used a sword? A dagger? That axe you picked?"

William scoffed but then scuffed his boot against the grass and grumbled to himself.

"You'll start with the basics today—conditioning and balancing. You must be able to control of your body before I let you near a weapon."

They all looked helplessly at Damien, but he threw his hands up.

"Hey, she's right."

William glanced at Leeyna, who fiddled with her hands beside him. She looked up and realized everyone was looking at her for a reaction. She shrugged. "I think we should do what they say, it's not like we can fight them over it."

Jenevieve stifled a laugh.

"Take them over by the river," Samara said, pointing to where the horses grazed. Damien nodded and clasped William on the shoulder before steering him away. Leeyna fell in step behind them.

Samara looked out to the hills beside them, searching for something. "I'm not sure where—"

"Hello, *best friend*," Ronan drawled from behind them. Jenevieve whirled around to find him standing a few feet away. Her eyes did a quick once over, and they settled on the hint of purple under his eyes that made it clear he hadn't slept.

Samara seemed to notice as well, her eyes slightly narrowing at him. He ran his hand through his hair, ignoring Jen and Samara's scrutinous gazes as he gave Emelie a smile that didn't quite reach his eyes.

"We're headed to the grove, you ready for a little nature walk?"

Emelie glanced behind him at the trees and gave him a tentative smile.

"Good," he said. He draped his arm around her shoulder and led her to the tree line.

"Alright, come with me, *chosen one*," Samara said. "Or would you prefer 'horse whisperer'? 'Wind dancer?'"

"I don't want to call myself *anything*," Jen said as she followed Samara to the foot of one of the nearby hills where the grasses thinned out.

"I hate to break it to you." Samara turned and faced her. "But people will eventually start calling you *something*."

Amazing. Just what I need—a nickname.

Samara lifted a shoulder in a half shrug and then pointed to Jen's feet. "Alright. Put your feet shoulder-width apart—good—now curl your toes and then relax them." Jen looked at Samara with a puzzled look. "We're building the feeling of being connected to the earth, without that assurance, you'll get knocked off your feet."

Jen sighed and started curling.

"Where did Ronan go yesterday?" She looked over to the grove where he disappeared with Emelie. Samara monitored her feet.

"Brooding, as I said."

"He's just standing in the dark, scowling?"

Samara cackled as she followed Jen's gaze to the trees.

"Goddess, I hope so, that's a hilarious picture."

"And you're not going to elaborate why he's *brooding*?"

"It's not for me to explain."

Jen scowled. So far all she knew about Ronan was his proclivity for showing up at random and dropping breadcrumbs of cryptic knowledge.

And he smelled of wildflowers and soil before a storm.

I hate that I know that.

She was yanked from her thoughts when her toes began to cramp, and she fell back on her heels.

Samara didn't seem to care.

"Now you want to imagine three points of grounding on the front of your foot, two on the pad, and one towards the arch," she instructed. "A triangle of balance."

Jen nodded as she looked down at her feet, imagining the shape outlined on the sole of her foot.

"Good, raise your arms for balance, and lift onto that triangle in your mind. This is to test the strength of your ankles. Weak ankles are the antithesis of balance."

Jenevieve held her arms out to either side and lifted herself onto the pads of her feet. Her ankles turned out slightly, her heels followed. Samara crouched down and maneuvered her ankles to line up with her toes and gently coaxed her shins directly over them. Jen grimaced as she held the position.

"Not that easy, huh?" Samara said from the ground. "Hold that position for thirty seconds."

Jen's eyes darted to the riverside, where Leeyna and William were doing the same thing, but Damien allowed them to hang on to each other for support. He turned back to Jen and gave her a thumbs up.

Bastard.

Jen was sweating through her shirt by the time she was on the ground doing rounds of sit ups, grumbling a slew of curses as she finished her final set. She sat up and rested her forearms on her knees.

She'd watched Damien training with his wooden dummies for years and never thought too hard about the amount of skill, or the physical toll, it took.

"Why are we training separately?" She swiped her arm over her face.

Samara crouched beside her, handing her a water pouch. "Don't drink too fast, you'll vomit."

After a moment of ensuring Jen was not, in fact, going to vomit, she said. "In order to connect with Taejja, you have to build a connection with your body, and the earth." She glanced at Damien. "He's a good teacher, but he doesn't know the intricacies of accessing magic."

Samara sat beside Jen and took the pouch.

"The foundational things are the same, but you and I will, in time, attempt to coax some of that dormant power out of you."

Jen stopped drinking and sat back in the grass, propped up on her elbows. The idea of accessing her power sent a flurry of emotions through her; on one hand, she was eager to learn magic, but on the other a dormant fear of what would happen when she did.

Since there's also an undetermined amount of ancient power floating around in my veins.

"So, you'll have me doing push-ups until I, what, accidentally shoot beams out of my hands?"

Samara smacked her with the water pouch. "Perhaps a slightly more nuanced version of that."

The sun was now fully over the ridge, with a soothing breeze blowing through the hills to wash away the day's heat. Jen's head dipped back.

"How far are we from Sachandes?" Jen laid the rest of the way down on the grass.

Samara lifted her hand to her forehead and looked towards the mountains in the distance. "About two more full days of riding; we'll arrive in the morning on the third day."

Jen reached into the pouch on her belt and pressed the stone to her hand.

Samara noticed. "The princess really didn't tell you anything?"

Jen sighed. "She didn't have time to—although I suppose she could've explained things in the years *before* a horde of monsters destroyed our village."

Like being the lost princess of a world I didn't know existed. That would have been nice.

"It sounds like she was doing what she thought was right." Samara rested her arms on her knees. "At least she had the sense to write *something* down, no matter how vague."

Jen's eyes narrowed; she hadn't shared the letter with her.

Samara shrugged. "Ronan."

Jen laid her arm over her eyes.

"That was private, he had no business—"

"He was trying to convince me to join you. I wasn't originally planning to." Samara leveled a look. "And were you not pressing me for information on *him* earlier?"

Jen crossed her legs, her hand tracing mindless circles in the grass.

Great. Now I'm a hypocrite.

"I'm sorry. The past few days have been—" she found a stick and snapped it between her thumbs. "Overwhelming."

Samara turned her head towards the river, her gaze far away. "For years now, there's been a noticeable shift working its way across the continent. Those who dwelled in the darkness have grown bolder. Dhokshas have planted themselves throughout the realms. Trust has been shaky at best."

"That's not how it's always been?"

Samara shook her head.

"This is different. Remember what Ronan mentioned when we spoke with the elders?"

Jen nodded.

An invasion—add that to the list of things to stress out about.

"I believe that is only *part* of it, but no one can get close enough to Vondur to confirm anything. Several kingdoms have attempted to send sentries to infiltrate the wards surrounding the peninsula; most don't return."

"Why are you telling me this?"

Samara turned to fully face her. "Because the dangers that threaten Etheria are very real, and the council is the only way to band the realms together into some kind of resistance." A look of disdain turned her mouth into a scowl. "But men are fickle. Pride and ego will be the death of Etheria as we know it, and it will lead us to war, either with Vondur, or amongst ourselves."

Jen glanced at her friends as guilt and shame blurred her vision like billowing clouds over a rain-soaked field. How could she tell them they had escaped the morai just to be thrown into a world on the brink of war?

"How can we convince the descendants that the threat is real?" she asked, her voice wavering.

Samara's expression turned serious.

"You."

"Me?"

"Your existence. Not only are you in the bloodline, but you came from Nimea, a realm that isn't supposed to exist. You witnessed an Echo, a *very* rare ability." She blew out a breath. "The Rhionnen were called to you, not just one, but the entire species. That's—unheard of."

Jen rubbed her hand over her face, a quiet groan rumbling in her throat. "But what does any of that *mean*?"

Samara rose and offered her hand.

"It means you are far more important than you realize."

CHAPTER 16

"*M*ama?*" she said with a gasp of disbelief. Fjora stood by the water, still as could be. A small smile formed on her lips.*

"Mama, how did you get here?" Tears streamed down her face. Her mother was here. Everything was going to be okay.

Fjora reached her arms out, beckoning Jen to come to her. Jen took off running. "I've missed you so much, I—"

A whistle of wind flew past Jen's ear and an arrow hit Fjora square in the chest. She choked on blood as she fell to the ground, a line of it pouring from her mouth. Jen's chest heaved and she sprinted to her.

"MAMA! NO!" She dropped to her knees, only this time, it didn't morph back into the dhoksha. Jen watched in horror as her mother gasped for air, the life draining out of her, blood trickled from her nose.

"No, no, no. no," she said as she pushed on the wound, begging it to stop bleeding. Her mother sputtered through fractured breaths.

Jen sobbed as Fjora took one final breath, and then her chest went still.

Jen's eyes opened to the sting of unshed tears and sweat coating her back. It was warm, too warm. Her skin felt like it was on fire.

The urge to steal into the night and take every bit of danger with her pulsed through her body, but she realized she was trapped beneath Damien's arm, draped protectively over her waist as he slept soundly beside her.

She carefully lifted it and got up quietly before reaching for her leather pouch, fumbling for the stone until it rolled into her hand.

Jen crept from the tent, the cool air relieving her overheated body as the moon floated atop the mountain peaks and amongst the stars, delicately twinkling as if painted by the hand of a deity.

That terrifying dream had haunted her every night since leaving the settlement, resulting in three consecutive nights of restless sleep that left her body feeling ragged. But no matter how hard she tried to push the images away, Fjora's lifeless body remained branded on the backs of her eyelids, and even though Jen knew it was only a nightmare, the reality that Fjora could very well be dead lanced through her.

Gods. Rhea, Darya, Jamie—did any of them survive?

Her skin was still too hot, and her breath grew choppy—raspy. She leaned over her thighs, forcing mouthfuls of air to enter her lungs. Tears collected in the corners of her eyes as panic thrummed between her gaping breaths, her body unwilling to cooperate.

Not again.

Her focus trained to her hand and the smooth, cold surface of the white stone. She rubbed it between her thumb and each finger, one by one, attempting to take a deep breath with each movement. Her eyes fell closed and she concentrated on the soothing slopes and cooling plateaus of the stone until the rest of the world went quiet.

She rose back to standing, her breath still shuttering, but more manageable than before. Until a chill caressed her skin, raising the hair on her arms.

Someone was watching her.

She peered up, finding the moon had bathed Ronan in haunting incandescence; he almost looked like a spirit from where he stood on the nearby hilltop, his mahogany hair blowing around his ears while light and shadow fought for dominance over his tan skin.

Jen glanced back at the stone, and when her gaze returned to the hilltop, he was gone.

Her eyes narrowed, but they were drawn to the Kalli mountains, their jagged peaks thrusting out of the cloud cover that cloaked them. Her skin cooled with the gentle breeze, relinquishing any remaining heat to the night sky as she listened to the crickets and frogs sing their nocturnal song.

"Are you alright?"

She jumped. Ronan appeared a few feet away.

"You scared me." She clapped her hand to her chest.

He looked ragged, like he hadn't slept in days—like her. His usually bright green eyes were dull and lacked the sparkle of arrogance they usually carried.

He took a small step towards her.

"Are you alright?" he pressed.

Something flashed behind his eyes; raw, vulnerable, and completely out of character—was that pain?

"Just—just a bad dream," she stuttered, waving her hand at nothing. She tilted her head. "Are you alright?"

The pain she'd seen a moment before vanished.

"I'm fine," he muttered, clenching his fists and walking towards his tent.

Jen followed. "Ronan?"

He froze with his hand on the flap.

She hesitated, but the unanswered question had been burning a hole in her mind since the first—and second time, she'd asked it. "Why are you helping us?"

His head turned, and for a moment—Jen thought he was actually going to concede and give her an answer. But then his eyes found hers.

"Not 'us'," he said. "You."

"But." Jen bit her lip. "Why?"

"I have my reasons."

"Care to share one of them?"

"No," he said, turning away.

Jen stepped forward. "Then, can you tell me where you've been going?"

"That's not your concern."

Jen forced a quiet laugh, attempting to break the tension. "Samara said you've been brooding—"

"Goddess fucking save me." Ronan flung the flap of his tent closed and faced her. "What is with the inquisition, Jenevieve?"

Jen opened her mouth and then closed it. His tone was strained, like he was holding himself back from snapping at her, but she didn't understand where it was coming from.

"You just haven't really spoken to me—"

Ronan scoffed. "The world, oddly enough, doesn't revolve around you."

Okay, fuck this.

"You mysteriously show up in a pub and decide to accompany us on this fucked up journey, yet I don't know anything about you." Jen waved a hand at him, trying to dissuade the tightening in her chest. "You're a stranger to me."

"It's better that way."

"Give me some peace of mind at least," she said. "Just tell me one thing about you—just one."

"I'm finding this conversation taxing."

A poisonous thought slithered out from the back of her mind as she bade her heartbeat to remain calm.

"Did—did I do something?"

Ronan's eyes flickered over her, a crease forming between his brows before he let out a heavy sigh.

"No." He looked out towards the river, his focus shifting far away. "You didn't."

She took that brief opportunity to close the distance between them. Whether it had to do with her or not; it was clear something weighed on him.

"What's going on with you?"

He dragged his gaze from the river. "You've known me for less than a week. How do you know this isn't who I am?"

Even though a timid voice shuddered in her mind, begging her to retreat, Jen reached for his arm, wrapping her hand around the lion tattoo. "You can talk to me. I'm your friend—"

Ronan ripped his arm away. "We're not *friends*, Jenevieve."

She staggered back like he had struck her. His eyes widened and immediate regret propelled him towards her. "I'm sorry—I'm—"

Jenevieve lifted her hand. "It's fine." She straightened her shoulders. "You're right."

"No, it's not fine." He pinched the bridge of his nose. "I didn't mean that."

"Forget it. You've made yourself clear."

"Goddess, I'm just exhausted."

"Yes, you've made that abundantly clear with your charming attitude."

"Jenevieve—"

Heat flashed beneath her skin.

"You weren't wrong, you know." Her heart hammered against her chest. "I haven't known you that long. Perhaps you plan to hand me over to Vondur and betray us all."

His mouth dropped open; her venom had shocked him, pained him. Maybe she wanted it to.

The pain she had sensed earlier returned to his eyes. "You really think that little of me..." he whispered.

She fought the guilt that threatened to claw its way through her. Jen didn't know where this spite in her own voice was coming from, she shouldn't fucking care how she made him feel. And yet, something in his tone pulled her gaze back to him.

He was looking at her, awaiting her answer—like it mattered.

A gust of midnight air swirled around them, sending a shiver down her spine. She tucked a strand of hair behind her ear and looked up at him through her long lashes.

"Should I?"

Before Ronan could react, she turned on her heels and walked back to her tent, leaving him in the dark.

Jen spent the rest of the night tossing and turning as images of Fjora with an arrow in her chest alternated with pained, verdant green eyes staring at her through the darkness.

We're not friends, fine.

After hours of failed attempts at sleep, light began to stream into the tent. She turned to her side to find Damien staring at her. His eyes were sleepy, but the intensity in them washed every negative feeling from her body, along with any thought from the night before.

Jen smiled lazily at him. He rubbed his calloused fingers along her cheek, as if she was the only thing he could see.

She still hadn't told him about Fjora—she hadn't told the others either. Jen was having a hard enough time accepting the princess revelation while simultaneously attempting to keep her wits about her. Damien would want to talk about it, work through it with her.

It was easier to shove it away from her thoughts—for now.

All I've seen is Damien coddling you.

Damien's hand traveled to her back, pulling her thoughts back to the man in front of her as he gently moved it up and down her spine. She leaned into his touch, soaking in the comfort of his scent, his presence.

"Are you ready for today?" he asked quietly, adjusting his head to lay in the crook of his elbow.

Jen caressed his cheek. "No."

He chuckled, pulling her closer to him. She rested her head on his chest as he wrapped his arms around her. His heartbeat was strong, steady.

He placed his finger under her chin and raised it to meet his gaze. "Everything will be okay, Bug."

"If it's not, at least I've gotten good at curling my toes," she said, doing exactly that.

Damien let out a soft laugh as he pulled her in for a deep, languid kiss. Unhurried, unencumbered by the nameless threats ahead.

After a few moments, he groaned, reluctantly pulling himself from her and rising from their place on the ground, turning back to wink at her before disappearing through the tent opening.

When Jen emerged a few minutes later, her eyes instantly snagged on Ronan loading up his saddle. He glanced at her, his tired eyes slowly looking her up and down as a muscle feathered in his jaw. She fought the urge to march over to him, to ask him what in *hells* that was last night.

But, as if sensing that inner battle, Ronan turned away to finish packing before she could convince herself to move.

Cold shoulder. That's mature.

They packed up the rest of the camp and mounted up.

"We're headed through the Forna Pass," Samara called.

We don't know what that means.

Jen's hand hovered over the leather pouch on her hip, her anxieties about reaching Sachandes scraping against her ribs. Samara's gaze followed her movement.

"The stone is working, Jen," she said. "Everyone is safe."

Jen nodded and looked back at her friends. Emelie flashed a weak smile beneath anxious brown eyes, and Damien threw her another wink. William leaned over in his saddle to give Leeyna's hand a squeeze—he had managed to only fall off his horse twice in the last three days.

Small victories.

They rode through the thinning grasses and rocky ground at the edge of the valley. The hills turned patchy, the earth beneath slowly shifting from grey stone and green grass to red-brown sand and clay. The Kalli mountains loomed closer as they made their way to the Forna Pass.

They came around the base of a stone covered hill and halted.

The red-brown sand and clay ascended into the beginnings of the expansive mountain range. But the exposed earth was not just the hue of clay. Layer upon layer of vibrant minerals rose from the earth, a rainbow trapped within the earth, flanking the pass as a shimmering echo in the morning sun.

Samara looked out into the pass to a narrow patch of green interrupted by a magnificent waterfall, collecting into a pool of effervescent blue-green water.

"The Fall of Grace, and the Sachandan border; this is the last stretch of the valley." She urged her chestnut mare to the gravel path that formed in the middle of the pass.

Jen coaxed Zarah alongside her. "I've never seen anything like this," she breathed, inhaling the smells of damp earth and blustering winds that picked up the dirt and spun it around the group.

She glanced behind her, drawing Damien's gaze away from the stunning landscape of the pass.

"Are you okay?" he mouthed.

She nodded, but her gaze drifted behind him towards the man in the back of the convoy. Ronan's verdant stare stood fixed straight ahead—a guise of indifference.

Jen turned back around, her grip tightening on Zarah's mane and his quiet question resounding in her ear: *you really think that little of me?* She kept her expression neutral, staring at the trail in front of her.

I can't think little of you if I don't fucking know you.

They continued for several hours, only stopping to allow the horses to graze and rest. When they approached the Fall of Grace, Zarah picked up into a trot towards the switchbacks along the side of the waterfall.

The group carefully made their way up, watching out for loose rocks and slippery patches of clay as they headed towards the plateau where the waterfall crested over the cliff, following the riverbend into the mountains.

The horses' hooves echoed off the walls of the mountainside as they came around a sharp corner.

Jen gasped.

"What is that?" Leeyna said, her voice filled with wonder.

A magnificent colossus of a female figure soared above them, straddling the river.

"The Goddess of Light," Ronan said.

She was impeccably carved to depict a flowing gown, with one hand holding a lily between her thumb and forefinger, the other extended to the sky, her head curved up to look out beyond the Sachandan border.

Her hair flowed down her back, with a diadem of baby's breath and precious stones wrapped around her delicate head. The embodiment of feminine power.

"The statue signals the end of the valley, Sachandes lies just beyond that tunnel," Samara said, gesturing towards the dark expanse ahead of them.

Jen reached down instinctively, her hand easily finding the stone in her pouch. She turned it over in her hand, letting it keep her calm.

Samara turned in her saddle, raising a skeptical brow as a silent conversation bounced between her and Ronan, who nodded slowly before scanning the skies.

Jen watched them, her nerves not at all abetted by the vigilance in Ronan's gaze as he kept it trained above them.

Am I still being tracked? Is the stone working? I think it's working—we haven't been attacked, that's promising right? Wait, am I breathing? I think I forgot to—

She forced a bout of air into her lungs. Samara looked over, her brows cinching and confusion crinkling the corner of her eyes. Jen gave her forced smile accompanied by an awkward thumbs up, a combination that only exasperated the confusion on Samara's face.

A thumbs up? What's wrong with me?

They followed the river into the tunnel, their path shrouded in darkness as the passage swallowed the light, the sound of the river their only guide.

Jen inhaled sharply.

A subtle thread wrapped itself around her and tugged gently as the hum of harmonious interwoven melodies flooded her ears, calling to her from the other side of the tunnel.

Zarah took off into a cantor as if she, too, heard the mystical hum. Jen hung on as the tunnel opened out and they emerged onto a ridge—and then all the air left her body on an exhale.

The Kalli mountains rose towards the heavens in never-ending sharp peaks of red-brown bedrock, the highest ones kissed with snow. They expanded to the west for miles, dropping off as epic cliffs into the Opaelian Sea.

The city of Quoxana was nestled within the valley. The river they had followed flowed through, fortifying the land and people who lived there.

Jen had never seen a city, not to mention one that densely populated. Thousands of stone houses and shops lined the maze of streets that intersected into massive squares punctuated by fountains. Ornate bridges embellished with flames of spun gold arched over the river to connect the two sides of the city.

Zaniya had been gray and worn—it held a humble crudeness. This was entirely different; the city radiated warmth—joy.

Jen searched for the palace, but Samara was already pointing to the eastern side of the mountains. There, built into the mountains themselves, sat the great palace of Sachandes.

A waterfall cascaded from the foot of the palace, as though the structure floated above the white water where the river was born beyond the mountain range. Marble columns were built into the many levels of the regal structure and emerald and gold flags hung from balconies, strung up on massive flagpoles.

And the flowers. Even from a great distance the blooms of thousands of colorful blossoms blanketed the balconies jutting out from the cliffsides, creating the air of perpetual spring.

If magic had not already been proven real, Jen would have certainly been convinced by the mere existence of that palace.

"Goddess, I missed this place," Samara murmured, looking out into the city.

Ronan rode up beside her. "When were we here last?"

"Ruymani, three years ago?"

Damien joined them, craning his neck to take in more of the city.

"Ruymani?"

"The Sachandan Festival of Light," Samara explained. "The entire realm erupts into an insane celebration with food, dancing, parades—*drinking*." She rolled her eyes towards Ronan. "When the sun goes down, the city is so heavily lit you can't even tell it's night."

"That could have also been the alcohol," Ronan interjected.

Samara shivered as if the memory of any sort of spirit made her cringe. "The last time we were here, we barely survived the party. We were all but dead the next day. Actually, I'm pretty sure we *were* dead for at least a minute."

"Sachandans party hard, and we like to think of ourselves as the life of the party," Ronan said, brushing a bit of dirt off his shoulder.

Samara stuck out her bottom lip. "We were sorely mistaken."

Jen stifled a laugh.

"If I remember correctly Ronan, I found you passed out in the fountain wearing a headdress and nothing else," Samara said, gesturing towards the middle of the city where a large fountain sat in the middle of one of the squares.

"Thanks for the blanket, I would have scarred someone."

Samara coaxed her horse forward and glanced at Jen as they started to move. "He did—*me*. I burned that blanket afterwards."

Jen snorted as they led their horses down the mountainside path into the city.

Quoxana was a flutter of life and prosperity; hundreds of people flocked the streets, shopping and socializing as the sounds of intense haggling blended with the squeals of young women running to embrace their friends.

They traveled along the river, passing by outdoor cafes with tables filled and street performers in the squares, one of which was a minstrel and his lute. Ronan dropped a few coins into the hat sitting on the ground in front of him.

They made their way through the cobblestone streets, until they were met with a pristine lake, from which the river flowed. The city center wrapped itself around the water's body, where families rowed small boats, children flew colorful kites, and young couples shared picnics in the grass along the water's edge.

At the other end of the lake stood the front of the palace. A double staircase of marble formed a bridge over the waterfall that poured into the lake, merging into a landing before becoming a grand set of stairs that led to the golden, ornate front gate.

Jen dismounted and ran her hand along Zarah's neck. She made her way towards the sandy gravel walkway, checking for her pouch and the sheathed dagger on her belt. Samara and Damien fell in step behind her, followed by William and Leeyna, while Ronan brought up the rear.

Silence fell over them when they reached the foot of the marble stairs. Jen clenched and unclenched her hands a few times, attempting to release the tension that was building in her.

She blew out a breath, looked up towards the front gate, and began her ascent. Jen reached into her pouch and retrieved the stone, rolling it around in her hand to keep her steady.

They made it to the landing where an elegant, golden gate stood guarded by two soldiers clad in emerald and gold uniforms. Suspicion turned their eyes to slits.

Jen stopped a few feet away, returning the stone to her belt. She straightened her shoulders and took two steps forward, feigning as much confidence as she could muster.

"My name is Jenevieve," she said. "Tell King Haythem, I wish for an audience."

The soldiers furrowed their brows.

"What business do you have with the king?" one of them barked.

Jen raised her chin.

"Tell him Fjora lives."

CHAPTER 17

NIMEA - The night of the attack

"**D**ON'T LOOK BACK!" Fjora implored. She ran behind Jen and the others; they were close to the hidden path into the forest. She scanned the tree line and spotted the crooked branch sticking out from it.

"THAT'S IT! LOOK FOR THE X!"

Fjora watched Jenevieve veer right into the forest, and a flood of fleeting relief drenched her. But the morai were still coming; their guttural sounds clawing at her ears. Jen and the others wouldn't make it far before they were caught or killed.

She grasped at her chest.

This is it.

In a desperate plea, Fjora yanked Damien back before he could follow the others.

"You have to protect her, Damien," she choked. The future of her homeland depended on Jenevieve's safety. Damien's eyes widened, looking past her at the horde closing in.

Fjora shook his arm. "Promise me. She's too important."

Confusion momentarily creased between his brows, but then he placed his hand over hers.

"You have my word."

Fjora exhaled sharply, knowing he would not let her fall into harm's way. She had watched the two of them dance around each other for years, but no matter what, he had never faltered in being there for Jen when she needed him—that much was certain. But she had no idea what he and the others would encounter on the other side of Bri. She was trusting him with Jen's life.

She let go of his arm.

"Now go. I'll hold them off as long as I can."

Damien opened his mouth to object, but Fjora was already running away from the tree line. She ripped off her cloak and pulled a pendant in the shape of a white flame from within her dress.

Fjora cupped it in her hands and whispered to it.

"Ufreijaa nuri."

Light exploded from the pendant, almost knocking her to the ground. She thrust her hand into the air and the light consumed the meadow around her, mimicking Jenevieve's magic—and drawing the horde's wrath towards Fjora.

They lurched away from the tree line and surged towards her. Fjora glanced towards the trees one last time, where Damien stood, wide eyed and mouth gaping.

"*Run*," she mouthed, her eyes rimmed red.

She gave him no time to react before she sprinted back towards the countryside. The light would only last a few moments. Her thighs burned as the field blurred beneath her feet.

"MAMA!"

Jenevieve's anguished scream resounded from the forest with heart wrenching desperation. Fjora's eyes stung, but still she kept moving.

The pendant was fading in her hand. She chucked it into the meadow and turned sharply back towards her house.

The morai dove to the ground, clambering for the fading light lost to the tall grasses.

She waved frantically at the panicked villagers desperately attempting to find their loved ones in the chaos. "GET INSIDE!"

Fjora darted up the path to the front door of her house as piercing shrieks echoed from the meadow.

She flung open the door and stumbled over the threshold. Two hands were instantly on her shoulders, hoisting her up to her feet. Jamie's face was filled with agonizing relief as he wrapped his arms around her and squeezed so tight, she thought her ribs may crack.

"It's okay sweetheart, I'm alright," she soothed, rubbing his back as he buried his head in her shoulder. She pulled away and wiped a tear away from his cheek.

Darya peered out the window. "Mama, what are those things?"

The fear in her daughter's eyes propelled Fjora around the table to embrace her, running a hand through Darya's hair before kissing her head. She glanced over at Rhea and Troi standing together by the hearth.

"They are—"

A screech burst through the cottage so violently they all dropped to the ground, grasping their ears to keep them from bleeding. Fjora leapt to her feet.

There, in the open doorway, stood a morai.

Its black skin absorbed any semblance of light, a dark void that swallowed any flicker of hope. Its large, black eyes scanned the room, narrowing on the family.

Fjora fought against the painful memories that shot through her mind; the sound of galloping hooves, the feel of trembling arms wrapped around her, a baby crying.

Her own screams.

She had seen these creatures before, but never this close. It took slow, menacing steps towards them. A ball of flame appeared in its hand, and he hurled it at the table, setting it ablaze.

Her daughters' screams speared through the jarring shriek of another morai on the rooftop, followed quickly by several more. The smell of smoke dragged Fjora's gaze upward, her eyes widening.

They're going to burn us alive inside this house.

She reached into her boot, retrieving a small dagger she kept hidden, and wielded it in front of herself and her family. The morai made a grating, high pitched sound, as if laughing at the feeble attempt to defend her kin.

Fjora pushed her family behind her as it stalked them around the room. The roof caught fire and the flames seeped into the house and fell like blazing raindrops of destruction.

The morai cornered them in the kitchen, another ball of flame appearing in its grizzly hand. It smiled cruelly. Jamie held Darya, who quietly sobbed into his chest, while Troi pushed Rhea behind him to block the blast.

Fjora flung her arms out and turned away, bracing herself as she whispered:

"Goddess, protect us.

Bring us to the light.

Guide our souls—"

A horn rang out in the distance.

Fjora's breath lodged in her throat.

It can't be.

But the creature froze, the ball of flame crackling in its hand.

Another horn. Another. Another—a chorus of brass that ascended higher until the morai began to scream out in agony. It clutched its head and swayed back and forth, as if the sound was burning it from the inside. It rammed through the house, engulfing itself in flames as it retreated, along with the morai on the rooftop.

But Fjora hardly noticed, for shock had momentarily numbed her senses.

How did they know to come?

Her focus snapped back as her children choked and gagged behind her, the flames licking up the cottage walls and the roof whining dangerously with strain. She pushed them out the door, and as soon as they reached the front gate, they collapsed to the ground, gasping for air and coughing up smoke.

Fjora peered up at the sky; the horde morphed and wove in chaotic shapes above them at the sound of the horns. They flew quickly and loudly back over the Forest of Bri, the shrieking slowly fading off in the distance.

She turned over on her elbows.

Her home was engulfed by flames.

There would be no saving it. She could only hope she had done enough to save Jenevieve.

Fjora awoke on a bed of coarse straw rubbing roughly against her skin. After they watched their home burn down, she had led her family to a nearby barn where they huddled together until they finally passed out from sheer exhaustion.

She knew she would have to explain everything to them. Who she was. Who *they* were. Where she was from.

Their faces and clothes were still covered in soot, the girls' hair in a mess of tangles over their shoulders. She reached over and gently caressed her son's face—her youngest, her only boy.

The look he gave her when she burst into the cottage, the fear and relief and anguish that contorted his face, replayed in her mind on repeat. A few rogue tears fell down her cheeks as she ran her hand through his golden locks.

She wiped her face and quietly stood, careful not to wake them. Fjora crept through the barn door, holding herself while she assessed the damage before her.

Her hand clapped to her mouth.

The countryside smoldered, and wagons were strewn about, some turned over while others were black and burnt. The tables from the feast were turned on their sides, having been used as a blockade during the attack. Food was scattered on the ground, the rodents already scavenging the remains.

Fjora looked towards the remnants of the bonfire and the scorch marks that plagued the ground. Her hands began to shake as she crashed to her knees.

Bodies.

Charred and maimed bodies, rendered unrecognizable, laid where her daughter had danced with her new husband. The beautiful memory was eviscerated, replaced with the smell of burned flesh and carnage.

She vomited.

A cold sweat shook her to her bones. The shock and horror of the previous night washed over her as she heaved again.

When there was nothing left, she wiped her mouth and weakly stumbled to her feet. She lifted her head, and through her dizzy gaze, Fjora spotted a figure at the tree line by the hidden path.

Who is that?

Her feet compelled her forward as several answers floated through her mind, but she would not allow hope to breach her fragile state. The figure was cloaked, their face hooded to remain concealed from her as she came closer. She could just make out the ivory underneath; her heart raced at the sight.

Fjora tried to keep her breathing calm, but her heart thumped loudly, blood roaring in her ears.

She stopped and waited, frozen.

Two battle-worn hands reached up and removed their hood. They slowly turned around.

"Hello, Fjora."

Fjora just stood there, her mouth agape as the figure spoke again, a smirk pulling at the corner of their mouth.

"It's good to see you."

She could only manage one word—a name.

"Naezara."

CHAPTER 18

A shadow of a distant dream from a life she left behind—that's what Fjora saw when she gaped at her old friend.

Naezara had always been striking, but perhaps the years without her somehow made her more beautiful. Her auburn hair was plaited into battle braids, revealing her elegant arched ears. Golden cuffs were clipped to the glorious, thick strands, and her vivid green eyes held slender peaks of gold, reflecting within them the heart of a fierce warrior.

In place of the bronze and ivory armor she donned the last time Fjora laid eyes on her, Naezara now wore an ivory tunic and pants embroidered with bronze thread.

Naezara arched a brow.

"Surprised to see me?"

Surprise was a vast understatement. Fjora launched herself across the remaining distance and threw her arms around her friend as a choked laugh escaped her. Naezara laughed with her, the stoic facade broken in an instant.

Fjora forced herself to let go, wiping away her tears.

Naezara ran her fingers gently over the fine lines of her friend's face, her eyes traveling to the wisps of gray hidden within ash-blonde hair.

"You got old."

Fjora pushed Naezara's hands away.

"You try living on this side of Bri. Let's see what it does to your immortal skin," she chided playfully.

Naezara folded her arms in front of her chest. "You Ascendiants and your damn vanity."

Fjora scoffed, but then her gaze shifted out to her decimated village, smoke still billowing from her cottage, along with many others. "The last time I saw you, I didn't think—"

"None of us did."

"I didn't know if you were alive," Fjora whispered.

Naezara pressed a hand to her chest. "I should be offended by the lack of faith in my abilities."

Fjora pointed towards the sky. "How did you—"

Naezara strolled toward her and cupped her face.

"You think we wouldn't notice the horde of demon bats?"

Fjora laughed sadly.

"They almost—I—" she tried to breathe. Naezara embraced her once more, and Fjora rested her head on her shoulder. They stood in silence for a moment, the rustle of the trees and the cracking of branches sounding around them.

"She got out," Naezara said.

Fjora let out a ragged breath, stepping out of the embrace.

"She—"

"They all did. I kept a few warriors with me to watch over them in the night. She led them out about an hour ago, I would assume they're on their way to Zaniya as we speak."

Fjora swept her hand to her head and started to pace.

"I should have prepared her," she whispered to herself.

"There was no way for you to anticipate the pulse enacting twenty years early."

"Naezara. I didn't tell her *anything*. She grew up not knowing who she was. She still doesn't know. She may not even find the letter I wrote her. Not that it was at all useful, I was in a blind panic when I wrote it."

"You raised her, protected her."

"Oh, and how well did I do with that?" Fjora snapped, guilt laced into her voice. "I kept her in the dark, and instead of telling her about her mother—about her father, I saddled her with the first bastard that showed me any kindness in this cursed land. I kept everything from her. I hid how important she is, who she is."

"Fjora."

"Yesterday she told me about the dream. I knew what it was. I should've dragged her to the forest right then."

"Fjora." Naezara grabbed her shoulders, forcing Fjora to look at her. "She's in Etheria. The fates have sung their song. You did your part, and you did it bravely, selflessly."

Fjora exhaled, her skin glistening with sweat. She paced away and began fanning herself. "What do I do now?"

Naezara smiled knowingly.

"You come home."

She froze.

"I—what?"

Naezara took a step towards her.

"You come home, Fjora."

Her eyes stung.

Home.

Home to Etheria, to Sachandes. Home to my people, my parents. Home to—

She looked at Naezara nervously, but, unable to meet her gaze, focused on the X carved into the tree behind her.

This is not the end of our journey, my love. I swear it.

"Did he know about the attack?"

Naezara looked down her nose at her.

"Who do you think sent me?"

Fjora shifted from one foot to the other.

"Why didn't he…"

Naezara put her hand up. "Before you start thinking he didn't want to come, he did. He was leading a scouting party on the Sachandan border; he sent word to me because he was too far away. He wouldn't have made it in time."

"You saved us." She grabbed her friend's hand. "Thank you."

Naezara gave it a squeeze before turning back to the path.

"I'll have horses waiting when you emerge from the Forest." She beckoned towards the village. "It looks like you have a lot of explaining to do before you embark."

Fjora turned around to find her children standing in front of the barn, watching her with weary expressions. Her gaze shifted back to Naezara, pulling her hood back over her head.

"Goddess protect you, Princess Fjora."

She returned to the barn where her family waited anxiously. Fjora kept a calm, maternal expression on her face, placed her arm around Darya's waist, and grabbed ahold of Jamie's hand. Together with Rhea and Troi, they silently walked to the remnants of their home.

They stood in front of the ruin; the smoldering had finally dissipated, the last of the smoke carried off by a gust of wind. Fjora opened the front gate and carefully walked into the ashes.

She approached the hearth as her family gathered behind her. They took in the house for a moment, their eyes rolling over the burnt walls and the roof that was reduced to a mess of dangling wood.

Rhea came up beside her mother and placed her hand on the charred mantle. "Tell us everything."

And Fjora did.

She told them all of it. Who she was, where she was from. They listened, eyes widening or rimmed red as she shared her story.

When Fjora finished, at least what she could tell them without putting them in significant danger, Rhea's brown eyes peered up at her from the singed couch. "So, you're a—a princess?"

Fjora cringed at the title, she had always hated it. "I'm the sole heir to the Sachandan throne."

Rhea ran her hands down her face and stared at her palms.

"And that would make us...*me*—"

"Next in line, yes."

The realization hit her oldest daughter so hard she slumped back into the couch and buried her face in her hands. Her muffled voice sounded through them.

"Are you telling us that we're *royal?*"

Rhea's hands dropped into her lap as her eyes fluttered around, visibly calculating her place in a royal bloodline of a realm they just found out existed.

"You didn't think we should know that bit of information?" she said, her voice growing shrill.

Troi placed his hand on his new wife's knee, although his face was rather green as he did so.

Darya, who now sat on the floor, leaned forward on her elbows. "Wait. Jenevieve wouldn't be your heir?"

Fjora shook her head. Darya paled. "She's not our—"

"Yes, she is." Rhea glared at her.

Darya wrung her hands. "That's not how I meant it."

Fjora sighed.

"Jenevieve *is* your sister. She has been my charge since the day after she was born. I love her as I love each of you, but, no, she isn't of Sachandan descent."

Jamie leaned against a fallen beam. "Our father…" He looked around at his sisters.

"No, Jenevieve is not his," Fjora said. "I arrived here thirty years ago as a heartbroken girl with a baby in her arms." She perched herself on the edge of a blackened armchair. "The pain was too much—too… raw." She chewed on her lip. "I met your father and threw myself into a life that would distract me, hoping that maybe it would dull the ache I carried around with me."

"Did it work?" Jamie asked.

Fjora smiled sadly at him. "It gave me you, didn't it?"

Darya hugged her knees to her chest and spoke almost to herself. "That means she protected us from a man that wasn't even her—"

Rhea reached down and squeezed her sister's shoulder.

"Her birth parents…" Jamie questioned quietly.

Fjora looked at the floor. "They were my dearest friends. They sacrificed themselves for their child, and I escaped with her through Bri."

"Mama…" Rhea pressed off the couch and took a step towards her. Fjora reached for her, noting the trembling in her hand. "It was a lifetime ago, my darling."

Jamie ran his hand along the beam.

"What happens now?"

Fjora rose to her feet. "I must return to Sachandes. There are things that have been set in motion that I cannot ignore."

"Are we to come with you?" Darya asked, a bit harsher than Fjora expected.

"Of course, we're coming with you," Rhea said, shooting Darya another glare.

"You may do whatever you wish," Fjora began. "You can rebuild this cottage and live a simple life. But it will not change who you are on the other side of Bri."

Darya's eyebrow shot up and Fjora straightened her shoulders, regality returning to her posture. Her eyes settled on Rhea.

"You are my heir, by birthright." She shifted her gaze to Darya and Jamie. "You are the future of Sachandes, and Etheria, whether you like it or not. But what you do with that is your choice."

She took Rhea's shaking hand. "You were not raised there; I will not hold you to its customs and traditions."

"How do we know we'll be safe once we get there?" Darya asked, her eyes defiant.

"You won't be safe," Fjora said bluntly. They all blinked, surprised at the crude honesty.

"The pulse that called the morai was twenty years early. The only explanation there could possibly be is that something bigger is happening. And if you think that whatever is coming will be contained to Etheria, that Nimea will not suffer as well, you are fooling yourselves."

Rhea looked down nervously at Darya, and then to Jamie.

"When do we leave?"

Fjora squeezed her hand.

Home.

I'm bringing my family home.

Her heart leapt from her chest as she said, "We gather what we can and leave at sundown."

Fjora moved carefully around fallen beams and splintered wood and noticed Jamie coming out of his room, holding something in his clenched fist. She approached him, and when he didn't meet her gaze, she cupped his hand within her own, willing him to loosen his grip.

He reluctantly opened his hand, revealing a miniature carving of a hawk, intricately whittled and sanded down from the wood of the oak tree that once grew behind their cottage. Fjora ran her finger along the bumpy feathers of its wings.

"You know, a hawk is meant to symbolize wisdom," she said softly.

Jamie met his mother's gaze, the lost little boy still adrift in the oceans of blue staring back at her.

"Did he ever love us?" he whispered.

Fjora's heart cracked as she caressed her son's cheek.

"Of course, he did, and I'm sure he still does."

He looked down to the figurine.

"Then why did he leave us?" His voice was barely audible.

She sighed. Jamie had been so young when his father left them—he was shielded from much of what her daughters had endured—but still, he suffered in his own way. And yet, there was a part of Fjora that didn't want her son to hate his father.

She ran her hand through his hair. "Your father has his own journey, his own demons to battle. They were too strong for him to fight alongside being a father."

"I just—"

"I know, darling."

She pulled him in, wrapping her arms around her boy. He was a sweet, kind person who somehow still turned out to be a good man, like her own father, who waited for her in Quoxana.

He turned to walk back to his room before stopping in the doorway. "Did you ever love *him?*" he asked over his shoulder.

Fjora clenched her jaw, thinking back to the father of her children, to the life she was forced into by fate.

She poured her broken heart into that charismatic Nimean, made a family with him, but when he suddenly found himself in a life he didn't want, he left. What a cruel twist of irony—and Fjora a delusional idiot—to think anyone could mend her heart.

"I tried, and for a time, I did."

Jamie didn't move.

"And this…Nelysar…"

Her eyes welled, and she spoke through the tears she fought to conceal. "Love is not a strong enough word to describe what I feel for him."

He nodded and then continued into his room.

Fjora clapped her hand to her mouth, stifling a choked sob. Not just for her son and his lost relationship with his father, but for the life with Nelysar she'd sacrificed—the love that knew no bounds and shattered her into a million pieces.

She let the tears fall silently, mourning the loss of her previous life, but she clung to the hope that something still waited for her on the other side of Bri.

They entered the woods at sundown, on a path she'd not taken in thirty years, and yet, her feet knew instinctively where to go. They had changed into traveling clothes, tunics or linen dresses paired with sturdy boots that would keep their feet dry.

Rhea trudged along quietly. Troi had decided to stay behind to help in the rebuilding of the village, and although it was noble, she was still heartbroken to leave him. Fjora assured her they would send for him when they were settled in Sachandes.

The familiar crunch of fallen leaves fell over her ears as her body remembered where to look for exposed roots that obstructed the path. Her family followed behind her, not quite as gracefully. The occasional yelp of pain or huff of frustration gave Fjora something to laugh about—in her mind.

She stopped them in a clearing to make camp, where she lit a small fire as they ate some of their provisions. Just beyond, she could see where the forest morphed into the gnarled maze, where the border of Etheria awaited them.

Rhea gathered her rucksack as a makeshift pillow and laid down next to the fire, the light of the flames dancing over her sad, dark-brown eyes.

"Tell us about Nelysar," she said, rather abruptly.

Fjora raised a brow.

Rhea pressed her lips together, clearly trying to keep her melancholy at bay. "Please? I need the distraction."

Darya nestled herself between the large roots of two neighboring trees beside Jamie, who sat with his back against a thick trunk.

Fjora glanced between the three of them. "Alright," she conceded.

Her gaze fell to the fire. "We met when I was twenty, during Ruymani—" She saw the looks of confusion on their faces. "Festival of Light," she amended. "It was the first time my parents allowed me into the city without any guards. I was accompanied only by one of my father's advisors."

Her eyes lit up as the images swarmed her mind.

"The city had this energy; it was—*alive*. The streets were crammed with people dancing, the fountains that sat in the squares had been enchanted by the Sachi into cascades of beautiful flowing fire that didn't burn if it touched you."

Rhea and Darya propped up onto their elbows, listening intently.

"We came to the largest fountain in the center of the city, the fire was roaring, it was so bright I had to block the light." She lifted her hands to reenact it. Her mind swept back to that fountain and her family faded away.

Her chaperone chuckled and gently lowered her hands.

"You won't be able to enjoy the festival like that, princess."

Fjora's cheeks flushed with embarrassment as she looked down and tucked her hair behind her ears.

She dressed to blend in, opting for a deep green linen gown trimmed with golden thread. Her long hair was pinned half up in graceful curls, the rest hanging down her back. A subtle crown of golden vines wrapped around her head and wove itself into her locks.

The citizens around her were so consumed with the festivities they didn't even notice her, some not knowing what the princess looked like to begin with. She became invisible and she enjoyed the freedom that accompanied that.

Fjora felt someone approaching and turned to see a striking woman strolling towards them. Long, auburn hair reflected strokes of gold in the fire light, her green piercing eyes drawing focus to her high cheekbones and thick eyebrows. Her hair was pulled back into one massive plait, revealing her arched ears adorned with several gold piercings along their slope.

Her chaperone's eyes lit up when he spotted her.

"Naezara," he said kindly, extending his arm to her. She clutched it with a curt smile in return. "Bastien. It's good to see you." Bastien released her arm and gestured to Fjora.

"May I present, Princess Fjora."

Naezara bowed deeply. "An honor to meet you, princess."

Fjora's cheeks reddened. "Fjora, please," she said. She never enjoyed the formality of her title, preferring to be simply, Fjora.

Naezara smirked.

"Fjora."

Bastien cleared his throat. "So how goes things in the Inbetween, General?"

Naezara laced her hands behind her deep blue tunic.

"Everything is going well; my brother has sent out scouting parties to the north to ensure the valley remains secure."

"Speaking of your brother, where has that rake wandered off to?" Bastien implored as he looked around the fire. Naezara waved her hand at nothing. "Oh, he's here some—"

An explosion of laughter erupted in the far corner of the square. Naezara hung her head low in exasperation. "Found him."

Bastien chuckled at the general's reaction. He gently pulled on Fjora's elbow.

"Come, we'll introduce you."

Fjora followed quietly beside Bastien as Naezara led them across the square.

"Why are scouting parties being sent out?" she asked him in almost a whisper.

He lowered his head beside her ear as they continued walking. "The pulse is due in eight months, Fjora. The entirety of the continent is on edge."

"But can't they just shield anyone from the bloodline that's left? There can't be that many of them."

Bastien halted them. His face was pained.

"I wish it were that simple. Over the last five hundred years, people of the blood began keeping their ancestry secret, even from their own children. They thought it would be safer if it wasn't acknowledged," he explained, running a hand through his long, pearl white hair.

"We send out scouting parties to protect the kingdoms from the morai and have established several safe haven fortresses throughout the land in case anyone needs to flee." He sighed. "It's the best we can do."

Frustration marred his expression. Clearly, he wanted to do more, but he was limited by the information he and her father had acquired over the years.

She reached down and squeezed his hand.

"You're trying to protect everyone, that's already so much to carry," she said kindly.

Bastien shook his head, snapping himself out of the solemn conversation.

"This is not the place for this kind of morbid talk. Come, let's catch up with Naezara."

They closed the gap with Naezara to find her rubbing her temples in annoyance. Fjora and Bastien joined her along with a group of women, surrounding someone—a man, by the sound of his laugh.

The women parted.

Perched on the side of a wooden table was an incredibly beautiful man. His auburn hair came to his shoulders with a few lazy plaits throughout and arched ears holding a single gold piercing. He had sharp features, high cheekbones, a pointed nose, and a chiseled jawline that could cut through the gold of Fjora's crown. His eyes were a bright green, ablaze with golden flames, and they were blazing into her.

Fjora attempted to swallow, but her throat dried up at the sight of him. He wore an ivory tunic that was rolled up at the elbows, revealing his sculpted forearms that were currently folded in front of him.

Naezara sighed loudly, bringing Fjora back from whatever trance she found herself in.

Bastien extended his arm. "It's good to see you in one piece."

The man returned the greeting, giving him a dashing smile, filled with feigned humility.

"I do what I can. It's good to see you, Bastien."

His gaze drifted to Fjora. Naezara stepped between them.

"Fjora, this is my brother, Nelysar."

Nelysar took her hand and kissed it, bowing deeply. She straightened her shoulders, acting as a royal to keep her blushing cheeks from becoming any more obvious.

"A pleasure to meet you," she said, feigning disinterest.

Nelysar peered up at her, his lips hovering over her hand, and she fought to keep her knees from buckling.

"The pleasure is mine, Fjora," he said, her name lingering over the tip of his tongue. He straightened to his full height, almost two full feet taller than her. He looked behind her where festival goers were beginning to dance. He arched his brow.

"Would you like to dance?"

She looked to Bastien for approval, which Nelysar noticed.

"I didn't ask him, I asked you."

Naezara scoffed. Fjora's eyes narrowed at the challenge in his voice.

"How could I say no to such charm?" she said pointedly.

His head fell back into a wolfish laugh. His eyes darted back to her, clearly enjoying the bite in her response.

He offered his hand to her, a challenge dancing in his eyes. A smirk ghosted over her lips, and she placed her hand in his.

Nelysar led Fjora to dance, where he continued their biting exchange, but their eyes softened towards each other with each spin and every pass.

Fjora finished. Darya and Rhea were now sitting up, fully engrossed in their mother's story. Even Jamie was listening, although trying not to make it obvious.

"The person you were talking to earlier—" Darya began.

Fjora smiled and rested her arms on her knees.

"Naezara, his twin sister."

"Do you think he's waiting for you?" Rhea asked.

Fjora shook her head, trying not to think too hard about it.

"I don't know."

Darya scoffed. "There's no way he isn't waiting for you. If your first meeting went like *that,* I can't imagine how insane the rest of it was."

Fjora laughed, running her hand through her hair. Her daughter had no idea just how accurate that was.

"Well, we'll find out soon enough," she said.

She laid her head on the rucksack, signaling the end of the conversation. The fire in front of her had dimmed to a few small flames. She fell asleep with faded memories swimming in her mind, and those enigmatic green eyes pierced her dreams.

When morning came, Fjora guided them through the gnarled thicket of the forest, moving slowly and deliberately so they could imitate her movements.

"Watch out for the low hanging—"

"OW."

Fjora stifled a laugh, "...branches."

They came to a descending slope, and she knew they were close to the edge of Bri.

They were in Etherian territory.

Her feet took off down the hill, trying to keep in mind that she had people following her. The entangled trees made the terrain difficult to move through and dark enough to doubt the time of day, but her momentum kept her moving.

The memories flooded back to her now with great strength as she ducked under branches and squeezed herself through the most enclosed part of the forest. She could hear her own anguished cries and see the tears streaming down Nelysar's face, feel the innocent infant in her arms. The images carried her until she came to an abrupt stop at the bottom of the hill.

Rhea, Darya and Jamie stumbled down after her before collapsing against several tree trunks. Darya keeled over with her hands on her knees, willing breath into her lungs.

Fjora raked her eyes over them to make sure everyone was in one piece, but her memories still echoed around her. She turned back to the opening in the trees where light poured into the thicket.

She found herself unable to move.

Home.

Tears stung her eyes. She was staring at both her past and her future within a doorway of twisted vines and whispers of memory.

Jamie clasped her shoulders from behind. She reached up to hold his hand, attempting to keep her emotions from boiling over.

She blew out a shaking breath—and stepped towards the light.

Etherian sunlight traveled up her body, warming her trembling limbs with an achingly familiar heat. She was waking up from a never-ending dream, a dream that she was ready to leave behind in the mangle of trees behind her.

They walked out into the clearing. The highest peaks of the Kalli soared in the distance just over the ridge that ascended before them. It struck a chord in her heart that she had long since silenced.

She ran.

"Mama! Wait up!" she heard Jamie call behind her.

But she kept running. Her legs knew where she was going and pushed her faster until she came to the top of the ridge.

Her hands flew to her mouth.

Etheria.

Her family trickled in behind her, each falling silent as they took in the view. All she heard was their panting breaths as the breeze picked up around them.

Around her.

She smirked and walked towards the edge of the ridge.

The wind of a spring morning whipped around her, wrapping her arms and legs in ribbons of zephyr. She stretched out her arms and leaned her head back, allowing the wind to dance with her, to welcome her home.

The air brought with it a gift for the lost princess.

It churned around her with more purpose, and Fjora sighed as she felt the shift, the magic of her home caressing her.

The charged streams of wind wiped away the fine lines and wrinkles of her mortal life, leaving her skin youthful and luminous once again.

A larger gust rushed through her hair, taking with it the streaks of gray that gave away her age on the other side of Bri, leaving lustrous ash-blonde locks.

Etheria stirred around her, returning her to her true self.

A daughter of the Ascendiants.

The princess of Sachandes.

She breathed in the return of her youthful glow and turned to her children.

Gaping mouths and sputtering sounds greeted her.

"Mama...?" Rhea breathed.

"What was—" Darya continued, her hand on her chest.

Fjora shrugged at her stunned family.

"Long ago, my people sailed across the Opaelian Sea from the distant land of Ascendia, a place gifted with extended life." She gestured to herself. "This is who I am, and who *you* are." Fjora turned back towards Etheria. "You are Ascendiants." She clasped the small emerald hanging from her neck. "You are Etherians." She looked back at them. "But you are first, and foremost—my family, and I vow to protect you with my life, *mo shaalis.*"

Fjora spotted a group of horses at the bottom of the hill, just as Naezara promised.

She turned and offered her hand to Darya.

"Come, we have a long way to go."

CHAPTER 19

SACHANDES: Present

The guards exchanged a nervous look, and then one of them addressed Jenevieve.

"Wha—What did you say?" His voice was higher than Jen was expecting; he couldn't be much older than her brother. But she stood firm, her gaze unwavering.

"Fjora. Lives."

Ronan stepped through the group and stood beside her.

"I suggest you let us through the gates. If I decide to proclaim that information through the streets of Quoxana, you may very well have a mob on your hands." He crossed his arms. "What'll it be?" he asked. "A group of seven? Or a mob of ten thousand?"

The soldiers paled and turned to each other for a moment, a silent discussion relaying between them.

"Do take your time," Ronan drawled.

They must have come to some sort of decision because a moment later they slammed their golden staves into the ground.

BOOM.

BOOM.

BOOM.

The gate slowly creaked open to a grand marble staircase lined with impressive columns of stone carved from the mountains. The cascading waterfall roared beneath their feet and a clear sky opened above as Jenevieve led them towards an imposing set of oak doors, which opened as they approached.

They stepped inside a great hall carved out of the mountain itself. High, cavernous ceilings dripped with chandeliers of woven gold adorned with emeralds, and great banners of deep green hung in rows, threaded with the golden sigil of Sachandes: a condor with its wings outstretched, superimposed over a geometric triangle, representing the Kalli Mountains.

A veranda stretched out on the other side of the hall, held up by more stone columns and hosting a breathtaking view of the beautiful Sachandan valleys. The floral scent of wildflowers arranged in intricate bouquets around the hall tickled Jen's nose, and although the sun warmed the hall, she could feel the cool relief of the stone that surrounded them.

Her friends gaped. You would think they'd have grown used to constantly being presented with new and awe-inspiring things, and yet, William's face was turning purple.

"William, breathe," Jen said.

As he gasped for air, Ronan came up behind him and clasped his shoulders. "Wait until you see the libraries," he whispered.

William sputtered. "There's more than one?!"

"If we lose William, we know where he went," Emelie laughed from a flower arrangement nearby.

Damien let out a low whistle as he came to Jen's side, and she was reminded that she still had yet to mention the princess revelation.

"This is where your mother grew up?" he murmured.

Oh, you have no idea how accurate that is.

But still, Jen couldn't imagine her humble, quiet mother running through the halls of a palace.

A princess of the realm.

"Why would someone ever leave this place?" she asked quietly.

Damien brushed his fingers against hers, drawing her wandering eyes to him. "I'm looking at it," he whispered, kissing her brow.

Footsteps echoed from the adjoining hall.

A man as tall as Ronan came hurtling around one of the massive pillars. His body was not quite as broad, but rather lean and defined by the emerald tunic hugging his figure. His pearl white hair came to the base of his neck, and arched ears pierced by a pair of golden hoops.

He came to an abrupt stop as his fiery, amber eyes widened. "Ronan?" he said in disbelief. "Samara?"

They looked coolly at him.

"For an immortal, you've certainly seen better days, Bastien," Ronan droned.

Bastien narrowed his eyes.

"At least I don't smell like a couple of stray hounds."

They glared at each other, a moment of tense silence stretching between them.

Jen nearly jumped out of her skin as laughter erupted from the three of them. Ronan and Samara crossed the room to Bastien, each offering casual hugs and for Samara a quick kiss on the cheek.

Bastien looked them over. "You two look awful."

"Always such a charmer, Bas." Samara swatted his chest.

"When was the last time you were here?" he asked. "Ruymani? Three years ago?"

Ronan rubbed his temples. "Mhm," he grunted.

Samara smiled widely. "With the—" she gestured to her head.

Bastien threw his head back and howled. "THE HEADDRESS. Goddess, Samara, *please* tell me you burned that blanket."

"And danced around it as it blazed," she joked, punching Ronan in the shoulder.

Ronan ran a hand through his hair. "Yes, yes. It was very funny," he grumbled. "Not at all a night I'd like to forget."

"Not that you can remember it anyways," Bastien said, arching his brow sarcastically.

His gaze shifted to Jen and the others and then back to Ronan. "Did you make some new friends?"

Ronan clasped his shoulder and led him over.

"This, Bas, is why we are here."

"You're not just here to drink at Lannas with me?"

Ronan chuckled. "There will be plenty of that, I assure you. But first, let me introduce you."

He gestured to each of them, Bastien warmly shook their hands, giving them a dashing, welcoming smile.

Ronan glanced at Jen, for the first time all day.

"This is Jenevieve."

Bastien took her hand and kissed it politely.

"She has a rather important message for you," Ronan continued. Bastien quirked a brow, looking at her expectantly.

Here goes nothing.

"Fjora lives," she said, her voice not as confident as before.

Bastien blinked.

"What?" he breathed.

Ronan nodded, watching the shock wash over him.

"It's true Bas, the lost princess is alive."

A sharp intake of air sounded from Damien and the others, their shocked gazes boring holes into the back of Jen's head.

I'll deal with that later.

Bastien shook his head and paced away from them. He stopped and turned back to them.

"How is that possible?"

Jen stepped forward. "I was given to Fjora to protect. She's been on the other side of Bri in Nimea with me and my family for the last thirty years—"

"NIMEA?!" Bastien paced again. "Nimea doesn't exist, it was wiped off the map."

"As I told your friend here," she pointed her chin at Ronan. "It very much exists. Those who stand behind me are living testaments."

Bastien turned towards the veranda, lost in thought. Samara crept up beside him, placing her hand on his shoulder. His head dropped before it turned to Jen.

"Why did you need to be protected?"

Jen looked back at Damien, who was eyeing Bastien like he expected the man to lunge at her.

"I'm in the bloodline," she said.

Bastien sucked in a breath and coughed harshly, like the words choked him. "Goddess, Ronan. Who did you bring to this palace?"

Ronan folded his arms and looked down at Emilie standing at his side. "Why do people keep asking me that?"

She gave a look that said *not the time.*

Bastien shook his hand in front of his face, trying to distance himself from the conversation. "How do I know that's true? Do you have proof?"

Samara cut in. "Bas—"

He directed his glare at her. "No, Samara. If I'm going to tell the king that his soul heir is alive, and that she's been protecting SOMEONE FROM THE BLOODLINE for the last thirty years. I need solid proof. I will not go to him if there is any chance that this is a mistake."

Jen exhaled and unsheathed her dagger. She presented it in the palm of her hands. Bastien's eyes drifted down to it, rendering him silent. She pointed the hilt to him, offering it.

"Is… is that—" he said in almost a whisper, his fingers reaching for it, but he hesitated.

Jen tilted the hilt further towards him, urging him to look at it. His glance moved back and forth between her and the dagger. She placed it in his hand.

Bastien raised the hilt to his line of sight.

"Where did you get this…"

"It belonged to my birth mother."

His eyes shifted back to Jen, his thumb running along the carved lily. "Do you know what this is?" he said like it was a wonder that he held it in his hands.

Jen arched a brow.

"A dagger."

Bastien smirked at the curt response. "This is not just a dagger. This is the tiishara."

William stifled a gasp.

Bastien glanced at him.

"I take it he's the scholar of the group?" Bastien raised an eyebrow at Samara. "Be sure to show him the libraries."

He turned back to Jen. "The tiishara is a very powerful weapon, the only one of its kind…exceedingly rare." He flipped the dagger in his hand before handing it back to Jen. "Make sure you keep it safe."

He considered her for a moment, before releasing an exasperated sigh. "I will speak with the King. I must figure out a way to break this news to him."

Ronan rubbed his chin. "Won't he be overcome with joy that his beloved daughter is alive?"

Bastien's eyes grew somber. "King Haythem is not the man you know from previous visits, Ro'." He began walking towards the veranda, Jen and the others following closely behind. "The queen fell ill two years ago and then passed without any warning. It broke his heart, and his spirit."

"I'm so sorry, Bas," Samara said, placing her hand on his back. He smiled weakly at her.

"He is a shell of the benevolent king he once was. He still wears his mourning attire; he refuses meetings with emissaries. He'll only speak with me, and that is using the term 'speaking' liberally." He looked out to the skies beyond the mountains.

"The condors don't fly anymore. We're blind to the rest of Etheria, to Vondur."

He turned to face them all, his appearance otherworldly with the Etherian sun silhouetting him.

"What exactly are you hoping to accomplish here?" he asked. "Do you simply wish to convey this news to him?"

Jenevieve wrung her fingers, her precarious show of confidence waning as her knees began to tremble. No, that was not all she wished of the king. She reached to her pouch and retrieved something from within it.

The letter.

She silently handed it to him. Bastien furrowed his brow as he hesitantly accepted the piece of parchment, keeping his eyes on her as he unfolded the paper. His eyes fluttered down and instantly widened.

His fingers traced the ink of the letter.

"Fjora," he whispered, his voice heavy with an unreadable emotion.

He covered his mouth with his free hand, and turned back towards the open skies, walking further out towards the golden railing that lined the balcony.

Hundreds of colorful flowers adorned the railings, and lush green vines climbed the pillars before melding into the mountainside. Bastien looked very much like a prince of spring as he read the letter to himself.

Damien appeared beside Jen. She shrugged at him, as if to say *what do I have to lose*?

Bastien's head shot up from the letter, and he turned slowly. His eyes met each of theirs, searching them for answers. He settled on Jenevieve.

"You mean to reconvene the Council of Suran?" he said with a quiet point.

"Yes."

"*Fjora* told you to do this?" He lifted the parchment in the air. Jenevieve joined him, gently taking the letter from his hand.

"The morai attacked my village, after the pulse came twenty years early."

Bastien rested his forearms on the balcony.

"I was told that when I arrived in Sachandes, the king would be kind and welcoming, which implied he would help me." She looked down at the letter. "Seeing as he is not in a…receptive state of mind, it seems that now falls to you."

Bastien was quiet, contemplating her words. He looked down at his hands.

"Fjora was like a sister to me. I did everything I could to protect her, to show her the ways of the world. When I thought she died I—" He looked up.

"I failed her. I should have been there that day, to help her, to find another way."

He turned towards Ronan and Samara, a grave look in his eyes.

"Something is shifting in Etheria. I know you felt it in the valley."

They both nodded.

He rose to his full height. "If Fjora is alive, and this is what she knew in her heart needed to happen, I will do my part to ensure it does."

Jen let go of the breath she was holding. She could feel the relief wash over everyone else as well. Bastien turned and gave Samara a smirk.

"I can make no promises. But I will do my best to arrange a meeting with the king."

Before Jen realized what she was doing, she threw her arms around him, embracing him tightly. He chuckled, his hands stiffly patting her back. She let go quickly, scrambling back a few paces.

He laced his hands behind his back, the model of noble stature.

"You shall stay here as guests. Allow me to show you to your rooms," he said, walking through the group and gesturing for them to follow him.

Jen stayed back for a moment longer.

She walked to the balcony and wrapped her hands around the golden railing, looking out into the expansive landscape of Etheria as the breeze billowed around her.

Ronan appeared beside her a moment later. She looked at him out of the corner of her eye and could sense that he was doing the same.

Several moments of silence stretched between them, and then Jen felt him subtly shift beside her.

"Well done," he murmured.

He turned quickly and walked away.

CHAPTER 20

Calcutta marble floors that looked like they had been cracked and put back together with molten gold stretched out beneath her from the bedroom and sitting area and into the bathing room.

Jen ran her hand along the soft upholstery of a forest green armchair, one of a pair, that sat before the marble fireplace, flanked by bookshelves built into the walls and lined with hundreds of books.

Across the room, a simple but intricately crafted breakfast table and chairs sat on the balcony reaching out over the cliff of the mountain. Long, sheer curtains of jade and cyan billowed between columns of stone that supported the high ceilings.

The room was lit by a golden chandelier adorned with emeralds as the ones in the great hall, though the space was already sufficiently well-lit by the sun spilling in.

Bastien mentioned that the climate of Sachandes was relatively mild year-round, and that most rooms and public spaces in the palace had the same open-air layout as hers, the coolness of the evening clearing the palace of any lingering heat from the day.

Jen nearly groaned upon spotting the biggest bed she had ever seen splayed out with dozens of feather pillows and lavish duvets all in various hues of green and gold.

This room was larger than her family's entire cottage.

Her brief moment of reprieve was drowned out by a wave of guilt that threatened to topple her over. How could she stand in a room this grand when she wasn't sure if her family's home still stood? When she wasn't sure if they were even *alive?*

Her feet moved of their own accord, and she found herself pacing around the far-too-big room.

Black, insidious eyes and membranous wings flashed behind her eyelids. Lucy's frightened sobs and Rhea's screams seared her ears. The desperation in her mother's twisted around the center of Jen's chest.

She jerked to a stop. No. Not mother—*protector*. And not just a protector, but a *princess.*

Legends and morai and shapeshifters and prophecies and bloodlines and a gods damned lost princess.

Jen scrubbed her hands over her face and looked down at the floor. "Fuck," she breathed.

She trudged over to one of the balcony chairs and sank into it with a shaky breath before bending over to unlace her boots.

Someone knocked on the door.

"Yes?" The word came out thinner than she wanted.

The doorknob turned and in strode Samara, who looked around the room and whistled in approval.

"They gave you the big room," she said, walking over to perch on the back of one of the armchairs. She glanced at Jen's unlaced boot.

"Don't get too comfortable, we're training in fifteen minutes."

Jen clenched her jaw. She was not in the mood for more toe curling and balancing. "We *just* got here," she muttered.

"There's a training ring on the other side of the grand hall," Samara crossed her arms. "You thought I was giving you the day off?"

"I thought we'd be able to rest for a bit," Jen grumbled.

"Vondur isn't resting, or did you forget about that?"

Jen tapped her finger on the table beside her, the endless parade of threats from the last week ricocheting against her skull.

"It's hard to *forget.*"

Samara tilted her head, as if noticing the change in Jen's mood. "The better shape you're in, the better vessel you'll be for your magic."

"Great, now I'm a *vessel,*" Jen mumbled to herself.

Samara pushed off the armchair. "*This* should be fun," she said as she walked to the door. "Fifteen minutes." She slipped into the hall.

Jen leaned her head on her hand and blew out another heavy breath. She stared at a spot on the floor, trying to push the haunting memories back behind that trusty granite wall in her mind, but the more she shoved behind it, the more the memories fought back.

Her brows cinched and she lifted her head, her fingers were tingling; like a thousand tiny sewing needles were pricking the surface of her skin. She rolled her wrist.

That's new.

Jen attempted to pass through the hall unnoticed, but with her less than clean traveling clothes, that wasn't a remote possibility. The men and ladies of the Sachandan court were a sea of jewel toned tunics and sweeping chiffon.

When the hall erupted into hushed murmurings that were not-so-subtly, directed towards her, Jen quickened her pace and practically ran towards the archway on the other side.

The marble floors of the palace were replaced by solid bricks of red-brown stone as Jen walked out into the courtyard.

The space was dotted with several training rings; the red-brown stone laid to form circles at several spots on the ground, colorful flowers and green hedges crawling along the perimeter, leading out to another balcony of woven gold.

The whole thing was built into a natural break between two smaller peaks. Jen peered up to the open blue sky, spotting a flock of massive dark-brown birds perched on some of the higher cliffs.

The same bird as the Sachandan crest.

Condors.

Her attention was drawn by the sound of footsteps as William bounded in with Leeyna close behind.

"JEN!" he called, his eyes wild. "They just showed me one of the libraries. ONE OF THEM!" He had his hands on his head, unable to process what he'd just seen. "THERE ARE SO MANY BOOKS. I couldn't read them all in a single lifetime if I wanted to. I mean, I'm sure there are subjects that don't interest me and so I could probably skip those—"

Leeyna placed her hand on his shoulder. "William is very excited about all the books. In case that wasn't obvious."

William went quiet. Leeyna followed his gaze to where her hand still lingered. She dropped it quickly, but not before a noticeable flush colored her cheeks.

Emelie and Damien arrived a moment later; she was showing him a page from the book in her arms, but he seemed distracted. When his eyes found Jen, he gave Emelie a passive smile and strode towards her, a question already in his eyes.

Damnit. He's going to ask about Fjora.

He lifted his hand to her cheek, concern creasing his brow as he searched her face for what she may be feeling—to be fair, she didn't really know, the princess revelation had been temporarily shoved behind the stone wall in her mind until she could figure out how to deal with it.

Damien's eyes widened before the question could make it to his lips. He dropped his hand. "You already knew?"

She sighed. Sometimes she really disliked how well he knew her. Jen's gaze fluttered down as she tried to string a sentence together, but Samara appeared from the archway on the opposite side of the courtyard, halting the conversion before it could start.

"Alright, my clan of misfits." Samara jogged to the center of one of the stone circles. "This is the training ring," she said, lifting her arms to present the area around her. "There are two others within the palace walls: one down by the dungeons, and another up on the top of the palace. This one is closest to everyone's quarters, and I can't be bothered to walk to the other ones, so here we are."

She nodded to Damien. He glanced at Jen; his eyes loaded with far too many emotions for Jen to take in at once—so she looked away. He huffed and grabbed William by the collar, gesturing for Leeyna to follow them to a ring across the yard.

Yes, I've known about my long-lost-princess–protector for days and didn't tell you because what the actual fuck do I do with that and, also, I was too busy trying to stave off recurring nightmares and constant panic attacks that I also failed to tell you about, okay, sorry.

Why couldn't I just say that? Oh, right. Because that's insane.

Ronan sauntered in from the great hall, trailed by a woman dripping in deep blue lace that he clearly didn't notice. She tugged on his arm and tried to pull his attention back to her, but he chuckled arrogantly, kissing her hand before he sent her, pouting, back inside.

He looked back to find everyone staring at him. He simply shrugged. "What, did everyone think I was a paragon of virtue?"

"I don't see how anyone could," Samara said from the wall of weapons.

Ronan blew her a kiss, and she gagged.

"Take your protege and leave us be," she said, waving her hand at Emelie.

He strolled across the courtyard and through the opposite archway. "Let's go, best friend."

Emelie gave Jen a quick wave before scurrying after him.

Samara joined Jen in the middle of the stone circle, her eyes narrowing on her like she was trying to decipher a puzzle.

Jen raised her brow. "What?"

Please don't ask me something I don't have the answer to.

The corner of Samara's mouth quirked up.

"Give me three sets of fifty lunges."

Fuck.

After a grueling warmup that Jen firmly believed should have been the entire session, Samara led her through eight numbered strike positions—checking her stance, fixing her posture, and being a general pain in the ass.

Jen threw a jab and held it. Her arm was beginning to tremble.

"Don't hyperextend your elbow," Samara said.

All that came from Jen was a grumble of curses and veiled insults.

Samara stretched her arms above her head and let them fall to her sides. "I see we brought *mature* Jen to the ring."

Jen dropped her shaking arms. "What is the point of this?"

She wasn't learning anything about the magic she didn't know she possessed until a week ago. She was punching air.

She glanced over at Damien drilling William and Leeyna. The former was keeled over the railing looking rather green.

Samara stared at her, hands on hips, waiting rather impatiently. "Alright then, give me a minute straight of one-two's."

Jen clenched her jaw but squared her shoulders and began the jab-cross combination, nonetheless.

Samara circled as Jen finished the first set, her hands falling to her thighs as she tried to catch her breath.

"Again. Faster."

Jen peered up. Samara loomed over her, a challenge twinkling in her dark eyes.

She pushed up from her legs and recentered herself.

"Go," Samara ordered.

Jen sliced her fists through the air with more intensity.

"I can see the anger, Jen," Samara barked. "Let it focus you. Use it. Shape it. Channel it."

She moved even faster as beads of sweat barreled down her face. A small fissure appeared along the bottom of her stone wall. Jen shuddered as a tendril of anger drifted up from the abyss, prodding at the crack before slinking its way out. It traveled beneath her skin, and the anger gave way to something deeper, stronger—her blood heating as it moved through her.

The last week had left her weak to defend against her own memories, and that ember of anger ignited into rage.

Damien stepped towards them, "Maybe that's enough—"

"Again!" Samara ordered over him, smacking two leather arm pads together and holding them in front of her, giving Jen a tangible target.

Wind rushed in from the mountain peaks and into the ring. It wrapped itself around her waist, twisted its way around her arms. The pressurized ribbons of air joined in her movements. She felt powerful—invincible. The world fell away, and the ring blurred around her. Fists pounded on leather, rage singing in her bones.

Her breathing grew steady—anger sharpened her mind. Faster and faster her arms moved until they became a blur before her eyes.

Eyes filled with clear, bright focus.

"Throw a hook—" Samara shifted the pad to shield herself.

"NOW!"

Jen hinged back and slammed against the pad. The air surged with her fist and blasted into the leather so hard she and Samara were thrown backwards from the impact.

She rolled, swinging her legs underneath her, planting one palm on the ground, the other extended behind her. Her breath sawed out of her—and she snarled.

The others froze.

Damien dropped his own leather pads, his lips parted.

The tingling returned to her fingers. She glanced down, her eyes widening slightly.

Smoke.

The kind that came from an extinguished flame. She turned her hand over, stretching her finger as the ripples of smoke floated away on the back of a wayward breeze.

Samara propped herself on her elbows, a wry grin on her face as her eyes fixed on the balcony overlooking the courtyard.

Jen slowly rose to her feet and dusted off her pants. She stepped into the center of the ring and looked up. Bastien stood on the balcony, his forearms draped on the railing, and an unreadable emotion on his face.

He eyed Jen carefully, thrumming the woven-gold railing under his fingers before silently disappearing back into the palace.

Damien was by her side a moment later. "Are you okay?" He examined her hands. "What was that?"

Jen winced; her knuckles were tender and starting to swell. "I'm fine, Sparky."

Damien's head snapped towards Samara. "Why did you make her do that?"

"I didn't make her do anything."

Movement pulled Jen's attention towards the archway. Emelie and Ronan had returned from wherever he had taken her. He whispered something in Emelie's ear, and she nodded, crossing over the training ring.

She retrieved a glass jar from a little black bag she didn't have before and offered it to Jen. "Rub this on your knuckles."

Jen raised a brow, but took it, her gaze shifting behind them to Ronan, still standing in the arch, picking at his nails.

She turned back to Damien. "Samara is right. That was all me."

He didn't look convinced, and a line appeared between his brows as concern spread over his face.

At least he doesn't look pissed anymore.

"I just coaxed her into a position to expose some raw power." Samara said, perching against a stone ledge along the perimeter of the ring.

"Bastien is attempting to get the king to meet with us. The backbone of his argument will be that Haythem's sole heir is alive. That she wasn't killed during the pulse. He won't go anywhere near the topic of the council if the king can't be convinced of that."

"So why the magic show?" William chimed in. He and Leeyna sat against the wall near the courtyard entrance.

Samara leveled a knowing look at Jen. "I saw the shift in you." She shrugged. "I took it as an opportunity to channel that fire behind your eyes."

You've got to be kidding me.

"You pissed me off on purpose," Jen stated.

"I would never do that." Samara winked. "And don't pretend like you didn't walk in here already wanting to hit me."

Jen shook her head. "I didn't want to hit you *that* hard."

"The king's most trusted advisor witnessed you wield Taejja with his own eyes," Samara said, as if that was supposed to clarify everything.

"I don't even know what that *means*," Jen murmured.

She glanced up. Ronan had stopped messing with his nails just long enough to find her gaze, his verdant stare considering her like she was a mystery he couldn't quite figure out.

Join the club.

Jen's eyes trailed to the ground as she fiddled with the glass jar, the flash of rage from earlier fizzling out to leave a hollow ache in her chest. A throbbing headache began to form along her temples—a consequence of holding up the stone wall while painful memories rammed against it.

Her fingers no longer tingled, but her skin was growing clammy with every passing moment that she awkwardly stood there.

She wanted to hide—to disappear.

I need to be alone. No one needs to see me like this.

Jen turned the jar over in her hand.

"I need to go apply this."

Before anyone could object, she turned on her heels and retreated through the archway.

CHAPTER 21

Steam was billowing from the bathing room when Jen returned from the courtyard. She tilted her head.

Who—

A young woman stumbled from the closet with a heap of colorful gowns draped over her arm, the fabrics so long, the short woman was nearly tripping over them. Her dark brown hair was swept into a plaited bun, her chocolate brown eyes widening when she spotted Jen.

"Oh! Apologies, my lady," she said with a curtsy, the bottom of her forest-green cotton dress bunching on the floor.

Jen smiled politely. "No need to apologize, and I'm not a lady," she said. The young woman looked confused. "My name is Jenevieve."

The maid smiled tentatively. "My name is Shyra."

"It's nice to meet you, Shyra," Jen said, unlacing her boots. She sat in one of the armchairs and removed them, noticing the gowns Shyra was laying on the bed. "Those are beautiful."

Shyra played with the lace appliques of one of them. "They are for you to choose from."

Jen pointed towards the bathing room. "Did you draw the bath as well?"

Shyra walked to the vanity that sat in the corner of the room, retrieving a brush from one of the drawers and placing it on top. "Yes, Miss."

"How did you know I was coming?"

Shyra chuckled.

"Lord Bastien had baths drawn for all of you, and a host of clothing brought to each of your rooms. He thought you would all like something—" She coughed, "cleaner."

Jen rubbed the back of her neck, acutely aware of how she must look—and smell. "He was right," she said as she stood. "Would it be alright if I had some privacy?"

Shyra smiled warmly. "Of course, I'll be back later to get you dressed," she said, walking towards the door.

"Oh, no, I don't need—" Jen started, but she was already gone.

She sighed.

Do people not know how to dress themselves here?

She shook her head as she continued into the bathing room, and as her hand ran over the length of her long plait, she grimaced at the tangles her fingers found.

Jen paused, raising her hands in front of her face. No smoke. No power-gusts of wind. Her eyes narrowed when she turned her hands over.

No swelling.

Her knuckles were still red, a few red splits peppered over her skin…but the swelling was gone—and so was the throbbing pain.

How is that even possible? If anything, my hands should look worse than they did in the training ring.

Her steps momentarily faltered in the doorway, her eyes leaping to the colossal marble tub filled with deliciously hot water, and then the open-air veranda beside it, held up by more columns and lined with a golden balcony.

But her thoughts continued to rampage through her mind.

Magical pulse dreams. Visions from trees. Dark creatures fucking everywhere. Herds of ancient horses. Power-wind and smoking fingers.

She passed by the two small steps ascending to the lip of the tub, where effervescent bubbles danced on the surface. She stopped to look at herself in the mirror.

Oof. I look rough.

Hair in a tangled mess, growing shadows under her eyes, dirt staining her clothes. Her gaze held that hollow ache, which had now seeped into her skin and extinguished any flame or enchanted wind that breathed power into her just a short while ago.

I wear the burden of an unknown destiny and mysterious fucking purpose well—is that a fucking twig in my hair?

Jen extracted the twig with a scowl and stripped her clothes off quickly, suddenly claustrophobic. Her hands swept up to cover herself out of instinct as though the walls were watching her, and she scurried to the tub.

Something between a groan and a sigh of relief escaped her as skin met water. She hadn't realized how sore she was until her aching limbs relaxed into the reprieve of the warm bath. She released her plait, sucking in a breath through her teeth as she attempted to free each knot with her fingers.

Note to self: pack a brush on the next life-altering adventure.

She plunged her head under the surface, blurring the world above her like brushstrokes of a watercolor painting.

Jen breached the surface and wiped the water from her eyes, and she startled. Damien was in the doorway, a small smirk on his lips. His gaze flickered with heat as he looked her up and down, but then shifted into something kinder, warmer.

She raised her brow, her body only visible from the shoulders up. "What?" Jen could have sworn his cheeks flushed.

Is there another twig?

"You're just—you're perfect."

Jen rolled her eyes and ran a hand through her damp hair.

"And you're an idiot."

He threw his head back in a deep, haughty laugh. Gods. That sound. Damien had two laughs; one, the most frequent, where he kept his mouth closed while his shoulders bounced up and down, like he was trying to contain a cache of bubbles, and the other one, the rarer one—and her favorite, that seemed to burst out of his chest like his body couldn't stop the visceral joy from escaping.

Jen couldn't help but smile as he approached her.

Damn him.

"You can't just let me say something nice?" he asked.

"No."

He sat down and propped his elbow on the ledge. Jen waded over to him until she was resting her head next to his arm.

His hand draped down to the surface of the water and swirled mindless circles. "So, Princess Fjora," he said quietly, but there was nothing accusatory in his voice.

Jen pressed her lips together, trying to find the words. "I've known since the meeting with the elders," she said. "I just...I needed time to deal with it." She huffed a laugh. "And then I didn't."

She expected frustration, annoyance—but instead, he just looked at her.

"Bug, I can't imagine what you're going through right now, and it's not fair for me to expect you to give me a minute-by-minute update every time you're thrown something new and terrifying." He sighed, his gaze falling back to the ripples beneath his fingers. "But I hope you know that you can tell me anything—I want you to."

I know. I've always known that.

But she didn't voice it, instead, silence stretched over the room for a few moments, and Damien kept his gaze fixed on the ripples. Jen waited for him to speak again, but he didn't; he just laid his cheek on his arm.

She could sense the next question. It was peering out from the damn winter-sky in his eyes.

"You want me to tell you what that was," she said, her eyes flicking towards the doorway. "Out there." Her gaze dropped back to the water. "You want to know what was going through my head."

"I have my speculations," he said, his voice low and calming.

She sighed, contemplating for a moment before turning to face him. "Honestly, there were a lot of things, but the rage..." She cleared her throat. "The rage was him."

Everything weak and vulnerable about Jen was rooted in memories of her father—he haunted her. The stone wall in her mind may as well have his name carved into it. But no matter how hard she tried to keep him behind it, he was always waiting just out of view for an opportunity to slither back out.

"That was my guess." Damien propped his chin on his arm.

Jen covered her face with her hands. "I don't know what happened. I usually keep those feelings under control, him, under control. I was already overwhelmed and exhausted; I didn't have the mental stamina to keep things at bay. It all burst through before I realized what happened."

"That's completely reasonable, Bug," he said kindly.

Damien had experienced the toll her father's actions had wrought on her, firsthand. He was the one she clung to when the shadows of memory threatened to consume her.

She shook her head, flecks of water splashing against the lip of the tub. "I don't want to lose control like that."

"It didn't look like you were losing control," Damien said pointedly. "If anything, it looked just the opposite."

"After all these years. I just—I don't want him to have that much power over me..." she whispered. "And what's worse," she said, finally meeting his gaze. "He's not even my real father."

I endured him, and it meant nothing.

Damien sat up. "He was real to you, to your family," he said. "If you're truly worried, then we'll figure out a way to help you let him go."

"It's not that easy—" she interrupted.

"I didn't say it was."

Jen sat silently in the tub, her hands moving methodically through the water. She had never known how to let things go. It wasn't something she did instinctively, despite her greatest wishes.

She held onto everything, kept it all in the back of her mind behind that wall. But things were starting to slip through the cracks, and it terrified her.

She glanced over at Damien, who looked like he was trying very hard to read her mind. She knew he had more questions, and it killed her that she didn't have the answers for him.

"You also want to know what I am," she whispered.

He brought his thumb to her jaw and stroked it gently.

"I wouldn't say what, but rather—who. And I've always wanted to know that." There was a quiet caress in his words, an earnest desire for understanding.

Damien cupped her cheek, and Jen held his hand against her. "You already know me better than anyone else in the world," she said.

He brought his other hand to her face, holding her in his palms.

"And yet there is still so much to learn," he said with a smirk.

He dipped his head towards her and kissed her gently, softly. His yearning to know her, to understand her, poured out of him.

But the question of who she was lingered like a shadow…a dark specter with an indistinguishable face.

He pulled away, pressing his head to hers as his thumbs caressed her cheeks, as if he could feel her unease. She breathed deeply, and the scent of unkempt pastures and smoke from a blacksmith forge wafted into her nose. Somehow, Damien still smelled like Nimea. Like home.

Her eyes flickered to the water and then back up to him.

"Do you want to join me?"

He gave her a rakish grin before standing up. "Nothing would make me happier—" he started. "But I didn't just come in here to watch you bathe."

She arched a brow.

"Bastien convinced the king to meet with us over dinner this evening."

Jen started. "Really?"

"I guess your wind dance worked in our favor."

She scoffed and sent water splashing at him. He chuckled and jumped back towards the door, folding his arms.

"And besides," he murmured. "If I joined you, I'd have you out of that tub and against that pillar in a heartbeat." He pointed to one of the columns through the bedroom doorway.

Jen followed his finger, her face growing warm.

He smiled wickedly. "Enjoy your bath."

He turned and disappeared through the doorway, his steps growing quieter as he slipped out into the hallway.

The dark specter returned to her mind, and along with it, that lingering question.

Who am I?

She exhaled and plunged back under the water.

The appliques of her gown were driving Jen crazy as she walked towards the great hall. Shyra returned after her bath to assist her in getting ready, pinning her golden hair into loose cascading curls around her face; half of it in an elegant bun, the rest flowing down her back. A small amount of blush was swept onto her cheekbones, her lips given a trace amount of a deep red stain.

She had never worn dresses this fine in her life, hadn't even seen or heard of the materials that they were made of. Jen had blindly picked the aubergine gown because she was partial to the color.

Elegant stripes of fabric wrapped over her shoulders and held the form fitting bodice at her waist. Tiered layers of chiffon sprung out from the underskirts, flowing with every movement she made.

She felt ridiculous.

Jen rolled her stone between her fingers; its presence having grown to comfort her. She placed it within the undergarments beneath her bodice, the coolness of the rock warming instantly to her skin.

Emelie was already waiting along with Samara, and wore a gown of similar material to Jen, with capped sleeves, in a gorgeous shade of midnight blue.

"You look stunning," Jen said, squeezing her hands. Emelie was quick to lift their hands to examine her knuckles.

"Jen—you're—you can't even tell you were hurt…" she said in disbelief. "Did you apply the salve I gave you?"

"I did…" Jen had applied it after her bath, but she noticed, as she smoothed a thin layer to her knuckles, that the redness had already faded, the small cuts along her skin, mended.

Samara walked over in an understated black linen gown trimmed with golden thread and peeked over Emelie's shoulder to look for herself.

She clicked her tongue. "That's curious," she said, releasing Jen's hands.

That's cryptic.

"What do you mean by that?"

The echoing of several pairs of shuffling footsteps halted the conversation. William and Leeyna fluttered into the hall, the latter flushed and fixing her hair, the former attempting to push wrinkles out of his sky-blue tunic.

Jen raised her eyebrows.

"Goddess, save me," Samara groaned as she rubbed her temples.

William took a step away from Leeyna and cleared his throat. "So, is everyone ready to meet a king?"

Emelie perched her elbow on Jen's shoulder.

"Seems to me you two are ready for something else entirely," she winked.

"Oh, leave them be," Damien said as he strode in.

He was in an emerald tunic, and his raven hair had been combed back, his cheekbones even more striking than usual. He looked the very picture of a courtier, as if he'd lived here all his life.

His eyes slowly took Jen in, settling on her face. His gaze softened as he slipped a hand on the small of her back and kissed her brow.

"Perfection," he whispered into her ear. Luckily, the flush that crept onto Jen's cheeks was well hidden by the rouge she wore.

Bastien appeared at the top of the grand staircase that split over the front entrance. He leaned on the railing of the landing that towered above them.

"You all clean up nicely," he said. "Come."

One by one, they climbed the marble stairs towards the buttressed ceilings of the great hall.

He led them down another hallway and into a large dining room. The walls were covered in massive floor to ceiling tapestries, woven intricately to reflect the histories of Sachandes and its people.

A long dining table extended through the middle of the room, covered by an immaculate emerald tablecloth and layered with a golden runner. Beautiful, ornate candlesticks dressed the table, along with vases of the most exquisite, deep-orange flowers.

There was a noticeable absence of the ever-present breeze, as there was no veranda off this room. Instead, a roaring hearth was blazing behind the unoccupied head of the table, emitting warm shadows across the floors.

Everyone wandered about the room, taking in the tapestries and the warmth of the fire. Jen found herself in front of the first panel of woven fabric. It depicted a star—a falling star. She lifted her hand to brush her fingers against the threads.

"Zethyna," Bastien said from behind her.

She yanked her hand back.

He chuckled softly. "It's okay, you can touch it." His eyes danced with humor as he came up beside her, admiring the tapestry with her.

"Zethyna is the star that brought magic to Etheria thousands of years ago. It crashed into Mount Naajin, and is said to have cracked open on impact, the raw magic that expelled from it forming into two deities," He pointed to the two figures next to the fallen star. One had sun-kissed skin, long, almost-white hair adorned with a crown of flowers and robes of flowing ivory and gold; the other, in stark contrast, had long, black hair, pale skin, a crown of glittering onyx stone and robes of black and deep violet.

"We believe that everything came from them. For a time, they used their limitless magic to create beautiful works of light, and of dark."

Jen's fingers ran over the rough threads.

"What happened to them?"

Bastien looked sadly at the woven deities.

"They disappeared a very long time ago."

Jen looked at him, genuine grief contorted his face. He shook his head and forced a smile to turn on his lips, gesturing back to the group.

"Shall we join the others?"

She nodded and took the arm he offered her.

They glided back to the group, and as they did, the large mahogany doors opened. Jen stiffened, expecting the king, but instead Ronan came sauntering in. Surprisingly, he was without a giggling companion for the first time since they arrived.

He walked up to Bastien and clasped his arm and then grabbed Samara by the hand, kissing it roughly.

"Lady Samara, you look *ravishing*."

"*Bleh*," she feigned disgust as she wiped her hand on her dress.

He looked around at everyone else.

"My, seems that bathing may be more powerful than magic," he said in jest. His eyes danced over Jenevieve in her chiffon gown. "At least for some of you."

"Charming as always, Ro'," Samara said, pushing him towards the long table.

Damien's hand tightened on her back. "I really don't like that guy," he mumbled.

Jen couldn't help the grin that slipped onto her lips.

"Really? You were being so *subtle*," she teased.

His eyes narrowed as he led her to the table. Jen stood to the left of the empty head seat, across from Bastien. Damien was to her left, Ronan across from him. He winked at him, and the muscles of Damien's jaw ticked.

Seriously?

They waited in silence, but after a few minutes, Jen looked at Bastien, silently inquiring what they were supposed to be doing. He glanced at her. He looked—nervous.

This is going to go well.

The imposing doors opened once again. When they realized who it was, everyone lowered themselves into a curtsy or a bow, as they'd been instructed to do. Their heads remained parallel with the floor as slow, deliberate footsteps clicked towards the head of the table. Out of the corner of her eye, Jen could see two hands press gently on the table.

Bastien lifted his head.

"Your Grace," he said.

"Bastien," the king grunted.

His voice was like gravel, as if he hadn't spoken all day. There was a monotonous, melancholic weight not only in his timbre, but in his aura. It was heavy with loss, with burdensome guilt.

Jen risked a glance at him.

He was already staring directly at her.

Oh my...He looks just like—Fjora.

She pushed the swell of emotion away.

The king's tan skin was creased around his eyes and between his brows, proof that at some point his face held expressions of joy and laughter. His ash-blonde hair that curled around his ears was streaked with bits of gray, his blue eyes, the hue of a clear ocean, were dull, lifeless.

Haythem was dressed in a simple black tunic, with intricate swirls of onyx satin that extended to the cuffs at his wrists. His belt held a long sword, but Jen suspected it was merely there for show, having remained sheathed for some time.

Jen wasn't sure what she was expecting, but if she hadn't been told he was the king, nothing about his physical or mental state would indicate his rank.

His eyes moved warily around the table at his dinner guests, before taking a seat in his high-backed, elaborately carved chair.

Jen followed Bastien's lead and promptly lowered herself into her own seat, followed quickly by the others at the table. Servants appeared out of thin air to pour wine from golden pitchers into crystalline glasses.

The tension only grew as the first course of some kind of soup was brought to the table. All that was heard was the crackling of the hearth or quiet slurping from deep spoons. Jen glanced at Bastien again. He was watching the king carefully, trying to assess his mood. After a moment of consideration, he put his spoon down.

He cleared his throat before crossing his hands on the table.

"Your Grace," he started. Haythem glanced his way. "This is Jenevieve, the woman I spoke to you about earlier." He gestured to her. The king didn't look at her.

"The woman who claims my daughter is alive," he said, disdain dripping from every word. Jen blinked and felt everyone's eyes land on her.

"I told you it was real this time, Your Grace," Bastien said with a bit more insistence.

The king snapped his head at Jenevieve. She had to keep from jumping at the sudden shift.

"Do you know how many times I've been told my daughter was alive?"

Jen tried not to tremble under his gaze, petrified of saying the wrong thing.

"Too many times to count. First, she was held captive in Ardovia. Then she was hiding with the water nymphs in the Inbetween, then she was boarding a ship to Ascendia." He was seething, but pain lived just behind his eyes. "Why should I believe truth exists in the words you speak, thirty years later?"

Decades of shattering disappointment plagued the king's voice. No, this wasn't the benevolent ruler she expected to meet. The loss of his daughter, and then his wife—this man had been wrecked. He couldn't fathom hanging on to any semblance of hope, he didn't have the strength anymore. She felt nothing but empathy for him.

Jen placed her hands on the table.

"Perhaps you didn't find her because you weren't looking in the right place." The king narrowed his eyes, but she continued. "For the last thirty years, Fjora has been in Nimea."

His head snapped at Bastien. "Did you allow some kind of mentally unstable *witch* and her coven to take up rooms in my palace?!"

Bastien threw his hands up defensively but spoke with more authority. "Your Grace, I implore you. Listen to her."

He nodded at Jen, encouraging her to continue. The king slowly turned back to her, stroking his beard.

Jen tucked a stray curl behind her ear. "Thirty years ago, I was born the night before the pulse." Haythem took a long sip from his glass. "My birth parents gave me to Fjora and sacrificed themselves so she could escape through the Forest of Bri. She settled in Nimea and raised me as her own."

Every time Jen was forced to tell that story, it felt like someone was stabbing her with a dull knife. The pain that her birth had caused so many people was something she hated living with. The broken king listening to her was one of those whose misery she was responsible for.

Haythem raised a brow.

"How can you be certain that she is *my* Fjora?" his voice grew softer, hesitant.

Jen looked at him with the utmost compassion.

"She looks like you," she said, her voice quiet.

He blinked several times. Jen could have sworn his eyes were rimming with tears.

"The ash-blonde hair…your nose." She tapped her eyebrow. "The way your brow arches as you decide whether or not I'm telling the truth…she did that a lot when I was a child."

Haythem ran his thumb along his jaw, considering her.

"If this is somehow true, where is she now?"

Jen looked down at her hands. How could she tell him that she wasn't sure Fjora was alive?

Damien gently placed his hand on her thigh, giving it a reassuring squeeze as she mustered the courage to look back up at the king.

"The pulse came twenty years early, and the morai attacked us. Fjora got us to the tree line and—"

Haythem's eyes turned to slits.

"And?"

Jen sighed. Grief seeped into her chest.

"The last time I saw her, she was running back towards the attack." She released a resigned sigh. "I don't know if she survived."

A sad smile fell upon the king's lips. "That sounds like her."

He sipped from his glass and swirled it in his hand.

"When was this?"

"About a week ago."

He sent an accusatory look towards Bastien. "How did we miss the horde?"

Bastien pursed his lips, clearly trying to choose his words carefully. "Your Grace, the condors don't—we're stumbling around blind. Unless I send out sentries, we have no idea what's happening beyond our borders."

The king leaned back in his chair, clenching the arms so tightly his knuckles turned white. He sighed deeply, shame and regret imprinted on his face.

"I have been remiss in my duties. There is no excuse for it."

Bastien placed his hand on the table and leaned forward.

"Grief comes for us all, even a king."

Haythem nodded his head, his thumb rubbing his chin. His gaze fixed back on Jen.

"Is this why you came all this way? To tell me my daughter may or may not be alive?" There was no venom in his voice now, only genuine curiosity.

Jen retrieved Fjora's letter from the pocket of her gown. She held it in her hands, her thumbs running over the worn parchment before she placed it on the table, gently sliding it towards the king.

"This next part you should hear from her."

He looked down at the letter like it was a *blade* she'd just pushed towards him.

He opened it slowly, the air so tense Jen almost wished she *did* have a blade to cut through it. Haythem's eyes widened and he dropped the parchment in front of him. He looked at Bastien, his mouth dropped open in shock.

Bastien smiled and nodded at him.

"It's her, Haythem."

The king's eyes were now rimmed red; a smile broke out onto his face as he brought the letter closer and examined it. "Fjora," he breathed. But his joy was short-lived as he continued reading.

Jen expected this.

Where is a herd of Rhionnen when you need them?

"The council…" he said incredulously.

Ronan cleared his throat.

"Your Grace. There has been a shift in the balance of Etheria's magic. Waelyn and Lutteala have felt it, their migratory timeline has been thrown off entirely. Dhokshas and kashyaks have been on the move in the last few years, infiltrating the realms and weakening trust amongst us. Some of my allies have even sworn they've seen raiding parties of *obari* along the southern borders of Senya."

Haythem scoffed.

"He's right. My sentries can validate his claims," Bastien said.

The king ran his hand thoughtfully along the pommel of his sword. "You believe war is a possibility?"

Ronan straightened in his chair.

"I think it's an *inevitability.*"

"You're a descendant, if you agree to uphold your ancestor's seat on the council, the other realms will fall in line," Bastien insisted.

Haythem jutted his chin at Jen.

"What is *your* significance in all of this?"

Jen didn't waver.

"I'm in the bloodline."

The king's breath hitched. "You're—"

"That's why Fjora was charged with protecting me, why she disappeared."

"Goddess." The king drained his glass.

Samara leaned forward on the table, having been a passive listener until her time to speak came. "The fates have sung their song. It is your choice; to listen or allow it to fall on deaf ears."

"You are asking me to risk not only my own life, but the lives of every Sachandan citizen whom I am charged to protect," Haythem said, his hands in fists.

"Their lives will be in peril either way," Bastien said.

Haythem ran his hands through his hair while he took a deep breath. After a moment, he rose from his seat. Everyone around the table fumbled to their feet.

"You have given me a lot to think about this evening," he said.

Bastien and Ronan looked at each other.

"But Your Grace—" Bastien sputtered.

Haythem put his hand up to silence him. "I will retire now."

Jen looked to Bastien for help, but his gaze remained on the king, disappointment slumping his shoulders.

She splayed her hands on the table. "We need you to lead the other descendants."

Haythem turned to her, his face kind, but stern.

"I will hear no more of this. I will not risk my people on the mere *possibility* of a threat."

Jen's face grew hot.

"But Fjora—"

"I will believe my child is alive when I see her with my own eyes. You cannot imagine the loss of a child, let alone the never-ending tortuous cycle of hope and heartbreak that has haunted me for thirty years," he snapped.

"She was my mother," Jen said, her voice losing its bite.

"No, she was *not*."

Haythem's chair scraped against the floor as he pushed away from the table and stomped through the doors, leaving everyone speechless.

Bastien looked around the table. "He—I—I'll be right—" he sputtered before running to catch up with the king.

Jen slumped into her seat, completely disheartened. She knew this wasn't going to be an easy meeting, but that discussion had taken a very sharp left turn and fell off a cliff into an abyss.

Damien sat down next to her as everyone else began awkwardly murmuring amongst themselves.

"I changed my mind," he murmured.

Jen looked at him warily.

"It's the *king* I don't like."

CHAPTER 22

Jen sat at the vanity in her room, her head pressed against her hand. After a painfully quiet meal following the king's abrupt departure, she immediately retreated to the seclusion of her bedroom. She was utterly mortified at how horribly that went.

She only wanted to do what Fjora asked of her. Jen may not know as much about the princess as she thought she did, but she did know that the woman who raised her wouldn't burden her with this unless it was the only choice.

But you could have at least warned me a little bit.

Jen grabbed her stone that sat on the vanity in front of her, mindlessly strumming it over her fingers as it gleamed in the light of the chandelier hanging above her head.

What am I supposed to do now? Sit around and wait for the king to change his mind?

Bastien never returned after following the king out of the dining hall, so that clearly hadn't gone smoothly. Jen let out a frustrated groan as her head fell back against her chair.

"You look like you could use one of these, too," a voice said from the doorway. Jen spun around to see Bastien standing just inside the door to the hallway, two small glasses and a bottle of amber liquid in his hands.

She rubbed her temples.

"You have no idea."

She joined him at the small table that sat between the two plush armchairs. He poured a small amount of the liquor into each glass and handed one to her.

He lifted his glass with a wry smirk. "To failed attempts."

Jen clinked his glass and let the amber liquid burn as she downed it in one long swig. Bastien arched his brows, and she pushed her glass towards him, tapping the rim.

He huffed a laugh. "Don't worry, we'll get him on board," he said, filling her glass.

Jen slung back the second glass.

"I'm sorry it was such a disaster."

Bastien leaned on the back of the armchair.

"It's not your fault that the king has been all but absent for the last few years," he said, glancing at her empty glass. "You should slow down."

She scrunched her nose at him and ignored him, pouring herself another. "He's been like that since the queen passed?"

Bastien nodded gravely, resting his forearms on the back of the armchair.

"After Fjora died—well—disappeared, Haythem and Eliana all but fused themselves together. Their love was already the bedrock of the kingdom, but this was something else. Haythem leaned on his wife and became almost too reliant on her." His head dropped as if remembering that painful time. "Two years ago, she fell gravely ill, and none of the healers could figure out what it was." He drained his glass. "We tracked down anyone and everyone on the continent that could have possibly helped…in the end…it wasn't enough."

Jen quietly grabbed the bottle and filled Bastien's glass. He gave her a sad smile. "He was once a noble and valiant king, but he has lost everything. He was a husband and father first. What happens to a family man when he no longer has one?"

Jen perched on the arm of the chair.

"When you ran out after him—I assume that didn't go the way you hoped?"

Bastien let out a pained laugh, his amber eyes seeming to gain back some life. "It was mostly groveling met with either silence or grunts."

Jen laughed softly. She had to. If she didn't attempt to find humor in their epic failure, she would spiral into a pit of despair with a sprinkling of shame and embarrassment.

"I'll drag myself into his quarters in the morning and attempt to talk some sense into him."

Jen rolled the stone in her hand, she'd forgotten she even had it. Bastien glanced down at it.

"What's that?"

Jen clenched it in her fist before offering it to him.

"Samara gave it to me back in the valley, it's supposed to conceal me— protect me."

He cocked his head and peered at it curiously.

"May I?"

Jen hesitated for a moment before handing it to him.

He considered it closely. "Samara gave you this?"

She nodded. Jen suddenly felt bare without it—vulnerable.

"Do you know where she got it?" he asked, weighing it in his hand.

She shook her head. "I think she had a healer or someone else enchant it…"

Bastien furrowed his brow, his fingers slowly moving over the smooth surface of the stone. "This is much more powerful than something a run of the mill healer could accomplish."

"What do you mean?"

He contemplated it for a moment longer and opened his palm to her. She plucked it from his hand, the comforting security returning to her.

"A veil like *that* is not an easy thing to conjure—"

There was a loud pounding at the door.

Before Jen or Bastien could respond, Samara's head peered between the door and its frame. "You two cheersing a job well done with that amber shit?"

Bastien didn't miss a beat.

"This *happens* to be the Ardovian rum Ronan gave me," he said, pressing the bottle to his chest.

"Did I hear my name?" Ronan called from the hallway. His face appeared in the space above Samara. Two floating heads.

"She's insulting your choice of gifts," Bastien chided.

Ronan looked down at Samara.

"Samara wouldn't know good rum if it smacked her in the face."

She craned her neck to glare at him.

"Don't make me come up there."

Jen clapped her hand over her mouth to conceal a snort. Samara eyed her. "As fun as it is to drink alone, we were thinking something less…depressing."

Bastien put the bottle down and clasped his hands.

"Lannas?"

The floating heads smiled mischievously.

"Lannas."

Bastien gave Jen a once over. "You'll want to change into something more comfortable."

Jen looked down at her chiffon gown.

"Comfortable for what?"

But Bastien was already striding towards Samara and Ronan. "Get changed and meet in the great hall," he called from the doorway.

"What's Lannas—" she yelled back, but they were already gone.

She glanced down at the stone in her hand.

If a veil like this isn't an easy thing to conjure, who did it?

Jen looked across the room at her reflection in the vanity mirrors and scowled. She squeezed the stone against her palm and stomped over to the massive walk-in closet to search for something acceptable for whatever Lannas was.

It took her longer than she anticipated to get herself out of the chiffon monstrosity. The first moment she wished for Shyra to assist her—nowhere to be found.

She opted for a simple lavender linen dress and comfortable brown boots. Her leather belt was fastened around her waist with the pouch containing the stone and an assortment of coins, and her dagger was carefully hidden within her room.

She came around one of the pillars and found Bastien waiting with Samara and Ronan. He glanced in her direction and smiled.

"Yes, much better."

Ronan and Bastien wore loose white shirts and black pants, Samara was in a deep blue tunic.

"Is it just us?" Jen asked as she settled between Samara and Bastien. As if she willed them into existence, Emelie and Damien came from the adjoining hall, both clad in more relaxed attire as well.

"No William and Leeyna?" she asked. Emelie gave her a knowing look as they approached. "William wanted to show her more of the *libraries*."

Sure. Libraries.

Damien winked at her, coming just close enough to brush his fingers against hers.

"Alright, time to show you the real Quoxana," Bastien said, clasping Ronan on the shoulder and steering him out the massive front doors and through the golden gate.

The walkway around the lake was lined with packed restaurants and cafes lit with lanterns that reflected in the water, a flowing river branching from it and weaving its way through the city, the same one they followed when they arrived.

Two cobblestone streets flanked the river, connected by dark oak bridges with animals and flower blossoms carved into the wood.

The streets buzzed with shops and vendors selling everything from spices to wool clothing to bathing salts. The sweet scent of lilacs and the savory scent of meat roasting on a spik nearby pervaded the air, making Jen's mouth water.

Children ran freely in front of their parents carrying shopping bags, young lovers held hands as they peered into shops selling fine jewelry, and groups of friends sat chatting at iron tables while they waited for drinks at one of the pubs.

Bastien walked up beside Jen as her eyes darted around, unable to take in everything fast enough. She peered over at him, pulling her focus away from the array of smells and sights around her.

"What?"

He smiled politely at a couple passing by.

"My lord," they said, bowing their heads.

"You remind me of Fjora, the first time I brought her out here without any guards." Bastien offered his arm, and she took it as he went on.

"It was Ruymani." He noticed Jen's confusion. "Festival of Light—which is only a few weeks away. Perhaps you'll get to see it." He veered them down another street away from the river, headed towards the city center. "Fjora loved this part of the city; the spice road." His eyes grew nostalgic. "She would stare at the colors and inhale the aromas; I never saw her so content."

Jen imagined a young Fjora being young and happy in her city, smelling colorful spices, surrounded by her people. A life ripped away to save a child that wasn't her own.

They walked around a fountain toward the other side of one of the main squares, where they stopped in front of a two-story house of worn wood, wedged between two shops.

A long porch extended the length of the building, dotted with chairs and tables, mostly occupied, with a matching balcony jutting out from the second floor. Patrons leaned on the railings, laughing with their companions and drinking from silver goblets. The entire thing was strung with small lights that dipped in arches all along the railings and the beams above their heads.

Bastien released Jen's arm and draped his own around Samara and Ronan, and together they walked up the front steps. She followed behind them, Damien and Emelie on her heels.

Ronan kicked the door open.

"SILVANO!" He bellowed to the barkeep standing behind the massive square bar in the middle of the room. Silvano spun around and scowled at the three of them.

"Who the fuck let you idiots in here?" He flung his bar rag at Ronan, but his scowl broke immediately into a boisterous laugh.

"We missed you Sil," Samara said as she lifted herself over the bar to kiss his cheek.

"Three years away from your favorite barkeep? I should hope so," he said. He nodded at Bastien. "Lord Bastien," he looked back at Samara. "He's not nearly as fun without you two."

Bastien rolled his eyes. "Thanks, Sil."

Silvano looked behind them at the rest of their party. "Did you all…make friends?"

Samara leaned on her elbow. "You're not the first person to ask us that today." She swatted Bastien's chest. "We're not social pariahs," she said as she beckoned Jen and the others to the bar.

Jen smiled warmly at the silver-haired man as she shook his hand. "It's nice to meet you, Silvano."

He scrunched his nose at the sound of his full name. "Sil, darlin'."

Ronan leaned over the bar, clearly searching for something. "Okay, wonderful, everyone knows each other. Can I get my rum now?"

Sil shoved Ronan back and grabbed the amber liquid from a shelf behind him. He gave Ronan his glass and offered everyone else goblets of Sachandan wine.

"We're high up in the mountains, the altitude will affect your tolerance. Best to start off slow," he warned.

From across the bar, a dark-haired woman wearing a deep blue gown that left very little to the imagination appeared beside Ronan. His eyes raked over her before leaning down to kiss her on the cheek.

"Margo," he said darkly.

She purred his name, before beckoning him to the second floor. He looked back at Samara and shrugged before following Margo towards the stairs.

The rest of Margo's party spotted Bastien and came running over in a fit of squeals and giggles. Bastien kissed each of them on the cheek, most of them turning a deep shade of crimson when he cast his attention towards them.

They swarmed him, pushing themselves between Jen and Emelie and Damien. Damien tried to elbow his way through, but when he stepped forward, one of the women stumbled backwards and rammed into him, spilling wine down the front of his tunic.

The woman spun around, completely mortified.

"Goddess, I'm so sorry!" she exclaimed, fumbling to grab a rag from the bar. Damien placed his goblet on the counter and wiped himself down with his hands.

"Oh, no, please let me help—my friends are so obsessed with Lord Bastien they become a stampede, and I didn't see you. I'm so clumsy I—"

Jen watched through the crowd as Damien smiled while the woman tried to clean his tunic.

"No, it's okay, accidents happen," he said as he took the rag from her. "You live at the palace, don't you? I think I saw you in the great hall."

She peered up at him, and then her eyes widened.

"Oh! You were in that group that arrived this morning," she said, her honey-blonde hair was plaited into a loose, whimsical braid, her dark brown eyes sparkling in recognition. "You all created quite a stir with your arrival."

Damien released a stiff laugh. "We were definitely *not* trying to create a stir of any kind."

The woman smiled warmly. "A stir is good! It keeps things interesting."

She offered her hand. "I'm Lyla."

He took it and smiled back at her.

"Damien."

Lyla flagged down Sil. "Well, Damien, since I spilled your drink, please let me get you another."

Jen leaned over the side of the bar to get a better look at the beautiful woman Damien was talking to—she was practically laying on the counter.

"He's just making friends, Jen," Emelie said, sipping from her goblet.

Jen slid off the bar top. "He deserves that though—something simple, easy. I mean just look at him." Damien flung his head back in that explosive laugh she loved as Lyla stifled a giggle.

"I want him to be happy."

Emelie placed her hand over Jen's and squeezed. "You deserve to be happy too."

Samara elbowed her way through the court ladies and grabbed onto Jen's shoulder. "Thank the Goddess, sane-ish people."

Jen shook off her momentary melancholy. "Is he always followed by a flock of women?"

Samara signaled to Sil before answering. "Bas is actually pretty mellow—see how he isn't actually touching any of them?" She gestured over to Bastien, whose forearms were resting on the edge of the bar. His eyes were kind, but he was clearly counting down the moments until he could recuse himself.

"Ronan is the peacock of the two of them."

Emelie cackled.

Jen's attention was pulled up to the second floor. Ronan and Margo leaned against the rail, one of his arms pressed against the wooden beam behind her head.

Samara followed her gaze. "How are things going with that?"

Jen snapped her head back. "What?"

Samara looked at her incredulously. "I heard you." When Jen looked at her like she still had no idea what she was talking about, Samara explained further. "Your argument in the valley."

Damnit.

Emelie looked surprised. "Your what?"

Jen groaned. "We had a bit of a—spat, the night before we got to Sachandes." She glanced back up at him. "And we haven't really spoken since."

Samara leveled a look. "Spat is putting it mildly."

Emelie looked dumbfounded. "Wait, why?"

Because he wouldn't tell me his favorite color and I accused him of planning to betray us all—that sounds very stupid in hindsight.

Jen buried her head in her hands. "He caught me at a bad moment—but—he's not innocent, he said some awful things too."

Samara leaned over the bar looking for something. "Yes, he's an arrogant peacock—as I said. But there are reasons why he acts that way." She grunted and leaned over further. "I suggest burying the hatchet, for all our sake."

I've been doing just fine with the cold shoulder.

Emelie chimed in. "He's been a wonderful teacher; he's patient and fun—
"

They are not going to let this go.

Jen groaned. "Okay, okay. I get it. I'll talk to him."

Samara peered up at him. "Here's your chance, looks like Margo has moved on—for now."

She snatched the rum bottle she'd been looking for and blew a kiss to Sil, who flipped a finger at her. She handed the bottle and a second glass to Jen.

"Don't go empty handed," she winked.

She found Ronan sitting in a large leather chair in front of one of several hearths on the second floor. He was swirling his glass, staring mindlessly into the fire. She approached quietly.

"Jenevieve," he drawled. His gaze didn't leave the flames.

Jen lifted the bottle of rum, his eyes shifted to it. "What do they say about Ardovians?"

A small, reluctant smirk pulled at his lips. "Absolutely shit people, but they do have their talents."

He exhaled through his nose, pointing his chin to the leather chair sitting opposite him. She placed the rum bottle on the table between them and sank into it as he removed the stopper and poured each of them a glass.

Jen's eyes wandered around the space. "Margo wasn't interested?"

He arched a brow.

"Did she look uninterested, to you?"

"She walked away."

"Were you watching me?"

"Yes."

His lips twitched. He took a sip from his glass as he leaned back in his chair. He considered her for a moment. "Margo left because I *asked* her to."

"Why?"

"I had a feeling you'd be making an appearance. And as much as I enjoy Margo, I would much prefer to—how did Samara phrase it—*bury the hatchet?*"

Jen glanced towards the stairs. "You heard us?"

He smirked against his glass.

"I have *excellent* hearing."

She leaned forward, feeling the warmth of the fire on her face. Ronan observed her carefully. "Damien made a new friend, it seems."

Jen took a long sip from her glass.

"He deserves to have fun—to be happy."

Softness flickered in the jewel laden troves of his eyes. "You don't think you deserve the same, do you."

It wasn't a question.

"How many of my conversations were you listening to?" Jen rose from her seat and rested her elbow on the mantle above the hearth.

"You are not alone in that struggle, by the way," he said quietly. She tilted her head. He leaned forward. "Accepting that you deserve happiness."

Her eyes dipped to the fire, tendrils of fear and anger twisting a gnarled knot in her chest and threatening to seep through her mental wall, but she shoved them back.

Ronan watched her curiously. "Why do you do that?"

"Do what?"

He pressed his glass against his temple. "Push the anger and fear away, that couldn't have been pleasant."

"I—"

He stood up gracefully and joined her at the mantle. "You don't have to tell me. I just figured if we were going to be friends, we could attempt some honesty."

Jen let out a strangled laugh and tucked her hair behind her ear.

"My anger…rage…it overwhelms me," she said, her voice small. "I'm completely blind when it comes forward, I keep it so heavily guarded that when it escapes its—volatile." The tingling sensation appeared and disappeared from her fingers. "It feels like the people who forced that on me… they still have power over me."

"And you want to find out a way to…*let it go*."

She thrummed her fingers on her glass.

Ronan grabbed the bottle and poured another two fingers of rum. He offered her the same, to which she nodded. "Do you want to know what I think?" he asked.

She took a swig, her silence confirming she did.

"Instead of thinking your anger—that *breathtaking fury*— is someone else controlling you, you should see it as a gift, a *powerful* gift." Jen stared into the fire as he continued. "I don't know what happened, maybe one day you'll tell me your story. But you can focus that rage; use it, shape it, channel it. You did that today."

"That wasn't on purpose."

"Exactly."

"Exactly what—"

He sighed. "Jenevieve, I've watched you for the last week. It's as though your body is waking up after a long sleep."

"I know…"

Ronan looked down his nose at her, his expression almost stern. "And I don't think it's something that should be *'let go'* or *dampened* in any way."

She drained her glass.

"What do I do? I don't know what it is, or how to control it."

He placed his glass back on the table and plopped down into his chair. "First, we go see Gaiana tomorrow afternoon. We need her for the council, but she can also help you finesse the Taejja."

She looked quizzically at him,

"The wind dance," he said, his eyes dancing with humor.

"I seem to be doing alright with that at least—"

Whatever that *is*.

"Yes, but I saw the smoke coming off your fingers, and although Samara can really piss me off, I would prefer it if you didn't accidentally set her on fire."

The color drained from Jen's face.

"Don't worry, we'll have a bucket of water handy."

She rolled her eyes at him and returned to her own chair. After a moment of silence, she looked over at him. "I'm sorry."

He raised his eyebrows. "What?"

"For the other night." She bit her bottom lip. "Although there's a lot I still wish to know about you, I didn't mean what I said…about giving me to—" She glanced around to ensure no one was listening. "Vondur."

Ronan leaned forward in his chair, his verdant eyes looking uncharacteristically uneasy. "That night, in the valley. You had a nightmare, didn't you?"

She blanched. "How did you know that?"

Something raw flashed behind his gaze. "Jenevieve, I—"

"JEN!"

She jumped at the sound of her name.

"Get down here! The band is about to start," Emelie called from the bottom of the steps.

"Leave Ronan to brood on his own," Samara snapped. They stood at the bottom of the stairs with their arms crossed.

Jen looked back at Ronan, but the raw unease had disappeared. "Go have fun." He waved his hand towards the stairs. "We can talk another time."

She smiled and fumbled to her feet; the wine and rum was starting to catch up with her.

Probably not a good idea to combine those.

She clung to the back of the chair as she walked behind it, pausing in front of Ronan. He looked up at her, and her heart stumbled a few beats, for within the verdant green—thin, violet streaks glowed around his pupil, and with the fire's light warming his face…Jen almost forgot to breathe.

That's new.

He lifted his brow, as if wondering why she was suddenly staring at him. She blinked several times, the violet streaks gone from his eyes, leaving Jen to think she'd imagined it.

She reached out her hand.

"Friends?"

Ronan slid his hand beneath hers and pressed a gentle kiss on her knuckles.

"Friends."

CHAPTER 23

Jen sat with her head between her knees at the breakfast table on her balcony. She didn't dare sit up; the room was spinning even behind her closed eyelids. It was a glorious summer morning, and she wanted nothing to do with it.

Maybe if she kept her eyes shut and just reached for a bland piece of—

"SHIT."

Her fingers ended up in a blazing hot cup of coffee. She shook her hand furiously, sucking the hot liquid from her fingers.

"Stupid rum," she hissed, the word making her nauseous.

When Jen had joined Samara and Emelie, the whole place exploded with music from a lively local band. She let the melodies sweep her away with her friends, her body swaying with no other thoughts but the music.

At some point, Emelie began yelling for shots, and so started the relay of dance—run to the bar for rum—dance—get more rum—on and on for several more hours.

When the pub closed for the night, Damien reappeared just as the girls were linking arms to stumble through the cobblestone streets.

He walked behind them to make sure no one fell down. And they didn't, although they may have wretched over a bush or two.

Now, she wanted to die.

Can whoever Goddess is come and take me to the afterlife please?

Jen's pathetic prayer was interrupted by a tentative knock at the door, Damien's head appearing cautiously in the doorway. The memory of him laughing with that beautiful woman sent a wave of jealousy crashing over Jen, threatening to send her to the ground, but she used the meager energy she had to stand instead.

Annnnd now there are black splotches in my vision. Terrific.

He took a few steps inside the room with his hands raised, as if approaching a wild animal. "How are you feeling?"

Jen thrummed her fingers on the table, her knees trembling slightly under her dressing gown.

"I'm fine," she said stiffly.

He came to the table, taking stock of the untouched food, and helped himself to a few grapes from one of the bowls.

"Why do I get the feeling you're angry with me?"

"I'm not."

He popped a grape into his mouth, a smug grin on his face.

"Bug, I've known you for most of our lives, and you've been angry at me for at least half of that." He pointed his thumb towards the door. "And you slammed the door in my face last night."

I...don't remember that. Whoops.

"She's pretty, you know," Jen said, picking up her coffee cup.

He tilted his head. "Who?"

Jen watched him over the rim of her cup. "The woman you were talking to all night."

"Ah," a feline grin pulled at his mouth. "Lyla."

"Yes, Lyla."

He took a step towards her, leaning on the back of the chair across from her. "I saw you chatting up Ronan—in a romantically lit corner of the pub."

A grueling headache was beginning to form along Jen's temples.

"We were burying the hatchet."

"Lover's quarrel?"

She scoffed. "You see right through me, don't you?"

He closed the distance between them, grasping her chin with his thumb and finger. "I know you're hungover, but you're being a brat."

Jen yanked her chin away and attempted to glide to the railing, but she doubted it looked at all elegant. She closed her eyes when she reached it, the sun far too bright, but a reprieving breeze blew her hair away from her face and soothed her clammy skin.

Damien walked up behind her, his hands dropping to her waist, squeezing gently. He lowered his mouth just below her ear. "It was just a conversation, Bug," he breathed.

Jen sighed. She knew, rationally, that she had no right to give him a hard time. He deserved to meet new people, have fun, take a break from the insanity they found themselves in.

"You—"

He leaned his head lower until his lips fluttered over her neck. "I had my eye on you all night, even with another woman's voice in my ear."

Jen leaned into him. His body was warm and strong, secure.

"Do you think I didn't see Ronan kiss your hand?" His hands wrapped around her waist and pulled back against him.

She smirked. "You saw that, huh?"

"I did." He placed his hands on the railing on either side of her. She turned around, his eyes blazing into hers. "And if you think," his voice was firm now. "For one second, that I would throw away a decade of fighting with you, of wanting you, of needing you—for a woman I've had one conversation with. You are gravely mistaken, Jenevieve."

Jen's eyes stung. He seemed to think she was jealous, but it was more than that. Seeing him with Lyla, the simple, carefree nature of their interactions, it left her feeling sad for him—that he was stuck with the complicated mess she brought upon them.

"Okay," she said quietly.

He bent down and leaned his forehead against hers, breathing her in. She sighed, the headache still throbbing, but his presence comforting her.

Someone cleared their throat from the doorway. Damien pushed away from her, revealing Emelie and Ronan standing a step inside the room. Emelie was blushing.

"Um. Do we need to come back later?"

Jen beelined it for the table to resume drinking her coffee.

"No, I was just retrieving Jen for training," Damien said. He glanced over to her with a wink. She put her cup down and darted across the room to the closet, fighting to conceal a groan as her body protested every single movement.

Wine before liquor, makes you…an idiot.

She emerged a few minutes later in a pair of brown pants and a green blouse and met Damien, Ronan, and Emelie in the hallway.

"You know, those do come with locks," Ronan said, his eyebrow raised to the doorknob, "for future reference."

Jen slapped him in the chest as they all walked, rather sluggishly, towards the courtyard. She noticed the slight grimaces and couldn't hold back her laughter.

"At least I'm not alone in my misery," she teased.

Samara waited with William and Leeyna in the training ring, a tray of goblets in her hands. William took in the state of them.

"You all look…"

"Like you had a wonderful time last night," Leeyna interjected, casting a sidelong glance at him.

Emelie held her head. "Yeah, we had so much fun. I think I'll be good for a while."

Samara chuckled as she offered the tray to them.

"Hangover brew. You'll still feel like shit, but you'll be able to stand up straight."

Jen accepted the goblet and took a tentative sip. Her hand darted to her mouth.

Don't you dare throw up. Keep it together.

It tasted like pond water, algae and dirt with just a hint of something akin to rust. Delicious.

"You thought it would taste good?" Samara asked.

Jen ignored her, setting her sights on William and Leeyna.

"What did you all get up to last night?"

William beamed. "We spent the evening in one of the other libraries, just walking around all of the different floors and through the stacks—"

"You can do more than just *reading* in some of those stacks William," Ronan said, a glint of mischief dancing in his eyes.

"OKAY. Time to teach me about more plants, *Ronan.*" Emelie shoved him away from the group as Leeyna choked on his joke.

"Oh, and Jenevieve," he said, his chin jutting down to a large bucket of water by Samara's feet. He wiggled his fingers. "Please don't set my friend on fire. I'm rather fond of her."

Samara looked at the bucket, her eyes widening in alarm.

"What does he mean—WHAT DO YOU MEAN BY THAT?" she shouted after him.

"Have fun!" he called as he disappeared beyond the archway.

Jen succeeded in *not* setting Samara on fire. She did, however, dry heave several times through their training.

And whine.

And curse.

Shyra must have come into the room while Jen was changing, because when she came out of the bathing room, she spotted a massive, golden pitcher of water sitting on the table on the veranda. Beside it; a tray of meats, cheeses, and a basket of bread.

Jen practically salivated.

Gods bless that woman.

She darted over and downed several glasses of ice-cold water, almost burning as it ran down her throat, and nibbled at a few pieces of cheese and gobbled down three rolls—her queasy stomach could only handle so much.

The headache she was battling had subsided a bit, but her body still ached and protested as she strapped on her leather belt with her stone and dagger in tow and walked towards the great hall.

She was supposed to meet Samara at the stables, but she had no idea where those were.

Haven't exactly had the chance to receive the grand tour yet.

Jen rounded one of the pillars only to ram into a courtier looking the other direction.

"I'm so sorry—" Jen reached for the woman she'd just clocked.

Lyla.

She was stunning in a flowing, sky-blue gown that made her dark eyes sparkle, her hair in elegant waves that framed her face.

Lyla grabbed onto Jen's elbows and steadied them. "No, that was me!" she said through a giggle. "I should really watch where I'm going—I'm a menace in heels."

Hells. Does she have to be this endearing?

"Don't worry about it–"

But Lyla had moved on already. "Oh, I'm so rude," she extended her hand with a warm smile. "I'm Lyla."

"Jenevieve," Jen awkwardly shook it, tucking a strand of hair behind her ear with her free hand. "Could you point me towards the stables?"

Once again, Lyla gave her a genuine smile, it was like standing in the damn sun after a winter-storm. She pointed towards the courtyard. "There's a flight of stairs by the archway over there, it'll lead you out the back of the palace, the stables are right there. You can't miss it."

Jen glanced over her shoulder. "Thanks."

Margo appeared with a group of courtiers and waved Lyla over from the other end of the hall.

"Nice to meet you!" Lyla said, running off towards her friends.

Jen let out a tense breath and quickly made her way to the stairwell.

Of course, I ran into her. Of. Course.

She came out into the valley. Ahead of her stretched a long, charming stable with a brown thatched roof, beside it an expansive, fenced pasture where a small herd of horses grazed peacefully.

Jen made her way to Samara and Ronan tacking up their mounts.

Ronan adjusted the saddle on his enormous, black Friesian as she walked over. "You ready?" he asked.

Jen shrugged. "To meet Gaiana and be rejected again—*sure.*"

Samara tightened the buckles around her dapple-gray. "This conversation will go differently, Jen. Gaiana is not Haythem."

I don't know what that means, but what else is new?

A harsh bark echoed from the barn, and a long-haired dog sprinted out, running straight for them. Samara leapt at it but missed—wiping out in the dirt.

It darted past them towards the stairwell, where Damien, Emelie, William, and Leeyna had just emerged. Without any hesitation, Leeyna crouched down and extended her hand towards the dog.

"Careful! That dog bites—" Samara shouted at them.

It slowed as it approached, the snarl disappearing as it pranced to her, rolling on the ground to expose its underside. Leeyna rubbed his stomach, unaware of any threat as a smile bloomed on her lips.

She looked up and her smile fell—everyone was staring at her.

"What?"

William stepped towards her, but the dog growled, baring its teeth. "She liked me first!" he scolded.

The dog remained at Leeyna's heels as they walked the rest of the way to the stable.

Zarah appeared outside the fence line, and the stable hands shook their heads in frustration. "She wouldn't let us put her to pasture. She tried to *kick* us!"

"Some creatures are not meant to be fenced in, Leith," Ronan said as he mounted his horse.

"Does Gaiana live in a palace like that?" Leeyna asked, gesturing to the mountains behind them.

Samara smirked. "No, Gaiana is not a palace kind of woman."

They mounted up and trotted towards the river a fair distance from the edge of the Kalli. In the distance, Jen could just make out a scattering of stone houses. People moved among them, carrying pails of water from the river or stoking fires that burned in the center of each small cluster. But as they drew closer, she realized the settlement was far more expansive than she had thought. The buildings grew more frequent, more condensed, more alive with activity.

Settled on the tiered hills that flanked the town center were more stone dwellings of varying shapes and sizes. There was no sense of uniformity, as if people had arrived over time and built whatever they pleased.

Samara raised her hand to her head and squinted.

A woman who looked no older than Jen was waiting for them as they dismounted. Long, dark brown hair was tied back, cascading behind her. Her stoic smile crinkled the corners of her deep chocolate eyes, her hands clasped at her midsection.

"Hello Jenevieve. Welcome to Sayllana," she said. Her voice was low, calm.

Jen started. "You know me?"

The woman smiled. "Gaiana is expecting you."

Jen glanced at Samara by her side, and then Ronan on the other—both shook their heads. No one forewarned Gaiana they were coming.

"Please." The woman gestured towards the town. "This way."

Jen tentatively fell in step behind her, Damien close by along with the rest of their party. She could smell the flowing water of the river and the embers of roaring hearths, the aroma of damp grass in the afternoon sun.

She quickened her pace and fell in stride with the woman leading them. "What's your name?"

The woman's eyes twinkled. "Rieshi."

"Do you work for Gaiana?"

The twinkle in her eye brightened.

"You could say that—she's my mother."

Jen raised her brows in surprise. "Oh."

Rieshi led them up the hill, past a few shops, a pub, and a cobbler who was sitting outside his front door, sewing the sole of a new pair of boots. He nodded to them as they walked by.

Jen expected them to head towards the three-story meeting house that sat at the bend in the river, where small boats were anchored to posts along the water's edge. But instead, Rieshi veered left, leading them through a narrow side street and into a quieter, more residential area.

The homes here became more inviting, dark wooden frames and paned windows lining the stone walls of each house.

They arrived at one of such houses nestled within a grove of trees. Jen followed Rieshi up the stone walkway to the front door. Before they could reach for the handle, it swung open.

A kind looking woman in swaths of mismatched fabrics stepped out, drying her hands off with a dish towel. Strands of her dark brown hair curled around her face, the rest of it plaited into a bun at the base of her neck.

"Hello Jenevieve, I've been waiting for you," she said, her deep brown eyes sparkling like Reishi's. She looked over at Samara and Ronan. "Samara." She nodded. "Ronan." She bowed her head slightly.

"It's been far too long." Ronan bowed his head graciously in return before stepping forward to kiss the woman on the cheek. She patted his face affectionately before returning her gaze to Jen.

"Gaiana…?" Jen asked. This couldn't be the leader of the Sachi, she was far too casual and…normal?

"Yes dear, that would be me," she said, again with an uncanny kindness in her voice. She swatted her dishrag through the doorway. "Well, let's not stand here all day. Come in, come in!"

They walked into an open sitting room, with woven textile rugs spread along the wooden floors, and an eccentric collection of colorful armchairs atop them. The kitchen's mahogany counters housed an abundance of exotic looking plants and piles of leather-bound books.

As they passed by, Jen abruptly stopped at the sink. From a large basin, a stream of water was pouring itself into a cast iron skillet, where a soapy rag washed it—on its own. She watched, mesmerized, as the rag moved in concentric circles.

Suddenly she realized all the small movements around her. The pages of the leather-bound books turned themselves, as if a gentle breeze was reading the worn parchment; one of the vined plants spontaneously grew from its pot and latched onto the kitchen wall before her eyes.

Aside from Samara showing her the water sphere back in the valley, Jen hadn't seen much magic up close. It was surprising to see something so powerful being used for—well—rudimentary household tasks.

Gaiana waved her hand towards the kitchen. "I was finishing up a few things when you arrived." She snapped her fingers, and in an instant, the water receded, the book closed, and the vines froze on the walls.

Jen looked from the kitchen to Gaiana, who was already in the large dining area with the others.

Who is this woman?

She followed everyone into the next room, where a hearth roared in the corner, a large pot hanging above the flames. A whimsical spiral staircase wound its way up to the second floor on the opposing side of the room, flanked by bookshelves occupied by hundreds of volumes.

William was already running his curious fingers over the bindings, turning his head to read some of the sideways titles. Samara and Rieshi sat at the corner of the table, while Ronan leaned against the mantle, picking at his fingernails.

Gaiana stood facing the open floor to ceiling windows in the back of the room. Jen swallowed and took a step forward, speaking through a held breath.

Let's get this over with.

"Gaiana, we have come to—"

"You have come to inquire if I will uphold my ancestors' oath, to join the Council of Suran."

She spoke to the window before slowly turning towards the room. Jen nodded her head.

Gaiana jabbed her finger at the mantle.

"Put that damned scroll away, Ronan," she chided, spotting him out of the corner of her eye. "I know what it is, you don't need to show me my great-grandmother's signature."

William gulped from the bookshelf.

"Great-grandmother? That would make you…how old…?"

Gaiana looked him over with quiet amusement. "It's *rude* to ask a woman her age, boy. But I'm sure you can venture a guess."

He sputtered, clearly wanting to answer, but afraid of offending her. She walked over to the large table and leaned on the back of her daughter's chair.

"We are similar to the Ascendiants, in that we were bestowed long life—"

"Ascendiants?" Damien asked, seated on the third step of the spiral stairs.

Gaiana seemed a bit surprised by his interjection and looked to Samara for confirmation. "They don't know of the Ascendiants?"

Samara dropped her head against her hand.

"They don't know of *a lot*."

Rieshi leaned forward, her palms pressed on the table. "Thousands of years ago, the Ascendiants came from another continent across the Ophelian Sea, Ascendia," she began. "Their land had been riddled with civil war. They all but destroyed themselves, and so some of them set sail to find a place to live in peace, settling in what you know as Sachandes." She smiled up at her mother. "Our ancestors were already here, cultivating the magic of Etheria as the shepherds of the Goddess."

Gaiana squeezed her shoulder.

"They sought friendship, as did we. And because of our respective lifespans, we were able to broker that over several millennia."

"The *treaty*," William said quietly. Rieshi nodded.

Gaiana lifted her shoulders. "All this to say—we are *old*."

Rieshi and Samara smirked at each other. Gaiana whipped her head towards them and feigned offense but winked as she continued.

"One of the abilities we were granted was to spiritually connect the animals of Etheria with those Ascendiants we deemed worthy of the blessing."

"I thought it was just the royal family?" Samara piped in.

Gaiana pursed her lips. "It ended up that way over time, but that was not the original intent. The pairing of a person and their animal counterpart is a delicate process, we are very selective of who we bestow that blessing upon. We have been fortunate that the royal bloodline of Sachandes has been consistently benevolent, unlike *others* on this continent," she sighed.

"No one outside the royal family has ever *sought out* the blessing, and so it has remained as it is to this day—" she stopped, her gaze suddenly fixed on the head of crimson curls against the wall.

Leeyna had been quietly absorbing the conversations around her. When she realized who was staring at her, she froze, her eyes darting around to the others.

The air in the room grew thick as Gaiana glided around the table, her eyes glazing over as she approached.

She gently took Leeyna's chin. "I see you prefer to be hidden from view, to live a life unnoticed and without a true purpose on the horizon," she said, her voice like a warm ribbon of honey. "That part of your life is coming to an end, my dear, and your journey will soon reveal more of its path to you…do not be afraid when a greater calling arrives…when a *blessing* reveres."

Leeyna looked like she wasn't breathing, her eyes swimming with an emotion Jen couldn't quite place. But Gaiana wasn't being hostile, rather, she was…assessing her, reading her, with an unsung ability.

William was strung like a bowstring, ready to pounce if Leeyna showed any sign of distress. But then, Gaiana's attention shifted to Emelie, standing to Jen's right.

Emelie froze as well, bewilderment etched on her face.

"You have the color of healing around you," Gaiana said, taking hold of her hands and clasping them within hers. She closed her eyes. "I sense something else as well." Her glazed eyes drifted over her shoulder, to Ronan. "You've been training her."

He nodded curtly, watching the scene closely.

"The aura of healing has been blended with something yet to be revealed; a brush of water painted through the hues of your future—the colors swimming together in a mysterious sea of refracted light."

She dropped Emelie's hands and turned fully. "I sense there are certain aspects of the training you are leaving out." His eyes widened slightly. "Bring them into the fold; she will need them sooner than you think."

He nodded once more, although not as assuredly as before.

Seriously, who is this woman?

Rieshi, sensing the tension that had come over the room, cleared her throat. "My mother can read people."

Damien stood up cautiously. "You mean like a psychic?"

Gaiana stepped away from the girls, who looked like the color had been leached from their skin. "No, not psychic." Her eyes cleared and the air returned to normal. "I can feel the presence of someone's spirit, see the broad strokes of their aura and occasionally a few blurry images. Over time, I've learned to piece them together, to decipher them."

Jen took a step forward.

"When we arrived, you said you'd been *waiting* for me."

Gaiana turned back to her. "Yes, I did."

"What did you mean by that…"

"After we saw the horde retreating north, I felt a presence enter Etherian territory. I couldn't be certain who it was, but it felt like an awakening within the earth."

"I was told to reconvene the council under the guidance of my mother. I wasn't expecting anyone to be aware of my arrival."

Gaiana raised her hand. "You misunderstood me. Etheria did not awaken because of your arrival, rather, it awoke because of your *return*."

"I can't be that important," Jen heard herself say.

"You are in the bloodline, my dear, your importance lives just beneath your skin. But your purpose in the grand scheme of this continent and its future remains to be seen."

Does she just…know everything?

Gaiana glanced over at Samara and Ronan. "You didn't just bring her here for the council."

They looked at each other, a silent conversation relaying between them.

It would be nice if they spoke out loud, but sure.

Samara rose from her seat. "She has shown an aptitude for Taejja; it's presented itself several times. We think she may—"

"You want her to be tested?" Rieshi asked in surprise, peering at Samara before her eyes darted towards her mother.

"What—tested…?" Jen fumbled.

Anyone care to elaborate?

Ronan stepped away from the hearth. "I told you we would try to enlist the tutelage of Gaiana to finesse your use of Taejja," he said. She was about to protest, but he made a downward gesture with his hands, imploring her to stay calm. "You *have* to be tested, just like anyone else."

Damien came to Jen's side, tension building in his jaw.

"What is this test you're referring to exactly?"

"To see which element of Taejja she responds to. Usually, unless you're Gaiana, there is one that calls to a person more than the others," Rieshi explained.

Jen wanted to crawl into a ball and disappear rather than have anyone witness her take some kind of magical test. She glanced at Gaiana. "What elements of Taejja can *you* use?" she nervously sputtered.

Gaiana looked almost amused at how uncomfortable she was. She jutted her chin back to the kitchen.

"What did you see on your way in here?"

Jen looked over her shoulder. "Um…the book, the basin, and the vines…?"

Gaiana put up a finger for each one. "Air, water, and earth."

Jen cocked her head. "Fire?"

Gaiana raised her brows towards the hearth. "Fire is the most elusive, hard to manipulate, and easy to lose control."

Ronan interjected before Jen could start to panic.

"But it *can* be controlled?"

Gaiana flicked her eyes over him. "With practice and the right state of mind, yes."

Droplets of sweat formed at the small of her back. Every day her magic flexed beneath her skin, and she knew, could *feel*, that it wasn't going to stop at tendrils of smoke.

What causes smoke?

Flames.

Luckily, Gaiana did not seem fearful at the prospect of fire, and that gave Jen the tiniest bit of hope that she could indeed learn to control whatever the fuck was building inside her.

Or Ronan can just follow me around with a bucket of water.

Damien laced his fingers with hers and squeezed gently, bringing her mind back to the room.

"Is the test dangerous?" he asked, his chest pressed against her shoulder.

Gaiana waved her hand. "No one has died in decades."

Samara scoffed. "She's joking——not very well, though."

She walked over and took Jen's hands. "I've done it. It's just a formality really. And besides——" she winked. "Don't you want to show her your wind dance?"

Gaiana raised her eyebrows, intrigue flickering in her gaze.

Jen sighed.

"When?"

Gaiana smiled and gestured to the back door of the house.

"Right now."

CHAPTER 24

Jen stood in a white chemise at the edge of a small clearing within the grove behind Gaiana's home.

After she agreed to the test, Rieshi whisked her up the spiral stairs to change into the clothing that everyone wore for their test. Jen insisted she keep her belt with the stone, and, luckily, Rieshi seemed to realize it was more than just an accessory and allowed it.

Her eyes flickered to the four massive trees that stood at the bends of a circle dug a few inches into the ground like a shallow elemental mote.

Each tree was carved with the Taejja symbol for one of the elements—air, water, earth and fire—as well as represented by something tangible within the circle. A windchime. A water basin. A pot of dirt. A pile of kindling.

Gaiana approached her. Gone was the eccentric warmth, now the leader of the Sachi people stood before her. Rieshi walked ceremoniously to her mother, her head down as she held a wooden bowl of white paint.

Everyone else gathered just outside the backdoor of the house, watching as she spoke.

"We are the protectors of this land." Gaiana dipped her fingers into the bowl and reached for Jen's forehead, painting a circle and two lines in a cross above her brows.

"Guide this child of Etheria as she crosses over into the elemental sphere."

She dipped her fingers again and took Jen's arm.

"Air."

White paint formed flowing lines that curved at the ends as a gust of wind. The tree that was carved with the same symbol glowed with recognition.

"Water."

Below the air markings, Gaiana drew pearl-white waves from wrist to elbow. Again, the tree with the matching symbol emitted a warm light from its carving.

She took the other arm.

"Earth."

Painted vines wrapped around Jen's bicep to her shoulder.

"Fire."

White flames appeared on her forearm.

One by one, the trees glowed as Gaiana painted the symbols onto Jen's skin. A trace amount of warmth returned to the Sachi leader's eyes, and she gently placed her hand on the small of Jen's back, guiding her to the edge of the circle.

"You will enter the elemental sphere," she murmured. "Once you are in the center, a barrier of sight will be placed around the perimeter. You will not be able to see us, but we can see you."

Jen was trembling. She looked back at the others, flushed against the walls of the house. Damien smiled at her, but concern swam within his gaze.

"We're right here, Bug."

She glanced over at Ronan and Samara, the latter giving an enthusiastic thumbs up. Ronan used his hand to mimic a deep breath, reminding her to do the same.

Her gaze returned to the circle before her and then drifted down to the markings on her arms.

"Open yourself up, and listen," Gaiana said quietly before shoving Jen across the line and into the circle.

Jen flung her hands out before she could wipe out on the damp ground. She regained her balance and looked over her shoulder just as a wave of pulsating magic swept around the grove, erasing her friends and Gaiana from sight.

Not only was she alone, but the sounds of nature; the flowing river, the birds in the trees, the cracking of branches—were gone, leaving the sound of her own breathing and a faint ringing in her ears; her mind's fabrication to swallow the silence.

What do I do now?

Jen took a few tentative steps into the middle of the circle, twigs and fallen leaves crunching under her bare feet. She looked around at each tree, searching for some kind of clue as to what she was supposed to do.

A small gasp escaped her.

A familiar thread wrapped itself around her and coaxed her forward. And then, a hum. The faint, melodious hum that had led her since she entered Etheria. It had found its way to her ear once more.

Open yourself up, and listen, Gaiana had said.

Jen closed her eyes and inhaled, allowing her lungs to fill before slowly releasing the breath. She let the hum guide her and the thread tug at her chest, turning her head as the forces grew stronger. Her eyes fluttered open to one of the trees.

Air.

She should have known it would be air. The gentle breezes and gusts of wind had all but spoken directly to her in the last week, an ever-moving source of kinship in an unfamiliar world.

Jen walked towards the wind chime that hung from a low branch into the circle. It was eerily still. Even without any wayward winds, Jen had never seen a wind chime hanging as though frozen in time.

Okay, what next?

She looked around as if Gaiana was going to pop out and walk her through this ludicrous test.

But Jen was on her own.

Her hand reached towards the silver chimes, her long fingers pausing just a breath away. Sweat collected along the skin of her palm and her heart threatened to break through her chest.

It's just a wind chime. Calm down.

Jen exhaled, and with her middle finger, she gently struck one of the dangling silver beams. It bounced against the others, erupting into a pleasant chorus of overlapping bell tones. Jen smiled, and the apprehension drained from her body.

She could manage this.

The tree began to vibrate, as if the frequencies of the chimes shook it to its roots. The leaves shuddered and reverberated as a stream of air flew around the low hanging branch that held the chime. The wind ricocheted through the silver beams before encircling her hand. It wove through the spaces of her fingers and swirled around her wrist, flowing over the painted symbol of its likeness on her arm. The tree carving lit up, and the dancing wind split into two streams, wrapping itself around her.

The air grew warm and heavy, the particles condensing until they shimmered with the golden light of the setting sun—magenta, burnt orange, violet—like brushstrokes painted across the air itself. She smiled broadly as the two streams swung her around the center of the circle, acting as an unseen dance partner.

The wind began to lose its pigment, retreating to the invisible force that Jen was familiar with. It guided her to the next tree, marked with the symbol for water.

She knelt before the basin, knowing immediately what she was going to do. With a devious smile, she placed her hand above the water, her palm facing the stillness below. Her eyes flickered shut and she quieted her mind.

The water began to stir and rose to slowly form a small column beneath her palm. She lifted her hand, molding the column into a sphere, before moving her hand underneath it, cradling it as it began to rotate above her fingertips.

In a flourish, she snapped her hand into a claw, the water shooting out into a small universe of droplets in the palm of her hand. The symbol on the tree illuminated as she came to her feet and blew on the droplets, they faded to mist and floated towards the third tree, etched with a carving of vines—earth.

Jen willed a stream of water from the basin to her hand, water and air becoming one as they wrapped around her like the coils of a snake.

She came before the pot of dirt and knelt, releasing the serpentine water. Her hand hovered for a moment, and before she realized what was happening, her hand warmed.

The glow. The faint white light.

From the barren soil, a green seedling sprouted and grew as if time accelerated, and the white petals of a lily bloomed into radiance, its strong aroma invading Jen's nostrils. Just like the moment in her garden, she reached for the silken petals.

Her heart seized, her body paralyzed with an onslaught of memories that laid siege to her mind.

The pulse. The morai. Her sisters. Her brother. Fjora. Lies. Rejection. Anger. Guilt. Fury. Pain.

And then something deeper barreled through her defenses.

Screams. Sobs. Fear. Violence. Abandonment. Rage. Rage. Rage.

The kindling at the fourth tree caught fire. Jen snapped out of the trance and rose before the flames, her chest heaving up and down with an unshakeable focus.

Her ears perked up, straining to hear the muffled voices coming from outside the circle, but she could barely make them out through the roaring in her ears.

"Goddess—" Rieshi breathed.

Then Damien's panicked voice cut through. "It's the fucking lily! Get her out of there!"

"She doesn't need anyone to *save her*," Ronan growled.

"The last time that damned flower showed up, the morai attacked our village, people *died*. It's what fucking started all of this!" She could hear him struggling, as if being held back.

A shuffle of feet, and then Ronan barked. "Keep him over here until the test is finished."

The voices fell away as the fire flashed within her eyes like a ring of scorched earth.

She stepped forward.

The flames grew wild, angrier, like it sensed her power as she drew near. The symbol on the tree glowed red and the fire *whooshed* towards the trunk and licked its way up the base.

She glanced down at her tingling fingers—the smoke had reappeared.

I wonder.

Jen lifted her hand in front of her face and coaxed out a drop of her rage, a mere tendril of an overwhelming shadow that bared down on her mind, but she held it back—and snapped her fingers.

A small flame ignited over her finger.

She stared at it, but before she could consider it further, a flurry of wind extinguished it like a candle.

Jen stumbled, her focus snapping back as her eyes widened in shock at the roaring fire consuming the tree. She flung her hand back to the basin of water and willed a stream of it to her, hurdling it at the inferno. It sizzled, doing next to nothing.

Her eyes darted to the lily.

Magic thrummed from the petals—an unknown power pulsating like a heartbeat.

An idea lanced through her muddy thoughts.

This had better work.

She sent a ribbon of wind around the lily and wrenched it from the soil, calling it to her before snapping her fingers and torching the silken petals.

Jen thrusted her hands forward, launching the lily ash into the air as she summoned a powerful torrent of air, slamming the ash against the tree.

The fire extinguished, billows of smoke spilling from the charred bark as the barrier around the ring fell away.

Her knees buckled, black splotches clouded her vision. Jen expected to crash onto the cold ground, but instead she fell into someone's arms.

Unkempt pastures, smoke from a blacksmith forge.

"Bug? *Bug?*" Damien shook her, his face contorted in panic.

He gathered her close, and as her vision returned, she spotted Emelie checking her for injuries or aches of any kind. If she was injured, she couldn't feel it. Her body was numb, perhaps a feeble attempt to shield her while it forced the rage back behind the wall.

Or maybe there was just an insane amount of magic coursing through her that her body had no idea how to reconcile.

She pressed her hand gently on Damien's chest.

"Careful," she grunted. "I'm delicate."

He choked on a ragged breath, and his head fell against hers. "Holy hells. You scared the fuck out of me," he said, kissing her head.

She breathed him in. "I like to keep everyone on their toes." Jen glanced around, "or on the ground, apparently."

Emelie held her hand, visibly relieved but still observing her closely. William and Leeyna stood behind her, looking on with concern.

Well, this is nice.

Gaiana appeared in front of her and handed Jen a glass of cold water. After a moment, the Sachi leader kneeled and took Jen's face in her hands.

Jen pushed her up and leaned against Damien's chest.

"Did I pass?"

Gaiana laughed. "You did far more than pass, my dear." There was an inexplicable shock in her eyes. "You are an iejja."

That…didn't answer my question.

Ronan wandered into the corner of her vision next to the charred tree. "You're certain?" he inquired as he considered the burnt branches.

"What is that?" Damien asked, his knuckles running up and down Jen's arm. She was grateful he was here to pose the questions she couldn't bring herself to ask.

"Manifester," Samara said, her voice almost a whisper.

Gaiana brushed her thumb over the painted circle on Jen's head. "Most of us who communicate with Taejja are wielders."

Rieshi stepped behind her mother. "Wielders are able to manipulate and harness an element of Taejja." She squeezed her mother's shoulder. "Only a powerful few are able to harness more than one." Gaiana smiled up at her daughter and squeezed her hand in return.

"Is that different from what I am?" Jen sat forward and rested her arms on her knees.

"A wielder is limited by the power of the element," Ronan explained from the tree. He turned to Jen and tapped his temple. "You are only limited by the power of your mind."

Great. Because my mind has been so reliable lately.

Gaiana pulled Jen to her feet. "You can call the elements to you, and they will behave and adhere to your commands and desires."

My desire is to summon the earth to swallow me whole.

"During the age of the Aylaenor, an iejja was personally selected and blessed by the Fates." She walked in step with Jen and led everyone back inside the house. "Since their departure from our world, there has been record of only one other iejja having existed, you are exceedingly *rare*."

Jen fought the urge to groan as she followed her up the spiral stairs to change out of the chemise. "What does that mean?" she asked as she pulled the loose white fabric over her head.

"It means you could have *absolutely* set Samara on fire," Ronan called as he clasped Samara's shoulders on the way into the house. She punched him.

"*Ouch*, I was kidding, sort of."

Gaiana chuckled and she handed Jen her tunic.

"It *means* that starting tomorrow, you will come to train with me. You will need help in harnessing and controlling that amount of power."

Jen was so overwhelmed by the notion of being some kind of rare magical manifester that all she could muster was a nod.

"Excellent. We will start tomorrow afternoon. For now—" She guided her back down the steps into the waiting arms of Damien. "She needs to rest," she said.

He nodded as he coaxed Jen towards the front door. They were almost down the pathway when she realized something.

"Wait!"

Gaiana and Rieshi stepped out of the doorway, eyebrows raised in curiosity.

"The council—"

Gaiana let out a cackle. "Oh, that. That was always a yes. My great-grandmother would come back from the Beyond and beat me senseless if I denied you."

With that, they disappeared into the house.

Jen was almost taken aback at how easy that was. No mystical horse calling, no painfully difficult dinner—

Samara passed by her as they made their way back to the main street. She winked.

"Told you."

Jen tried to conceal her fragile state when they reached the stables, swatting Damien's hands away when he reached up to help her dismount, but she ended up practically falling into him.

"I've got it," she mumbled.

He grabbed her waist to steady her. "If you say so." But his expression told her he was nervous to let her walk by herself, like even a whisper of a breeze would knock her over.

She stepped out of his grip and started back towards the palace. Something flaked between her eyebrows. Reaching up, she felt the dry, crusted, painted circle underneath her fingers.

She stretched her arms out in front of her and scowled at the swirls of paint that adorned them, realizing she was walking towards a palace of courtiers who already thought she was odd.

Now, she looked like a sacrificial virgin.

Why didn't I ask Gaiana for a rag or something? Why didn't it occur to me to wash off the paint?

She attempted to rub it off as she trudged up the stairs and into the palace, leaving a flurry of white flecks behind her. Completely consumed by her thoughts and, also, wanting to avoid the sneers and judgment of anyone in the vicinity, she didn't bother to look up until she was a fair way inside.

"Jenevieve?"

The warm, familiar voice stopped her dead in her tracks.

Jen slowly lifted her gaze from the floor.

Her breath caught in her throat.

Fjora.

CHAPTER 25

Jen took an instinctive step back, but her trembling limbs ended up pressed against Damien, who became deathly still behind her. Emelie, William and Leeyna gathered at his back, unease pulsating from them.

The last time she thought she'd seen Fjora, it was a dhoksha. She watched it die with an arrow in its chest.

This had to be another trick. Somehow, she'd been tracked, even with the stone in her pocket. Jen glanced at Samara. She subtly shook her head.

This wasn't a dhoksha.

"Bug," Damien whispered over her shoulder. "Look," urging her to look back at Fjora.

She heard them before she saw them. Three sets of quiet feet padded across the marble floor and stood behind Fjora. Her eyes widened at the sight of them.

Darya.

Rhea.

Jamie.

Emelie gasped quietly as Jen took a small step forward, holding on tightly to Damien's hand. Fjora smiled and reached her arms out from beneath her cloak.

"Darling."

A choked sob ripped from Jen's throat, and she crumpled to the ground. Fjora was already moving, her siblings close behind. They dropped to the floor, pulling her between them in a mess of tears and soft laughter.

They made it out. For the last week she had lived every moment with the crushing thought that they were dead. That she would never hear her brother's laughter or fight with her sisters.

They were alive.

Fjora cupped Jen's face and rubbed her cheeks with the pads of her thumbs. Her eyes glimpsed the painted circle, and her gaze filled with pride.

"You were tested." There was no question, just an adoring observation.

Jen looked up at the circle, a bit cross eyed, before speaking through a sniffle. "Just now, actually."

Samara stepped towards the huddled group on the floor.

"She's an *iejja*," she said as she bowed. "Your Highness."

Fjora's eyes snapped to Samara and then back to Jen. "Wha—"

But Jen found herself staring at the shocked woman before her. The fine lines and wrinkles that held the years of their life in Nimea were gone. And there were no signs of grey in her ash-blonde hair, just lustrous blonde locks and a youthful glow.

They looked the same age.

She reached up and ran her thumb down Fjora's temple, where a wrinkle once lived.

"I think you have some explaining to do, *Your Highness*."

Fjora smiled and helped Jen to her feet. She launched herself at Jamie, embracing her baby brother tightly. Damien and Emelie jumped in and took each of them into their shaking arms.

Jen returned to Fjora, holding her hands tightly.

"How did you—"

Fjora stroked her cheek as the greetings and embraces around them reached William and Leeyna with strings of kind words and animated explanations from her family.

"I will explain everything, but first I must—"

"Fjora."

Everyone's eyes shot up to the balcony. Bastien stood with his hand clenching the golden railing. When his eyes locked on her, he took an instinctive step back, just as Jen had.

"Hello Bas," she said, her voice echoing off the walls.

He walked slowly down the marble stairs like he was afraid she would evaporate if he moved too quickly, while Fjora broke away from Jen and the others.

His pace quickened as he neared her, and she matched him just the same. Bastien jumped a few steps from the bottom and scooped a laughing Fjora into his arms, swinging her feet clean off the ground.

He put her down and grabbed her face, his eyes wide and wild.

"How—*How*—" Tears welled in his eyes. "Call for the king! Immediately!" he ordered the guards by the entrance of the hall. He turned back to her, a tear falling down his cheek. "I thought you were—Fjora, I'm so sorry."

Fjora gazed up at the man that was more her brother than any other title he held. "No, *I'm* sorry Bas. I never wanted to put you through this."

"We tried to find you—we looked everywhere—Nimea?!" He sputtered, stroking her thick ash-blonde plait.

"Everything happened so fast." Fjora placed her calming hands on his chest, her eyes looking down at her boots. "There was no time to send word—it was too dangerous."

Bastien placed his finger under her chin and looked at her, his eyes still not quite believing it. "You're here now." He kissed her forehead. "You're safe." He brought her into his arms. "You're home."

His brows cinched at the young people who appeared behind her. "Who have we here?" he said, attempting to sound casual.

She threaded her arm through his and led him over. "Bastien, these are my children." Fjora smiled nervously.

She walked over and put her arm around Darya. He couldn't hide his shock as his gaze moved to each of them until they landed on Jen, who had her hand around Jamie's arm. She gave him a small nod.

"Children…" he said in almost a whisper.

Fjora caressed Darya's cheek.

"This is Darya," she said. She pointed her chin. "Rhea." Jen leaned her head on her brother's arm as Fjora gestured to him.

"And my son, Jamie."

Bastien considered each of them, attempting not to appear too shaken by this revelation. His eyebrows raised suddenly as if he had a striking thought.

"Children—so, you have a husband? Is he with you?" he asked, glancing around the hall as if someone would appear around one of the columns claiming that title.

Jen looked sadly at her siblings, who stared at their shoes.

Fjora shook her head. "Not anymore."

Bastien took in the flashes of regret in her eyes, and the evasive looks of her family. He reached out to her. "It sounds like you have a lot to tell me."

"I do, and I will," she said, clasping his hand. "But I—my parents—" She glanced up the stairs. The king had not arrived yet.

Bastien flicked his gaze to Jen for a moment, who knew exactly what he was struggling to tell Fjora.

Her mother.

How does he tell her the queen is dead?

Fjora noticed the exchanged looks between them.

"What's going on?

The guard Bastien had sent earlier appeared at the balcony. He shook his head. The king was not coming.

Fjora scoffed. She pushed past Bastien and stomped up the stairs, her cloak sweeping the ground behind her. Jen and her siblings followed suit, leaving Bastien blindsided at the foot of the stairs.

"Wait! Fjora, hang on!" he shouted, scrambling to catch up with them.

Jen hastened to her mother's side. "There's something you should—"

"No, Jenevieve. I need to see for myself."

She spoke in a tone that Jen did not recognize. It was strong, sharp. The sound of a spitfire princess who was determined and unrelenting. Nothing like the docile, maternal voice Jen had grown up hearing.

Fjora arrived at the tall, ornate wooden doors of the king's private residence, her family halting right on her heels. The guards that stood on either side looked at her as if she were a ghost.

"Open the doors," she ordered. Shock paralyzed them, but Fjora was undeterred.

"NOW."

It was a command from the heir to the throne. They did not hesitate to obey her this time. Bastien had just made it up the stairs. "Fjora—" he pleaded breathlessly.

Fjora raised her chin and marched into the suite, not even bothering to wait for the doors to be fully opened. Her regal stride faltered the moment she entered the room. She threw her arm out to stop her family from going any further.

It was mourning personified.

The room was sullen, as if all of the happiness and life had been sucked out by the Goddess of Darkness herself. The columns that held up the beautiful, open veranda had been hung with heavy, black velvet curtains. They snuffed out any breath of light or awareness of the outside world.

The air was stale. It smelled of old food and forsaken hope, the only reprieve being the roaring fire of the massive stone hearth. But even that made the room feel almost too warm—heavy with grief.

Fjora looked around the room, dreading the suspicion that was now confirmed as truth. Black banners hung from the ceiling, mourning clothes piled on the deep emerald sofas and strewn about the floor.

The fact that she had not been tearfully greeted as she'd entered her parents' room.

Her mother was dead.

She knew it in her bones.

Her blood turned to ice as Bastien quietly came up beside her. She glanced at him out of the corner of her eye. He lowered his head in sorrowful confirmation.

"When…" she breathed.

He turned towards her. "Two years ago," he whispered, his voice somber.

Fjora's gaze found the massive emerald armchair that sat in front of the hearth. Sitting in it was a slumped over figure, seemingly asleep, the light of the flames casting shadows on his face.

"He's been like this ever since?" she said quietly, fighting back tears.

Bastien nodded.

"Losing you, and then your mother…it was too much. He's not the man you remember, Fjora."

She wouldn't—couldn't—believe that. She couldn't accept that her father had just given up living. He had always radiated with a passion for life and pulsated joy and laughter. He didn't belong in a tomb of his own making. She would not allow that.

She was home.

Fjora glided quietly across the room. When Bastien and her family attempted to follow, she raised her hand—a silent command to let her go alone.

She walked past the walls of bookshelves; all shrouded in darkness. Her feet hit the emerald and green carpet that covered the center of the room, evoking childhood memories of playing with her parents on the soft fibers. She lifted her chin away from the floor as she found herself a few feet from the armchair—and her father.

Her heart was beating as fast as a hummingbird and her eyes burned. It had been thirty years since she had seen him. She had resolved to never see him again in this life. And yet, here he was, asleep in his favorite chair.

His black shirt and pants seemed disheveled, and the small streaks of gray in his hair glowed in the fire's light.

His chest moved slowly up and down, lost in dreams of a sad and lonely existence.

Fjora knelt in front of her father, and she willed her trembling hand gently onto his knee. "Papa," she whispered.

Nothing.

She carefully shook his knee, attempting to coax him awake.

"Papa," she said a bit louder.

He stirred.

"I'm—I'm home."

His bleary eyes opened one at a time, but not fully. A sleepy grin spread across his face, and he lifted his heavy hand to her cheek.

"Goddess has seen fit to give me a beautiful dream tonight," he murmured, his eyes becoming heavy again.

Fjora placed her hand on his, tears pooling in her eyes.

"It's not a dream."

He blinked. His thumb caressed her cheek, as if assessing the flesh he touched.

"No." He tried to pull his hand away. "Goddess taunts me with a vision of my child."

Fjora pulled his hand back to her face and reached into the bodice of her dress. She pulled out the necklace she wore, a gold chain with a simple emerald encased within delicate golden wings. Her mother had worn the same one.

He sucked in a breath.

"It's me, Papa," she said, running her thumb over his hand. "Goddess doesn't taunt you. She brought me back to you."

Tears fell silently from the king's eyes.

"*Mo—mo shaali.*"

She nodded, her eyes burning.

A desolate cry erupted from Haythem. He slid off the armchair and onto the floor in front of his child, his hands frantically touching every inch of her face.

Fjora let the tears fall and her father was there to embrace her, laughing through each sob that racked their bodies.

"I missed you every day," she whispered through her tears. "I'm sorry, Papa. I'm so sorry."

He kissed her hair and rubbed her back to sooth her. "Oh, *mo shaali*—my darling. My brave, strong child. My heart cannot bear your apologies."

A throat cleared behind them.

The king jolted when Jen and four others appeared behind his daughter. Fjora looked lovingly at them before turning back to her father.

"Papa, you've met Jenevieve already?"

Haythem gazed at Jen, his eyes lacing with regret and apologies. A compassionate smile bloomed on her lips. He glanced back at his daughter and nodded.

"Well, these are the rest of my children, your grandchildren."

Haythem struggled to his feet, bringing Fjora with him. He hadn't let go of her since she knelt by his chair. He struggled to find the words, but Jen could see the warmth awakening behind his eyes. The dullness that plagued them was melting away as his family came before the fire to greet him.

He kissed the cheeks of his granddaughters. He shook hands with his grandson. But he never let go of Fjora's hand.

She leaned her head on her father's shoulder as Jen padded across the room to one of the heavy curtains blocking the setting sun.

"What do we think?" Jen asked. "Should we let in some light?"

And she yanked the curtain down to the floor.

CHAPTER 26

Every heavy curtain came down, restoring a bit of light and fresh air to the room, and with it, life returned to the king. He called for a comically large amount of food to be sent up from the kitchens, while Fjora gathered everyone onto the balcony. There were plates laid out, piled with roast turkey, herbed potatoes, and a myriad of sauteed greens.

They drank wine from crystal glasses and watched the sky melt into the magenta and orange of the Etherian sunset.

The conversation was stilted but filled with warmth and love as Haythem slowly emerged from his grief laden shell.

Still, the king did not let go of his daughter's hand, which made it impossible for either of them to eat anything, though neither of them seemed to notice.

Fjora held her father's hand just as tightly as he did hers.

Jen imagined that neither of them believed they would ever have a moment like this again—that they were both afraid to let go, as if it were only a beautiful dream they might soon wake from.

She glanced at Rhea, Darya and Jamie sitting around the veranda. It was uncanny how much they looked like the king, Fjora's resemblance even more striking.

They looked like a family.

A royal family.

The bloodline of the Sachandan throne sat before her, and suddenly Jen found herself peering in through a window at a life that she was not a part of. At a family that was not hers.

Nothing in her life was ever meant to be hers, save for the loneliness that had crept its way into her mind and wrapped itself around her heart. Save for the darkness she had gained from her father that now resided behind the stone wall.

He wasn't her father. Gods. That should have given her some kind of relief, but instead a flash of anger rippled under her skin. She had protected her family for nothing. Shielded them for nothing. Allowed herself to be shattered into pieces, for nothing.

"Darling," her head snapped up and found Fjora watching her. "Everything alright?"

Jen painted a soft smile on her lips. "I'm just happy for you," she glanced at her siblings. "And you as well."

Jealousy wove itself within the threads of loneliness and threatened to strangle her, but Jen swallowed it and shoved it away.

When the wine ran out, Haythem led Fjora and his grandchildren to her old apartment down the hall, which had remained untouched since her departure.

Jen took that opportunity to slip away, her warring emotions fighting against the back of her skull, a throbbing headache settling in.

She walked along the hall and down the grand stairs towards her room. She was, of course, relieved that her family was safe and where she could watch over them—and that they had a loving grandfather who was a king, and a mother who was *actually* their mother, and a palace to live in, and a future that looked bright and shiny and filled with endless possibilities.

Her jealousy bubbled up again in her throat.

Stop it, Jen. They deserve to be happy.

For her entire life, the happiness of her family and those she cared about had come before her own, because that was how she wanted it. Why was she allowing her own loneliness to tarnish this moment that her family sorely needed?

Because she had nothing now, save for the scars that no one sees, save for that stone wall in her mind that struggles to keep the shadows from looming over her thoughts.

She walked into her room and closed the door, leaning back against it with a labored sigh. But then—her body jerked to attention.

Something was off.

A strange stillness pervaded the room, as if the air was suspended by spools of invisible thread. Even the sheer curtains that hung from the columns found an unsettling silence.

She padded slowly across the floor, cautiously searching for the source of discontent. Everything seemed to be where she left—

Her gaze shifted to the vanity beside the veranda. To her hairbrush, sitting on the wrong side of its dark wooden surface.

That's not where I left it.

She inched her way towards it.

Maybe Shyra moved it while I was gone…

But she saw no other evidence that Shyra had even been in the room since she left that afternoon.

Her heart thrummed in her ears, there was something strange and alluring about the brush, and her hand instinctively reached for it until her fingertips were all but touching the ornate handle.

Cold, golden metal met her hand.

A distorted ring tore through her ears and grated against her mind, and she stumbled forward with a wince. A flash of blinding light flooded her vision.

Jen was flung to the ground.

She whipped around onto her elbows and realized quickly that she was no longer in her room. Her arms scraped against rough stone, and a circle of insidious flames roared around her.

She was trapped.

Her gaze shifted along the stone floor and stopped. She broke out in a cold sweat. A pair of heavy worn boots stood just a few feet away.

She knew those boots.

Dread pooled in the pit of her stomach, her eyes working their way up to settle on the figure's face.

No.

Long before she entered Etheria, he had been the face of her nightmares. Her reason for erecting her wall of protection, her reason for throwing herself in front of her family. This was the face that haunted her before the dark creatures and ominous voices.

Childlike fear threatened to drown her. She was a young girl again, cowering on the ground under the terrifying, wild eyes of her father.

His harsh, angular face contorted with violent rage.

"You fucking bitch," he snapped.

Jen started to crawl back but splitting pain erupted from her back. "AHHH," she cried. She reached behind her and brought her shaking hand to her face.

She was bleeding.

She looked down and found herself in a cream-colored linen gown. But it was ripped to shreds, dirt and blood smeared over the fabric.

He stomped towards her, his boots landing heavily on the ground, sending trembles through her body. "Papa, please—" she begged.

She looked around frantically, but there was nothing there. "Mama," she tried to whimper, but nothing came out, as though fear had rendered her vocal cords useless.

Tears pricked in the corners of her eyes. She knew how this ended. He would break her. He would destroy her. He would ignite a rage she would never learn to control and leave her with scars that would never heal.

It would be so easy. A disjointed voice whispered just above her ear. She snapped her head towards it, but there was no one there.

Let the darkness in Jenevieve. You could stop him. The voice came again, but this time it brought something with it, and her hand was suddenly wrapped around cold stone.

A hilt.

She looked down, the tiishara in her grasp.

You should have protected them.

Guilt thrummed in her bones.

She tightened her grip on the hilt and struggled to her feet, shuddering at the phantom wounds. She bent low in her thighs, angling her feet into a fighting stance.

You failed them.

Her eyes swung to the vicious man in front of her. He laughed. "Are you going to kill me, daughter?"

Blazing hot fury pierced through her. He was panting like a rabid hound, more animal than human.

And she could put him down.

"Jenevieve? Jenevieve?"

A different voice crashed through the ring.

"Come back. Hey."

She shook the voice from her head and lifted the dagger, but her father was already charging at her, his body moving like a disjointed puppet.

Visceral fear ripped through her as she let out a desperate cry, her dagger slicing through the air—

"WHOA!"

A strong hand wrapped around her wrist.

The ring of fire and her father disappeared as her vision cleared.

She was in her room.

No blood. No flames. No father.

Air flooded her lungs, and she heaved in breaths like she had just come up for air after nearly drowning. Her eyes caught the dagger and the hand firmly holding her wrist above her head.

"Ronan?" she choked.

He stood within an inch of her face; she smelled wildflowers and soil just before a storm. He was real, and so was his hand firmly planted on her waist.

For a moment, his eyes flickered with concern, searching her face for signs of life, his thumb caressed her hip and his lips parted slightly as if he wanted to say something. But instead, an arrogant smirk slipped into place.

His eyes peered up at the dagger.

"I know I'm an arrogant bastard, but stabbing me is a little dramatic, don't you think?"

Jen's hand went slack, and the dagger fell to the ground with a loud clash against the marble floor. Her body trembled, struggling to pull her back to reality.

Ronan tilted his head, watching her inner battle within the hazel hue of her eyes. When it was clear she wasn't going to move, he let go of her, bending down to pick up the dagger, his eyes never leaving hers.

Jen glanced towards the veranda, where the curtains had returned to their billowing movements in the evening breeze.

Her eyes widened—she must still be dreaming.

A hooded figure stood in the shadows behind one of the sheer emerald curtains. The bottom half of his face contorted in a jeering grin.

Jen clapped her hands to her mouth and stumbled back in terror. Ronan shot up from the ground and whirled towards the balcony. He was out at the columns before Jen even realized he moved, searching the area, the dagger posed to strike.

Ronan slowly prowled back into the room, his eyes taking in every corner of the space. He paused at the vanity and looked down at the hairbrush. His eyes narrowed.

"It's been cursed."

Jen sank onto the edge of her bed and clung to the edge of the mattress. "What?"

He carefully plucked one of her hairs from the bristles and examined it in the light of the chandelier above them.

"Whoever spelled it used your hair."

Her face grew hot while her skin grew clammy. She squeezed her eyes shut as her breathing grew shallow, her lungs fighting to take a full inhale.

Why is this happening?

When she opened her eyes, Ronan was standing in front of her. He crouched down and placed the dagger on the sheets beside her, and then his cool hands found the overheated skin of her cheeks.

"Breathe. *Breathe.* You're safe."

He placed one of his hands over her heart and inhaled slowly, silently commanding her to breathe with him. Jen forced the air through her nose and out through her mouth, her chest rising and falling against his hand.

Before she realized what she was doing, she placed her own hand over his heart, matching her breath with his, feeling his strong heartbeat beneath her fingers. Something rolled over Ronan's expression, but he stayed still.

Together they breathed until her heart returned to normal and the heat left her skin.

Ronan lowered his hands and rested his forearms on his knees. He glanced at the brush.

"What did the curse provoke?"

Jen ran her hand through her knotted hair.

"Nothing…it was nothing."

He arched a brow. "That nothing tried to *stab* me."

She whipped her head towards him. "I'm so sorry. It wasn't *you* I was seeing—in there." She waved her hand at the vanity.

He reached up and tucked a strand of hair behind her ear. "Do you want to tell me who it was?"

She bit her bottom lip. A part of her did. A part of her wanted to share who was in that terrifying ring of fire, to confide in Ronan as she had Damien and Emelie. But speaking those words made it feel far too real, and the realization that her father had followed her here, that he still haunted her, was too much to reconcile.

And I don't need anyone else to know that broken part of me.

Ronan rubbed the back of his neck, a small, emphatic grin tugged at his lips.

"It's alright. I understand," he said as he stood back up. Jen didn't know why, but she believed his empathy. Somehow, she felt it.

He was being kind.

This day is getting scarier by the second.

"Why would someone curse me?" she asked quietly, her eyes darting back to her vanity. Ronan leaned on the column behind it, his brows furrowed in serious thought.

"It seems someone wanted to lure you."

"To what...?"

"To give into darkness. They probably wanted to see how easily they could sway you, and they did it by using your own mind against you."

Jen looked down at her hands. She had fallen prey to it so quickly and hadn't even put up a real fight. Every day she felt her mental defenses slipping under the weight of a new and frightening power or threat either within her or against her, the integrity of the stone wall waned under the constant rattling of her increasingly unmanageable inner turmoil.

She was exhausted.

"I can't possibly be that important," Jen said, almost to herself.

Ronan pushed off the column and pulled out the chair in front of the vanity. He sat down and glared at her.

"I'm going to ignore the 'I'm not important' bull shit for now," he said through gritted teeth. He ran a hand through his hair. "You came blazing out of Nimea after the pulse came early. You are in the bloodline, you ride a Rhionnen mare." He blew out a heavy breath as if his next words blew his mind. "And you are an *iejja.*"

He rubbed his hand over his face.

"Gaiana said that Etheria awoke when you returned." He leaned back in his chair, a ghost of something painful flickering over his face. "Not all of Etheria is good." He glanced back at the brush. "Some of it is darker than your most insidious nightmares."

His tan skin grew pale like hers and his jaw clenched under the weight of his thoughts.

Jen bit her lip. "I don't...want to burden anyone with this."

Ronan huffed a laugh, running a thumb along his jaw. "Again, I'm going to ignore the self-deprecating shit—for now. But I won't share what happened here with anyone, not unless you ask me to."

"Thank you," she said quietly, her hands fiddling in her lap.

His eyes lowered to the pouch on her hip. "You still have it?"

Jen nodded.

"The stone should continue to conceal you," he said, pointing his chin at the tiishara. "Find a new place to hide that. Someone clearly knows about the bloodline, and we don't want them to get anywhere near it."

"We?" Jen said, her head lifting to meet his gaze.

"Don't get sentimental—I'd just like to avoid being stabbed."

She rolled her eyes at the return of smug arrogance in his voice. Gone were the gentle concern and unsettling empathy, he was back to his regular, infuriating self.

He took a few steps towards the door. "I'll do my best to find a way to protect your room from any… unwanted guests."

The bedroom door flew open with a whoosh of tulle and chiffon and a collection of pained grunts. Ronan raised his brows in fleeting surprise as Shyra came barreling into the room with a ridiculous pile of ball gowns. She dropped them on the plush armchair and nearly jumped out of her skin when she saw that she wasn't alone.

"OH! Goddess, save me, I didn't see you Miss Jenevieve," She turned nervously to Ronan. "Lord Ronan."

He winced at the sound of 'Lord.'

Shyra looked Jen up and down. "Miss Jenevieve, you—ehem— well—I'm going to—umm —draw you a bath," she sputtered before scurrying into the bathing room.

Jen looked down at herself. She was covered in dirt, flecks of white paint, and caked dust from the king's suite. She hadn't changed since coming back from Gaiana's.

Ronan snorted.

"I didn't have the heart to point out, well." He gestured to her. "We were having such a nice moment."

He strode towards the door, stopping at the armchair and the pile of appliques and absurdities. "Ah, right. The Ball of the Forgotten, to honor the lost princess. It's in a few days, although—" He frowned as he lifted a particularly garish piece of orange chiffon. "I suppose it's The Ball of the Found, now? Doesn't have the same ring to it, does it?" He dropped the chiffon as if it bit him and pointed at it with a scowl. "Not that one."

He left the pile of tulle and continued to the door. "I'll send for Damien, I'm sure he'll love the opportunity to protect you from any monsters under the bed."

Jen scoffed loudly and hurled a pillow at him, missing, but not by much. He smirked as he opened the door, glancing back over his shoulder.

"There she is."

And he was gone.

CHAPTER 27

"**O**uch."

Shyra whipped around Jen in a blur of excitement. She was hand sewing several more colorful lace appliques onto the ball gown that Jen found herself trapped in, and she wasn't being gentle.

Trapped was a strong word choice. She had picked this gown after Shyra forced her to model almost a dozen other—louder, options after Ronan left the room a few days ago.

She was wrapped in layers of flowing mint green and jade chiffon. The delicate cap sleeves held up the boned corset bodice, more soft green chiffon concealing the bodice in an elegant cross down to her waist.

Jen had never worn a corset before, and although she enjoyed the curves it created, she was pretty sure she would be passed out on the ballroom floor before the evening concluded.

Breathing must not be considered essential here.

"This color is splendid on you," Shyra beamed, finishing with the last applique. She steered Jen to the vanity to fix her hair, picking up a silver hairbrush.

"This is new?"

Jen's eyes widened slightly before quickly scrounging for a believable excuse.

"The other one broke," she said nonchalantly.

The other, cursed, brush is indeed broken—on the side of the mountain...where I chucked it.

Shyra eyed it suspiciously before picking it up. She began brushing back smooth waves of hair into elegant pins, leaving it mostly down. Jen watched her work in the reflection of the mirror.

"So, the Ball of the Forgotten, it was to honor Fjora?" she asked, in desperate need to fill the silence.

Shyra smiled.

"Mhm. After she disappeared, the king and queen refused to hold a royal funeral. Instead, they held a ball. They had all their guests release hundreds of golden lanterns into the sky in the hopes that if she was out there, perhaps she would see them and come home. It's really, quite beautiful to see them floating over the mountain peaks. I used to watch from my village as a child," she explained.

She put down the brush and opened the jewelry box next to the mirror, retrieving a pair of gold teardrop earrings and a necklace to match.

"After a few years, the ball took on a life of its own. People started using it to honor their *own* lost loved ones, so they, too, are never forgotten."

Shyra's eyes grew wistful as she clasped the necklace at the nape of Jen's neck. "But we also celebrate that we are still here, the ones who carry on their memory," she said, placing a hand on Jen's shoulder.

Jen found her gaze in the mirror. "Will you be honoring someone tonight?"

Shyra nodded. "I release a lantern for my father."

Jen reached up and squeezed her hand in return. She understood what the loss of a father felt like. In more than one way, unfortunately. They shared a quiet moment before Shyra laughed softly through a sniffle.

"Oh, Goddess. This isn't the time for such sad conversations!" She grabbed Jen's hands and pulled her from her seat. "You look incredible!"

She spun her in a playful circle, fluffing the skirts as Jen laughed softly and followed the momentum of the gown.

"That she does."

Jen stopped spinning and looked towards the open doorway. Damien stood in a sunset orange tunic, his hair combed out of his face, the winter-sky of his eyes even brighter than usual.

The corner of her mouth pulled up in a smirk. "You don't look bad yourself, Sparky."

Damien hadn't left her side since Ronan retrieved him a few nights ago, but even then, she had only told him about the vision, not that someone had entered her room and cursed one of her belongings. That deep rooted fear of being a burden prevented her from mentioning it to anyone, even him.

She pranced over to the vanity and retrieved her stone, placing it in the bodice of her gown. Damien leaned against the door frame, his gaze fixing on her as she crossed the room.

His eyes were striking against the color of his tunic; it almost took her breath away. He gave her a devilish grin, like he knew what she was thinking.

"Am I making you swoon, Bug?"

Jen rolled her eyes.

"Every minute of every day."

His head fell back in a warm, explosive laugh, her favorite, and then he offered his arm to her. He kissed her on the cheek as she took it. "You really do look incredible," he whispered, his nose nuzzling her ear.

They passed through the great hall and into the courtyard. The weapons and training gear were now out of sight—not quite the aesthetic for an elegant ball. Damien led her under the archway into the adjoining hall.

"Hey!" a voice yelled from the courtyard. "Wait up!"

Emelie ran through the archway, her cerulean tulle skirts sweeping the floor behind her. She was wrapped in the same color Gaiana had sensed, the aura of healing. But there was nothing *healing* about her when she rammed into Jen.

Oof.

"Damien," Emelie gasped, giving him a once over. "Is there really a blacksmith under there?"

He wrinkled his nose as he laced Jen's arm back through his.

"You look great too, Em," he said, offering his other arm.

The three of them moved through the secondary hall, where a set of open, floor-to-ceiling doors revealed the grand ballroom beyond. Damien attempted to weave them through the crowd of courtiers; all dressed in bright colors and elegant fabrics as they glided around the room to greet one another.

Jen caught sight of Margo, in another seductive number, this one a deep royal purple with silver chains draping over her shoulders and down her chest. Next to her stood the ever-stunning Lyla, in a beautiful tulle gown that made her look like a sunset, layers of warm yellows and burnt orange framing her in a ray of light.

They walked through the doors to a landing at the top of a grand marble staircase, the ballroom stretched out before them. Marble floors were lined with grand columns that held up the ceiling where half a dozen golden chandeliers bathed the room in warm light. Long banners hung between the chandeliers, alternating in emerald green and gold.

A massive veranda jutted out into the cool evening sky on both sides, one looking out to the never-ending Etherian landscape, the other to the bustling streets of Quoxana. Both were filled to the brim with stunning arrangements of deep orange flowers laced with green and gold ribbons. Piles of flattened lanterns awaited in every corner.

In the middle of the room, around which the dancing and socializing orbited, was a majestic golden statue, melded into the shape of a mighty condor with its wings extended towards the sky.

Jen descended the stairs with Damien and Emelie, passing several couples who were already out on the dancefloor as dozens of gowns spun in an effervescent waltz.

"Jen!"

William and Leeyna waved them over from a tucked away corner of the room. Jen breathed a small sigh of relief at the secluded spot.

She let go of Damien to hug Leeyna, who dazzled in a stunning off-the-shoulder gown of scalloped lavender chiffon.

"Where have you two been?" Emelie teased as she released William from a tight embrace.

"Ronan's been dragging me to the libraries—not that I'm complaining."

"And I've been out at the stables," Leeyna added, looking out into the valley on the other side of the veranda. "I don't know. I can't be inside all day," she said, fiddling with her fingers.

"She's been very one with nature, lately."

Jen jumped when Samara appeared behind her.

"Are you just skulking around the palace watching us?" Damien leaned against the wall beside Jen.

"Yes, there's nothing I would rather be doing," she waved her hand in their direction.

"Your concern is so touching," Emelie said, her head falling dramatically on Samara's shoulder.

Samara awkwardly patted the top of her head.

"What are you and Ronan looking for in the library?" Damien asked. He hooked his finger around Jen's wrist and pulled her to him. She raised her brow in surprise but nestled into his chest.

"He's had us scouring the stacks for anything on the pulse and all sorts of curses, he's been a bit insufferable about it, actually," William said.

Ronan kept his word...he hasn't told anyone.

"What have you found?" Jen asked, a little too insistent. Damien glanced at her, his fingers digging into her waist.

"Well—"

"Anything about the curses?"

"Umm…" William scratched his head uncomfortably.

"Easy Jen, we're at a party," Damien said, tugging her hand. She hadn't realized she moved so close to William. She took a quick step back and rubbed her temples.

"I'm sorry." Her eyes trailed around her circle of friends. "I'm just exhausted, I'm not myself." Damien's fingers relaxed and moved to rub her back.

Yes. Harass your friend at a ball because you're so desperate to know why someone cursed you. Good job, Jen.

The orchestra finished the last note of the previous waltz, the room filling with the sounds of polite applause and crinkling chiffon as the courtiers and guests found their next partners or wandered off to gossip on one of the balconies.

Jen looked towards the musicians, lost in thought, and watched the strings re-tuning in preparation for the next round of dances. When she turned back, her eyes flickered down to Damien's hand outstretched and waiting for her.

She peered up, and her heart nearly stumbled at the affection in his gaze. He raised a thick brow in a question. Jen glanced back down, and after a moment, she placed her hand in his. He gently traced his thumb over her knuckles as they walked out onto the dance floor.

She looked over her shoulder to see her friends watching them, bittersweet nostalgia hanging over them like the cloudy mist of another life. Emelie even fanned herself to complete the memory.

Damien wrapped one of his arms around her waist. He pulled her close, eliciting a small gasp from her. She looked around to see the other courtiers glancing over at them.

"People are staring at us," she said quietly.

He pulled her closer, his nose dipping to her ear. "It's just you and me," he whispered. "Two people enjoying a dance. Let them stare."

Her lips parted in recognition as he pulled back. Rhea's wedding, before everything they knew about the world came crashing down.

Damien squeezed the hand that rested in his as the music began.

Jen stiffened. "Wait, we don't know this dance."

Damien gave her a lop-sided grin. "Then we'll create our own."

And he began to move, bringing her with him.

The violins and cellos coaxed the guests into another waltz, the melody ascending into an upbeat jaunt that filled the dance floor with an effervescent spirit.

Damien swung her around, loosely fitting into the basic steps of the waltz. Her body began to relax as they turned about the room. They stepped on each other's feet and bumped into other couples, but soon the rest of the ballroom fell away as Jen let herself laugh.

Damien spun her and yanked her flush against him.

"That's my favorite sound."

"My laugh?"

He moved them into a clumsy turn, attempting to follow the other dancers. "Your *happiness*."

Her cheeks warmed under his gaze, but something shifted behind his eyes. "Which is why I know there's something you haven't told me." He spun her again. When she returned to his arms, a rush of guilt betrayed her body.

She sighed.

"I wasn't completely honest about the vision."

Damien's shoulders grew tense as they continued turning. She looked away, opting to let her eyes fix on the walls rather than look him in the eye.

"I *did* have a vision… but it—"

BOOM.

BOOM.

BOOM.

Their attention snapped up to the top of the grand stairs. Two guards standing on either side of the balcony had slammed their golden staves into the floor, halting all movement and conversation instantaneously. Anticipation grew palpable as everyone waited.

Two figures slowly glided through the doors. Jen smiled when she saw them.

Fjora on the arm of King Haythem.

The hall erupted into quiet gasps and whispers.

They stood stoically at the top of the stairs. Fjora looked absolutely royal, donning an emerald-green gown of satin, with flowing skirts billowing out from the bodice and embroidered with swirls of gold along with the sleeves that wrapped around her slender arms.

Her hair was pinned into a romantic bun at the nape of her neck, stray curls framed her face, and an emerald crusted golden tiara adorned the top of her head.

King Haythem stood proudly beside her wearing a golden tunic layered with a deep green cape, connected by a thick golden chain. The cape was embroidered like Fjora's gown, making them a matching pair, completed by the golden crown with a large emerald encased in the middle.

Not a thread of mourning black in sight.

He took a step forward, bringing Fjora with him.

"My friends," he said, his voice booming through the hall. "We have much cause to celebrate this evening, for our lost princess has been found."

The tension in the room broke as the stunned guests cheered at the announcement.

Haythem put his hand up to quiet them, but a warm smile bloomed over his lips. "Goddess has seen fit to bless this kingdom. After the devastating loss of our queen, she saw fit to bring our princess home."

He looked over at his daughter, love shining in his eyes.

Jen looked around the room of shocked faces—some were crying with joy, others embraced each other. Fjora had truly been beloved by her people, it was clearer now that a whole host of them were standing in front of her.

Jen's heart clenched. It was one thing to be aware of Fjora's life before, it was another to see the ramifications of her sacrifice playing out in front of her.

The lost princess of Sachandes.

She turned back to the King and Fjora, who had shuffled to one side of the stairs.

What's happening now?

"Not only have I been reunited with my daughter and heir. I have also been introduced to the continuation of the royal bloodline." He gestured to the doorway. "My grandchildren."

Jen's face fell as the room collectively gasped. Dressed in various shades of green and embellished gold, looking slightly overwhelmed—

Rhea. Darya. Jamie.

They walked halfway down the stairs and stopped when they were level with the king. He and Fjora walked over to join them.

He kissed his daughter's cheek and then raised his hands in a grand gesture. "I give you the royal family," he announced.

"*My* family."

The room erupted into applause and rowdy cheers, the air thick with joy and hope for the future.

A dull, aching pain gnawed at her chest. Jen had gone from feeling like an outsider within her own family, to finding out they weren't her blood, and now they stood without her, presented to the world as a united front that she was not a part of.

Jen tried to conceal any reaction, but Damien wasn't fooled. He leaned over and kissed her brow, wrapping his arm tightly around her waist.

"I'm sorry, Bug."

She blinked away the sting in the corner of her eyes.

"It's fine. They look happy, that's all that matters."

"You deserve that too—"

"I'm tired of people saying that to me. I'm fine. Please." Jen couldn't take the pity; it was just making the ache in her chest more unbearable.

Haythem clasped his hands.

"Music! Lanterns! Let us truly celebrate!"

The orchestra started back up, the strings sweeping into a buoyant melody that filled the room as Haythem and Fjora ushered her siblings down the remaining stairs.

Jen peered back as Damien led her off the dancefloor; the crowd parted as Fjora graciously greeted her people, Rhea, Darya, and Jamie following close behind.

The ache shuddered through her, threatening to steal her breath, so Jen did the only thing she could do.

She shoved it behind the stone wall.

CHAPTER 28

"Jamie, stop fidgeting," Darya chided, swatting his hand away as she tried to button the top clasp of his tunic. He was all but trying to claw his way out of it.

"Be nice, Darya. This is much more formal than he's used to," Fjora said, coming to her son's side to rub his back.

"You're coddling, Mama," Rhea said from one of the columns beside them.

"I am *not*," Fjora retorted, taking a step away from Jamie.

Alright, maybe a little.

"He can deal with a few high placed buttons while Darya and I suffocate in our gowns." Rhea ran her hands around her waist, taking a strained breath through the boned corset before giving her mother a sarcastic thumbs up.

"I think you two look beautiful," Fjora said, reaching for Darya's hand. She took it and pressed her cheek against her mother's, feigning a pout.

"It's okay, Mama. We all know Jamie is your favorite.

Fjora scoffed but didn't correct her.

Jamie shifted uncomfortably from one foot to the other, glancing several times away from and then towards the massive doorway that led to the ballroom. They stood in the empty adjoining hall, listening to the sound of the festivities echoing into the quiet space.

"Darling, don't be nervous," Fjora said.

Jamie furrowed his brows. "This just—this just feels wrong without Jen."

"It *is* wrong without Jen," Rhea said, crossing her arms over her bodice.

Fjora sighed. She'd gone to Jen's rooms several times in the last few days, but she was either not there or passed out in her bed. It was becoming very clear that she was avoiding her, and she couldn't blame her. Fjora hadn't prepared her for any of this. She should have been training her to fight, teaching her about Etheria and the brutal history with which her destiny was intertwined.

Jen would have needed to return here eventually, even if the pulse hadn't come early. It had always just been a matter of time before Vondur made its move, but Fjora had no idea when, leading her to believe she might never see her home again when she left Nelysar to escape through Bri.

Many details of her life had faded into a blur over the last thirty years, but not him. That last wrenching glimpse—his figure among the trees, closing the path with tears of his own heartbreak—was burned into her memory like a brand.

She shook her head, pulling herself back into the hall with her family. "I tried to collect her earlier, but she wasn't in her room."

They looked unconvinced, and she let out an exasperated sigh. "After everything she's been through these past few weeks. I'm sure the last thing she wants is to be the center of attention at this ball…"

Am I trying to convince them, or myself?

She was interrupted by the sound of heavy footsteps clicking across the hall. Her face broke into a smile. "Papa," she said as he came to her side.

He took her chin. "I still can't believe it, *mo shaali.* I keep waiting to wake up from this wonderful dream."

She took his hand and kissed it. "Maybe we should spar. You'll be convinced I'm real when I've bested you."

He let out a deep laugh and offered his other hand to her.

"You must be real. In my dreams you were much demurer."

"Your dreams must have been *painfully* mundane," she jabbed. He laughed again as he led her towards the ballroom.

They came to the open doors and paused. Haythem turned to his grandchildren. "Wait here until I announce you. I'll make it as quick as possible. I'm not a fan of these sorts of royal obligations, but." He winked at them. "Duty calls."

Fjora felt the weight of tension leave her children when they realized their grandfather didn't care for formal entrances either. "I'll see you in a minute my darlings," she said.

BOOM

BOOM

BOOM

She flinched at the ground-shaking slams of the guard's staves. Haythem chuckled and patted her hand. She couldn't stop her heart from fluttering as they walked out to greet their court.

A court she hadn't seen in thirty years.

The crowd broke out into hushed whispers as Haythem began to speak. Fjora only half listened, taking this moment to scan the room for Jenevieve.

Goddess, there was so much tulle. It was like staring into a bowl of colorful candy floss, her eyes straining as she continued her search.

The crowd erupted into applause. She glanced over to see her father beaming at her.

Oh, whoops, that must have been about me.

"This ball was started as an attempt to find you, *mo shaali*, and over the years it has turned into a beautiful tradition for all those who wish to remember and honor their *own* lost loved ones."

Fjora placed her other hand on her father's arm. He nudged her towards the side of the grand staircase, she hadn't realized they'd descended halfway down already.

I really need to pay more attention.

She glanced once again at the crowd.

There.

She spotted Jen watching from the dancefloor with Damien close beside her. Before she could lock eyes with her, Haythem spoke again.

"Not only have I been reunited with my daughter and heir. I have also been introduced to the continuation of the royal bloodline." He gestured to the doorway "my grandchildren."

The court gasped as Rhea, Darya and Jamie walked down the stairs. A tingle of pride spread through her as her father pulled her along to stand in front of Rhea and the others. He held up his hands in a grand proclamation.

"My family."

Fjora immediately found Jen in the crowd when it erupted into thunderous applause and watched her face fall. Damien whispered something to her and kissed her brow. In an instant, a fake smile lifted over her daughter's face, the facade that Jenevieve hid behind when she didn't want to feel pain.

"Music! Lanterns! Let us truly celebrate!"

Haythem began his final descent into the ballroom, bringing Fjora and her children with him. She let him lead her, all the while watching as the tiny bundle she was charged to protect disappeared into the sea of chiffon.

Fjora mindlessly greeted the line of courtiers that had gathered at the foot of the stairs. She recognized most of them, feigning grace and gratitude for their prayers and love while they curtsied or bowed. Her eyes darted from her children, who stood next to her shaking hands and receiving unabashed adoration from the court, to Jenevieve, or at least in the direction of where she'd been.

I need to find her, explain that my father had just gotten carried away.

"You look like you're enjoying yourself," Bastien mused. She gave him an acknowledging grunt but didn't look at him.

He stepped in front of her.

"Fjora?"

Her eyes continued to search the room.

He gently rubbed her arm. "Are you alright? I know this might be a bit overwhelm—"

Her gaze finally settled on him. "Jenevieve."

Bastien tilted his head. "What about her?"

"She just watched that whole thing," Fjora said, waving her hand towards the stairs. "I need to make sure she's alright."

Bastien placed his hands on her shoulders. "I'm sure she's fine, Fjora. She's with her friends in the corner over there." He gestured to the opposite corner of the room.

Fjora followed his hand, but she couldn't see her through the crowded ballroom. Her gaze shifted back to Rhea, Darya, and Jamie. They seemed fine enough, but an abundance of guilt crept under her skin.

"I—this is too much. I may be used to this sort of attention, but they aren't. I should—"

Bastien tightened his grip as she tried to move towards Darya.

"Listen to me," he said firmly. "One: they're your children, yes, but they are also adults who chose to come with you. They're *fine.*"

She tried to look away, but he followed, holding her gaze.

"Two: Jenevieve is okay. I will check on her in a bit, but she's with Damien and the others. You don't need to worry about her at this moment."

"But…"

Bastien took her hand and laced it around his arm.

"You've been gone for thirty years, Fjora. Let yourself be welcomed home." He began leading her across the ballroom.

She looked back at her children. "Where are we going?"

"*They're fine*, Fjora. Let Haythem shower them with affection. From what you've told me; they've been sorely in need of it."

She blew out a breath and stopped resisting, moving across the room with Bastien, stopping occasionally to receive anything from a cordial welcome home to a tearful embrace.

The ballroom spun around them, a whirl of shifting gowns and dissonant gossip dripping from every corner as they made their way to the edge of the dancefloor, where the room opened out onto the veranda overlooking the brilliant night sky.

Bastien glanced at her out of the corner of his eye, chuckling. "You have the same look you did that first night of Ruymani."

She whipped her head towards him. "I do?"

"Mhm. Utterly captivated and fascinated."

A small laugh escaped her. "Well, it's been a while since I've seen so much tulle in one place."

"It's all a bit garish, isn't it?"

Fjora snapped her gaze towards the familiar voice, her breath catching in her throat as Naezara rounded the corner and approached them.

"You look better than the last time I saw you," she said, embracing Fjora tightly.

"Etherian air does wonders for the skin," Fjora mused.

Naezara clasped arms with Bastien.

"Did the scouting parties find anything?" he asked.

"The obari have begun to encroach on Lutteala, in addition to the threats on the Senyan border," she said, crossing her arms in front of her chest.

"What do you think they're doing?" Bastien asked, rubbing the underside of his chin with his thumb.

"We think they may be searching for something, but not before destroying anything in their path. Fucking mindless foot soldiers."

Fjora looked between them.

"Well, this all seems ominously familiar."

An eruption of laughter came from the column on the opposing side of the veranda, and she froze.

That…that can't be…

Naezara groaned while Bastien nudged her with his elbow. "So does that," he murmured, but Fjora's heart was beating so loudly she barely heard him.

Her gaze met Naezara, who tilted her head towards the laughter. "He's been waiting for you," she said, a smirk tugging at her lips.

Bastien, once again, placed Fjora's hand around his arm, and, along with Naezara, guided her across the veranda.

It was achingly familiar, an ode to a moment of her past she had replayed in her mind over and over, except now as she drew nearer to him, her heart hammered against her chest, blood roared in her ears.

She'd been thinking about this moment for thirty years. She had dreamed about it, longed for it. Built it up so intensely in her mind there was no way this would—

The group of women that surrounded the column parted when Naezara and Bastien brought Fjora forward.

Her throat went dry, her knees buckling beneath her.

Nelysar leaned against the marble, arms folded over his ivory tunic. Sharp features and auburn hair, a single gold bar through the arch of his ear and green eyes alight with golden flames—flames that burned into a part of Fjora's soul she had kept carefully hidden for so long.

Bastien let go of her and retreated a step, leaving Fjora exposed in the middle of the group of women, who were rooted where they stood, watching the scene unfold.

The air was charged like a lightning catcher.

She couldn't move, paralyzed by the sudden dread that this was all a dream.

I'm going to wake up at any moment.

But then, Nelysar pushed off the column and strolled towards her, far too casually, like this wasn't a moment he had played over obsessively in his mind as she had. Fjora lifted her chin to maintain some semblance of regality. He stopped within a foot of her, his eyes narrowed slightly.

That's when Fjora noticed it.

He was trembling.

A heavy silence fell over them, threatening to crush them both under the weight of the longing that hung between them.

He silently offered his hand. Her lips parted, but words failed as her gaze remained locked on the hand in front of her.

The corner of his lip turned up.

"Would you like to dance?"

His low tenor sang into her bones, a sound that had only lived in her memories, she had almost forgotten the effect it had on her. Fjora tried to keep her breath steady, but, Goddess, it was him.

She glanced at Bastien, and Nelysar noticed.

"I didn't ask him, I asked you."

Naezara scoffed, completing the memory. Fjora's eyes narrowed at the challenge in his voice. She arched a brow. "How could I say no to such charm?"

And then he smiled, and Fjora's heart burst. She forced her expression into one of indifference as she placed her hand in his.

Goddess, save her, she was touching him. He traced her knuckles with his thumb, the small caress nearly bringing her to her knees right there, but the look on his face told her he was attempting to maintain the same level of decorum as her.

She recognized every glance, every subtle shift—reading him as well as she had all those years ago. Every unspoken word, every flicker of feeling— she knew them all as if they were etched into her soul.

He's real.

Nelysar led her onto the dance floor, his eyes never leaving hers, even when their path forced the other dancing couples to part. Both were unaware of anyone else in the ballroom.

He turned to face her, and slowly wrapped his hand around her waist, pulling her close. She placed her hand on his shoulder, stepping a bit further into his arms, her breath catching as he dipped his head to her ear.

"Fjora," he said, his voice wavering.

She swallowed before pulling back to meet his gaze.

"Nelysar."

They began to move, the dance coming back to them as the romantic melody swept through the air like the hushed breathing of secret lovers. It enveloped them, their bodies sinking into each other, their facade becoming more difficult to maintain.

She glanced over at her family. Her worlds were melding together; the life she had, the one she was forced to create, and the one she now returned to.

Guilt and loss and love flooded her heart. She'd left this life—left him, thinking she would never return. And when she did return, her mother was dead. Jenevieve was struggling under the weight of the burden her destiny holds; her children were now royalty and attempting to adjust. She was dancing in a room with people who thought she was dead just moments ago. She was a ghost to them, a corporeal memory of a tragic time in her kingdom's history.

Her chest heaved, her thoughts overwhelming her. Nelysar watched her closely, too closely; yearning permeated off him.

"Fjora…" he said, squeezing her hand.

She snapped her head towards his. The loving concern in his voice gutted her. How could he want her now? She wasn't the same person, she couldn't be.

Goddess, how can he bear to even look at me?

She stumbled back. He caught her, his hands firmly around her waist, holding her steady.

"I can't do this," she whispered, and forced herself out of his arms. His mouth dropped open, lost for words. She turned and marched off the floor towards the veranda.

She needed air. She needed to calm herself down. But a voice called out behind her.

"Fjora. *Fjora.*"

Nelysar followed her as she beelined it for the lanterns, she needed something to do with her hands.

She grabbed the flattened lantern and jerked it open.

"Such a gentle touch."

Nelysar stood a few feet behind her, his arms crossed over his chest. The way he observed her was so natural, so intimate, it pained her.

She glanced behind him and found Jenevieve in the corner of the room, the facade of happiness placed carefully over her as loneliness came off her in waves.

She narrowed her eyes at Nelysar.

"I need to be alone."

He closed the distance between them and gently took the lantern from her. He quietly assembled it as she watched him, his fingers nimbly working around the thick paper.

He handed it to her when he finished, and as she took it, he placed each of his hands on top of hers. Together they held the lantern between them. The flames that licked within his green eyes warmed his gaze.

"You will never be alone again, *mo nuri*."

Mo nuri.

She all but fell over. She had only heard those words in her dreams for so long. She wanted to fall into his arms and never let go. But instead, she ripped the lantern from his hands and walked toward the balcony.

"Don't call me that."

CHAPTER 29

Jenevieve stood beside Emelie and Damien, barely paying attention to the conversation her friends were having, her eyes fixed upon a blank spot of the wall across from her.

"Jen?"

Her focus was yanked back at the sound of her name.

"Say that again?"

William gave her a quizzical look. "I asked if you wanted to join me in the library sometime over the next few days. I know you like to do things yourself."

She feigned a smile. "As long as I'm not intruding."

His forehead creased. "You can't intrude in a public space, Jen."

"I just don't want to get in the way, is all."

"You're not getting in the way," Leeyna said, grabbing her hand.

"Sure," she said, her eyes wandering over to the dance floor.

Earlier, Damien had asked her to dance again, but after watching the presentation of her family—the *king's* family, she wasn't feeling up for it. Honestly, she wanted to leave the ball entirely, but there was no way for her to slip away without anyone noticing. The flicker of disappointment in Damien's eyes certainly didn't help.

A flush of sunset tulle and chiffon caught her eye from across the marble floor.

Lyla.

She was standing in the corner, alone, Margo having left her to dance with a courtier in a deep blue tunic. She was fidgeting with her gown, clearly uncomfortable and in need of something to do.

Damien glanced at her, the moment fleeting, but Jen knew he noticed her standing by herself. Jen bit her bottom lip; she wasn't up for dancing, Damien clearly wanted to, and Lyla was standing there looking beautiful with no partner.

She pushed down the twinge of self-inflicted jealousy and came to his side, facing the dance floor with him.

"You should ask Lyla to dance."

He whipped his head towards her so fast he almost knocked himself over. "What?"

She sighed.

"She doesn't have anyone to dance with, look at her."

Two lines appeared between his brows. "I saw."

"Just…I know you two are friendly. Go be a friend to her."

He turned to face her. "I'm not going to *leave* you here."

She released a stiff laugh. "Then you'll be standing here all night. I want you to have fun, Damien."

His eyes flashed to Lyla and then back to her.

"I don't—"

"It's just one dance. And *look*." She jutted her head to the bottom of the grand stairs, where Bastien was ushering her siblings in their direction. "I'm about to have more company."

He grabbed her chin, glancing from her siblings, to Lyla, and then attempted to find anything behind the mask that lingered in her eyes.

"You're sure?"

"Do I need to push you over there myself?"

"No need for that," William said as he and Leeyna joined them. "We were going to join the dancing when the next one starts. We'll walk over there with you."

Damien still looked unsure, but he nodded curtly at them. His thumb caressed her jawline. He kissed her gently, barely pulling away as he said, "I'll be right back," against her lips.

He let go and turned on his heels to make his way across the room, William and Leeyna close behind him.

Jen had no right to feel the tightness in her chest when she watched him walk towards Lyla. She told him to go. But she wasn't expecting to see Lyla blush when he offered his hand to her, or, to realize her sunset gown was almost the exact color of Damien's tunic, making them appear as a matching set.

"Did you just send Damien to dance with another woman…who's wearing a matching gown?" Darya asked curiously as she appeared at her side.

Well, when you say it like that—

"That was an interesting choice," Rhea said, her brows furrowing with confusion.

"He deserves to have fun," Jen said, gesturing down at herself. "I'm not the best company at the moment."

Jamie glanced between his sisters, looking uncomfortable as a grimace formed on his face. "Jen, we didn't want to do that entrance without you."

She threw up another fake smile, this one almost painful.

"It's okay, I know," she said, placing her hand on her brother's shoulder.

A small flicker of sadness flashed over the ocean-blue of Darya's eyes. "Have you been avoiding us?".

Jen shifted uncomfortably.

Gods, she has the king's eyes.

"It's not that I've been avoiding you—"

"She's been training," Emelie piped in from behind her. Jen blew out a quiet breath, grateful for the assistance.

Samara stepped over as well. "She trains every morning with me and then visits Gaiana in the afternoons."

"Who's Gaiana?" Rhea asked.

Samara stifled a groan. "Oh, good. Another herd of people spat out of Nimea with no knowledge in their pretty little heads."

"Samara!" Emelie elbowed her in the ribs.

Samara winced. "What? I said they were *pretty*."

Bastien chuckled as he passed through Rhea and Darya.

"Come dance with me, you don't play well with others," he winked.

She scoffed and took his hand. "*You* don't play well with others," she grumbled.

"Let's work on those comebacks, shall we?" Bastien teased, spinning her under his arm and out towards the golden statue.

Jen let out a strained laugh. She scanned the room for Damien and Lyla but instead found a pair of bright green eyes staring at her from across the room.

Ronan leaned against a large marble column, his mahogany hair swept back, and his stubble trimmed enough to see his chiseled jawline. Margo was dangling on the arm of his midnight blue tunic, trying to engage with him, but he kept his gaze on Jen.

It was almost a relief to see him—*almost*, but she let herself genuinely smile anyway, and her heart warmed a little, a welcome reprieve from the sadness that had been eating away at her all night.

"Who is *that*?" Darya asked, looking down her nose at him.

Jen gave him a small wave. "A friend."

His head dipped towards Margo, and he shook it. She scoffed loudly and stalked off with a few other courtiers. His gaze returned to Jen, and his lips turned up into a grin as he pushed himself off the column and began his stride towards her.

When he was halfway across the room, he halted at the opening to the veranda, his eyes fixed up towards the sky. Jen raised her brows in confusion.

Is he looking at the lanterns?

She took a few steps towards him, peeking around one of the other columns. Hundreds of paper lanterns had been released into the sky, floating in a golden sea of prayers and hope that ascended over the mountain peaks and towards the heavens. She had never seen anything quite so tragically stunning in her life.

Her gaze drifted down to the balcony, where she found Fjora standing with Nelysar. But she wasn't looking at him, her sight fixed on Jen—the same expression she had right before the morai attack.

"What the fuck do you mean, 'don't call me that'?" Nelysar followed her to the balcony. He grabbed her wrist and pulled her back to him.

"I'm not the same person I was when I went through the forest," Fjora choked out.

Thirty years without him. Thirty years of trying to forget him. Thirty years of knowing he wouldn't want her if she ever returned.

"I've been with another man, Nel." Her eyes welled. "I had to try to make a life there."

His gaze bored into hers. "You don't think I know that?" he seethed. "You don't think I thought about that when I let you leave. When I forced you through that forest? When I shut the barrier between our realms?"

"I had children with him. You can't tell me you're okay with that?" She pointed to the ballroom. "A walking reminder of the life we were denied?"

He deserves better than me. A failure.

"What did that realm do to you, *mo nuri?*" he breathed.

"Please stop calling me that," she pleaded.

"I will call you that until my last breath on this earth, and even then, I will whisper it from the Beyond until our world fades into obscurity."

Nelysar let go of her wrist and gently wiped away the tears streaming down her cheeks, such a tender gesture that threatened to shatter her.

Fjora looked down at the lantern in her hand, and more desolate tears fell. "My mother is dead."

"I know." He caressed her cheek. "I was there."

Her tearstained gaze shot up to meet him. "You—you were?"

He nodded solemnly. He carefully took the lantern from her hands and held it in front of her. He closed his eyes for a moment and willed the wick to ignite with a small, white flame. The lantern glowed before them, casting their faces in a golden warmth.

"I was told her time was coming, and so I made my way here. I sat at her bedside with Haythem and Bastien as she took her final breaths." He stared into the flame. "I thought…I thought that since you were so much a part of me, that I carried your heart with me every moment—maybe— in a way…you were with her too, in the end."

She stared at him. This man, this Regal, had loved her so much he had sat by her dying mother as she left this world.

"I can't believe you did that," she whispered, looking down at the lantern.

He lifted it and raised his brows in a silent request. She nodded tearfully, and together they released the lantern into the sky. In honor of her mother, Queen Eliana.

"She would be proud of you, Fjora. As your father is. As I am." He took her hand and placed it on his own cheek.

"I'm not worthy of your pride. I failed." More tears slid down her cheeks.

He kissed the inside of her palm and released it to hold her face in his hands. "No, you didn't." He kissed the tears from one of her cheeks.

"You sacrificed everything to protect the child." He kissed the tears from her other cheek. "You kept her safe. You raised her as your own." He kissed her forehead. "And when the time came, you returned her to fulfill her destiny." He pulled back, his eyes glistening.

"You came *home*."

She looked down. "But my family—"

He lifted her chin with his finger. "They followed you into Etheria. Which makes them brave, and strong," he whispered. "That means they are more *you* than anyone else. And that's all that matters to me."

She was quiet for a long moment. Then she looked at him with a small gleam in her eye. Hope.

"You…you still want me?"

A low growl rumbled in his throat and one of his hands found the nape of her neck.

"Yes."

"You…I—"

He placed his other hand on her waist and leaned his head against hers. "When we were at the edge of Bri, I swore to you that our journey together was not over, and I meant it," he breathed. "That last moment of you with a babe in your arms haunts me to this day."

She breathed him in.

"No matter how hard I tried to push you from my mind, you refused to leave." She placed her hand on his chest, feeling his heart beating as fast as hers. "I shouldn't have been surprised."

Nelysar's voice cracked. "My life has been a shell of hollow existence…an empty husk, without you. And now that I have you back in my arms, I cannot—" The sound he made was almost a moan. "—*will* not, let you go again." A tear ran down his cheek.

"I love you, Fjora. And I have longed for you every moment of every passing day. Please, *please* tell me you still love me, too," he said through another fallen tear.

She rubbed her nose against his.

"I never stopped, Nel." His breath hitched. "I loved you through every moment we were apart, and I will continue to love you until my last breath on this earth."

His lips crashed against hers in a kiss with the power to erase the years they were forced apart. Her lips parted for him, and his tongue swept in, desperate to remember every inch of her. She grabbed the front of his ivory tunic and pulled him closer, feeling his body flush against hers.

His hands roved down her back, the lust and love in their kiss drawing out breathless sounds of desire.

And then he froze.

Fjora fell against him. When she looked up at him, wildly confused, he wasn't looking at her. She followed his gaze to the sky, flooded with a sea of golden lit lanterns.

But there was something else. Something was weaving through the lanterns further out in the sky. Something big. Something dark.

Her eyes widened.

She whipped her head to the ballroom and found Jenevieve standing by one of the columns.

"Run," she mouthed.

Fjora snapped her head back to Nelysar, alarm contorting his face. She pulled up her gown to reveal two thigh straps, a dagger sheathed in each one. She flicked them into her hands and raised a defiant brow.

A wicked smile appeared on his face as he unsheathed his sword.

"That's my girl."

Her brow twitched before she faced the crowd of people who hadn't noticed what was flying straight for them.

"MOVE!" she screamed, and she sprang into action.

CHAPTER 30

"*Run,*" Fjora mouthed to her.

And then it came.

The screech that shook her to her core, the horrifying sound she heard when they fled Zaniya.

The kashyak, riding its salyaat.

The dark beast seemed to swim around the lanterns, its reptilian feathered body slithering through the sky. It flew closer, descending upon the palace.

A flood of people spilled into the ballroom from the veranda, Fjora's voice booming over the panicked screams in a command to move. She lunged to the edge of the ballroom and faced the creature with Nelysar and Naezara at either side. Blades drawn. Stances low and ready to defend.

Jen turned back to Ronan, and he lurched forward, sprinting across the room, reaching for her.

The screech came again. Louder. Closer.

"Jen!" Emelie yelled from behind her.

Jen swung her arms back, summoning a torrent of wind to push Emelie and her siblings out of harm's way. But she misjudged her strength, slamming them against the wall with a *thud*. She whirled around, and a twinge of pain twisted in her chest at the sight of shock and fear etched into her siblings' faces.

Emelie pressed off the floor and waved her off with an unspoken promise to look after them. Jen nodded, shoving the fearful looks from her siblings behind her mental wall, and whipped back around to the havoc in front of her.

She searched for Damien in the unfolding chaos, and quickly found him across the dance floor, him and William having thrown Leeyna and Lyla behind them. But his eyes were on her, terror and pain lancing through his gaze.

Before she could yell for him, the ground shook with the impact of the salyaat as it landed on the veranda, its claws scraping into the marble floors.

Jen heard Fjora snarl at the beast, any trace of the gentle homemaker from Nimea long gone.

Terrified cries rang out as the room was enveloped with a thick, dark smoke, rendering the entirety of the court blind. Jen's eyes stung as she stumbled forward into the smog, but the ominous clouds numbed her senses. She instinctively reached in front of her and hit something warm, an arm.

Ronan appeared in front of her, radiating with rage and the smallest whisper of fear that drove into her burning eyes.

He leaned into her space. "When the smoke clears," he whispered, grabbing her hand and squeezing her fingers tight. "Don't. Move."

She choked on the smoke. "What?"

The smoke began to dissipate, and as it did, the air around them seemed to grow heavy and still. The hair raised on the back of her neck as she felt the tingle of magic on the surface of her skin.

An unfamiliar metallic taste touched the tip of her tongue. Ronan stood stock still beside her and murmured, "dark magic."

She immediately felt it scraping along her mind, attempting to subdue her, but her own power pushed against the foreign enchantment as she glanced around the room.

Oh, gods.

No one was moving.

Nausea churned in Jen's stomach.

Everyone was frozen where they stood, as if cast in stone—except for their eyes. Hundreds of panicked eyes darted around the ballroom, aware of where they were but unable to move.

Ronan tensed beside her as the sound of footsteps came from the top of the grand stairs.

Her blood turned cold. Her skin slick with sweat. She recognized the figure from the pulse, from the nightmare that started it all. He'd been kneeling before his master.

A Knight of Eseer.

"According to legend, the Knights of Eseer were once people, but Heltior consumed their souls for power and left only darkness within them," William had explained.

"Well, well," the Knight drawled, his voice like a dark velveteen rope wrapping itself around the ears of his puppets. "What a lovely celebration."

His disinterested expression wandered about the room, taking in the grandeur he had halted.

He stood with his hands clasped behind his back, wearing a black tunic. His long, raven hair was tied back to show his jagged cheekbones and disturbingly pale skin. But what caused the chill to run down Jen's spine was the black paint on his face.

Obsidian paint was brushed around his eyes and over the bridge of his nose to look like a mask. Three long lines broke up the left side of the disguise, revealing pale skin beneath. Although his face looked bored, he felt dangerous. Power rippled from him like waves of heat coming off damp ground.

He strolled down the stairs, taking his time as the crowd of frozen courtiers looked on, paralyzed.

The kashyak slid down its salyaat, beginning a slow, unnerving entrance into the ballroom. It snaked around the sea of tulle, finding its way to Damien. His eyes darted to Jen, and the fear she saw in them almost broke her deception, but Ronan's fingers brushed against hers, urging her to stay still.

It inhaled Damien indulgently before slithering its way around Lyla and Leeyna. Jen could practically feel them trembling from across the hall as it slithered its gray, scaly body against each of theirs.

It stalked toward William and flicked its forked tongue over the skin of his cheek. He squeezed his eyes shut until the creature slinked away to torment other guests.

The Knight came to the bottom of the stairs, rolling up his sleeves to his elbows to reveal tattoos of black, jagged vines wrapping up his arms. His power channeled through them, Jen could sense the invisible vines of magic weaving through the room, keeping everyone in place.

He peered over at the king, who stood just a few feet from the bottom railing.

"King Haythem," he stretched out the name. "It's so nice to see you out of your mourning attire," he lingered on every word. "I know Etheria wept when your queen dropped dead."

The king attempted to break through the paralysis, his anger bulging out of his eyes, but it was no use. The Knight began to circle him like a predator.

"Two years was an awfully long time to forget your duties." He feigned a bow. "Your Grace." His lips curled into a disturbing smile. He turned and extended his arms to the ballroom, addressing the crowd.

"The fact that my associate and I—" He gestured to the kashyak, still slithering through the crowd as the salyaat released a visceral screech from the veranda, "were able to walk right into your realm is a testament to how weak your king has become. How pathetically sad—a macabre shadow of the once valiant King Haythem."

Haythem flushed rouge in anger or shame, perhaps both. The Knight came within inches of him, his expression a condescending contortion of disappointment.

"Where is Orion, my king?" he murmured. "Your majestic condor and his flock would have seen me coming." He took a long, slender finger and caressed the king's cheek. "Such a shame."

He whipped back towards the ballroom and clapped his hands.

"But this is a celebration, is it not?" His head snapped to the veranda, where Fjora stood with Nelysar and Naezara.

"The beloved Princess Fjora found her way home at last." He meandered towards them, his head tilting to Nelysar. "She found her way back to her Regal, reclaiming her title as the royal whore of the Inbetween."

Fjora glared defiantly.

The Knight chuckled before swinging himself towards the corner, where Jen stood in front of her siblings. "But not before she opened her legs for another." He looked back at Nelysar with a sympathetic grin. "That has to sting a bit, knowing she fucked another man, a *mortal* no less." He looked at the wall where Rhea, Darya and Jamie were frozen.

Jen could feel their fear overwhelming them as he slinked towards their trembling bodies.

He stopped.

His head turned slowly in Jen's direction.

"There you are." He lunged toward her, inhaling her deeply. He released a euphoric sigh. "Oh, you smell of delicious power."

Jen paled.

The stone…he shouldn't be able to sense my magic.

Her eyes flickered to his forearm; within the jagged vines, a long, curved trident was inked with an eye in the center of the prongs. He raised a brow; a sickening smirk curled on his lips as he lifted his arm to her.

"You've seen this before?" He clicked his tongue. "Of course, you have." He ran his fingers over the tattoo. "It came to you in a dream." He licked his lips. "A pulse."

Sweat pooled at the small of her back.

The Knight spun around to the ballroom.

"You are harboring a child of the blood!" he bellowed. "The delicious power I sensed is of an ancient, *light* magic." He rubbed his chin thoughtfully. "And if that formidable blood runs through your veins—"

He slammed his fist into Ronan's ribs. Jen broke immediately to catch him, falling with him to the floor as he grunted and collapsed.

The Knight's smile turned vicious. "You are immune to my enchantments."

Jen held Ronan steady as the air returned to him.

Kiara, the Aylaenor…the power to rival Heltior…

They shared a look.

Is light magic.

"What do you want?" she spat, pulling Ronan up with her.

The Knight took a few steps towards the golden condor in the middle of the ballroom. "I came for *you*, Jenevieve."

She blinked.

"You know me?"

He ran his hand along the condor's wing. "I know all about you, Jenevieve of Nimea."

His eyes turned to slits as he turned about the room, landing on a group of courtiers in the middle of the dance floor. Still bearing his cruel smile, he curled his hand and lifted it with a jerk.

Jen gasped as the men and women were hoisted into the air. They sputtered and gasped for air; he was strangling them with a subtle squeeze of his fingers.

He raised his brows at her.

"Stop me, *bloodliner.*"

Jen's mouth stood agape. She looked at Ronan, but his eyes were locked on the floating victims before them. Their lips were turning blue, their gasps becoming weaker.

"That's enough," Ronan said with venom.

"Hmm."

The Knight let go and the courtiers dropped to the ground with a sickening cascade of thuds. He prowled towards Ronan, circling him in utter fascination.

"You are not of the blood," he murmured. Ronan clenched his jaw. "Oh, you are something else entirely. You even seem…familiar, somehow."

A muscle feathered in Ronan's jaw.

Jen stepped forward. "What do you want with me?"

His head snapped to her, his eyes alight with malice.

"I want to see that stunning bloodline magic, your kind are so rare, you see," he taunted. "But." His eyes wandered slowly up her body. "There is something else lurking beneath your skin…oh," he rolled his neck. "I can feel it—"

He licked his lips, his eyes flashing something malicious before he flicked his hand.

Jamie was thrust into the air, gasping for breath.

"No!" Jen screamed.

"Jenevieve, who summoned a horde of vicious morai to her innocent village," the Knight sneered.

Another flick, and Darya was in the air, tears streaming down her face in horror.

"Stop!"

"Jenevieve, whose birth killed her parents."

Another flick, and Rhea was dangling by her siblings.

Jen tried to summon anything within her. A gust of wind, a trickle of water, a beam of light—anything.

But nothing came.

Ronan raised his hands towards her family, but the Knight waved his arm and slammed him into the column beside them. He crumpled to the floor.

"No!"

"Jenevieve, whose birth *ripped* Princess Fjora away from her kingdom, away from her lover. Her life."

Another flick and Fjora was flung into the air.

Nelysar leapt forward. "Stop this!"

The salyaat reached out its razor-sharp claws and swiped him and Naezara across the veranda, slamming them into the balcony as the lanterns floated in the distance behind them.

"Should have known those *insufferable* Regals weren't enchanted."

Jen's family sputtered for air, clawing at their throats. She threw her hands up again, trying to summon anything to save them, but fear strangled her magic. The crack along her mental wall reopened, deepening as anger once again began to crawl out from the abyss.

The Knight watched her, and his eyes grew sinister.

"Jenevieve, whose father *never* loved her."

Her blood heated under her skin, tendrils of that anger seeping through the crack. Her nostrils flared.

"Jenevieve, who shielded a family that was never *hers*."

Her breathing grew heavy, fear fading as several more rage-fueled wisps joined the others, the stone wall trembling as her control waned.

"Enough," she murmured.

"Jenevieve, who hides her true self behind a *pathetic* facade."

Blood roared in her ears.

"Enough," she growled.

Another flick and Emelie was jerked into the air.

"Jenevieve the *unwanted*," he mocked.

"Enough," she snarled.

Another flick of his wrist. William and Leeyna went flying towards the ceiling.

"I said—"

"Durche yahvak!" he shouted. He waved his arm and Damien lurched into the air.

"I SAID ENOUGH!"

Jen screamed as a flood of fire expelled from her body in an explosion that shook the room, blasting a hole through her mental wall as power erupted from her.

Not powerful light—but raging flames.

Bastien leapt forward and flung his arms out with a massive shield to block the crowd from the waves of fire. Ronan lunged to catch her family and Emelie. Naezara sprinted to catch Damien and the others with a wave of her magic. A wounded Nelysar caught Fjora before they both fell to the ground.

Jen crashed to her knees, gasping for air. Ronan dropped to her side, pulling her up by the arm. The fire went out, leaving the ballroom hazy with thick smoke.

It vacillated around every soul in the room, slowly forming itself into a thick, sweeping tunnel.

Not a tunnel.

A serpent.

The faint shape of a serpent slid around her ankles and coiled up her body, giving her a parting embrace before evaporating into thin air.

All eyes landed on her, every expression laced with shock. Fear.

The Knight appeared with the kashyak on the back of the salyaat.

"That was interesting," he said, his lips curling into a macabre grin. "It's only a matter of time, Jenevieve."

The beast gave a final blood curdling screech before it leapt from the veranda and took off into the night sky, leaving massive welds of cracked marble in its wake.

As soon as the creature was airborne, the enchantment lifted and all in attendance collapsed from their statuesque prisons. The hall erupted into a mess of moans and cries of agony.

The sounds lanced through Jen's soul.

I did this. Not the Knight. Me.

Her hands began to shake. She peered up at Ronan with red rimmed eyes, cloudy with magic—with shame. He held her gaze, the hand that held her up tightened around her waist and his lips parted as if he wanted to say something.

But before he could, Damien and Fjora came hurtling towards them. Ronan gently handed her off to Damien. Fjora cupped Jen's face in her hands.

"Jenevieve—talk to me, *mo shaali.*"

Jen met her gaze and saw it—love, too fierce, too much. It overwhelmed her. Fjora glanced helplessly at Damien, and he nodded, pulling Jen against his chest.

"I'll be right back." She kissed Jen on the cheek and ran to Rhea, Darya and Jamie, examining each of them meticulously.

Ronan returned a moment later and clasped Damien's shoulder firmly. "Are you alright? Are they?" He jutted his chin towards Lyla, Leeyna and William.

Damien stammered. "I—I don't—" He glanced back at them before his pained gaze fell back on Jen, who still shook in his arms.

Ronan gestured towards the stairs. "Get her out of here. I'll check on the others."

He turned and his face fell. Emelie was on the ground beside Samara a few feet away, her legs blistered and burnt.

"Fuck."

He ran over and scooped her into his arms. She let out a strangled cry before she went limp. Emelie rose with him as he said, "Check on the others and meet me at the healer's corridor, bring anyone who needs one." He took off with Samara.

Horror pooled tears in Jen's eyes as she watched him disappear up the stairs. "Did I do that?"

"Shh. Come on, Bug, let's get you out of here," Damien said quietly, coaxing her in the same direction.

"My family." She pushed back on Damien's hold and limped towards the corner.

They have to be okay. They have to be okay.

They stood in a tight group, holding onto each other as Fjora soothed them. King Haythem was at their side, his hand clasped around Jamie's shoulder.

She reached for Darya. "Are you all—"

Darya flinched.

Jen yanked her hand back.

Her sister *flinched.*

Darya realized what she had done and quickly tried to redact it.

"Jen—I—"

Jen shrunk into Damien's arms and turned away from her family. Fjora called after her, but it sounded like her voice was underwater, and Jen was swimming further and further away.

I did this. I did this. I did this.

Damien led her up the stairs, the murmurings and harsh whispers of the court crashing against their backs. His grip on her tightened, and they moved quicker until they made it out into the hall. As they silently walked from the courtyard to the grand hall, a voice called out to her.

"Jenevieve."

Jen looked over her shoulder.

Gaiana and Rieshi stood in the archway of the courtyard.

Damien held her close as the women approached. They were in eccentric gowns of mismatched patterns and fabrics, their hair pulled back into loose buns.

Gaiana glanced down at Jen's trembling hands and offered her own steady ones.

Jen looked down nervously. "I don't want to…"

Rieshi shushed her gently as Gaiana took her hands.

"You won't hurt me. It's alright," she said kindly.

Damien rested his cheek on Jen's head, and Rieshi rubbed her arms in a soothing pattern. Gaiana closed her eyes and ran her thumbs along Jen's knuckles.

The trembling in her hands faded away and a soothing warmth flooded her body like warm water on a winter's night. She looked up at Gaiana, her eyes welling with gratitude.

"What was that?" she whispered.

Gaiana rubbed her hands. "Just a way to calm you."

Jen's head throbbed as her mind attempted to patch up the hole her rage had created. It was like stumbling out of a fog, the haze still blurring the edges of everything that had just happened.

She stared back down at her hands.

"I…I lost control. I didn't mean to—"

Gaiana held her hands firmly. "We know."

Shame drowned her. "I hurt people," she whispered, her heart twisting in knots at the thought of Samara's broken body.

"Not on purpose, Bug," Damien breathed into her hair.

Gaiana and Rieshi nodded in agreement.

Fear rubbed up against her bones, whispering beneath her skin.

"He knew who I was…he knew about the bloodline."

Gaiana caressed her cheek with a sad smile. "And he will not be the last." She took her chin and held her gaze. "You must not be afraid, Jenevieve."

CHAPTER 31

amien opened her bedroom door and led her inside. Jen pulled herself from his arms and made for the bottle of amber liquid Bastien had left by the hearth.

She poured herself a glass and emptied the contents in one swig. She set the glass down and leaned into the back of one of the armchairs, her knuckles turning white around the upholstery.

Damien crept up beside her and silently poured himself a glass, emptying it in one swig as she had. She could feel his gaze on her face, trying to read her as she stared into the crackling fire.

Gaiana had calmed her body, but that all-consuming shame and fear still plagued her thoughts—her heart.

He placed one of his hands on top of hers, his thumb gently running over her knuckles. She looked down at the gentle caress, then peered up to where his kind eyes waited. After a moment, he tugged her towards the bed, sitting her down on the edge.

He knelt in front of her and carefully ran his calloused fingers down her calf and around her ankle, lifting her foot to rest on his thigh.

She watched him through hooded eyes, mindlessly wringing her hands in her lap. He unlaced the deep green slipper and pulled it from her foot, placing it gingerly on the floor beside them before lifting her other foot to do the same gentle task.

Jen glanced over at the new silver hairbrush gleaming in the moonlight. "It was more than just a vision," she whispered.

Damien stilled. She took his silence as a sign to continue.

"It was a curse...a trap...set for me."

He rose to his feet then took a few steps towards the veranda, crossing his arms in front of his chest.

"What do you mean, a trap?" he asked quietly.

Jen looked back down at her hands.

"It wasn't like the Echo, or the dream of Fjora. I wasn't watching from the outside…It was… it was happening *to* me. It felt like a world that exists in that moment before waking from a deep sleep—like half a dream siting on the edge of reality."

He walked further towards the balcony. His raven hair reflected ripples of blue in the light of the Etherian moon, his lean body casting a long shadow into the bedroom.

"Why?" he asked as he turned back to face her, the moonlight surrounding him like a halo of iridescent light.

Gods, he is so beautiful.

"To lure me…to give into darkness."

"Why would someone want to do that?"

Jen shook her head. "I…I don't know."

"What do you mean you don't know?"

She sighed and let her head fall into her hands.

"I mean I don't know, Damien."

"What did the curse use to lure you?"

Jen dropped her hands and stared at the floor. When she lifted her head to meet his eyes, realization dawned on him when he saw the hollowness reflected in hers.

"Fuck."

He strode over to her and came to his knees, his hands gripping her thighs. "Tell me what happened," he implored. "Please."

She squeezed her eyes shut and tried to force the memory back into her mind. "There was a ring of fire." She extended her hand as if painting a picture in the air.

"I was on the ground, and then he was there. Towering over me, cursing at me."

Damien gently squeezed her legs, the light pressure keeping her tethered to reality as she recalled the curse.

"I had the tiishara—it—it appeared in my hand." She opened her palms in her lap. "There was this voice in my head, taunting me…goading me, and then he came at me, and I was going to—" She covered her mouth.

"Hey. Hey, it's okay," Damien placed a hand on her cheek. Jen looked at him, completely desolate.

"I was going to kill my father, Damien. If Ronan hadn't pulled me out—"

"What do you mean Ronan pulled you—"

Panic rose in her voice. "No, no. He was just passing by. I must have looked like I was having a fit or something. I had the tiishara *in* my hand, not just in the vision but here too. I almost stabbed him. Please don't be angry."

Damien grabbed her other cheek and shook his head quickly.

"Jen, hey, no. I'm not angry. I'm glad someone was here to pull you out." Relief washed over her. "Do I think a little maiming would bring him down a peg or two, sure." He shrugged as Jen choked on a weak laugh.

Her face fell.

"I fell into that dark place so quickly. I didn't even fight it that hard…"

He moved his hands to her arms, caressing them slowly.

"You were taken by surprise, Bug. Give yourself a little grace here."

Jen was quiet for a moment. "I'm sorry I didn't tell you."

Damien arched a brow. "Why didn't you?"

Her lips trembled. "Because I didn't want you to be afraid of me."

He rose to his knees to be eye level with her, his eyes stealing into hers. "How could I *ever* be afraid of you?"

"The Knight said that the bloodline was supposed to possess light magic, but what I just did in there—"

He shook his head fervently. "You are the best person I know. You are kind. You are selfless. You are *good*," he said. "Whatever is happening here doesn't change who you are—even magic."

Jen pulled his hands from her face and held them within hers. "Whatever is happening here is much bigger than you think, Damien. I can feel it stirring under my skin. The pulse, the Arc, the visions, the trap, the Knight, the council. All of it is leading somewhere, and…"

"And what?" Damien laced his fingers with hers.

Tears fell down her cheeks.

"And you deserve better than to be shackled to me."

Damien frowned. "What in hells does that mean?"

More tears stained her cheeks.

"You deserve a happy life, Damien," she cried. "A beautiful, wonderfully happy life."

He tried to wipe her tears, but she pushed his hand away.

"I see how carefree you are with Lyla, how easy it could all be if you weren't burdened by a complicated past and an ominous void of a future. I didn't mean to drag you into this, I'm sorry."

She never wanted to put him in danger. Had she known what she was walking into, Jen would have never allowed him to come. He was too precious to her.

"You could go back to Nimea, live a peaceful life and leave this mess behind you. I would understand," she said through wretched sobs.

Damien held her hands and gently pulled her to her feet. She kept her gaze down, but he tipped her chin to meet him.

"I can't do that," he said quietly.

"Yes, you can." She clutched his tunic, desperation coursing through her. "*Please.* I need you safe."

He pressed a finger to her lips.

"I can't do that, Bug," he said, his voice low. He removed his finger and caressed her cheek with it. "Because…"

His voice turned to a whisper.

"I love you."

Her breath caught in her throat.

"You…"

His other hand moved to her waist.

"My heart has always belonged to you. I have loved you since the moment I saw you beneath the trees all those years ago," he said. "I have loved you and hated you. Protected you and betrayed you." He squeezed her waist in a silent plea for forgiveness.

"I have watched you shield the ones you love, witnessed you remain kind despite the darkness that followed—that still haunts you." He leaned his head against hers. "I am in awe of you. Gods, how could I not be?" His voice grew serious. "Maybe my life *would* be easier if I went back to Nimea. But I wouldn't have you. And that, I will not accept."

A single tear fell down her cheek. Damien gently wiped it away, lowering his head until his lips were a breath away.

"Whatever is coming, we will get through it together. It's just you and me, remember?"

Jen finally looked up, and the conviction, the devotion in his expression nearly brought her to her knees.

"I am not going anywhere. I'm with you until the end, and when that comes, I will meet you between the trees. Just like we promised."

She released a breath she didn't realize she'd been holding and stood in silence for a moment, absorbing every syllable of his words into her weary heart.

He knew her so intimately. His presence wrapped around her like a warm shield of security and love, and Jen wanted so desperately to feel safe. Damien had always been a haven. He and his beautiful, unyielding heart.

She needed him. She loved him, too.

He let her go, his brow crinkling in deep thought, and turned on his heels towards her closet. She stood there mildly bewildered until he reemerged a moment later, holding a delicate white nightgown in his hand. He brushed past her and gently placed it on the edge of the bed.

He turned to face her, and suddenly he looked a bit…anxious.

She tilted her head.

"Do you want me to…to stay tonight?"

Her heart melted at the uncertainty in his question. Despite the heaviness, she smiled and nodded her head. She watched his body relax, and then he offered his hand to her.

She padded over to him, thinking he was bringing her close to kiss her, but her breath hitched, when, instead, he turned her around, her back pressed against his chest.

He slowly moved her hair away from her neck and lowered his head to the tender spot below her ear. He planted a painfully delicate kiss, her body heating at the small touch.

"Let's get you out of this gown," he whispered.

She swallowed hard as he began to unlace the corset bodice. He grazed her neck with his teeth as the ribbons loosened one by one.

"When I saw you in this, my first thought was—" He kissed her shoulder. "Beautiful." She shuddered.

"My second thought was—" He nipped her ear, and a small gasp escaped her lips. "I wonder what it would look like on the *floor.*"

He released the bodice and the gown fell to the ground, leaving her breasts bare and only thin undergarments between them.

His fingers fluttered over her hips, the touch so light it sent shivers down her spine. "Much better," he murmured.

His hands wandered over her stomach, making idle circles as they rose up her torso. She leaned her head into the crook of his neck, her back arching for him as his nimble fingers found their way to her peaked breasts.

He sighed in approval as he caught her nipples between his thumbs and index fingers, rubbing them together in an achingly slow movement.

Gods, the way he touched her, like he knew exactly what her body needed, what she craved.

She moaned into his touch. "Damien," she breathed.

He groaned at the sound of his name on her lips. One of his hands trailed down to the band of her undergarments while the other stayed fixed on teasing her. She tilted her hips against his hand, urging him on.

She felt his smile on her neck as he trailed kisses down to her shoulder. His pace was unhurried, as if they had all the time in the world to unravel.

He let his fingers lower beneath the band, and he sucked in a breath when he felt the slick wetness waiting for him.

"Hells," he breathed.

She shuddered as he slowly moved his thumb in lazy circles over the most sensitive part of her. She could feel his own arousal harden against her backside. She grinded against him, trying desperately to find more friction. He growled and turned her around, capturing her mouth with his.

His kiss was deep and languid. She wrapped her arms around his neck and opened for him, their tongues intertwining with a tenderness that made her heart ache.

I love him—I love him beyond words.

He nudged her to the bed and gently lowered her onto her back. He climbed over her and placed his hand on her face, holding her gaze before kissing each of her cheeks. He softly nipped her bottom lip before lifting onto his knees to remove his tunic.

His beautifully sculpted chest glowed in the moonlight. She knew every ridge and dip of his muscles by heart. But still, she propped herself onto her elbows and reached out her hand.

Damien watched as her fingers met his abdomen, hunger deepening the hue of his eyes as her hand continued to wander over the terrain of his body. His head fell back, and he breathed in deeply, relishing her touch.

Jen leaned back onto the mattress, and he came with her, gently taking her hand and pressing a kiss to the inside of her palm before lowering to her neck.

Her breath grew ragged as he worked his way down, kissing between her breasts and over her navel.

He knelt between her legs, kissing and nipping her inner thighs until she was writhing under him. He chuckled, the warm air from his laugh echoing deep within her. A small whimper left her lips.

"Gods I missed this," he breathed, and his tongue dragged right up her center. The world exploded around her as she gripped the sheets and bowed into him.

And then he was devouring her. Long, luxurious licks as if he were a starving man, longing to taste every drop. He spread her thighs wider and flicked his tongue over the bundle of nerves atop her apex.

Her hands flew into his hair, feeling his head move between her legs as he gripped her thighs firmly. She could feel him moan against her as pressure began to build.

"Damien," she breathed.

He sucked the bundle into his mouth and plunged two fingers inside her, drawing out a desperate cry. He flicked his tongue faster and pumped his fingers in and out, finding the rhythm that would push her over the edge.

Jen felt her body tensing, aching for release. She wrapped her fingers in his hair and breathed, "Please."

He withdrew his fingers and held her open. "I know what you need." His tongue lowered to that bundle of nerves, moving back and forth until her body convulsed. He moaned against her once again, and her vision blurred as her climax careened through her body.

Her back bowed off the bed and she called out his name as his tongue and lips continued to move against her, wringing out every bit of pleasure from her body.

He removed himself for a moment, and while she panted in the aftermath of her orgasm, she heard him remove his pants and drop them to the floor before returning to her.

Damien kissed her passionately, the taste of her arousal on his tongue, fueling her own fervor. His eyes were hazy with lust, but still, it was love that pierced through—that lived in his unwavering gaze.

He positioned himself over her and placed himself at her entrance. He was looking at her for permission. Instead of nodding, she pulled his face to hers.

"I love you," she whispered.

The look on his face was one she would hold forever in her memory. The awe, the disbelief, it all shone brightly through that winter-sky in his eyes—like he couldn't comprehend what she had just confessed.

Whatever restraint he was holding onto snapped. He groaned at the sound of her reciprocation and sheathed himself inside her.

He swallowed her moan with a deep kiss that enveloped them both. He moved his hips, rocking in and out of her in a slow, deliberate tempo. He lifted himself onto his elbows and watched as she became lost in the fullness of him.

Jen was consumed. They were a tangle of limbs and teeth and lips as she moved her hips in time with him. She felt her body tensing again, each thrust rubbing that sensitive spot between her thighs.

She wrapped her arms and legs around him and pulled him further inside her as he bucked his hips faster.

"I love you so much," he breathed into her neck.

She kissed his neck and moaned into his ear. His entire body shivered as his pace became wild and untamable.

Jen felt herself nearing the edge and rubbed herself against his hips. "Please," she whimpered.

He reached between them and rubbed his thumb in frenzied circles, catapulting her into her release.

She screamed his name as her world shattered and reformed under his hands. He kept his fingers moving, pushing her further over the edge until he let out a sound between a moan and a cry. He called her name as his own release came over him, collapsing on her as his body shook.

They held each other close as their heart rates slowly returned to normal. Damien caressed her cheek, rubbing his nose against hers.

He unsheathed himself and pulled her against him, his arms enveloping her. She scooted closer, entangling her arms within his and settling into their embrace. He pressed his face into her neck, kissing her gently.

She sighed contently and turned her head to look over her shoulder. "Why did you bring me a nightgown?" she asked.

He chuckled into her hair.

"I was trying to be a gentleman."

He pulled her closer, and at that moment, Jen didn't feel afraid. The guilt and shame that had flooded her senses was gone, and the fear of the dreadful unknown floated just out of reach.

She knew this feeling wouldn't last forever, but she would relish it while it did. For now, she would sleep soundly in the arms of the man who loved her.

Jenevieve awoke to the peaceful sounds of Damien breathing behind her. His arms were still draped over her, as if they hadn't moved an inch all night.

It was quite the contrary, as he had woken her up several more times in the night to make slow, passionate love to her, his need insatiable.

Not that she was complaining.

The sun shone through the curtains, and when Jen peeked her head up, she found a breakfast tray sitting on the table. Shyra must have snuck in earlier and left it for them.

With as little movement as possible, she slid out from Damien's arms and threw on the nightgown that was still laying on the edge of the bed.

Gentleman my ass.

Jen smirked to herself and padded across the room to assess the tray of food. She poured herself a cup of coffee, topping it with a splash of cream and one sugar cube. She stirred it with a small golden spoon and wandered onto the balcony to admire the Etherian morning.

A small herd of horses grazed near the stables and the beginnings of a peaceful glen peeked out behind it. The river branched out into smaller streams and ponds of crystal-clear water, stretching through the valley and out of sight.

She felt a presence behind her, and a moment later, Damien stood with his hands on the railing on either side of her. He rested his chin in the space between her neck and shoulder, quietly looking out into the distance with her.

His bare chest brushed against her thin nightgown as he folded his hands in front of her. She reached her hand behind her to caress his hair.

"Morning," he breathed into her ear.

She laughed softly.

"Morning."

He turned her around, caressing her cheek, his eyes still heavy with sleep. "Sleep okay?"

"When you let me, yes," she said, arching a brow.

He wiggled his eyebrows and leaned down to kiss her, much more tenderly than she was expecting. He grabbed her hand and pulled her back towards the bedroom.

Jen giggled and placed her coffee cup on the table as they passed by. "I just woke up, Sparky," she teased.

He gave her a wolfish grin but didn't lead her to the bed. Instead, he brought her to the armchairs by the hearth.

He pulled her against him. "I would love nothing more than to never leave this room ever again," he said as he placed his hand on the nape of her neck. "And there will be many more repeats of last night." He rubbed his nose against hers. "But it seems you have somewhere to be."

He tilted his head towards one of the chairs. Jen reluctantly pulled her gaze from him and looked down.

Draped over the top of it was a set of dark brown fighting leathers, and a note.

She furrowed her brows and carefully unfolded the paper.

It said only one word.

Roof.

CHAPTER 32

Jen pulled at the skin-tight fighting leathers as she made her way up what must have been a thousand stairs to the rooftop training ring, her legs screaming in protest most of the way.

Damien had helped her into the leather before he dressed himself and, rather reluctantly, kissed her goodbye, slipping out to get ready for his own training with William and Leeyna.

She was surprised that Samara was able to train today, given the state she had been in the night before.

Maybe I didn't actually maim my friend.

Her mind was still attempting to mend the hole her rage had blasted through the stone wall. Her attempts were aimless, her mind too exhausted to keep the memories of the ball from barreling right in.

Onyx talons scraping the marble floors. Raging flames heating her skin. Burnt flesh assaulting her nose. Black twirling vines. Darya's flinch.

She shook her head, trying desperately to knock the thoughts out of her mind. But it was no use, they returned to her as soon as Damien had left, as if his presence had been some kind of dam keeping everything from bursting through.

She huffed up the last few stairs and emerged onto the rooftop.

Miles of jaw-dropping, mountainous terrain stretched before her, a breathtaking view framed by a clear blue sky that showed no trace of the darkness that had consumed the palace the night before.

Jen turned towards the ring, expecting to see Samara impatiently waiting for her.

She stopped.

She did not expect to see Fjora and Nelysar, in matching leathers, standing in the center of the ring.

"Where's Samara?" Jen asked curtly.

Nelysar stood facing the valley looking down his shoulder at Fjora, who watched Jen with an anxious strain in her eyes. She took a tentative step forward.

"She's still healing, but we didn't think you should miss a day of training."

"We?" Jen said with more bite than she meant. She ignored the tightening in her chest at the thought of Samara still in pain because of her.

Nelysar turned around, his hands crossed over his chest and his fiery green eyes watching her carefully.

"We."

Gods. The man was huge. She had seen him in her dream, and briefly again last night, but she hadn't had the chance to fully take him in. His powerful body towered over Fjora, the top of her head came to his chin. His long auburn hair was plaited on one side and a single gold bar gleaned from one of his arched ears.

Jen stood under the weight of their expectant gazes, and, after a moment, she sighed heavily and pulled at the front of her leathers.

"What's with these?"

Fjora's body relaxed.

"You should have always been wearing them, but I understand the journey here didn't allow for that," Nelysar said.

Jen inched her way towards the ring. This training yard was much larger, with several other training rings spread out across the stone floor. Every ring had its own stockpile of weapons and gear, and there was the addition of sporadically placed tables and chairs with jugs of water and glasses.

"Isn't your *sister* the warrior?"

Fjora snorted. Nelysar smiled warmly at the sound, before raising a brow at Jen.

"She'll love that you said that. Yes, Naezara is the general of the Inbetween forces."

"The Warriors of Kiara?"

His eyebrows shot up.

"They are the elite faction of our forces."

"And they are all Regals."

Nelysar glanced at Fjora, who looked equally bewildered.

Jen lifted a shoulder. "I saw the Warriors when I was fleeing Nimea." Jen pointed to his ears. "The arched ears and ivory under their cloaks."

"Well, we don't *just* wear ivory." He gestured to his dark brown leathers. "That would severely limit our wardrobe."

"You're a Warrior then?"

Something about the way he rubbed the back of his neck told her he wasn't expecting to be grilled with questions this morning. Fjora watched quietly, eyeing him as he answered.

"For a long time, I was, but there came a time when my abilities were needed elsewhere."

"Like holding open a barrier."

A flinch of sadness rolled over his features. "Amongst other things, yes."

Jen looked down at her feet. The image of Fjora and Nelysar clinging to each other as he held the barrier open scraped against her mind.

She rocked back and forth on her heels, looking down at the ground to conceal how uncomfortable she felt. Fjora seemed to notice and took a tentative step towards her. "Jenevieve, about last night—"

Nope.

Jen blew past them towards a cart of equipment on the outskirts of the ring beside them. "I don't want to talk about that."

Her mind was still piecing itself back together. She couldn't handle reliving the havoc her magic wrought on that ballroom of innocent people. She couldn't risk the darkness seeping back out when her mind was still so fragile.

She swung a leg back and started a set of lunges.

Fjora and Nelysar followed her.

"Darling, I—"

"Don't call me that," Jen snipped.

Fjora winced while Nelysar peered down at her.

"That's the *second* time I've heard that in twelve hours."

Fjora ignored him and kept her gaze fixed on Jen.

"I tried to find you before the ball. We wanted to do that entrance as a family."

Jen paused. *That* wasn't where she thought this conversation was going, but it wasn't exactly a reprieving pivot.

She resumed her warmups. "Then you got what you wanted."

"Jenevieve. You are a part of this family."

Jen stood up and crossed her arms.

"Am I?"

Nelysar stepped between them.

"Alright, that's enough." He pointed to the training ring. "Both of you in the ring."

They both put their hands on their hips and glared at him in defiance. His eyes bounced between them.

"Well, you sure look like family from here."

Jen dropped her hands immediately.

He cleared his throat and ran a hand over his plaited hair. "Okay. Let's just breathe."

Nelysar closed his eyes and took a deep breath. He cracked one eye open to see neither woman following his lead. "Or… not." He exhaled. "Let's just start with reviewing the sparring movements, and then you can hit each other."

"Why am I even up here?" Jen gestured to the ring. "Shouldn't I be learning to use my power? Isn't that the entire *point* of all of this, especially considering I just learned that apparently, I possess ancient, light magic?"

Nelysar traipsed towards her. He looked her up and down, examining her. "You're depleted." He leaned forward. "That blast of power left your body ragged and exhausted."

Rude.

Jen clenched her fists.

"In order to wield that kind of power, your body must be able to physically support it, and that comes from this." He gestured to the ring.

She turned on her heels to stomp away, but her steps faltered on the stone and her gaze fell back to Nelysar.

"Last night, that was a Knight of Eseer, wasn't it?"

He glanced at Fjora and then back to Jen.

"Yes, it was."

She released a sigh and ran her fingers over her bottom lip.

Nelysar considered her carefully. "That wasn't the first time you've seen one of them."

"No. It wasn't." She rubbed her temples. "He was able to—to freeze everyone. What was that?"

"An extension of Heltior. When they swear fealty, a whisper of magic is gifted to them, allowing them to temporarily tap into specific areas of his power stores."

That's new, and terrible. Shocking.

"Swear fealty—"

Nelysar crossed his arms, a flash of disdain flickering in his eyes. "The Knights of Eseer *chose* to follow him. You saw the trident on his arm."

The same trident from the pulse.

A wave of nausea fluttered through her stomach. Even with the small amount she'd learned, she knew Heltior consumed their souls for power, which didn't seem like something one would volunteer for.

She ran her hand over her messy bun.

"Why did the kashyak come?"

Fjora's eyes darted to her. "You know what that is?"

"One of them tracked me from Zaniya."

Fjora looked horrified. "Tracked—"

"After I witnessed an Echo from the Tree of Whispers."

Nelysar froze, his mouth dropped open.

"You…" he breathed. "You *what*?"

She rubbed her hands over her arms. "I touched the tree and the vision just *happened*."

"That's—" Nelysar seemed lost for words.

Jen threw up her hands. "I know, I know. *Rare*."

"What was the Echo?"

She looked nervously at Fjora, who watched her closely.

"Kiara giving birth—the beginning of the bloodline."

Nelysar kept a neutral expression, but Jen could have sworn she saw the blood drain from his face. "You saw Naedyra."

Her eyes widened at the sound of that name.

"How—"

His expression didn't change.

"Naedyra was my mother."

Mother.

She thought back to the echo. She had very clearly watched Kiara take her final breaths, but Naedyra had just…disappeared down that stairwell with the midwife.

"She—you—" she sputtered. "How *old* are you?"

Fjora appeared at Nelysar's side, her chest leaning against his arm. "Jenevieve," she warned.

Jen jerked her head back with an accusatory brow. "Really? *That's* where the line is?"

Nelysar wrapped his hand around Fjora's. "It's alright, *mo nuri*," he said to her. He turned his focus back to Jen. "Old."

Jen scoffed at the answer.

Immortals think they're so funny with their vague answers to simple questions. Hilarious.

He chuckled and squeezed Fjora's hand before jutting his chin back to the training ring. "That's enough chatting, for now."

Fjora and Jen stood on opposite sides of the ring as Nelysar worked them through a series of drills. He was a good teacher, Jen had to admit. He was patient but firm and had a way of correcting her without making her feel like a complete idiot.

When he showed by example, his body flowed like a dance, his muscles moving with an instinctual current that was mesmerizing to watch.

After a particularly grueling set of kicks, Jen rested her hands on her legs, trying to catch her breath. She glanced over and saw sweat dripping down Fjora's face, which made her feel better about her own exhaustion.

Nelysar walked over to Fjora and tucked some stray hairs behind her ear. "You're doing well, *mo nuri*. It's coming back to you; your body remembers."

Jen shot up and fought against the black splotches blurring her vision. "You've trained her before?"

Nelysar looked proudly at Fjora and playfully nudged her with his elbow. "Sure did."

Another reminder of how my existence ruined her life.

"Can we get this over with?"

Nelysar glanced at Fjora, who gave a resigned nod. He retrieved a roll of thick fabric from the cart of gear and wrapped each of their hands. He directed them to their sparring positions and said, "To be clear, sparring is not real fighting. I'll call out the combinations and you'll take turns striking and blocking. Clear?"

They both gave a short nod. He looked between the two of them, looking entirely unconvinced. "Alright then. Jen, you'll strike first."

They took their positions, angling their bodies and setting one foot in front of the other. They lifted their hands into fists and listened for his command.

Nelysar stood at the edge of the ring.

"Jab, cross, hook, cross."

Jen stepped forward and threw her jab. Fjora moved to block before shifting to intercept the cross.

"You look my age, now," Jen grunted.

Actually, she looks a little younger.

"I'm an Ascendiant, but I was cut off from the—perks, of my lineage when I fled behind the wards of Bri. As you know, there is no magic in Nimea."

She turned her body and landed a hook on the shield Fjora formed beside her head, the strike fueled by the mention of her home.

But was it every truly my home? It certainly wasn't Fjora's.

Nelysar paced around them, watching their form and, well—ensuring no one threw a real punch. Jen's eyes darted to him before she finished the combination. Fjora extended her hand to block the final cross.

"Rhea, Darya and Jamie—they're Ascendiants as well."

"Half...but yes, they are."

Nelysar barked out the next combination.

"Fjora; hook, cross, hook."

They reset their stances, their fists raised. The morning sun beat down on the ring as the women circled each other.

"And Rhea is your heir."

"I suppose so..."

She leapt forward. Strike. Block. Strike. Block.

"It clearly wouldn't be me, since I'm not actually your daughter. I have no claim, not that I want it."

"Why would you say that?"

Nelysar called out to them.

"Jen; jab, cross, hook, knee."

Jab. Block. Cross. Block.

They were sweating through their skin-tight leathers. Jen missed the thin fabric of her tunics, the armor making her feel claustrophobic.

"No one would want to see me on a throne, anyway—a *bloodliner*."

Hook. Block.

"Don't say it like that."

Jen latched onto Fjora's shoulders and threw her knee into the awaiting block. She released her hands and pushed herself back, her breath growing shallow.

"Like what? Like it's some kind of curse? Like it makes me dangerous?"

Fjora raised her hand to silence the oncoming combination command from Nelysar. She reached for Jen's hand.

"You are so much more than the bloodline, my darling."

Jen ripped her hand away and paced towards the other side of the ring.

"I saw you, you know." She turned to Nelysar. "Both of you."

Fjora frowned. "What do you mean?"

"The night you took me through Bri."

Jen looked at Fjora. "I watched you beg him to go with you." She shifted to Nelysar. "I watched you hold open the barrier and proclaim your love." Her voice cracked as her eyes found Fjora's. "I watched you crumble to the ground and sob with a babe that wasn't even your own."

Fjora clenched her jaw. "I remember it quite clearly, Jenevieve, and I do not wish to relive one of the worst days of my life."

Nelysar stepped to Fjora's side and placed his hand on the small of her back. "We did what we had to do for the good of Etheria."

"I'm the reason you left your life, your family, *him*." Jen thrusted her arm at Nelysar.

I destroyed her life.

"I'm the reason you didn't get to say goodbye to your mother. I'm the reason my parents are dead. I'm the reason why people were hurt last night." She put her hand on her chest. "Samara isn't here to train me because I *hurt* her."

The words got caught in her throat. She felt something pressing against her heart, but it wasn't rage, nor was it darkness.

It was sorrow.

How can I be expected to wield light magic, when pain and death follow me at every turn?

"You didn't mean for that to happen," Fjora said.

Jen rounded on her.

"Why didn't you tell me anything? I had no *idea* who I was. I still don't! You didn't train me. You didn't educate me. You didn't even tell me Etheria was real. You let me believe it was a legend that lived in the pages of an old book."

Fjora closed her eyes tightly and released a sigh. When she opened them, her gaze was clouded with regret.

"I was young, and my heart was shattered. I tried Jenevieve, I truly did, but I know I failed you."

Jen couldn't bear the look on Fjora's face, the genuine admission of the mistakes she made and the burden she now carried. Her gaze shifted out to the vista beyond the ring.

"Did you think I couldn't handle it?" Her voice croaked. "That I was too weak? Too soft-hearted?" She was almost whispering.

"It had nothing to do with you, sweetheart."

Jen's attention jumped to Nelysar.

"Tell me what's happening," she demanded, pointing her chin towards the valleys beyond the training ring. "Out there."

Fjora tried to interject. "Jen—"

"No." She raised her hand. "I deserve to know."

Nelysar looked at her. "You do."

"Nel."

"It's alright, Fjora."

He looked out over the valley. "Since the age of the Aylaenor, light and dark forces have existed in Etheria, two opposing powers that both repel and depend on one another, delicately balanced on the tip of a needle." He walked towards the edge of the ring.

"A thousand years ago, Heltior committed an act that went against the laws of nature and thrusted that balance into chaos. He took it further and murdered the Council of Suran, polarizing the entire continent and destroying that delicate balance."

"What does that have to do with what's coming now?"

Nelysar turned to her. "Everything."

"For five hundred years he has been laying the groundwork for an invasion, and if he succeeds, the conflict between those who follow the light and those who dwell in darkness will come barreling towards us in a cataclysm of unimaginable carnage."

Jen turned pale. "War."

Nelysar nodded gravely. "The war of our time is inevitable," he said. "It will come for us all."

"Can we stop it?"

His eyes brightened at the togetherness implied in her question, but quickly his face grew somber. "That is the sobering thing about the inevitable—there is no escaping it. We can only prepare and brace ourselves for the impact."

Jen crinkled her brow. "That sounds like giving up."

Nelysar straightened. "It isn't, but there is only so much we can do when those who seek to destroy us remain hidden within the shadows," he said. "I have to think of my people."

"I have people, too. People that *I* need to protect." She stared down at her boots. "I know the bloodline is meant to rival Heltior, but—" She touched her heart. "There's something wrong with me…something's missing…the light feels…dim…"

Useless.

Nelysar slowly walked towards Jen until he was within a foot of her. She craned her neck to look at him, her eyes filled with utter defeat.

"You were always meant to wield the light, Jenevieve. Fate simply delayed your receiving of it, that's all." He placed a gentle hand on her shoulder.

"But make no mistake," he said, his eyes twinkling as if lost in the past. "Your presence, your destiny—"

Nelysar glanced at Fjora, and they looked as if, for a moment, they were sharing the same memory. He turned back to Jen, the corner of his mouth raising in a small grin.

"You are the hope of this world."

Jen's eyes darted to his hand on her shoulder, then flicked up to meet his. "I'm no one's hope."

His face fell as she pulled away and fled toward the stairs, the weight of her guilt and pain clawing up from the abyss she had tried to bury it in.

CHAPTER 33

"Jenevieve—yoohoo!" Gaiana shouted from the edge of the elemental circle.

Jen's attention snapped back to Gaiana, who was pointing to the ground in front of her with an amused expression on her face. Jen peered down and realized she'd flooded the entire circle, her boots almost fully submerged in ice cold water.

Gaiana had tasked her with simply filling the three buckets that sat on the ground in front of her. It'd been easy enough to summon the first droplets into the bucket, like slowly turning on the faucet in her mind, allowing the Taejja to travel like an iced over river through the warmth of her veins.

She had only been training for a few days, but she discovered that each element had a different bodily sensation associated with it.

Water was icy veins. Air prickled the surface of her skin. Earth felt like her bones were pulling power from the very ground on which she stood. Fire, well, fire felt like her entire body was being engulfed in flames.

They had been working on isolating each element, and today was water. But after the physically and emotionally grueling training session earlier that morning, her focus was completely shot.

It felt like someone had reached into her mind and broke the faucet, the water now gushing as an uncontrollable flood.

She shook her head and lifted one of her boots out of the water.

"I'm sorry."

Gaiana curved her palm down, and the water receded into the ground, like the earth was absorbing it. "It's alright, my dear. The ground was looking parched anyways," she said with a wink.

Jen blinked rapidly. "What the—"

Gaiana stepped into the circle, her hands folded in front of her. "I simply returned it to the earth," she said with a mischievous grin.

Jen looked down at the overflowing buckets and pressed the heels of her hands into her eyes. "I'm sorry. I can't seem to focus."

Gaiana gestured to the circle around them.

"You are safe in this circle. The elements are contained within the wards around it, you can explore your power without fear here."

She sat on the ground, her multi-pattern linen skirts bunching up around her. Jen joined her, folding her hands in her lap.

"Do you want to tell me what's making you sad today?"

"I'm not sad," she said quietly.

Gaiana arched a brow. "My dear, magic is rooted in emotion. and Taejja is no different." She leaned back on her hands.

Jen idly played with the dirt in front of her.

"What do you mean by that?"

Gaiana closed her eyes and took in a deep breath, a serene smile curling on her lips. A gentle gust of wind blew between them, weaving its way around her outstretched arms.

"Air responds to empathy, *compassion*." She allowed the tickle of wind to wrap around her fingers before she released it with a flick of her wrist.

She tilted her head. "Why do you think it was the first element to show itself to you?"

Jen shrugged.

Gaiana placed her hand on the ground in front of her. She rubbed a gentle circle with her palm and pulled her hand up. A small seedling sprouted from the earth.

"Earth responds to humility and strength." Her fingers grazed the delicate leaves. "Together, those qualities create grounding within the soul," she spoke with the inflection of one telling a story to a child. Her eyes were alive with magic, while Jen continued to pick at the dirt.

"I shouldn't be able to summon it if that's the case."

Gaiana placed her hand over the seedling and pulled her hand up once more, bringing the whimsical bloom of a daffodil to life. She plucked it from the ground and reached over to gently place it behind Jen's ear.

"Invoking any sort of magic forces us to journey inward, my dear. You would not be able to summon it if the potential for stability and balance wasn't already there, pulsing somewhere deep within you."

She took Jen's hand and glanced at the overflowing buckets. Jen followed her gaze and released a tense sigh.

"Let me guess, water responds to sorrow?"

Gaiana chuckled, lifting her hand with a sway to summon the water from the buckets. It flowed into a ribboning stream, bright streaks of iridescent light glinting off its surface in the late afternoon sun. "It responds to sorrow, yes. But also, to fear, and in the opposing direction, peace."

The ribbon of dancing water wound around them until Gaiana guided it back to the bucket with a splash. She rested her head in her hands and patiently waited for Jen to speak.

"I…um…" She wrung her hands, trying to find the words. "I'm sad, yes. But more than anything, I'm…I'm afraid." Her voice grew small. "I'm afraid I'm something to fear—that I'm dangerous."

Gaiana scooted closer and placed her hands over Jen's.

"I try so hard to keep the anger—the *rage,* at bay, to hide it from the world. And then last night…with the Knight…I—I thought maybe the bloodline magic would appear—that *light* magic would save everyone, but then," she stammered. "The fire…it *hurt* people, it didn't save them, and it felt—dark," Jen said, her eyes wide with fear and anguish. "The fire felt my rage…"

Gaiana shook her head again.

"Fire does not respond to rage, Jenevieve, it responds to *passion*. And *you* decide what that means."

Jen opened her mouth to interject, but Gaiana continued.

"Right now, yes, it is presenting as rage. But passion is not just reserved for anger." She patted Jen's hand. "It is also reserved for beautiful emotions, and that, in my humble opinion, is where true power lies."

Jen looked down at their hands.

"I just feel angry and sad and guilty all the time. It's too heavy."

"But you also feel *love*."

Jen peered up at her.

"You are the child of Aiyla and Lior. Even though there may be darkness present, there is also radiant light that has nothing to do with magic, and you received that from *them*."

Jen stifled a gasp. "You—you knew my parents?"

She hadn't heard anyone, but Fjora, speak her mother's name, and she'd never heard her father's until now.

Gaiana ran soothing hands over hers. She smiled sadly. "Yes, I did. And they were good people, Jenevieve."

Jen's eyes stung with tears, but Gaiana did not let go of her. "They loved you so much. You were conceived out of *love*, my dear. They knew the risks, but they wanted you so very badly."

"I don't understand," Jen whispered.

Gaiana released a sigh, as if she was deciding whether to continue. "During her pregnancy, your mother and father traveled to Senya, along with Fjora, Nelysar and his sister." She smiled to herself. "They were inseparable."

"They headed to the Tree of Awakenings. There, your mother received a vision."

I don't like where this is going.

"They were told that the child she carried would be a powerful iejja, but there was something else as well."

Jen's heart slammed against her chest.

"The child would signal the end of the bloodline, and she would become the bridge between the forces of light and the forces of darkness, emerging as the *Oshara*, a being of prophecy that would bring balance back to Etheria."

I'm sorry, what?

Jen yanked her hands away. "You're telling me that a war, not just any war, but an existential clash between magical forces is barreling towards Etheria, a continent I have known about for a few weeks, and I am supposed to—" She swallowed the lump forming in her throat, "be its savior?"

No. Absolutely not.

She shot up from the ground and marched towards the house, but Gaiana grabbed her arm.

"Jenevieve—"

Jen whirled around. "No. *No*, Gaiana. I can't do it. I can't be the Oshara." She shook out her hands to keep them from shaking. "I am not a being of prophecy." She paced back and forth.

"I taught music. I had a garden. I had a home with a family and a mother who made apple cakes and wasn't a lost princess of a world that existed in legends."

She stopped, dread crashing into the pit of her stomach.

"Did she know?"

Gaiana tilted her head, unsure of the question.

"Did Fjora know I was the Oshara?"

Gaiana hesitated, Jen stepped toward her. "*Did* she?"

"She was with Aiyla when the vision came, yes."

All the air *whooshed* from Jen's lungs. The sting of betrayal stabbed her heart and threatened to cut it out of her chest. Fjora had known. For thirty years she knew and did nothing—said *nothing*.

Her head began to spin, and then her legs crumbled beneath her, but Gaiana was there to catch her. Jen peered up into deep, compassionate brown eyes.

"There's no one left," Jen's voice cracked. "I'm the last one."

"Yes, dear."

"They are all dead." Jen shivered. "He murdered them all."

Gaiana placed her hand on Jen's cheek. "Not all of them."

Tears threatened to fall from the corners of her eyes, but she blinked them away. "But why me? I'm too broken to wield the light…too tainted by my own darkness. I'm the wrong choice. I'm—I'm no one."

Gaiana held her gaze.

"There is, within each of us, a battle that no one sees, our own set of demons to reckon with," she said, running the back of her hand along Jen's cheek. "But Etheria called upon you, *chose* you, for a reason, Jenevieve—do not let it fall upon deaf ears."

This isn't happening.

Jen peeled off her sweaty leathers and threw them into the laundry basket. Her muscles ached as she gingerly pulled on a soft, lavender dress.

This is a dream. A very long, terrifying dream.

She loosened the tie from her hair and let her golden waves cascade down her back, scrubbing her scalp with her fingertips as she walked into the bedroom.

The room was silent, save for a few birds chirping outside on the veranda. Every time silence found her now, the same faint ringing sang in her ears to fill the void, as if her mind was trying to protect her from her own thoughts.

She rolled her stone in her hand and walked aimlessly about the room. She leaned on one of the marble columns as the weight of the last day bore down on her, the stone a cool relief beneath her warming skin.

Why did I even ask? Not only am I the last in an ancient bloodline, now I'm a prophetic being meant to save a continent.

Her eyes stung as she held the stone against her navel. She took slow, deep breaths through trembling lips. Her resolve was about to slip away when she heard a soft knock at the door.

She shoved herself off the column and blinked back the threat of tears as Emelie cautiously entered the room.

"Jen…" she said, scanning the room.

Jen tensed. On top of the revelations the day had thrown at her, she wasn't sure where she stood with her best friend after last night—or with anyone.

Emelie spotted her and bolted across the room. To Jen's surprise, Emelie threw her arms around her in a tight embrace that threatened to release the tears she held back.

"Are you okay?" Emelie asked, her arms still firmly wrapped around her.

What a question to ask.

Jen gently removed herself from the embrace and tried to bypass the question. "Have you seen anyone else since last night?"

Emelie lifted a brow in light exasperation, but answered, nonetheless. "I have. Everyone is fine, a little shaken up, but physically no one is hurt."

Jen fiddled with her fingers. "Except Samara."

Emelie pursed her lips.

"Ronan and I were with her all night; she's going to be okay."

The clanking of china and stumbling feet pulled their attention to the door. "Oh, Goddess, Miss Jenevieve, Miss Emelie," Shyra said as she hurried over to place the golden tray on the table.

She walked over to Jen and grabbed her hand, worry etched into her kind face. "Are you both alright? I can't believe it, a Knight of Eseer in the palace," she said, shaking her head in disbelief.

Jen squeezed her hand and gave her a reassuring smile. "Everyone is okay, Shyra. Did you release your lantern?"

Shyra let go of her hand and went to work setting up the tea. "I did, I released it from here," she said, gesturing to the balcony.

She spooned tea leaves in two cups. "First the scouting parties, now a Knight brazenly entering our realm. It's only a matter of time before—"

It's only a matter of time, Jenevieve.

The Knight's parting words echoed in her ears.

"Before what?" Emelie asked.

Shyra stilled for a moment, like she hadn't realized she spoke out loud. She stood up straight and idly swiped at her apron. "Maids talk," she said in a low voice, her eyes darting around as if someone were eavesdropping.

"Word is that Vondur is sending out more scouting parties; Lutteala has reported sightings of kashyaks roaming the skies, and foot soldiers seem to be building strongholds along the valleys in the north."

Nelysar was right. An invasion is coming. And then, war.

Emelie padded over to the table. "What does that mean?"

Shyra's face grew solemn.

"It means, the fates have sung their song."

Act 3

There is a song upon the horizon, where light and shadow merge within the hues of twilight—a stunning kaleidoscope of death and dawn.

CHAPTER 34

Jen flung out her arms, the wind rushing over them as she and Zarah galloped towards the stables. Around them, the valley's lush grasses rippled like a living sea in the cool breeze of early evening, while the red-brown peaks of the Kalli rose like sentinels around them.

She could just make out the training yard on top of the palace.

A grimace twisted her features.

Since their one and only training session—and the discovery, almost two weeks ago, of betrayal and her role as a prophetic *bridge*, she had all but avoided not just Fjora, but most everyone.

She had discovered the third training ring hidden in the bottom levels of the palace, and had chosen to train there, alone.

Of course, Damien and Emelie would never allow her to become a complete recluse and so made excuses to check in on her. Damien took it a step further and spent every night with her, holding her close while the world faded into peaceful obscurity.

And it killed her that she couldn't bring herself to tell him anything. She didn't know how, at least, not yet.

How do you tell the man you love that you are the last of an ancient bloodline destined to bring balance back to Etheria, but not before the war of our time wreaks havoc upon us.

Jen dismounted and ran her hand along Zarah's neck; she had begun going for late afternoon rides after her sessions with Gaiana. There was something exhilarating about galloping through the valley with reckless abandon, something Jen sorely needed. The pressure of the Oshara was weighing heavily on her. Not to mention, she hadn't confronted Fjora yet.

"Alright, go on," she said as Zarah nuzzled her shoulder. Her beautiful horse whinnied before galloping back out into the valley.

Gaiana emerged from the stables to untack the chocolate-brown horse tied to the fence. She had warned Jen that she was going to ride up to the palace after their session.

"To light a fire under that stubborn king's ass."

They had hoped that something useful would come from the horrific night at the ball, that perhaps Haythem would return to his former valiant persona and agree to join the council. But unfortunately, it seemed to have the opposite effect.

And Gaiana was not a patient woman.

Jen wandered around the side of the long, weather-worn building to discover Leeyna brushing a gigantic, black stallion—Ronan's Friesian, Bear.

That really is an oddly perfect name for that mammoth of a horse.

She held her breath and walked over, her boots crunching in the sand and pebble mixture that surrounded the stable. She hadn't seen much of Leeyna since the ball and half expected her to flinch at Jen's presence the way the courtiers had begun to.

But Leeyna looked over and a radiant smile consumed her entire face. Her long crimson curls blew freely in the breeze, the freckles on her fair skin more pronounced than usual.

A territorial growl came from between her feet, where the stable dog stood alert to Jen's presence. Leeyna scowled at him.

"Oh, hush," she scolded. The dog whimpered before he lowered himself to the ground, his eyes still wary.

Leeyna must have sensed Jen's unease, so instead of speaking, she reached into the small wooden crate beside her and retrieved a second brush. She offered it to her with an understanding smile.

Jen took it gratefully and situated herself on the other side of the steed. They quietly ran their brushes across Bear's shiny, onyx coat, with only the sounds of moving bristles and the distant whinnies of the other horses in the pasture.

Leeyna seemed perfectly content to continue in silence, but it was leaving Jen with her own thoughts for too long.

She cleared her throat.

"Can I ask you something?" she asked softly, her gaze stayed fixed on the brush strokes.

"Mhm," Leeyna hummed from her side of the horse.

Jen's hand dropped by her side. "Why did you come with us?"

Leeyna slowed her hand. Jen quickly amended. "I'm happy you are here. Truly, I just, you had a life in Nimea, a family business and—"

"I was betrothed," Leeyna said through a sigh.

Jen lifted her arm and started brushing again. "You were?"

"To a man my father's age," she sighed. "I was due to travel to his village the day after your sister's wedding."

Jen stepped under Bear's neck.

"So, when you came with us…"

"I saw an opportunity." Leeyna ran the brush along the horse's back. "I didn't want the betrothal. Gareth was well off and agreed to help my family's business in exchange for my hand. But he wasn't…" Two lines appeared between her brows. "He wasn't the kindest man."

Jen ran her hand along Bear's neck. "I'm sorry to hear that."

"When the morai attacked the wedding and everyone was running for cover, there was this voice in the back of my head, telling me I *needed* to follow you, like a whisper coming from beyond the trees," she tapered off.

Oh good, someone else is hearing voices. That's comforting.

"I left the betrothal ring on one of the tables and let them all think I died in the fires."

"Does William know?"

Leeyna's cheeks flushed. "I confided in him in the forest before we crossed over. He's been so understanding and kind."

"And *handsome*."

The flush was now crawling up Leeyna's neck. She quickly cleared her throat.

Jen returned to her side of the stallion. "I'm—"

I'm sorry you escaped a betrothal just to be thrown into a never-ending cascade of dangerous encounters and an imminent war.

"If you say, 'I'm sorry', I'm going to throw my brush at you." Leeyna stuck her brush wielding hand above the Bear's back for emphasis.

Jen snorted at the feigned threat before Leeyna appeared in the space beneath the horse's neck, her face more serious now.

"I've thought a lot about this." She patted Bear's chest. "For one reason or another, I think we were all meant to take this journey with you."

They whipped their heads towards the sound of distant voices coming over one of the nearby hills. Jen's face fell when she saw who it was.

King Haythem and Fjora, trailed by Nelysar and Bastien.

She quickly averted her gaze to the ground in front of her.

"They've been coming out here every few days," Leeyna explained as she ran her brush through Bear's thick mane.

"Why?" Jen tried to ask nonchalantly.

"I think the crypt is out in those hills somewhere."

Jen attempted to stay hidden behind Bear's tall shoulders, but then she heard a familiar voice calling out to the group.

"Haythem! We need to talk, you old coot," Gaiana shouted.

Bear spooked and reared against the lead rope. Jen and Leeyna dropped their brushes and leapt back to avoid his flailing hooves. Leeyna waited a moment before grabbing the halter, attempting to calm him down.

The dog yanked the brush from her other hand and took off behind the stable. "Hey!" Leeyna yelled. "Come back here!" She ran after him, disappearing behind the stable as well.

"Leeyna!" Jen followed her, catching a glimpse of her light blue dress as it vanished around a bend in the stream. "Wait up!"

She stopped abruptly when she felt the subtle pull coming from her chest and heard the familiar hum in her ears.

A thread wrapped around her and gently coaxed her forward while the faint, melodious hum once again branched into cascading harmonies and dissonance.

She continued by the stream until she came around a steep hill and found herself in the opening of a glen, with hills of emerald grass and grey stone that sparkled like silver rising to flank the valley. The sky had melted into exquisite shades of burnt orange and magenta, the moon climbing slowly as the sun breathed its last whispers of light.

The stream poured into a small lake of deep blue-green water. Subtle ripples billowed out from the stream's source as if brought on by the gentle touch of a willow branch.

But Jen didn't notice the beauty around her.

The hum and the thread disappeared, and all she could see was her friend standing still with the dog at her feet.

And an enormous Etherian wolf standing at the water's edge.

For a moment, nothing moved. The air was still, as if it were afraid to conjure even the faintest breath of a breeze.

The wolf lifted its head from the lake's surface and stood at the daunting height of a large horse, its long fur a deep brown that echoed crimson in the faint glow of the moon, illuminating its striking eyes. One green. One silver.

Its piercing gaze was fixed on Leeyna, who hadn't moved since Jen found her standing far too close to it.

Jen started to take a step forward when an arm shot out in front of her.

"Don't."

Gaiana appeared beside her.

"What do we do?" Jen whispered. She was trying to stay level-headed, but she had no desire to tell William that she let his love get eaten by a giant wolf.

Gaiana rubbed her chin.

"We do not interfere."

Jen looked dumbfounded. "What?"

Gaiana pointed at the wolf, who hadn't so much as glanced in their direction.

"That is Selene."

"It has a *name?*"

"*She* is the alpha of the Etherian wolves. A queen, some might say." She cast a sidelong glance at Jen. Realization dawned on her.

"Wait…" She looked back at the wolf. "That's—"

Gaiana nodded.

"The bond of Queen Eliana."

"There was this voice in the back of my head, telling me I needed to follow you, like a whisper coming from beyond the trees."

Jen stood agape. That day they met Gaiana, the prophetic moment with Leeyna in the house—this was it.

"She disappeared when the queen died and hasn't been seen in two years."

Leeyna let the bristle brush fall from her hand into the grass and humbly faced her empty palms to the alpha.

"Something called her back?" Jen looked on as Leeyna took slow, deliberate steps towards Selene, her breath steady.

Gaiana folded her hands in front of her.

"Someone."

Selene mirrored Leeyna, her large paws sinking into the damp earth. They walked towards each other, matching step for step until Selene towered over her, casting her in shadow.

Leeyna lifted her hand and extended it towards the wolf, who bared her terrifying canines in an assertion of dominance. Jen clapped her hand to her mouth in a silent gasp.

Leeyna tilted her head without an ounce of fear and whispered in a voice Jen did not recognize.

"Selene."

The wolf tilted her head curiously. Leeyna remained still, keeping her hand extended to allow the wolf a moment to study her. Selene closed her eyes and moved her head forward, placing the bridge of her nose against the open palm of Leeyna's hand.

Together, they stood beneath the rising moon and the setting sun as a warm glow emanated from her fingers and into the dark skin of the wolf's snout.

Gaiana sucked in a breath and reached for Jen's hand. "I have never seen this—the bond happening without ceremony."

Jen placed her hand on Gaiana's arm. "This looks like a ceremony to *me*."

Selene stepped back from Leeyna and stretched her front legs until she was in a deep, solemn bow. Leeyna responded in kind, hinging at her waist into an equally low bow.

"What is going on here?"

Gaiana and Jen spun around to Haythem and Fjora standing in the opening of the glen, Nelysar and Bastien a few paces behind them.

Haythem's eyes were wide as he watched Leeyna with his wife's bond, an unreadable emotion flickering over his face. Gaiana took a purposeful step towards him.

"What does it look like to you, Haythem?"

He glanced at the wolf, and then back to her. He clapped his hand to his cheek.

"That's—that's not possible."

Fjora tugged at her father's sleeve. "Papa…"

He shook his head, his eyebrows furrowed into a hard line. He pointed his trembling finger at Selene.

"That is *Eliana's* bond."

"Eliana is *gone*, Haythem," Gaiana said emphatically. "Selene has no bond."

Haythem marched towards Leeyna, but Jen stepped in his path. His sharp gaze found hers. "Move."

Jen lifted her chin. "Leeyna was led here. She did not seek out the queen's bond," she said. Fjora's eyebrows shot up at the defiant tone in her voice.

"Don't you see what's happening here?" Jen looked back at Leeyna, who was now stroking Selene's deep brown coat.

Haythem followed her gaze. He scoffed.

"You have no idea what you are talking about."

"Papa. *Enough*," Fjora said as she placed herself between them. For a fleeting moment, her eyes flickered over to Jen before returning to her father. "Listen, *please*."

"Etheria senses something," Gaiana spoke clearly and without an ounce of patience. "Bonds like this don't just happen, Selene could *feel* Leeyna." She gestured around her. "Don't you recognize this place?"

Jen looked back at Haythem, who rested his hand on the pommel of his sword and sighed heavily, his head hung low.

"Eliana received her bond in this glen." His chin jutted towards Leeyna. "On that spot."

Jen bit her bottom lip.

"Haythem," Nelysar said quietly. He came beside Fjora and took her hand. "We know you loved Eliana, we *all* did. But you must find a way to carry the grief, because the world has not stopped moving."

He placed his hand on Haythem's shoulder.

"In all my years, I have never once seen a spontaneous bond. This is a sign—one we cannot ignore. Selene sought out another bond because she can sense Etheria spinning towards a greater conflict."

Fjora gazed at her father. "It's time, Papa."

He looked around the small circle of people, and then back to Leeyna and the wolf. He took a step towards them, but stopped in his tracks when Leeyna turned to face him.

Selene loomed as a shadow behind her, that one silver eye glowing brightly in the growing moonlight. They seemed in that moment—*as one*.

A single tear fell from the king's anguished gaze.

When he turned back, Jen stood just a few feet from him. Her fixed stare held compassion, but not a trace of weakness.

As he approached her, his expression softened.

"I wasn't always this man," he murmured as he looked over his shoulder. "This…shell." He looked past her to his daughter. "But what kind of man was I? If I couldn't protect my child? My wife?"

Jen folded her arms over her chest. "I understand what it's like to fail at protecting the ones you love. But Goddess has given us a chance to atone—to do better."

She had never invoked the Goddess, and she didn't yet understand the significance, but the slight widening of Haythem's eyes told her it was the right thing to say.

He stepped back, and in a flash of metal in the moonlight he unsheathed his great sword. The king held the blade in his hands, his eyes never leaving Jen's.

He knelt.

Those behind him stood rooted in shock. Silent tears rolled down Fjora's cheeks as Nelysar held tightly to her hand. Bastien stood beside them, watching intently.

"I, Haythem II, descendant of King Soryn, vow to uphold the oath of my ancestors. I will join the Council of Suran. Sachandes will stand with you in the days ahead. This I swear."

He bowed his head.

"Ufreijaa nuri."

Jen gazed down at the king, and then at the moonlit glen where the silhouette of a woman and her wolf cast a magnificent shadow over the tranquil lake. And beyond that, the brilliant stars twinkled with triumphant light over the night sky.

CHAPTER 35

Jen sat at the table the next evening, her eyes narrowed in concentration. Damien watched her from the balcony, his expression dancing with amusement as he sipped his tea.

"How's it going—"

"SHH!" Jen hissed.

She placed her hand over the golden pitcher sitting in front of her. She closed her eyes and summoned the icy chill that coated her veins and flowed down into the palm of her hand. She opened her eyes to the pitcher slowly filling itself with crystal clear water.

She squealed.

"LOOK LOOK LOOK!"

He chuckled and pushed off the railing, strolling over to her just as the water started to bubble. Jen's eyes widened as the pitcher began to shake with boiling water. She snatched it up and shoved Damien out of the way to fling the contents of the pitcher over the balcony. A gust of wind blew through and reduced it to steam before carrying it off into the golden sky.

She spun around and hugged the empty pitcher to her chest. Her eyes darted around the balcony as a guilty smile tugged at her lips. Damien arched a brow.

"Were you trying to turn the balcony into a hot spring?"

The pitcher fell to her side as laughter exploded from her. She slid down to the marble tiles in a fit of giggles.

Damien smiled broadly at the sound and went to sit beside her. He draped his arm around her and kissed her brow as she came out of her giggle fit.

"You're in a good mood this evening," he said, caressing her shoulder with his fingertips.

"I need to find little things to laugh about," she said through a faint chuckle. "If I don't, I'll actually lose my mind." She placed her hand on his knee. "And we got Haythem to agree to the council. At least we're doing okay on that front."

He rubbed his nose against hers.

"Who would have thought, Leeyna the wolf whisperer?"

She looked over at him, this beautiful, raven-haired man who loved her, who had risked everything to follow her and protect her—and yet, she was keeping things from him.

But she knew him and knew him well. If he found out about the Oshara, about the war, he would leap into action and put himself in harm's way to keep her safe. Jen was having a hard enough time keeping herself from falling apart, she couldn't risk something happening to him, she wouldn't survive that.

But the guilt gnawed at her stomach like a rabid animal trying to escape.

I need to tell him.

"Damien," she said. He lifted his head, and the look in his eyes momentarily stole the breath from her lungs.

Gods. Why does he have to look at me like that?

"What are you guys doing on the floor?"

Their eyes shot up to Emelie with her hands on her hips, looking down at them curiously.

Damien pulled Jen to her feet.

"She was showing me some of her magic tricks." He winked.

Jen nudged him with her shoulder, but when she looked back at Emelie, she noticed the sober expression on her friend's face.

"What's wrong?"

Emelie fiddled with her fingers. "William wants to see us all in the library, *now.*"

Damien glanced over at Jen, his lips forming into a hard line.

"Well, that was short lived."

They walked in the opposite direction of the great hall until they reached the ornate oak doors that led to the main library.

Marble columns lined the center of the room, holding up the dugout ceiling that was interrupted by a massive skylight. The room was cool from the red-brown stone that hosted the endless tomes. Although there were many levels perched atop one another, there was an intimacy to this library. The glow of the sconces and candles bounced off the bookshelves and stone, giving the cave-like space a warm ambience.

Directly beneath the skylight stood one of the library's many long tables, the one where William and Ronan stood side by side, poring over piles of scrolls and volumes. Leeyna sat at one end, intensely reading a roll of parchment.

They made their way towards them, the sound of their steps bouncing off the stone walls.

Jen caught sight of Bastien coming out of one of the stacks. She veered away from Damien and Emelie to fall in step with him. He arched a curious brow.

"Can I help you carry those?" she asked.

He wrinkled his nose and stopped a few strides from the table. "I think I can manage the last few feet," he said with a grin.

Jen laughed awkwardly. He gave her an expectant look, like he knew she was trying, and struggling, to say something else.

"I—" she started. "I wanted to thank you."

"For what?"

She fiddled with her hands. "At the ball, you saved all those people when I—"

He tilted his head. "When you were provoked by an unhinged Knight?"

She nodded. "I'm sorry…about the fire—."

"Why in Goddess' name would you apologize for that? I'm just sorry you missed *him*."

Jen tried to hide her surprise as they approached the table. He was being so understanding; she expected at least a *little* ire.

William smacked Ronan's hand, "Don't dog ear the pages, you big *brute*," he scolded. Ronan scowled as Jen propped one elbow on each of their shoulders.

"So, what's the danger of the day?"

Ronan glanced at her elbow. "You seem *calmer*."

The last time she'd seen him was through red rimmed eyes clouded by magic and shame. He had held her trembling body so tightly, becoming the only thing that kept her from collapsing to the ground.

And he hasn't spoken to me since.

William shrugged her off and put a scroll in front of her, pulling her focus back to the present.

The council scroll, from the Arc.

"Why am I looking at this?" she asked.

William leaned on the table and sighed heavily. "Because we have a problem."

Jen picked up the scroll and looked at it closely.

"We haven't reached out to all of them, but we know who we're looking for right? What's the problem?"

William looked over at Ronan, who took the scroll from Jen and placed it back on the table. He tapped his finger on the corner of the age-stained parchment.

"There were two signatures here."

They all leaned in closer.

"What?" Damien asked.

"They've been erased."

Leeyna shook her head. "But why?"

"Is there a realm we missed?" Emelie asked as she slid the parchment over to her.

Jen stood up straight and ran her fingers over her lips.

And then it hit her like a smack in the face. The realm where she was hidden away. Behind the Forest of Bri within the rolling pastures and a hill with two oak trees. She dropped her hand and pulled the paper back to her. "It's Nimea."

Silence.

"It has to be," she spoke again, tracing her finger over the blank spaces.

Damien stared at her. "How do you know?"

She peered up at her friends, who were looking at her like she had grown three extra heads in the last two minutes.

"When Heltior was exiled, Nimea was cut off and made to look like it was wiped off the face of the continent." She looked between Ronan and William. "Right?"

They both nodded.

"But that would imply that before that, they were very much a part of Etheria. They would have been part of the council—had descendants. But the signatures would have been wiped away along with Nimea." She lifted the paper in the air. "Who else could it be?"

She glanced over at Ronan, and something akin to pride echoed behind his eyes.

"Shit. So, what do we do?" Damien asked.

"Can the council convene without them?" Emelie thrummed her fingers on the table.

"I have an awful feeling that what's coming will not stop at the Forest of Bri," Bastien said, his mouth twitching into a frown.

The inevitable war that I haven't mentioned to my friends yet.

"How the fuck do we find the descendants?" Damien growled.

William thumbed through a pile of parchment next to him. "We start looking for very, very old shit." A collection of exasperated groans sounded off around the table.

Everyone, save for Jen and Ronan, slumped into ornate wooden chairs and began sifting through the papers and books on the table.

She peered over at a pile of worn, leather books that were beautifully embossed with flecks of gold and silver. "What are these?" she asked Ronan.

He looked over rather absentmindedly. "Shit about the old religion. I don't know why we grabbed them."

"The old religion?"

"People used to worship the Fates before the star fell."

They broke out into a flurry of conversations. Jen was thumbing through a pile of parchment when something made her pause.

A faint, high pitched ring cut through the clamor. She looked around the table, but no one else seemed to hear it. She turned her head and the ringing intensified. Her gaze shifted to a book at the bottom of a heap in front of her.

Jen pulled it from the stack, revealing its faded gold covering, embellished by framings of white thorns. Her hand gently grazed the surface of the book.

She sucked in a breath when one of the thorns pricked her. A small drop of blood pooled on her fingertip and fell onto the golden cover.

Jen watched, captivated, as the book absorbed her blood. And then, the book snapped open to a page towards the end. She sucked on her bleeding finger as she leaned over the text.

"The time will come when the hubris of good and the shadow of evil will bring forth a power long thought lost. Only when a child of light and a child of dark become one in tandem shall those that were lost be found, and the legend of light and shadow shall be known."

She looked up from the page to find everyone had gone silent. Her eyes darted around the table. "What?"

Damien looked gravely concerned. "Jen, what *was* that?"

Jen furrowed her brow. "What do you mean?" She looked at Emelie, whose face had gone pale. "Was I reading out loud?"

William cleared his throat.

"Out loud... and in another language."

Jen stepped back from the book. Ronan slid it in front of him before giving Bastien a pointed look.

"She read from the Book of Prophecy."

Bastien's eyes widened. "Shit, really?"

Ronan turned around and perched on the table.

"You found that right here?" He jutted his chin to the tabletop.

"It was with the other books..."

Ronan shook his head. "That book is not housed in this library."

Jen sat in the chair behind her and rested her arms on the table.

Now I'm summoning magical, blood-drinking books.

Bastien pulled the book across to him. "Do you know what language that was?"

Jen closed her eyes and rubbed her temples.

"I didn't even know I was speaking another language."

"You were speaking *Eaydriir*," he said.

William sputtered loudly. "WHAT."

Jen jumped at his reaction.

"Anyone want to tell me what that is?"

Bastien pushed the book towards her, watching her with fascination. "It's a dead language."

Ronan looked down at her, the corner of his lip pulling up.

"The language of the Aylaenor," he said, tracing his hand over the golden book. "Of your ancestors."

Jen stood up, her mouth agape. "This just looks like the common tongue to me," she breathed, gesturing down to the title of the book.

"It is *anything* but common," Ronan said.

Her gaze dragged from the book to his enigmatic green eyes as his lips formed into a wry grin.

For days she had been inside her own head, convincing herself that she was too weak, too susceptible to darkness to wield the power of her bloodline—to wield *light*. But reading their language, *her* language, it lifted something from her chest—the weight of the burden her destiny forced upon her shoulders…and it allowed a small thread to fasten itself to an idea she didn't dare entertain until now. Hope.

Maybe I just needed to find this, to find a connection.

Her eyes drifted back to the book, and she released a heavy sigh as her hand met the border of the gold covering.

A crease formed between her brows. She tried to lift her hand, but her fingers wouldn't move, as if fused to the faded cover. She winced as that thin thread of hope was suddenly engulfed with a thick ribbon of black smoke—her mind swallowed by darkness.

Thick, black boots stomped through wet grass. A black, hooded cloak blew in the frigid air as rain drizzled from a cloudy, night sky. The figure made their way towards a small, unassuming cottage, a soft light streaming from the window as the smell of firewood mixed with the dampness of the rain-soaked ground.

Jen closed her eyes and leaned on the table.

"Jenevieve?" Ronan murmured, an edge of concern in his voice.

Now, she was inside the cottage, standing by the hearth, the fire crackling as a young woman, with long, white-blonde hair, chopped vegetables at the kitchen table.

Jen gasped.

Kiara.

Her head jerked up, the knife still in her hand—and the front door burst open as the hooded figure stormed through the doorway.

"What's happening?" William asked.

"I will not go down the path you have chosen—I can't," Kiara said, her voice pained but unyielding. "It's too late."

"What do you see?" Ronan asked, dipping his head to try to find her gaze, but her eyes were squeezed shut.

Kiara lifted the knife towards him. "I know what you are, now, what they call you." Her eyes filled with tears. "Heltior."

The figure said nothing, but instead, reached for their hood.

Jen stumbled back as her breath fractured. Ronan placed a steadying hand on her back.

It was a man…and his eyes—ripples of green and brown merging together in a striking hazel hue with a ring of scorched earth circling his pupil…

A low, fragile whimper cracked in her throat.

Are mine.

Jen screamed out in agony as something white hot lanced through her mind, violently hurling her onto the floor.

Damien leapt over the table. "JEN!"

Kiara's screams consumed her, horrible, heart-wrenching cries pounding into her head.

STOP—PLEASE—

A heavy weight bore down on her like someone was on top of her.

THIS ISN'T YOU! PLEASE—DON'T DO THIS!

Jen struggled under the invisible force; she writhed and pushed to no avail.

HELP ME—ESEER! HELP!

She clawed at her head, trying to force the horrendous sounds out of her mind.

NO—NO—NO—PLEASE!

The pressure released and screams faded away. Jen gasped like she was coming up for air after nearly drowning, coughing and wheezing as she sucked in labored breaths.

Damien shook her shoulders, panic piercing through his eyes.

"Jen? Bug?"

She pushed away from him and scrambled to her feet to find everyone staring, horrified.

"I'm…"

Kiara's words from the Echo rang in her ears.

He can't find out about her. Hide her away…please.

Jen stared down at the table, denial wrapping around her lungs and squeezing as the truth took hold.

No. It can't be true.

She clapped her hands to her mouth.

Heltior sired the bloodline. He—he raped her.

"Bug…"

Kiara died giving birth to her rapist's child.

"Jenevieve," Ronan said through a wince.

For five hundred years, he has been after his own kin—the only power able to rival him…is his own.

This was too much. She tried desperately to push the onslaught of secrets and betrayal and prophecies and impending war behind the poorly mended wall in her mind.

The reason I've fallen to my inner darkness so easily…why rage and pain are so quick to consume me.

She squeezed her eyes shut, a sound between a moan and cry scraping out of her throat as Kiara's desperate cries and the weight of Heltior's body speared through her ears and crushed her heart.

His blood runs through my veins. I am dark. I am dangerous.

She ran.

"Jen, wait!" Damien called.

She sprinted out of the library and down the hall. Those wretched screams lashing at her skull. She turned the corner towards her room and rammed into Fjora, her siblings right behind her.

"Jen?" Fjora's eyes flashed with worry as she quickly reached for her hand, but Jen threw herself back towards the wall.

Her vision was going in and out of clarity, her heart was racing so fast she thought she may pass out. Her siblings stood behind Fjora, and she could feel their apprehension like a dull sting along her skin.

"You knew," she cried, betrayal careening to the front of her mind. "You knew who I was the whole time."

Fjora's eyes grew wide. "How—"

"You were there. You were with my mother when she found out."

"Let me explain—"

"You betrayed me. You kept everything from me. My parents. My power. My destiny. All of it."

Rhea, Darya and Jamie watched from behind their mother, their apprehension morphing into fear.

She snapped her anguished gaze to them.

"I know you're all afraid of me, alright?" she bellowed. They winced at her rough tone.

She tried to suck in a breath. "And you should be—"

Jamie stepped towards her with his palms up. "Jen…"

"I tried so hard to protect you and it was for *nothing.*" She clapped her hand to her forehead. "I suffered for *nothing.*"

She looked at Darya, utterly devastated. "You flinched—" Tears welled in Darya's eyes as she watched her sister break down. "I tried to protect you most of all—and now—"

Her body was shutting down, her hands began to shake, and shadows encroached on her vision. Her feet were moving before she realized she was running again.

"Jen, stop!" Fjora ran after her, but Jen ran faster. She flung open her door and slammed it shut, locking it behind her. Fjora banged on the door.

"Jen! Jenevieve! Please, let me in."

Jen held the door shut as her breath came out in rapid wheezes—her chest constricting with every attempt to draw in more air. She clapped her hand to her mouth to stop the sobs from escaping.

"Jen—" Fjora's voice cracked. "Let me explain, please."

She heard Fjora crying against the door, and it only made it harder to stop her own tears. "Please." Jen pressed her hand against the wood. "Leave me alone."

I'm dark. I'm dangerous. I'm broken.

Fjora shifted outside the door. After a quiet moment, Jen heard a small, desolate sigh.

"I love you," Fjora said quietly. "I'm sorry. I failed you—I failed *them,* in so many ways, and there is no excuse except for my own weakness."

Her footsteps receded back down the hall, and when they were completely gone, Jen crumbled to the floor.

She held herself as the sobs crashed over her, like she was the rock and her tears a tempest of unrelenting waves. Her agonizing moans poured from a part of her heart that she kept shut, now hurled open and laid bare on the floor.

She wept for Kiara and the tragic end of her life. She cried for Damien and her friends who she had unknowingly thrust into danger. She ached for her siblings who carried scars that she could not heal. She mourned for Fjora and her lost life. She longed for the parents she never knew.

The pain seemed endless as heartbroken tears fell for the ones she loved. But none reached her own sorrow—her own torment.

Jen sat in a heap on the floor for what felt like an eternity, and when her eyes fluttered open, she realized she wasn't alone.

Shyra stood a few feet away, waiting quietly, her hands folded in front of her with patient compassion etched into her tan skin.

Jen looked up through tear swollen eyes.

"I'm...I'm so sorry Shyra—I didn't know you were..."

But Shyra simply walked over and offered her hand. Jen stared at it, and then weakly accepted. She was pulled to her feet and gently led to the plush armchair in front of the blazing hearth while a comforting numbness settled over her. Jen lowered herself into the chair, and Shyra disappeared, returning a moment later with a glass of water in her hand.

She didn't ask for any explanation, nor did she try to comfort her. She simply sat down on the rug in front of the chair and placed her hand on Jen's knee.

They sat in silence while Jen sipped on her water, and when she was finished and felt the exhaustion seeping into her bones, Shyra helped her ready herself for bed. She brushed Jen's hair at the vanity and draped a nightgown over her head, all the while maintaining a comfortable quiet.

When Jen laid her head on the pillow, her stone placed on the nightstand beside her, she reached for Shyra's hand.

"Thank you," she said, her voice hoarse and weak.

Shyra knelt beside her, an emphatic smile tugging at the corner of her mouth.

"Fate comes for us all," she said quietly. "But your destiny—" She squeezed her hand. "Lies within the courage of your heart, and the conviction of your soul."

She rose to leave, but paused, her eyes gleaming as she looked down.

"Ufreijaa nuri."

CHAPTER 36

Jen cursed at the stab of pain that shot through her knuckles after slamming a rather aggressive jab against the training dummy.

She really had no desire to be down here.

After a night of fitful sleep, filled with echoing screams and a hooded figure revealing her own eyes beneath its shroud. Jen dragged her aching limbs out of bed and forced herself down into the dreary basement training facility.

The smooth red-brown stone ceiling was lower than in the rest of the palace, and aside from two arched windows hewn into the stone wall to her left, the room was dimly lit with sconces placed intermittently around the room.

Fantastic lighting to accompany her mood.

Although the puffiness from her tears had calmed down overnight, her eyes were still smudged with dark circles. She forced herself down here because she thought hitting something would make her feel—well, *anything*.

Images from the library still faintly haunted the back of her mind. She couldn't shake the awful burden of weight pressing on top of her. Nor could she forget the look on Fjora's face when confronted with her lies and betrayal.

Her breath turned ragged, and she faced the training dummy. She wailed on it. Blow after blow she landed on the cloth covered wood until she hinged back and slammed her foot through the center, sending it crashing to the ground.

She pressed her hands to her knees and sucked in air through clenched teeth, her skin glistening with a thin layer of cold sweat.

"Damn, what'd he do to you?" an amused voice came from the doorway.

Jen glanced over to find Ronan leaning on the frame of the old wooden door. She scowled at him and went to pick up the flattened dummy, keeping her back to him as she did so.

Yesterday he saw, along with everyone else, the beginnings of her spectacular breakdown. She had no desire to show anyone any more weakness.

"I'm not in the mood," she barked, dragging the dummy back to an upright position.

He lifted one of his hands in defense.

"Easy, Fury, I come in peace."

She finally turned back to him, her brows furrowing into a harsh line. "What in hells is *Fury?*"

He smirked. "It's what I've decided to call you."

She crossed her arms and scoffed.

"I don't *want* a nickname."

He stepped into the room. "Would you rather I call you 'Weepy'?"

"Fuck you."

He winked at her. "There she is."

She put her hands on her hips as the remnants of yesterday's tears threatened to escape. She blinked rapidly and ignored the burning behind her eyes.

"What do you want, Ronan?"

He pressed his lips together and looked down at his other hand. She hadn't noticed the mug. "What's that?"

"Poison."

She rolled her eyes.

Ronan smirked before he took a few more cautious steps forward and handed it to her. He cleared his throat.

"It's tea."

Jen looked at it suspiciously. He huffed. "It's not actually *poison*, Jenevieve. It's to calm your nerves."

She swirled the contents of the mug before taking a small sip, the scent of chamomile and valerian root flooding her nose and warming her chest. She glanced at him curiously.

"How did you know I was here?"

He chuckled and ran his hand through his dark-brown hair.

"I followed the smell of smoke and rage."

"Hilarious."

He closed the distance between them and perched his elbow on the training dummy. He looked down at her. "I wanted to show you something."

"And what would that be?"

"Something I think you need…and perhaps will enjoy."

"I don't know." She pulled at the frayed cloth on the training dummy. "I'm pretty busy at the moment."

He pinched the bridge of his nose and exhaled dramatically.

"Do you have to be so difficult?"

"With you? Absolutely."

Ronan's eyes narrowed, and he grabbed her elbow. She instinctively tried to pull away, sending the contents of her mug pouring over her hand. "Careful, you big brute. You're spilling my poison."

He grumbled under his breath as he pulled her out of the room.

He let go of her arm and led her through several winding passages until they came out into an arched tunnel lit by a row of torches on either side. Jen looked towards the light pouring in from the opening on her right. "Is that…"

"Quoxana, yes." He tilted his head in the opposite direction. "This tunnel runs directly under the palace," he said as the sound of their steps echoed off the walls. "It's usually used to transfer goods or move horses into the pasture."

She fell in step beside him, sipping her tea as silence came over them. After a few minutes of staring at her shoes, she looked over at him. His face was strained, his lips pursed.

"What?" she asked.

He slid his hands into his pockets. "I was contemplating asking you about yesterday."

Her spine stiffened. "What about it?" she asked quietly.

Ronan pulled on her arm and brought them to a halt. He crossed his arms and looked down his nose at her.

"I'm never going to demand answers from you. I'll never make you share something if you aren't ready," he said sincerely. "But as someone who lives with their own demons, I will always listen without judgment. As I've said, I have *excellent* hearing."

He looked at her earnestly. "I will simply ask if you need my ear, or my sword."

Jen shifted her weight to peer up at him. "I'm…"

He raised his eyebrows expectantly.

"I'm afraid I'm turning into some kind of monster."

He rubbed his chin and considered her for a moment before taking a step closer, dipping his head beside her ear.

"Who says that's a bad thing?"

Jen's eyes drifted down, clenching her jaw to fight off a ripple of emotion that threatened to cascade down her cheek. Ronan must have noticed, because his voice turned gentle.

"What makes you think that, Jenevieve?"

She bit her lip, the confession on the tip of her tongue as she took a deep, shaky breath, bracing herself for his reaction.

"Heltior sired the bloodline," she whispered.

Ronan looked at her as if she had just told him what she had for breakfast. "Alright."

Jen looked up at him, her brow raised in confusion. "That's all you have to say?"

Ronan tilted his head, as if trying to see inside her mind.

You don't want to see in here right now, trust me.

Her lips parted subtly, and his eyes dipped down before shifting back to hers. "I have lived with true monsters, Jenevieve. I have seen the foulest creatures that walk this earth." He stood upright, putting distance between them.

"But you, you are *exactly* the kind of monster this world needs."

Jen nodded, the only acknowledgement she could muster. Ronan pointed his chin towards the opening of the tunnel. "Come on, Fury." He started walking backwards, lifting his hands beside him. "What kind of monster are you?"

He turned back around, and she scampered through the tunnel to keep up with his long strides.

Well, that was…easy? Anti-climactic?

When they emerged from the tunnel, the mid-morning sun was blinding. Ronan led them down a stone path lined with angular box hedges. She glanced over, noticing his stubble had grown into the beginnings of a short beard and his hair was longer than usual.

She looked away. "Can I ask you something?"

"Hm?"

"Why didn't the Knight's magic work on you?"

A muscle feathered along his jaw. Jen had thought about this several times over the last few weeks and couldn't figure it out. He didn't have the signature arched ears of the Regals—so what was he?

They came to a set of stone stairs flanked by columned arches which were wrapped in vines of ivy and small colorful blooms. She waited for an answer as they descended the shallow stairs, the plant life around them growing wilder by the step.

Ronan stopped her a few steps from the bottom.

"The answer to that question is complicated."

Okay, well, I just told you I am the descendant of evil incarnate.

Jen opened her mouth to speak. "But…"

"And now is not the time," he said over her, a mischievous grin playing over his lips. "Now, a little birdy told me that in Nimea, you had a garden?"

Jen blinked.

That is not where I thought this conversation was going.

"Um… I did."

He took her elbow and pulled her down the last few stairs and around the corner to the end of the stone path.

She clapped her hands to her mouth.

Beneath the side of the palace sat a magnificent archway leading to rows upon rows of flowers and herbs, vegetables and fruit trees.

A garden.

The low stone walls were overgrown with moss and vines, like the valley tried to draw it back into its wild heart. The glorious sun shone through the glass ceiling, held up by ornate golden arches protruding from the surrounding stone.

She looked at Ronan, but words seemed to fail her. He gave her a lopsided grin and took the mug from her hand. "This birdie also told me that it was how you centered yourself—found some solace."

Her eyes burned as she looked at the massive plot of wild earth.

"It was."

Something moved at the edge of her vision. Ronan waved his hand in that direction.

"Here's the little birdie, as we speak."

Jen beamed when Emelie arrived through a second archway.

"Jen!" She ran up to them, a basket hanging in the crook of her elbow. She threw her arms around her, the basket barely missing Ronan.

"I'm so glad he brought you! I've been wanting to show you this place for weeks," she said as she gleefully pulled Jen into the garden. Jen couldn't wipe the smile off her face as Emelie continued. "This is the healers' garden." She pointed to the archway from whence she came. "It's connected to their corridor."

"Is this where he's been bringing you when you train?" She nodded over at Ronan, who leaned in the entryway, picking at his nails.

"Every other day or so."

Ronan strode over to them and playfully draped his arm around Emelie. "She's doing well and has a natural gift."

Emelie clasped her chest in feigned surprise. "Was that a compliment?"

He shook her shoulder. "Don't get used to it, best friend."

"Well, that's rude," a voice echoed from the healers' stairwell.

Jen whirled towards the door. A figure sauntered out of the shadows and into the morning light. "All this time, I thought that was *me*."

Samara.

Emelie smiled and threw her arms out. "Surprise!"

Jen stared at her.

Uninjured. Healed.

"What?" Samara raised her hands. "No hug? Isn't that what you people do?"

Jen choked on a laugh and launched herself at her, and for once, Samara embraced her just as tightly. Her body flooded with relief; she was okay. Samara was okay.

She pulled back to look her over. "I'm so sorry. I didn't mean—"

Samara gave her a stern look.

"Please don't tell me you've spent the last few weeks in a guilt spiral." Jen tried to respond but Samara tilted her head at Ronan and Emelie. "Has she?"

"Yes," they said together, selling her out immediately.

Jen's eyes narrowed at them, but they smiled coyly. Emelie shimmied out from under Ronan's arm and linked arms with her friends.

"Come with me girls, you're in *my* territory this morning," she said, leading them down a row filled with the familiar purple hues of lavender.

Jen looked over her shoulder at Ronan.

Thank you, she mouthed.

He gave a shy smile and nodded before turning on his heels, strolling out of the garden and back towards the palace.

Emelie knelt by a long bed of the soothing flowers, Samara and Jen perching beside her. "We'll harvest some of this and then plant a few new herbs over in that empty bed." She waved vaguely across the garden.

She handed them each a pair of gloves and some sheers, but before Jen put on the gloves, she sat on her knees and stretched her hands into the cool earth. She felt the dirt filling the underside of her nails, inhabiting every crevice of her fingers.

A cathartic sigh left her body.

And in that moment, she felt a small gust of calming wind wrap itself around her. A content smile formed on her face, and with every curl of her fingers within the soil, she felt a little more at ease.

Jen skipped through the great hall with her basket of lavender blooms, her favorite. She smelled of dirt and sweat and every herb she had rubbed between her fingers.

The dozens of courtiers socializing in the hall looked at her as if she were insane, and maybe she was. She didn't care.

Samara and Emelie trailed behind her.

"Jen!" Emelie said through a giggle.

"Wait for us!" Samara called through her hands.

She scuffled her way to her bedroom door and even found herself humming a nameless tune as she opened it. She looked back into the hallway with an all-consuming smile as her friends hastened to join her.

Her arms flew out and she spun herself into the room, dancing to the unknown song in her head.

She stopped with a jolt.

The basket fell from her hand.

Lavender spilled onto the marble floor.

Drawers were flung open. Clothes strewn about the room. The mirror of her vanity cracked. The mattress and bedding ripped to shreds as if a beast had burrowed into it.

Her room had been ransacked.

But Jen didn't see any of that.

No.

All she could see was on the carpet by the veranda.

A young woman, with soft brown hair.

Lying in a pool of blood.

Shyra.

CHAPTER 37

She knew her friends were speaking to her, but they were muffled—distorted, like they were swimming away through murky water.

Jen found herself on the floor, her knees steeped in blood, her hands wrapped around Shyra's cold fingers.

Emelie was crouched by Shyra's head, dipping her ear close to her blue lips, checking for any signs that she may be alive. But Jen knew, felt it.

She was gone.

Samara was speaking sharply at Emelie, but the words were dulled by the time they reached Jen's ears.

She slowly glanced towards the door, her neck turning as if moving through damp clay. Two blurry figures were running toward them—one with hair like dark wood, the other with hair like lightning—but still, everything moved as if time itself had sunk into the clay with her. The figures came into focus as they dropped to their knees.

Bastien and Ronan.

They both looked at her, asking important questions, but she only returned a vacant stare. They were swimming through murky water.

She turned back to Shyra.

I release a lantern for my father.

Jen's shoulder was moving—shaking. Someone was trying to get her attention.

But she wouldn't turn away.

Two strong fingers grabbed her chin, and all at once, time resumed, and the voices surfaced from the deep waters.

"Jenevieve."

It was Ronan who had her chin, his voice clear and urgent. She looked up at him in a daze. He searched her face, looking for signs that she hadn't gone catatonic.

"Jenevieve, what happened?"

Her throat felt like sandpaper.

"I…"

"She was like this when we got here," Samara explained, watching Jen carefully.

Dead. She was dead, and she had died alone.

"This room has been turned over," Bastien said as he sat back on his heels.

"Why would someone do this?" Emelie asked, her eyes welling as she wrung her hands in her lap.

Ronan kept his hold on Jen's chin, but his gaze dropped down to Shyra. His eyes widened before they returned to Jen.

"Her neck," he murmured.

Jen looked down. Sure enough, across the width of Shyra's ashen neck, was a singular, deep slash. Blood barely trickled from the fatal wound, as most of it was already spilt on the floor around her.

She blinked rapidly, a breath shuddering out of her.

"Where is it?" Ronan asked in an urgent whisper.

Bastien and the others looked between them.

"Where's *what?*" Samara asked.

Jen's eyes shot up to meet Ronan. She fumbled to her feet and tripped over her blood-soaked dress to the marble stone floor beneath her bed.

The plush emerald rug was upturned. Jen's heart plummeted into her stomach.

No. No. No.

One of the marble stones had been ripped up and tossed by the foot of the bed frame. Jen reached her trembling hand into the hole it left, her fingers finding nothing but cold, uneven stone.

She turned back to Ronan, her expression one of panic.

"Fuck," he hissed.

Bastien looked on, his face etched with concern.

"What?"

"The tiishara, it's gone."

She pulled herself onto weak limbs and looked down at Ronan.

"Is…Isn't my room protected?"

He looked away, as if ashamed. "Yes."

"Then how was someone able to get in here?" her voice trembled.

Ronan pushed the heels of his hands into his eyes and let out a frustrated snarl. He sighed heavily and returned to her waiting gaze. "No one who holds ill intent should've been able to get in here," he said, his eyes flickering over Shyra and back to Jen.

"So, what does that mean?" Emelie asked, subtly trying to wipe the blood from her hands.

"It means dark magic has penetrated the palace," Samara said solemnly. "Someone was able to conceal their true intentions and walk right in."

Ronan slammed his hands on the ground with a loud curse, splattering blood further on the marble floors. He stood up and marched over to Jen.

"This was not supposed to happen," he muttered. "You were safe in here." His head dropped. "I'm sorry, Fury."

"It's not your fault—"

"Yes. It is. You entrusted me with your safety, and I failed," he said, his eyes boring into hers. "I will figure out what went wrong, and why someone wanted the tiishara so badly that they were willing to kill for it."

Samara stood up behind them. "What…what do we do?" She glanced down at Shyra.

Bastien cleared his throat. "I'll take her to the healer's—"

"There's nothing to *heal*," Jen snapped. Ronan wrapped his hand around her wrist.

"They also handle… death, Jenevieve."

He nodded to Bastien, who gently wove his arms under Shyra's cold body. When he stood, she fell limp—her arm draped down towards the ground. Her hair was caked in blood, her lips a bluish hue.

"Wait," Jen said, stumbling over to him.

She brushed her hand along Shyra's lifeless cheek that once held a soft, rosy warmth. She reached for the arm that hung down, gently placing it over her chest. She squeezed her hand, as Shyra had the night before.

"I'm sorry," she whispered.

She nodded at Bastien, who pursed his lips before heading out of the room. When he reached the door, he almost knocked into Fjora, who came running into the room. She looked at the body in Bastien's arms, and the scene before her. Her mouth dropped open as she processed what she was looking at.

"Wha—what," she sputtered as Bastien hung his head and left with Shyra.

Samara glanced at Jen, her eyes locking on the blood-soaked carpet. When it was clear she wasn't going to speak, she took a few steps towards Fjora.

"The palace has been compromised, princess."

Fjora looked between all of them. "Compromised—"

Ronan raked his hands through his hair. "This isn't just a crazy Knight making a fucking scene at a ball, Fjora." His direct tone made her flinch.

He pointed at Jen. "Her tiishara has been stolen, and someone has been *murdered* in her room. A room that was *warded*." He crossed his arms over his chest. "There's a traitor in the palace."

"What would you have me do?" Fjora regained a bit of composure, her voice became firm, regal. Ronan stomped over to the table where a bottle of amber liquid sat. He took a long drag directly from it and turned back at the princess.

"Cancel Ruymani," he said. "Lock the palace down and get Nelysar here to seek out the traitor."

Fjora clapped her hand to her cheek and shook her head. "We can't cancel Ruymani."

"Why the fuck not?"

Samara inched towards him. "Ronan, watch how you're speaking to her. She's the princess."

Fjora put her hand up to stop her. "No, it's alright." She glanced over at Jen, who still stared at the floor. She sighed. "We can't cancel Ruymani because it's already happening. The entire realm is already starting celebrations. It's impossible."

Ronan clenched his fists. "Fuck Ruymani," he snapped back and charged towards   the   door.

"Where are you going?" Samara shouted at him.

"I need to hit something, and then I'm going to the fucking library because the only answers I can seem to find here are buried under a mountain of dust." He growled and stomped out of the room.

Emelie, Samara, and Fjora turned their focus to Jen, whose gaze remained fixed.

They said her name, at least she thought they did, but she couldn't hear them, not clearly, at least. Their voices faded as the last of her focus slipped, and the faint sounds plunged back into the deep ocean of her mind.

Muffled.

Distorted.

Underwater.

Jen sat at the vanity, staring at herself in the cracked glass. It seemed fitting—the break in the glass reflected on her face, as if she, herself, were fractured.

Samara, Emelie and Fjora stayed with her for a while. They had retrieved a few buckets and cleaned most of the blood off the floor. Jen had watched from the seat she found herself in, fiddling with the silver brush that Shyra used to sooth her just the night before.

They tried to speak to her, but she said very little, mostly some variation of 'I'm fine.' There were so many emotions swimming in the endless abyss in her mind, that all she could do was float at the surface.

When they finally left, Jen found herself sitting at the vanity for a long while, as if waiting for Shyra to come rustling through the door in her cheerful manner.

But she wasn't coming.

Her unfocused gaze drooped down to the carpet. Though most of it was cleaned up, the blood remained a crimson stain on a verdant canvas.

She needed to clean it. She needed to clean it now.

Jen ran over to the bucket someone left behind. She plunged her hand into the cold water and retrieved the scrub brush from the suds.

She scrubbed.

In fast, frantic motions, she scrubbed the rug. She wasn't even sure if was helping, but she needed to do *something*.

Jen ran the bristles through the plush carpet with a force that would likely damage it. Her face felt hot, and beads of sweat appeared at her hairline. Her arm ached, but she continued scrubbing.

"Bug...?"

A faint voice came from the door, followed by thumping footsteps, and then Damien was crouched beside her.

She didn't look up.

"Emelie told me..." He tried to get her to look at him.

"I have to clean this up," Jen said quietly.

Damien knelt on a clean spot of marble.

"I'm so sorry—"

"Shyra would hate this mess."

"Jen… hey…" He placed his hand over hers and stopped the brush. She paused, staring at their hands. Damien pulled the brush from her hand and laced his fingers with hers.

"She was so cold—like her soul warmed her from the inside, and now it's gone," she said. "She was innocent. And someone murdered her because she was in *my* room."

Damien squeezed her hand. "I know, Bug."

Jen's brows furrowed. She pulled her hand away.

"Where were you?" She looked over at him, his eyes filling with a hint of something she couldn't place.

"I was—"

She rose to her feet. "I needed you. And you weren't here."

He stood to meet her eyes. "After training, we went into the city."

"We?"

"William, Leeyna…"

Jen pressed her lips together. Damien sighed.

"We ran into Lyla and Margo…"

"Sounds like a fun group."

"They wanted to show us the city, how it looks when everyone starts celebrating Ruymani."

"So, when I was dealing with a dead body in my room, you were out, what? Having a grand time with Lyla?"

Damien was watching her, reading her. He scratched the back of his neck and gave her a knowing look. "What do you want me to say here, Jen?"

She walked over to the table by the hearth.

"Nothing at all."

He marched over to her as she poured herself two fingers of rum and tossed it back in one go. "You don't think I feel guilty for not being here? How was I supposed to know? I thought you were with Gaiana like you always are in the afternoons."

"Glad to know that you're making *friends*."

Damien recoiled. "I'm not just sitting here at your beck and call like some kind of pathetic lap dog.

"That's not what I said."

Damien raked a hand through his hair and took a few steps back. "I'm trying to have some semblance of a life, to find at least a little fun when I'm not dealing with all of this shit."

"Sorry it's been so rough for you. Glad you have someone to lean on."

"You *made* me dance with her. You *wanted* me to be her friend. And—"

"She's easier to be around. Not like me and all my shit."

He groaned and looked back over at the blood stain and the brush on the ground. "Enough, Jen. I'm sorry I wasn't here, alright? I can't change that. I've earned a fucking break from—"

Jen winced at that. Damien's eyes widened with instant regret.

"Bug, I didn't mean it like—"

Jen wrapped her hands around the back of the armchair and stared into the hearth. "You're right. You deserve a *fucking break* from me." Her eyes burned. "So, leave."

Damien took a small step towards her.

"I'm not going…"

She rounded on him, her eyes flooding with unshed tears. "GET OUT," she screamed.

Damien stumbled back in shock. His mouth dropped open, but she forced herself to ignore it. Whatever was happening now involved murder. She wouldn't have him anywhere near it; she needed to protect him, even if he hated her for it.

At least he would be safe.

"Please," she said, her voice barely a whisper. "Please, go, Damien."

The hurt in his eyes cracked something deep in her chest, but after a moment, he blinked the hurt away. His shoulders grew tense, and Jen watched as his armor slipped over him.

"Fine."

He turned on his heels and walked to the door. Jen thought he might turn around, say something—fight with her. But he just sighed heavily and left without looking back.

She stood watching the door for a moment, still thinking he might come back. But he didn't. Her eyes welled, but instead of allowing any tears to fall, she marched over to the bloodstained rug and knelt beside the bucket.

She scrubbed until the water ran red.

CHAPTER 38

s the sun vanished behind the hills, the room seemed to hold its breath, a thick fog hanging over the room, heavy with the burden she alone had to carry. Jen sat at the table by the veranda, her golden hair in messy waves from the bath she forced herself to take. A simple cream dress wrapped around her body and draped to the floor.

Her breath came in long, slow inhales as she stared out into the vast terrain of the valley.

It is easier to feel nothing, than to feel everything all at once.

A familiar breeze pushed its way through the room of forgotten time and gently wrapped itself around Jen's shoulders. It ribboned about the veranda and into the room, collecting the thick air and condensing to reflect brilliant golden light as it streamed towards the bedroom door.

Jen watched curiously, until something else joined the magical interlude.

A thread wrapped around her and pulled her to her feet. And then, a faint, melodious hum. Just a small whisper of a voice, soon joined by another, and then another until the chorus of harmony guided her across the room.

The door opened on its own as the stream of light floated towards it, beckoning her to follow. Jen watched, her brows fixed in low arches until she felt her feet moving, her mind melding with the hum that she had learned to follow.

She took a step outside her door, but her ears perked up at a familiar voice down the hall.

"Damien! Where's the fire?" The voice said.

Lyla.

Jen peeked her head out. Sure enough, at the other end of the hall stood Lyla in a magenta gown, and Damien.

Her heart lurched.

Lyla tilted her head, her brows arching with concern.

"Everything okay?"

He cleared his throat.

"Everything's fine. I'm just headed to Jen's room."

"Taking her to Ruymani?"

Damien nodded, shifting from one foot to the other.

Jen jolted just as his head snapped at a *bang* from the open doors of the library down the hall. Damien ran towards it with Lyla on his heels.

He peered inside the doors and exhaled as if something truly taxing was waiting for him. "I should go in there." He glanced at Lyla. "Maybe, we'll see you later."

She looked at him for a moment and then gave him a warm smile before heading back the way they came.

When the sound of rustling magenta chiffon disappeared, Jen stepped out of her room. She took a few steps in the direction of the library.

"What are you doing in here?" She heard Damien's voice echo against the library walls.

"I'm in no mood, Damien."

Ronan's low grumble rippled into the hall. Jen quietly crept towards the library and pressed herself behind the open door.

"Looking for something?" Damien asked.

"If you must know, I'm trying to figure out why the ward failed."

"Need help?"

Jen could practically feel Ronan's eyes searing a hole into Damien's head.

"*What* are you doing?"

"I may not know what most of this is, but I have a pair of working eyes." Ronan scoffed. "And Jen's safety is more important than anything, so, I'm offering my assistance."

Even after everything I've put him through—and after I kicked him out…Gods, I don't deserve him.

Wood creaked as someone plopped down into a chair. "The issue is—" Ronan groaned, "I don't know what to look for."

"That must be hard for you," Damien said, sarcasm dripping from his voice.

"You think provoking me is helpful?"

"Didn't say it was, but it's enjoyable."

There was a moment of silence, and Jen knew they must be glaring at each other. Ronan let out an exasperated sigh. "Okay, fine." Papers shuffled over the table. "I'm trying to figure out how someone was able to mask their intentions and slip through the ward."

Jen risked a glance around the door. Damien was perched on the end of a table, while Ronan had his hands pressed against a pile of parchment; he looked exhausted.

"What if they were already wearing a mask?" Damien suggested.

Ronan arched a brow. "You mean like a dhoksha?"

"Maybe."

Ronan pulled at his disheveled hair. "If there are dhokshas crawling around the palace, I'm going to lose my shit."

Damien bent down to pick up the broken lamp, most likely the cause of the crash Jen had heard earlier. He placed it on the far corner of the table.

"Where does Heltior play into this?"

Ronan thrummed his fingers on the parchment in front of him. "I don't know." He mindlessly flicked through an open spell book. "The curse, the ball, Shyra—they're all too subtle for him."

"Murder is *subtle*?" Damien asked.

Ronan leaned on the table, the wood groaning beneath him. "If this *was* him, he would have burned down all of Sachandes to get to her, not just send an unhinged Knight to scare her."

Damien turned to the table. "That means…"

Ronan locked eyes with him.

"Heltior doesn't know about her."

Jen's shoulders sagged against the door.

Well, that's one *not-awful thing to cling to.*

She tilted her head as Ronan kept speaking. "If it wasn't him," he murmured. There was a moment of heavy silence. "*No*—that's not possible," he said to himself.

"What's not?"

"SHH. Let me think," Ronan said sharply.

Jen rested her head on the door, but as soon as she did, the hum in her ear grew louder, demanding to be heard. The thread around her pulled more insistently, coaxing her towards the ribbon of light streaming into a set of nearby stairs.

She glanced between the library and the stairwell. She didn't want to leave them. She wanted to burst into the library and apologize to Damien and stop Ronan from ripping out his hair—to tell them both she wasn't worth the pain.

But the pull was too strong, her mind was cloudy with fear and betrayal and looming darkness, and her resolve was weakened. The gentle thread and the melodic hum had always led her where she needed to go on this journey—she had no reason to doubt it.

The men's voices faded into nothing as the pull and the hum overtook her senses, and she followed.

Down.

Down.

Down.

Until she found herself beneath the palace by the dungeons and her isolated training ring. Her skin grew clammy as it led her through the passageways Ronan had shown her. The iridescent reflection of the streaming light bounced off the stone walls, illuminating the path of her bare feet.

She emerged into the tunnel lit by sconces on either side. Jen glanced to her right and was greeted with Quoxana and the bright celebration of Ruymani. Fountains spewed magical fire instead of water, casting sparks into the twilight. Dancers in bright colors and towering headdresses moved in time with pulsing drums and fluttering flutes.

The smell of grilling meats from hundreds of street vendors filled her nose and the jubilant laughter of children and families threatened to overpower the humming in her ear.

But then she turned her head slowly to the opposite end of the tunnel, where the glowing light led towards the valley. The humming grew louder, and the thread pulled as she padded away from Ruymani.

Jen came out into the open, the stone under her feet turned to lush grass, cold and damp between her toes. The stream of light wound its way around her and a hazy smile turned up on her lips as she spun with the wind. Her arms opened and her dress billowed around her.

Around and around she spun, lost in the radiant light and the intoxicating weightlessness that fluttered in her chest. She moved further into the valley and away from the palace until she was a sphere of light within the darkness of night.

The humming grew louder and louder until it felt like a hot iron driving into her head. Jen clapped her hands to her ears and urged her body to stop spinning as the feeling of weightless dancing disappeared into noise. She winced as the light spun around her.

The humming and the light reached its crescendo, and when she flung her hands out, the sound died, the sphere of painted wind disappearing along with it.

Ice-cold dread slammed into her stomach.

They approached under the moonlight, like serpents in the night. Six kashyaks surrounded her, their salyaats menacing at their backs.

She darted her eyes around the circle.

How could I be so stupid?

Jen kept her breath steady as one of them slinked over to her.

"We...*click...click...click*...know it is you...Jenevieve," he rasped. He reached a hand of gray-scaled skin towards her face and caressed her jaw. She held her breath and attempted to keep perfectly still.

He breathed her in as his hand continued lower...down her clavicle...between her breasts...past her navel. She kept her chin high, but fear pierced through her when his blackened nails found her belt—with her stone in its pouch.

He licked his thin lips, and with one jerk of his hand he ripped the belt from her waist and threw it, releasing the veil that protected her.

The kashyaks inhaled deeply, and then they swarmed her. Their rough skin rubbed up against her body, forked tongues lapped at her in a frenzy to devour.

Thin hands grabbed at her hair and at her dress. All she saw was a horrific collage of pointed teeth and black, soulless eyes coming at her from all directions.

A cry tore from her throat and her hands shot out. A wall of hard wind expelled from her, slamming her assailants to the ground.

"Now, now, my friends," a slippery voice called from beyond the circle. The kashyaks slinked to their feet and parted, their heads bowed to the ground.

Her chest heaved as Jen turned towards the voice.

The Knight from the ball revealed himself, not a trace a black paint disguising him this time; his black hair shimmering under the moonlight and a crude smile splayed across his pale, pointed face.

"My apologies, they are not used to the scent of such—" He licked his lips. "Power. It can be quite—" He rolled his shoulders. "Intoxicating."

Sweat pooled in the small of her back.

He tilted his head. "I did not get the chance to introduce myself when last we met." He bowed. "*I* am Mobius."

The same, metallic taste from the ball flooded over her tongue as his dark magic wove its way towards her mind, wisps of power slithering up to her defenses, poking and prodding against the white stone. Jen trembled, using every ounce of energy she had to guard her mind.

"Hmm." Mobius hummed.

Jen sagged as his magic retreated from her head.

Mobius circled her, his hands folded behind his back. "I see we don't have that same *bite* we had at the ball." He came up behind her and spoke into her ear. "Where are those beautiful, rageful flames, *Jenevieve?*"

She cringed. "What do you want with me?"

Mobius spun around and landed in front of her. Jen was taken aback by the manic nature of the movement, and that's when she noticed.

Something about him was off. He wasn't the domineering presence he had been at the ball. His eyes were too wide, his shoulders too straight, his smile too bright. It was unsettling, like the last vestiges of his sanity were cracking.

"My master wishes to speak with you," he said, his voice lingering on every word.

Her breathing stuttered at the word *master.*

Oh, gods—maybe Damien and Ronan were wrong.

Her body seized. Fear sent shivers across her skin, but she straightened her shoulders. "I'm not going *anywhere* with you," she said, but her voice was not as venomous as she intended.

Mobius chuckled, and the sound scraped up against her like nails on a chalkboard.

"I thought you would be…less than enthused." He looked towards the palace. "Which is why we have a dhoksha following your family." He lifted his hand. "One signal from me and they will die an *excruciating* death." He relished the word, as if he longed to give the signal.

"You're bluffing," Jen seethed, but her heart thumped wildly.

His head tilted like a curious bird. "Oh, am I?" Mobius tossed something to her. She caught it, and when she looked down, she let out a small gasp.

A small, intricately carved figurine. A hawk.

Jamie.

Jen cradled it in her hands, running her thumbs over the sanded bumps of its wings. Her body trembled. "Do not *touch* my family."

"*That,* is entirely up to you." Mobius looked up at his hand.

There was no question in her mind. She wouldn't let Mobius, or any other creature of darkness, near her brother. Her sisters. They were not hers by blood, but at this moment, that didn't matter. The instinct to protect them was stronger than anything else.

She lifted her chin, her resolve steady.

"I'll go."

Mobius smiled with too many teeth. "Excellent choice."

He nodded to one of the kashyaks. It skulked up to her, and before she could protest, two cuffs of black alloy, holding several symbols she didn't recognize, connected by a crude metal chain, appeared on her wrists. She pulled against it, trying to summon the elements to her.

Nothing.

Panic galloped through her chest as Mobius clicked his tongue. "The cuffs are just a…precaution. They nullify your magic." He shrugged. "I can't very well unleash an *iejja* on my master." He stepped forward and yanked on the chain, pulling her up against his face. "It would get in the way of his plans," he breathed.

He dragged her over to his salyaat, who let out a screech into the empty valley. He strapped her to the back like the spoils of a hunt, which it seemed, she was.

The beast took off, its massive wings bleeding into the night sky as they flew further away, soaring over the palace. The city was oblivious, celebrating its Festival of Light while Jen flew towards her fate.

And then, a voice cried out from far below.

"JENEVIEVE!"

CHAPTER 39

The winds whipped her cheeks, leaving her face numb and her eyes watering.

Her moment of resolve was fading quickly, finding itself replaced with terror that all but paralyzed her. Heltior waited for her. The sire of her bloodline, the monster whose darkness dwelled under her skin.

The fate she could not escape, she now willingly approached.

Her family would be safe. Her friends. Damien. She had to hang on to that, however naive it was. This wasn't for nothing. It was for *them*.

Her stomach churned as the salyaat banked to the right and leveled out over the valley, ascending higher until Jen could hear the stars whispering above her.

She lifted her head.

Wait. Those weren't the stars she was hearing.

"What is this?"

Her breath caught in her throat. Damien. How was she hearing Damien's voice? She glanced around and only saw the black-feathered tail of the salyaat slicing through the sky.

Her mind felt as though it was being torn in two directions, part of it here with her on the back of the salyaat, the rest reaching towards a different presence.

Wildflowers and soil before the rain.

"Shit. This is—" paper shifted over wood. "The bloodline."

Ronan, his deep timbre shivered and echoed against her skull. She closed her eyes on a wince, and suddenly a flood of images careened against the backs of her eyelids.

She lowered herself to look at it clearly, hundreds upon hundreds of names in a never-ending tree destined for extinction. Damien touched the faded ink.

She was in the library, and Damien stood beside her, but that could only mean…

Jen looked down and saw tan hands pressed against the table, mahogany hair fell in front of her line of sight, and she felt a sigh like it was coming from her own lungs.

"It just…stops," Damien said, his voice quiet.

Ronan pursed his lips. "The Blood War."

His voice ricocheted in her head. She was watching this from Ronan's eyes. But, how?

Damien hung his head low, sadness filling the space behind his winter-blue eyes.

"Her family…"

Ronan nodded, matching the sadness in his own expression. His gaze fell to another roll of parchment. He grabbed it from Damien and unrolled it, his eyes doing a quick scan. "This was with the bloodline?"

Damien nodded, but as he caught a glimpse of it over Ronan's shoulder, his expression shifted. He snatched it from Ronan's hands, staring at it in stunned disbelief. "What is this?" he breathed.

Ronan snatched it back. He read it more closely. "The time will come when a powerful iejja will return from forgotten lands as a child of the blood and become the bridge between the forces of light and forces of darkness, emerging as—" He lifted his hand to his mouth.

"The Oshara."

Damien paled. "What is that?" he asked quietly.

"A being of prophecy said to signify the end of the bloodline." He hung his head low. "And dawn will rise in an age of reckoning."

Damien paced back a few steps, rubbing his face. "This means…" He looked over at him and stopped mid-sentence. "Hey, are you okay?"

Jen had to bite down on her lip to keep from crying out. It felt like someone was reaching inside her and squeezing her lungs with jagged claws, scraping against her ribs and setting her blood on fire.

Fear. It was fear she felt. But not like anything she had ever experienced––this was violent, visceral, and not just her own, but another's compounded and smashed like an avalanche of uncontrollable terror.

The images blurred with the suffocating pain.

Ronan was frozen at the table, his eyes squeezed shut, his shoulders trembling. His hands were like vices on the corner of the table, holding him in place until he let out a gasp and stumbled back.

Damien caught him by the arms, and when he whipped around, his eyes were wild.

"What?" Damien jumped back in alarm.

Ronan was already bolting for the door.

"We have to go. NOW."

Ronan sprinted out of the library, Damien on his heels. They cleared the corner and veered towards Jenevieve's open door. Ronan ran in and stomped through the room—into the bathroom—the closet.

"Jenevieve!" he called.

Damien barreled in behind him. "What's going on?"

"Shit," Ronan said to himself before running out the door.

"Ronan, hang on!" Damien lurched after him.

They made it to the grand hall, completely devoid of people. Ronan stopped so suddenly Damien plowed into him.

"Fuck! Will you stop doing—"

"SHH!" he hissed. He pointed out beyond the veranda. "Listen."

They fell silent for a minute, hearts booming in their chests. Damien turned his ear towards the open skies of the valley.

"What is that?"

The beating became louder until it was clear something big was flying nearby, and then they heard it.

The screech.

Jen sucked in a breath, her wrists pulling against the cuffs. They had heard the salyaats carrying her away.

"Go!" Damien yelled. They raced down the nearest stairs.

They came hurtling out towards the stables just in time to see the herd of salyaats slithering in the distant sky.

"JENEVIEVE!" Ronan screamed.

She hadn't imagined the voice calling for her. Gods. They had been mere moments away from being in the crosshairs of Mobius and the kashyaks. Jen released a sigh of relief.

"Wha—" Damien clapped his hands to his head. "Why was she even out here?!"

Ronan looked at the moon kissed ground, crouching down beside something in the grass.

Her belt.

"She was ambushed," he kept his voice steady as he gingerly grabbed the belt and pouch.

Damien did no such thing. "What do we do? Where are they taking her? Are they going to Vondur? Do we need horses—"

"Damien. Goddess, save me, get ahold of yourself," Ronan rose and marched up to him, shoving the belt into his hand. "They aren't going to Vondur." He pointed to the north of the valley. "That's the way to Vondur, they flew east."

Jen furrowed her brow. If she wasn't going to Vondur, where was Mobius taking her?

"THEN WHERE THE HELL ARE THEY GOING?" Damien shouted, his arms flailing. "HOW DO WE FIND HER?"

Ronan grabbed his collar and shook him hard. "Stop fucking yelling," he growled. "I'm going to ask you to do something that's not in your nature. Calm. The Fuck. Down. Don't fucking act like you're the only one on the continent that wants her safe." He shoved him back.

Damien stumbled back, clutching Jen's belt before kneeling in the damp grass.

Ronan paced back and forth, wracking his brain until he came to a sudden stop. His head dropped towards the ground.

"Shit."

"What?" Damien said, his voice shaking, but not quite as panicked.

Ronan rubbed his hands over his face and groaned. "There may be a way to find her and get to her at the same time."

Damien shot up from the ground. "Then let's go."

He started towards the stables.

"It doesn't involve horses."

Damien turned around, looking wildly confused.

"Fuck. Fuck. Fuck." Ronan muttered to himself. He gave a resigned sigh. He walked up to Damien and held his hand out. "I need the stone."

Damien looked at him warily, but gave him the stone anyway. Ronan rolled it in his hand. "I have to warn you, I haven't done this in a very long time."

"Done...what?" Damien said while Ronan took a few steps away from him.

He held the stone firm in one of his hands and closed his eyes. He held out his other hand and inhaled deeply.

"Jenevieve," he whispered.

The air in front of him crackled, like beads of static on a piece of metal. He closed his eyes tighter and breathed in the charged energy that surrounded him. He clenched his jaw. and with a sweating palm, he flicked his wrist sharply up and down.

A concentrated crack of thunder boomed, and his eyes shot open. Through a panting breath, he sighed with relief.

Damien inched forward.

"What in the ever-loving fuck is that?"

Black mist was settling in the corners of her vision, she couldn't make out what Damien was looking at, but he looked thoroughly unconvinced.

"It should lead us right to her."

"SHOULD? I need more assurance than that."

Ronan shrugged. "I told you I haven't done this in a while. It'll only stay open as long as I can keep it that way. So, we should move quickly." He started walking towards it.

"Don't come for me, you idiots," Jen murmured.

She hoped they wouldn't be so stupid as to follow her, unarmed, and in a blind panic.

Damien crossed his arms over his chest.

"Absolutely fucking not. I'm not walking through that thing."

Ronan stared at him before pinching the bridge of his nose.

"Do you want to be the hero or not?"

Before an answer came, a cloud of mist enveloped her vision and the men disappeared.

"No!" Jen's eyes shot open, and she reached out.

But they were gone.

The salyaat landed with a thud on the outskirts of an abandoned fortress hidden within the hills outside of the Sachandan border.

The stone walls were covered in vines and layers of moss. The square towers were crumbling, their stone facades torn open to expose hollow rooms and skeletal stairwells.

In another life, the fortress would have been magnificent, but now it just looked haunted—cursed. Mobius hoisted Jen off the salyaat's back and dragged her through the grass and mud. It was eerily quiet, like they were the only ones there.

This doesn't look like the evil lair of a terrifying tyrant.

They entered an old stone courtyard. Jen could feel a subtle, familiar vibration from the air in front of her.

A veil.

Mobius extended his hand and tapped it, dissolving it to reveal the horrifying reality beyond.

Hundreds upon hundreds of morai flew through the ruins of the fortress, some perched menacingly on the tiered arches of the courtyard. Droves of kashyaks and dhokshas watched her approach, and in an instant, they were upon her.

They ripped at her dress and licked at her body as they lifted her and carried her through the archways.

"Try to leave her in one piece," Mobius called after them.

Jen kicked and scratched the vile creatures, screaming out as they assured their grip on her. They brought her into the remains of a great hall, the open space doused in darkness save for the moon casting a haunting light off the grey stone walls.

Above her were endless levels of stone walkways surrounding a massive unlit chandelier.

The frenzy of kashyaks dropped her roughly on the ground before a large stone dais. She struggled to her feet just as Mobius and the kashyak from the ball passed her and climbed the dais steps.

Jen spat on the floor, her eyes beacons of hatred. But Mobius simply cackled, and the entire hall joined in an eruption of disturbing, maniacal laughter.

She looked around at the dark creatures that stood at her back, and the horde of onyx wings that loomed above her.

This is what hell must look like.

Her gaze returned to the dais, where Mobius raised his hand to quiet the chaos that echoed through the cavernous room. He remained silent as he folded his hands in front of him, a sick grin twisted on his face.

"Welcome, Jenevieve," a voice rang out from the shadows behind the dais.

Her blood ran cold in her veins.

She knew that voice.

The sound of clicking shoes ricocheted off the stone floor as a figure emerged from the darkness. Her eyes widened and her throat went dry, trying to grasp what in hells was going on.

She watched the figure drift to the collapsed throne, their grin gleaming—too white, too wide, and utterly detached from their deadened eyes.

Amber eyes. Arched ears. White hair.

Bastien.

CHAPTER 40

“I’m sure someone convinced her to go into the city, *mo nuri*,” Nelysar said. Fjora stood in the doorway of Jen’s empty room. She heaved a sigh when she saw the stain on the carpet from the day before.

“I should’ve had someone remove that rug right away,” she scolded herself.

Nelysar took her hand and led her out into the hallway. “You can take care of that in the morning, alright?” He led her towards the great hall, but saw the guilt cloud her eyes. He pulled on her arm to stop them.

“We can ask someone before we head out, hm?” he said, caressing her cheek.

She nodded gratefully.

He kissed her tenderly and rubbed his nose against hers before continuing towards the hall. Not a soul was there, save for an irritated young woman with olive skin and long black hair. Fjora tilted her head as they approached.

“Samara?”

Samara jolted.

“Princess.” She nodded at Nelysar. “Nelysar.”

“Why aren’t you out in the city?” Fjora asked.

Samara scoffed. “I’m waiting for Ronan. He was supposed to meet me when he was done in the library—”

Nelysar tugged on his earlobe. “We just passed the library and there’s no one there.”

“Of course not,” Samara said, rolling her eyes.

Fjora smiled warmly. “Maybe he’s collecting Bastien?” She gestured towards the stairs. “Come with us, we’re walking towards my rooms anyway.”

They made their way up the grand staircase and veered left towards Bastien’s rooms. When they arrived, the door was slightly ajar.

"Bas—" Samara said as she knocked on the door. She peered inside. "What the—" She flung the door open and marched inside. Fjora and Nelysar followed her, their eyes widening as they took in the room.

Clothes were strewn about the floor, piles of books had been knocked over, scrolls and bits of parchment blew in the evening breeze from the veranda. The forest-green bedspread was crumpled in a pile at the end of the mattress.

Nelysar walked precariously around a wad of tunics. "Is he usually this…disgusting?"

Fjora and Samara shook their heads as they tried to conceal their shared concern. Samara found herself by the hearth when something caught her eye. She bent over to retrieve a small packet of parchment. Her brows furrowed as her fingers flicked through it.

"Princess," she said without looking up.

Fjora joined her, and when Samara gave her the papers, she collapsed into the large leather armchair behind them.

"Why was he tracking Jen's movements…" Samara asked, her hands crossed in front of her chest. Nelysar crossed to them, looking over Fjora's shoulder.

"He was tracking *all* of you," he said, reaching down to point to another page. Fjora sat silently with the parchment in her lap.

"Look at this," Samara said quietly, she picked up another pile of parchment. "He recorded the conversations he had with Jamie." She offered it to Fjora, but Nelyar took it, his eyes turning to slits as he examined the conscriptions.

"I don't—why would he…" Fjora stammered, she held a hand to her cheek.

She turned to the next page and let out a guttural gasp. Nelysar snatched it from her lap, and when he saw what was on it, he whispered. "Goddess, save us."

Samara peered over his shoulder.

"Is that…" she started, clapping her hand over her mouth in disbelief.

The parchment was filled with dark ink sketches of the same symbol. Over and over as if someone was fueled by a wicked compulsion. Layers of roughly drawn arched tridents with an insidious eye in the middle of the three prongs.

"Heltior's insignia," Nelysar whispered. He flipped the page over and hissed, casting it into the fire. He yanked Fjora from her seat and pushed her towards the door, Samara right behind them.

"We need to find your father," he said urgently.

As they fled the room, the sheet of parchment slowly burned from the edges, but the inked script still oscillated in the light of the ominous flames.

Durche yahvak.

Darkness reigns.

The kashyak yanked Jen back as she flailed against her chains.

"You BASTARD!" she screamed. The creature kicked her behind the knees, and she dropped to the hard stone floor with a painful *thud*. Mobius let out a deranged cackle from the corner of the dais, the last vestige of sanity gone.

Bastien placed his hand to his chest, feigning offense.

"Come now, Jenevieve, I thought we were friends," he mused, a sick grin curled on his lips. His once warm face was different now, sinister. His cheekbones were harsh against the moonlight, as if someone had carved them out of pale stone. His strikingly beautiful amber eyes were now malevolent pools of wicked flame.

"I trusted you. We all did," she seethed.

He picked a piece of lint from his black tunic, reeking of indifference. "Well, that, my darling girl, was clearly a grave mistake."

She glared up at him, her pupils bursting into rings of blazing fire. "What is this place?" she barked, her chest heaving.

He flung his arms out to his court of dark creatures. "Why, this is one of the safe haven fortresses," he bellowed through the hall, a jagged chorus of rancid laughter rang out. "Used to shelter the bloodline and their kin." He dropped his insidious gaze to her. "Well, when there were more of you."

She thrashed against the gray scaled hands that dug into her shoulders, holding her in place. "You would betray Sachandes? The king? Your home?"

He chuckled. "That place was *never* my home." He lifted a brow towards her. "It was my *prison* for over two hundred years."

Jen's mouth dropped open, and he reveled in it as he continued. "Centuries ago, I was dispatched to the benevolent court of Sachandes to dismantle the realm from within."

"But—"

"You dare interrupt him, *bloodliner*?" Mobius snapped, tilting his head in a most unnatural position.

Bastien held his hand up as if he were consoling an errant hound. "It's alright, my friend, Jenevieve is just curious."

He turned his focus back to her.

"I was tasked with befriending the young heir, to become so valuable to him that when he ascended the throne, he would bring me with him as his most trusted advisor." He winked at Mobius, who giggled like a deranged child. "Little did he know, I was sent to *destroy* him."

Jenevieve tried once again to yank herself from the kashyak that held her, but in a flash, he had his hand in her hair, jerking her head back, exposing her neck. He slid his forked tongue down her sweat slicked skin, moaning into her ear. A whimper escaped her throat.

"That's enough, my pet," Bastien scolded. It kept its hand in her hair but backed off.

"Anyway," he said. "All was going reasonably well. Thanks to you, Fjora disappeared, and the realm grew restless with the constant searches for her."

He sighed as if he were pained.

"But then Eliana grew suspicious of me."

Jen's eyes widened. "You…you poisoned the queen."

He shrugged. "It was exactly the catalyst I needed to plummet Sachandes into disarray, breaking the king's spirit to the point that those insufferable condors stopped surveilling from the skies." He arched a brow at her. "And I was able to keep my *true intentions* hidden."

Realization struck Jen so hard she almost keeled over.

"It was *you*," she breathed. "*You* cursed me." She pointed to Mobius. "You sent that psychopath to the ball." He gave a mocking bow.

"You—" The words got caught in her throat. Her eyes burned but she blinked the hot tears back. "You murdered Shyra," she choked out.

He traipsed down the steps at the front of the dais, not reacting to her realizations. He rolled up his sleeves one at a time.

Jen's heart sank, her eyes fixing on his arms.

Tattoos of jagged vines surrounded a long, curved trident with an eye in the center of the prongs on his left forearm.

"You're a Knight of Eseer," she whispered.

He came within a foot of her and gave a satisfied nod to his tattoos. "One of the very first to join the noble cause." He leaned down next to her ear. "I apologize for Shyra. She was simply in the wrong place at the wrong time." He licked his lips. "Nothing personal."

He lifted his head, and she spat in his face.

"MURDERER."

He stood up straight and wiped her spit from his face with two fingers. Jen's stomach turned as he sucked her saliva from them.

Then there was searing pain.

Bastien smacked her so hard her head bashed against the stone floor. Her vision blurred and then more pain followed, this time in her ribs as he kicked her so violently, she cried out, gasping for air.

He was about to strike again when a dhoksha appeared at his side. It whispered something in his ear and scampered off.

Bastien's smile grew unhinged. He whistled to the kashyaks behind her, and they roughly pulled her up to her knees. Her head was spinning, her breathing labored.

"It seems we have some guests joining us."

She could hear the faint scrapes and grunts from outside the great hall. They grew louder and louder until the thrashing and cursing was undeniable.

Jen's heart plummeted as Damien and Ronan were hauled into the room by a conclave of angry dhokshas.

Fjora and Samara raced after Nelysar towards the king's suite.

"Fjora!" a desperate voice pleaded from the grand staircase.

They jerked to a stop. Rieshi was halfway up the grand stairs, struggling to hold up her mother. Nelysar ran down and slipped Gaiana's arm over his shoulder. "What happened?"

Rieshi clung to her mother. "She sensed some kind of shift and then she started seeing things, she won't tell me what—"

They reached the top of the stairs and Gaiana grabbed onto Fjora's hands.

"The one who was invited to the table shall surely poison his hosts," she said, her eyes glazed, her voice husky.

Fjora eyed Nelysar and Rieshi, but Gaiana held tighter. "The hope of this world threatens to burn in a blaze of dark despair," she gasped.

"Gaiana…" Fjora tilted her head to get her attention. Rieshi clapped her hands over her mouth, watching her mother in horror.

Nelysar came next to Fjora and took Gaiana's face in his hands, her eyes unfocused. He placed his fingertips at her temples.

"Come back, Gaiana," he whispered.

Her eyes cleared as she stumbled forward. Her head snapped around until she came back to Nelysar, her face relaxed. "Well, hello, you beautiful piece of—"

A collective sigh of relief cut her off. Nelysar winked at her. "Nice to have you back, beautiful."

She glanced at Fjora. "You hear that? He thinks I'm beautiful."

Fjora let out a stiff laugh as Nelysar wrapped an arm around her waist and kissed her brow.

Rieshi embraced her mother. "You scared me. What *was* that?"

Gaiana regained her focus and fixed her sight on Fjora. "It's Bastien, he's deceived us all."

Fjora nodded, her eyes rimmed red. "We know, Gaiana."

"He has Jenevieve," she sputtered. "There were moss ridden walls…grey stone floors…dhokshas and kashyaks *everywhere*…"

"What does he want with her?" Samara asked, her voice shaking.

Gaiana looked back at Nelysar.

"He means to burn the bridge."

Nelysar's eyes grew wide. "We need to find her." He peered down at Fjora. "We need Orion."

"JEN!" Damien cried as he was yanked towards the dais.

His eyes filled with tears when he saw her battered state. He fought madly against chains on his wrists and the group of dhokshas that held him.

Behind him another gang of dhokshas brought in Ronan, but he wasn't fighting them. They seemed almost nervous as they pulled him across the room.

It was only when he saw the state of her that his composure slipped for barely a moment, his nostrils flaring.

"Ah, the valiant heroes have come to call," Bastien announced as he walked back up the steps of the platform. The two men were brought to either side of Jen.

"And it seems the villains have emerged from the shadows," Ronan drawled.

Bastien laughed. "As someone who knows the shadows well, I'm surprised you didn't see me, old friend."

"Perhaps I'm not as clever as I make myself out to be, Bas."

"No, perhaps not." Bastien perched on the crumbled throne.

Jen winced through the pain in her ribs.

"Why am I here?" she asked through clenched teeth. Damien once again tried to reach for her, but the dhoksha yanked him back. Ronan kept his uninterested gaze on Bastien.

"You were an unexpected inconvenience, *my sweet,*" Bastien drawled. He plopped down on the crumbling throne and rested his head on his hand. "Fjora was long gone, the queen was dead, I was essentially king consort, and the realm was *finally* collapsing in on itself." He gave an exasperated sigh. "Imagine my surprise when a child of the blood showed up at the palace on the back of a Rhionnen attempting to reconvene the council." He rubbed his temples.

"You haven't answered my question," Jen snarled.

A smile slowly pulled on the corners of Bastien's mouth, he kept speaking as if he didn't hear her.

"Then I saw your raw power, and the darkness that stirred. And after your brother confided in me." He pushed a finger to his lips. "Oh wait, he's not *actually* your brother."

Jen bared her teeth.

Bastien shrugged and pushed up from the throne. "Then there was that stunning display with the Book of Prophecy in the library, I knew at that moment I needed to act." He took a step back. "But poor Shyra discovered me in your rooms, and well—" He gestured to his hip.

The tiishara.

"I knew, at that point, I wouldn't remain undetected for much longer. So, plans were altered and here we are. I know, it's all a bit *dramatic*," he said with a tilt of his head.

Mobius cackled, his eyes bulging out of his head.

Bastien smirked before fixating on Jenevieve. "The power of the Aylaenor runs through your veins, and yet, darkness is where your power *thrives*." He walked down the steps towards her.

And yet?

Jen kept her face fixed with disgust, but a thought pushed towards the front of her mind.

Oh, gods.

"You have been so resistant to its seductive pull. Haven't you thought of all you could do if you…" He came within an inch of her face, "embraced it——embraced who you are?"

He knows.

She glared at him, but her heart stuttered as she tried to figure out how he could have possibly figured it out.

"I realized I had an opportunity," he continued.

Damien lunged at him.

"Has that worked for you yet?" Bastien asked him, his smile growing. He stalked around Jen, his hands lacing behind his back. He came behind her and breathed into her ear.

"You already teeter on the precipice, and by dawn—" he chuckled sadistically. "I will have broken you so thoroughly that giving into darkness will be your only relief from this world. And from those shattered pieces I will meld you into a formidable weapon and present you to my master. And you will *want* to do it."

Jen jerked her head away.

"Why not take me to Heltior now?"

Bastien threw his head back in a deep, maniacal laugh.

"You think I speak of *that* brute?"

Jen blinked rapidly, her confusion fueling his mania.

"Oh, my dear Jenevieve, Heltior is the *least* of your concerns," his head snapped to Ronan. "Isn't that right, Ro'?"

Ronan watched him closely.

"You've played a long game, Bas," he said, his voice low and clear. He took a step forward. "But so have I."

Bastien rubbed his chin. "Is that so?"

Ronan's eyes gave nothing away.

"Durche yahvak," he said.

Bastien's brows shot up before they quickly settled to an expression Jen couldn't place. She snapped her gaze to Ronan.

I've heard those words.

Bastien's gaze found the dhokshas that held Jen and Damien.

"Take them to the dungeons. I need a word with my *old friend*." He turned to Jenevieve. "You have quite the night ahead of you, my dear. I'll see you soon."

They were hauled back towards the stairwell. Jen cried out as she fought against them. "Ronan!"

He didn't turn back to her, not even when she continued to call his name as she was dragged down to the bowels of the fortress.

CHAPTER 41

"Haythem!" Nelysar shouted.

Fjora and the others darted into the king's suite to find he was not alone; Rhea, Darya and Jamie were all seated by the hearth.

Haythem rose from his seat.

"Nelysar, what's the meaning of this?"

Fjora struggled to fill her lungs. "It's Bastien," she panted. "He's taken Jenevieve."

The king's eyes widened before he shook his head.

"Why on earth would he do that?"

Samara came forward. "We were just in his rooms, Your Grace. It was overturned." She brought forth a few pieces of parchment. "He was tracking us all, and…"

Haythem reluctantly took the papers. "And?"

Her eyes found Jamie, standing behind the armchair where Darya was seated. "He recorded your conversations," she said to him.

Jamie went pale. "He—why?"

She looked at him sympathetically. "He seemed to deem the information valuable."

Darya turned in her seat. "What did you tell him, Jamie?"

He shoved his hands in his pockets. "Just stuff about Nimea, our lives there… and…well, he asked about… father."

Darya jumped to her feet. "That was none of his business!"

Rhea rushed to Jamie's side and placed a hand on his shoulder.

"He didn't know, Darya."

Nelsar pushed past Samara. "He's a Knight of Eseer, Haythem."

Haythem's eyes looked like they were about to bulge out of his head. "Don't be ridiculous." He chucked the papers onto the table beside him.

"Bastien has been at my side since I was a boy. He kept the realm afloat after the queen—" his voice wavered.

Nelysar came to the table and looked solemnly at the king.

"Durche yahvak," he murmured.

Haythem blinked. "What did you just say?"

"You know what I just said, Haythem, and so does he. There were parchments filled with those words, written by a madman."

Haythem scoffed. "There must be some kind of explanation—"

"I felt a shift, Haythem." Everyone turned as Gaiana spoke inside the doorway. "As if his facade was ripped from his body. He fled the palace and kidnapped Jenevieve."

"She's in the bloodline, but..."

Gaiana crossed over to him. "Jenevieve is not just in the bloodline." She glanced at Nelysar. "She is the end of it." Her eyes shifted to Fjora. "And not only is she an exceptionally powerful iejja..."

Fjora grabbed onto Nelysar's sleeve and spoke the words that she had known since that day at the Tree of Awakenings with Aiyla.

"She is the Oshara."

Gaiana nodded. "We cannot lose her. She has a destiny we must protect at all costs. Bastien will try to sway her—break her."

She fixed her determined gaze on the king. "You know what you must do."

Haythem stared at her, a wave of apprehension cresting behind his ocean-blue eyes. He stomped over to the veranda, crossing his arms tightly over his chest.

Fjora followed quietly behind him, placing her hand on his arm and looking out into the valley with him. "Call for him, Papa."

His head hung low, shame plaguing his features.

"He won't come. I abandoned the bond."

She arched her brow. "Only one way to find out," she said as she gave her father a gentle push towards the balcony.

Haythem grasped the golden railing, his chest heaving in a great sigh as his head bowed humbly towards his realm. He inhaled deeply and lifted his chin, his eyes closed.

"Orion," he whispered.

Silence.

No one moved as the king waited.

After a moment, Haythem turned back to Fjora, a look of somber defeat etched into the lines of his face.

But then, his brows cinched together, and his gaze snapped back to the valley, hearing something the others could not.

Out of the darkness, the intrepid beating of magnificent wings filled the room until something enormous landed on the railing of the veranda. Haythem threw his hands up to block the torrent of wind as papers flew everywhere and the fire in the hearth danced, threatening to snuff itself out.

A majestic Etherian condor stretched its wings, spanning almost half the balcony.

Orion.

Fjora choked back an elated sob. Haythem's shoulders slumped in relief as he walked cautiously towards the railing.

"Hello, old friend," he breathed.

Orion tilted his head warily. Haythem extended his hand towards the condor, and it jerked its head to nip at his fingers.

He sucked in a breath, yanking his hand out of Orion's reach, but his expression remained soft.

"I know. I'm sorry," he cooed.

Haythem raised his brows in silent permission, and it was then that Orion bowed his head. The king raised his hand once more, his palm finding the weathered beak of his companion.

A warm glow appeared, reigniting the bond.

He let out a heavy exhale, and as if Orion could hear his thoughts, he ruffled his feathers, ready for orders.

"Find her," he said quietly.

Orion stretched his dark-brown wings, and with one massive flap, he was airborne. He flew into the night sky, but not before the rest of his flock joined in the aerial search, their majestic silhouettes cutting through the nocturnal glow of the moon.

Haythem turned back to the room and looked directly at Nelysar, his gaze focused—clear.

"Call the Warriors."

Jen and Damien were dragged down the uneven steps and into the dank darkness of the dungeon. They thrashed against their captors as they were forced along the hallway until they reached a row of iron clad cells.

They removed the chains from Damien's wrists and threw him into one cell, and then shoved Jen into the adjoining one, their bodies cracking when they hit the stone floor.

She held her head and winced, trying to get her bearings as her vision cleared. There was a pile of musty straw and a small chamber pot in the corner—it reeked of mildew and rusted metal. Shadows crawled up the walls. Darkness embraced every corner of the windowless prison.

A groan sounded behind her.

Jen stumbled to the bars. "Damien," she choked.

He clambered to his feet and ran to her, his hands desperately reaching for her.

"Jen." His hands hovered over her face, like he was unsure where it was safe to touch her. "Are you hurt?" he asked, his voice hoarse. "What did they do to you—"

The chain between her cuffs rattled against the iron bars as she lifted her hands to his cheek. "You shouldn't be here."

"Me? What about *you?*"

Jen looked down to the dirty floor. "I'm so sorry. I'm sorry I kicked you out after—"

His eyes welled. "*No*, I shouldn't have left. I let my ego—"

"I was trying to protect you," Jen said, her eyes stinging as she looked at the crazy, idiotic man that she loved so much. "I couldn't bear the thought of you getting hurt."

He ran his thumb over the scrape on her cheekbone. "*I* was supposed to protect *you* and I let you walk right into an ambush." His head hung low with shame.

"They threatened Jamie, my family," she said, grabbing the bars. "I chose to go, Damien."

He shook his head. "I would have gone with you."

She let a tear fall down her cheek. "I wouldn't have let you."

He wiped it away and let his forehead rest against hers through the bars, his hand lacing into her golden hair, holding on for dear life. "When will you accept that I would do anything for you?"

Gods. I love him.

He dropped his hands and took a step back, releasing a sigh. "I need to tell you something." His eyes found hers. "Your return to Etheria, it signals the end of—"

"Damien." Jen grabbed the iron bar beside her head. "I already know—"

"Jen? Damien?"

Their heads snapped to the cells opposite them. Her heart plummeted into her stomach. "Emelie?"

"We're here, too," another voice said from a neighboring cell.

Emelie and Leeyna emerged from the shadows of their dim cells and draped their arms through the bars.

Jen stared in disbelief. "I—" she sputtered. "Where's William?"

"I'm back here," he called from the darkness. "You know, I don't think I particularly care for Ruymani."

Jen crossed her cell, clutching her chest as the initial shock simmered into confusion. "H h how are you all here? Why…"

The reason dawned on her, and her body seized with dread. Bastien meant to break her, and she was looking at the tools he planned to use.

"Oh, you know, good old-fashioned drugging." William was sitting on the floor against the bars in the back of his cell, his legs crossed as if this wasn't a life-threatening situation.

"We were in the city for the festival. Someone must have slipped something into our drinks," Emelie said, her brown eyes bloodshot.

"We woke up here," Leeyna finished. "Where is *here,* by the way?"

Jen ran her hands up and down the bars. "We're in a safe haven fortress."

Damien joined her. "That's ironic."

"Anyone want to tell me *why* we're here?" William asked.

Jen sighed, tightening her grip around the bars until her knuckles turned white. "It was Bastien." Their eyes widened. "He's a Knight of Eseer, he's been behind everything; the ball, my curse, Shyra…it was all him."

Emelie held her arms around herself. "But why?"

"He means to break me, to…" She scuffed the floor with her bare foot. Damien reached through the bars and squeezed her arm. "To turn me into a weapon."

"Then, why are *we* here…" Leeyna asked, but as soon as the words left her, her face drained of color. "Oh."

Jen began pacing around her cell, fighting a shiver as the dampness that clung to her feet climbed its way up her legs.

Of course, I'm not wearing any fucking shoes.

"I'm not going to let anything happen to you," she said. "I never should've let any of you follow me here. I should have sent you home the moment we left Bri."

"Do you really think we would've let that happen?" Emelie asked.

Leeyna let go of the bars and crossed her arms. "We said we're with you. Those weren't just meaningless words."

William grunted as he fumbled to his feet. "The trip back is annoyingly far anyway." Leeyna shot him a sharp glare. "I'm kidding, sort of," he amended quickly.

"Where's Ronan?" Emelie asked.

Jen glanced at Damien, and he cleared his throat. "Bastien has him, but we don't know what's going on up—"

The sound of heavy footsteps silenced them. They held their breath as a shadow appeared in the stairwell, travelling up the wall until a familiar shape landed at the bottom. Ronan's broad shoulders took up almost the entire hallway as he sauntered towards the cells.

Jen let out a relieved sigh.

He's okay. Everyone is okay.

"Oh jeez, you scared us," Emelie said, clearly feeling relieved as well. "We were so worried."

He didn't look at her.

Jen's eyes turned to slits, suspicion twisting in her chest.

Something was wrong.

Ronan wasn't in chains, and he came alone. His hands were laced behind his back as if he were traipsing through the Sachandan court.

"Ronan?" Damien asked nervously.

He was silent as he approached Jen's cell, looking at her through the bars with a smooth expression of indifference. He revealed a set of old iron keys from behind him. A small flutter winged in her chest, breaking through the suspicion.

Did he find a way to escape?

The door unlocked with a *click*, and when it creaked open, he stepped inside with her. Jen took a step back, his movements didn't feel like him, the Ronan she had come to know, had come to care for. This felt…threatening.

"He's ready for you," he said, his voice flat.

No. This isn't happening.

"Ronan…"

He stepped towards her. "Let's go."

Damien hissed, his brows snapping together as he leapt towards the bars, violently shaking against them. "YOU TRAITOR!"

The others stood agape, stunned to silence.

"What's going on…" Emelie asked, her voice shaking like she already knew the answer.

Damien jabbed his finger at him. "He's fucking working with Bastien. He betrayed us just the same."

Jen's stomach turned. "You wouldn't," she said, unable to mask the hurt in her expression.

He couldn't. Not after everything that's happened.

"Don't make me say it again," Ronan said, disdain dripping from his voice, a sound he had never levied at her.

Rage bubbled under her skin, but the metal cuffs trapped her magic, holding it hostage within her own body.

Oh, fuck this.

She hinged back, bringing her chained wrists with her, and punched him square in the jaw, knocking him against the bars.

Surprise flashed across his face as his hand rose to the split in his lip. A chagrin grin curled in the corner of his mouth, and he lunged at her, wrapping his large hand roughly around her arm, wrenching her out of the cell. She fought against him, but his grip only tightened as the others began to scream for her.

Damien banged against the bars with all his strength, beating them like a madman. "JEN!" he screamed.

Ronan got in his face, his green eyes filling with malice. "I suggest you fortify your minds and prepare yourselves, friends." He glanced over at the others. "You're all in for a rough night."

He ripped Jen away from the bars and hauled her down the hallway, her friends' desperate cries echoing through the dungeon.

"Ronan! Stop, please!" she begged. "Why are you doing this?!"

He said nothing as he dragged her up the steps. Her nails cracked and bled as she clung to the walls, the railing, anything, but he was too strong. He practically lifted her up by the chains of her cuffs.

She cried out, the metal cutting into her wrists. Ronan's grip loosened, and for a fleeting moment, she could have sworn she saw something flicker behind his eyes. But then he changed positions, his hands grabbing her waist to carry her the rest of the way up the stairs.

Bastien slid in front of them, a devious smile forming on his lips. "Welcome back, Jenevieve," he drawled.

She writhed against Ronan's hold on her.

Bastien tsked. "Save that for later my dear." He ran a long pale finger down her cheek.

"You fucking—"

Bastien blew a silver powder into her face. Her eyes burned as she choked on the remnants of it. Her arms went limp, her body growing heavy just as her knees gave out. Bastien's white hair grew fuzzy and distorted—and then the world went dark.

CHAPTER 42

"""W""ake up," a distorted voice taunted. "Wake up, Jenevieve."

Her eyes batted open, and even in her dazed state, something felt wrong. Her joints ached, and when her vision fully cleared, she realized her arms were strung up to a tall, thick wooden pole.

Shit. Shit. Shit.

Panic coursed through her body as she pulled against the restraints, but they held firm. Her head darted around to her surroundings.

She stood in a clearing, the ground covered with dirt, but she seemed to still be inside. There were walls flanking her, but they were uneven and crumbling, much like the rest of the fortress—but these walls were brown.

Is that clay? Dirt?

She peered around the pole, and her blood went ice cold when she saw a tunnel swallowed by a black abyss looming in front of her.

"Up here, dear girl," the distorted voice now rang clear. Her disoriented gaze rose to meet Bastien, with Ronan and Mobius on either side, standing above her.

She was in a massive pit.

"Seems you may have given her too much," Ronan murmured. Bastien waved his hand dismissively. "No, see? She's fine." He looked down at her. "You're fine, yes?"

Jen went to throw a scathing retort, but when she opened her mouth, nothing came out. She tried again, and again. Her lips moved, but her vocal cords refused to vibrate. Fear set in as her wide eyes met her malevolent host.

"Oh my, are you rendered—*speechless*?" Bastien mocked. Mobius cackled beside him. "Our objective this evening is to break you, oh mighty *iejja*. And what better way than to dismantle you piece by piece." He took a step forward, looking down into the pit. "This first task is to break down your *mind*. And who better to help us than your quizzical friend and his lovely beast wrangler."

Alarm seized in Jen's chest, her eyes going wide as she scoured the pit for her friends. Bastien watched her with a macabre grin.

Suddenly her head began to spin, like her mind was being stirred in a cauldron. She fought off the need to vomit as it spun faster, her consciousness pulling away from her body like honey from a comb. She clamped her eyes shut to find some reprieve, but when she opened them—she was staring down at her own body.

Slumped against the pole.

"You should have a front row seat for this," Bastien's voice danced around her. She realized, to her horror, that she was looking at the scene through his eyes. He'd pulled her consciousness into his own.

No. No. No.

"Oh, yes indeed," he drawled. His mind caressed her with invisible ropes of demented magic, holding her still.

Jen looked back at her unconscious body hanging from the pole, and after fighting the non-corporeal urge to pass out, she tried to get her mind back on track.

She was in the middle of the long pit, and when she casted her gaze in either direction…

A maze.

She was looking at a maze, and her body was at the center.

Rough grunts and shouts came from the eastern entrance. Two dhokshas dragged William into the maze and shoved him into the dirt before snickering their way out, the exit sealing itself behind them. His head snapped around, panic pulsing through him so strongly he was shaking.

But she didn't watch him for long as the western entrance filled with the shadows of two more dhokshas, hauling a far too quiet Leeyna into the maze. She didn't struggle, but her face was blotchy—she'd been crying not a moment ago and she held herself like she was trying to keep her own panic at bay.

Bastien's voice boomed over the pit.

"Welcome, my friends," he said, clasping his hands together.

Their heads snapped up. William clenched his fists.

"You find yourselves in the Maze of Morlache, a training pen for Etherian soldiers before it was converted to a safe haven fortress." His hands rose beside him. "Your task is simple. Find your way to the middle of the maze—to *each other*." He made his bottom lip quiver.

"Such a simple ask, Bas," Ronan quipped.

"You think I should make it *interesting*?"

Ronan arched his brow.

Bastien chuckled. "My friend thinks I've made this too easy. But don't fret."

A sinister chuckle wrapped around her mind as two dhokshas struggled to pull a massive ornate hourglass to the edge of the pit. They pushed it upright, and when Bastien snapped his fingers, the top half filled with red-brown sand, a daunting mound of passing time.

William and Leeyna's mouths dropped open.

"You have a time limit." He looked at Ronan. "Should we say... five minutes?"

Ronan rubbed his chin. "Seems reasonable."

Bastien held up his hand. "Five minutes. After that—"

A thunderous roar shook the room. Leeyna and William froze. A twisted grin pulled on Bastien's lips. "After that." He cleared his throat. "I will release my pet. He is so very starved for entertainment down there."

William breathed heavily through his mouth, his skin glistening with sweat. Bastien turned toward the dais before putting a finger in the air. "One last thing, and it's rather important."

He said the next bit straight into Jenevieve's trapped mind as well. "Cheating will be tempting, but I will warn you. There will be consequences."

What in hells does that mean?

"Begin."

Dhokshas and kashyaks swarmed the perimeter of the pit, their maniacal jeers and screams filled the hall as they clamored over each other to watch.

William immediately started shouting.

"Leeyna! Leeyna, are you alright?"

Relief flooded Leeyna's face as she yelled back. "Yes! Yes, I'm alright! Are you?"

William looked up at the hourglass. "I've been better."

"What do we do?" Leeyna shouted, taking in her surroundings.

He paced back and forth, pulling at his short, brown hair like he could yank the answers from his scalp. His head jerked up to scan the walls ahead of him.

"Etherian soldiers were connected by mind-melding, so they could work as one entity on the battlefield—" he was interrupted by a slightly higher pitched Leeyna.

"The short version, William!"

"The Maze of Morlache was used to fortify the connection. Each side is mirrored—we have to do the opposite of each other." He clapped his hand to the back of his head.

"But we don't know the path!" Leeyna shouted, her voice shrill.

"We're going to have to work by trial and error. I'll shout your direction and mirror you," he said, his voice shaking. "Ready?" he shouted.

Leeyna braced herself. "I hope so," she said.

"GO!"

They sprinted into the maze.

"LEFT! RIGHT! RIGHT AGAIN!" he yelled.

They quickly worked a third of the way through. Bastien crossed his arms. "Well, this is boring." He tilted his head to Mobius. "You're on."

Mobius shrieked in excitement and stepped forward. With a flick of his wrist several of the maze openings crumbled into piles of rubble, blocking their paths.

William came to a screeching halt. "Shit, my path is blocked!"

Leeyna halted as well, gasping for air. "Mine, too!"

They both turned on their heels and ran another way but found only dead ends.

"I'm trapped," Leeyna choked. She whipped her head around the maze before glancing up at the hourglass. "We're running out of time!" she yelled, almost hysterical, now. "How do we get through?"

William looked around frantically, his hands clasping his head as he searched the collapsed corridor, desperate for any way to get through.

Something in the adjacent corner caught his eye. It reflected in the dull light of the pit as he shook his head in disbelief.

An axe.

He sprinted over to it, and when he picked it up, he froze.

"Vondurian steel," he breathed. He yelled across the maze. "Leeyna! Look around! Do you see anything on the ground!?"

Leeyna staggered around the rubble and choked on a sob when she saw something gleaming from the ground. "YES! Yes, I see a blade." She picked it up and clenched it with both hands. "What do I do with it?"

William ran to the wall next to the crumbled path. He ran his hand over the red-brown stone—wait. It wasn't stone. He rubbed his fingers together. "The walls are clay," he murmured before he yelled out with overwhelming respite. "THE WALLS ARE CLAY! We can cut through them!"

"I don't know if I can!" Leeyna cried.

"We're running out of time, you have to!" he commanded. "Take a few steps back to get a running start. You can do this. I'm right there with you!"

Leeyna fumbled back a few steps. "Okay," she said through trembling lips.

"Whatever happens, you keep moving! Understand?"

They're going to make it. They're going to be okay.

But her thought was stifled by a low, sinister laugh.

"Remember what I said about cheating?" Bastien murmured. She felt her mind churning until he expelled her, hurtling her back into her own body.

She jolted, gasping for breath.

"RUN!" William shouted from within the maze.

Their weapons clashed through the clay walls.

Jen winced. Her dress ripped as searing pain rippled down her back like someone was carving jagged lines with a red-hot knife.

Her body lurched against the invisible swordsman.

She tried to release a scream, but once again, no sound came, and neither did any reprieve from crying out in pain.

And then something worse.

A terrifying roar came from the wall behind her. Fanatical screams and jeers from the crowd of dark creatures sang out from around the pit. The ground shook as something large crashed into the maze.

Bastien shouted into the pit. "It seems my pet didn't want to wait. You should pick up the pace, my friends!"

"FASTER!" William bellowed.

The ominous thuds of the horrifying beast plagued Jen's ears as her mouth dropped open and tears cascaded from her eyes, another pair of searing lines maiming her back. She writhed against the assault, but when she looked over her shoulder, no one was there.

The axe. The blade.

Bastien warned against cheating the task and then forced them into doing just that. Jen looked up through her welling eyes to see him staring down at her with a malicious sneer.

Their weapons are enchanted.

Every strike to the maze was a strike to her body.

The beast crashed through the walls, its growls rumbling in her bones. With every sound of crumbling clay, she couldn't tell if it was the beast or the blades. She couldn't anticipate the slashes, couldn't prepare herself for the pain.

"WE'RE ALMOST THERE!" William yelled.

Jen thrashed against the restraints as a third pair of scorching cuts carved themselves between her shoulder blades. She opened her mouth and clenched her entire body as wretched sobs attempted to escape her, to no avail.

They couldn't hear her screams.

The beast grew louder, plowing its way towards the center.

"KEEP GOING!" William's voice echoed just behind the closest wall.

Jen's vision blurred, surrounded by black mist. The pain was too much. The last wall of the maze smashed on either side of her, and she could just make out Leeyna and William blasting into the center of the pit.

Bastien flicked his wrist just as the last torrid slashes flanked her spine. A guttural, torturous scream exploded from her. She wailed, clinging to the pole as blood poured from her open wounds, dripping down her back onto the ground.

William and Leeyna stopped dead in their tracks.

"Oh gods, Jen!" Leeyna yelled.

They dashed over to her, but they stopped short, their mouths dropping open at the sight of her back.

William looked down at his axe, and then the shape of her lashes. He dropped it, the muffled clang of metal hitting the dirt at his feet.

Jen shivered as she attempted to breathe, moans crawling out of her throat as her head drooped between her arms.

Leeyna looked at her own blade in horror. "Was—did we—" She clapped her hand to her mouth, tears streaming down her cheeks. "We *cheated.*"

Jen tried to shake her head. "It's...alright...you didn't." She sucked in a breath through her teeth, fighting the urge to cry out. "You didn't know," she said weakly.

The beast pummeled through the wall behind Jen, the force knocking William and Leeyna to the ground.

Thunderous jeers came from the crowd around the pit.

"A boruut," William said, clearly having trouble believing it.

The gargantuan creature loomed in the middle of the dirt pit. Its black, thinning fur haphazardly covered its gray, weathered skin. It thrashed its massive head, the curved, onyx horns above its black eyes destroying more of the walls around it.

Long, sharp teeth snapped and snarled at them. Its enormous claws digging into the upturned dirt. Leeyna fumbled to her feet, her fearful gaze bounced from Jen, to William, to the boruut. She gulped and took a cautious step forward.

William rose slowly, inching his way over to Jen. "What are you doing?!" he whisper-yelled.

Leeyna shushed him.

The beast bared its teeth but didn't come closer. Jen bit her lip hard as she tried to look over her shoulder, any movement stretched the lashes carved into her back.

Leeyna dropped her sword and exposed her palms.

The commotion above them went silent.

Her breath became slow and calm as she approached the bear-like creature. It sniffed in her direction and shook its head, like it didn't understand her scent. She raised her hand towards the beast, lulling it with a croon.

It blinked at her. The creature closed its eyes and stretched its head towards her hand…

A great bellow came from behind her. William charged at the creature, and before it could move to attack, he skidded onto the floor beneath it, and shoved Leeyna's sword up into its neck. Leeyna lurched back as blood splattered onto her face.

The boruut released a disturbing scream before its eyes rolled back and it crumpled to the floor.

"NO!" Bastien screamed. The crowds of creatures erupted into angry shrieks.

William crawled out from under the animal, heaving and wiping the blood off his face, but when he stood and looked at Leeyna, it wasn't gratitude he found on her face, it was anger.

"What did you *do*?" she seethed.

"What?"

"It wasn't going to hurt us!" she yelled. "You murdered an innocent animal!" She fell to her knees in front of the boruut.

A pack of dhokshas leapt into the pit and rushed William and Leeyna, yanking them back towards the tunnel.

"Leeyna!" he cried.

"William!" she screamed.

They were dragged past Jen, bloodied and semi-conscious.

"JEN!" Leeyna yelled. Her name echoed through the pit as they were pulled into the dark abyss, but she could barely hear anything, the pain of her maimed back overwhelming her, leaving her mind in shambles.

Bastien had won this round, her mind was indeed, broken.

Jen exhaled, and her body collapsed against the pole into sweet oblivion.

CHAPTER 43

Jen came to and found herself not in the dungeon with the others, but a small, quiet room. The space was so still, she almost forgot where she was.

Almost.

She laid on a dusty cot, her eyes still bleary.

A stream of moonlight flooded in through a long, narrow window across the room. Jen pushed herself up—but the moment her muscles flexed, pain tearing through her back like a blade. She gasped and collapsed, her body refusing to move. A tear ran across her nose and onto the thin sheet. When she followed its path, her eyes caught on something sitting on the floor.

A small, clear vile. And next to it, a few flowers that looked like tiny daisies. She whimpered as she gingerly reached her arm down and retrieved the vile, removing the stopper with her mouth to smell its contents.

She turned up her nose.

Alcohol.

For my wounds? But who would help me here?

Jen moved to push herself up again, slowly this time, practically biting off her lip to stave the searing pain. She grabbed the edge of the cot and braced herself, taking a deep breath before reaching her shackled hands over her shoulder.

An agonizing cry fell from her as she poured the alcohol over her wounds. She moaned and cursed as the liquid slid down her back, disinfecting the deep lashes. She looked down at her cuffed wrists and the empty vial.

Her breath cleaved from her chest.

A visceral scream clawed out of her throat, and she threw the vial across the room, shattering it against the wall.

The wooden door flew open, and Jen jumped to her feet, fighting the bout of dizziness that accompanied the quick movement. Bastien and Ronan stood in the doorway with their arms crossed.

"Time to go," Ronan said, his expression indifferent.

Jen spat on the floor in front of him. "Fuck you."

She could have sworn she saw the corner of his mouth twitch.

"There she is," he retorted, his lips in a firm line.

Bastien looked between the two of them before blowing out an exasperated breath. "Well, if you two are quite done with." He waved his hand. "Whatever *this* is."

He strolled over to her. She kept her chin high and her face in harsh lines of disgust. He whipped out his hand and blew the same silver powder into her face.

The world went black once again.

She swam through the dark recesses of her mind until she broke the surface, coughing over a cold stone floor. Her dress was ripped and frayed, blood staining the delicate fabric.

Jen turned on her elbows and saw she was back in front of the dais. Her mind was fragile and her body weak from blood loss, but still, she forced herself to her feet.

She was still Jenevieve, not some soulless dark weapon. Bastien stood above her, an arrogant smile on his face. Ronan and Mobius were posted on either side. Bastien's gaze flickered towards the dungeon stairs. She followed his gaze and her heart plummeted.

Emilie was being brought up the stairs.

She was pulled through a sea of dhokshas and kashyaks, who leered and grabbed at her, but Emelie's head remained high as if immune to their darkness.

One of the kashyaks brazenly ran their hand up her thigh.

"Don't touch her!" Jen yelled, but Emelie's gaze turned to steel, and she gave no reaction. She was pushed towards the dais where she ignored Bastien entirely and fixed her attention on Jen, who stood with her hands cuffed in front of her.

"Are you alright?" she asked.

Jen shook her head. "Never mind me, what about you? William and Leeyna? Damien?"

"Damien has all but destroyed his cell—"

Bastien stepped to the edge of the dais. "Ladies, we are in the middle of something, if you don't mind."

Emelie fumed. "I do mind, you fucking traitor."

"Well, well," Bastien mused. "I was not expecting such a sharp tongue from our resident *mother hen*." He descended the steps and strolled over to her. "I was just reminiscing with our dear Ronan, about our night at Lannas." He curled a tendril of her hair in his fingers. "That was one for the books, was it not, Ro'?"

"Indeed," he said.

Bastien leaned towards Emelie's ear, her nostrils flaring. "I happen to remember a moment later in the evening." He ran a finger over her cheek. "When you started demanding shots from our friend Sil." He started back towards Jen.

He reached into his pocket and retrieved a small glass bottle from his tunic. He twirled it in his hand, looking almost fascinated by it.

"It's not exactly Ardovian rum." He winked back at Ronan.

When he offered it to Jen, she backed away, the backs of her legs pressing against the bottom step of the dais. Mobius appeared behind her, his cold hands wrapping around her shoulders. He held her in place as Bastien stepped closer.

He grabbed her cheeks with his fingers and forced her mouth open. "But it still has a good kick," he breathed into her face.

"Bastien," Ronan said in a low voice.

"No!" Emelie cried.

Jen thrashed against his hand, but he tightened his grip and emptied the contents down her throat.

He held her mouth shut and forced her to swallow the foul liquid. She fell to the ground, her knees hitting the weathered stone floor as the liquid burned as fire down her throat and tumbling into the pit of her stomach.

"What have you done?!" Emelie ran to Jenevieve's side.

Bastien meandered back up the steps. "I've started the next task, dear." He raised a hand to the hall, where a large wooden table appeared before them. It was laden with glass bottles, a mortar and pestle, knives, and a myriad of ingredients.

An apothecary table.

Bastien turned and looked down his nose at her. "This task will break down her body. If you don't create an antidote for our dear Jenevieve." he shrugged. "She will die, and her death will be on your hands."

Emelie frantically examined her, looking for any immediate signs of what poison was used.

"What is your plan here, Bas?" Ronan asked, rubbing the stubble lining his jaw. "She will be a useless weapon if she's *dead.*"

Bastien patted him on the back and arched a brow. "We'll just have to hope that your star pupil shines, my friend."

Jen lurched forward, her stomach tying itself into violent knots as she dry-heaved over the floor, but Emelie held her steady.

"Time is of the essence, Em," Bastien chided.

Jen crouched on her hands and knees, her face contorting. "G...g go— I'm...okay." She waved her hand towards the table.

Emelie bolted to it and quickly took stock of what was in front of her. She breathed heavily and grabbed the mortar and pestle.

"Okay. Okay. Okay."

Her eyes darted around the table. "Just start with a generic antidote, Emelie," she murmured.

She grabbed a jar labeled 'skin of lizard' and chucked a piece into the stone bowl. Next, 'nettles of aniseed.' She started pulverizing the ingredients into a fine powder when Jen groaned.

Jen's skin grew slick with sweat. She was boiling hot and ice cold at the same time. Her body started to tremble, and she folded herself into the fetal position.

"Talk to me, Jen!" Emelie ordered.

Jen screamed and the fortress shook with cackles and jeers from the eager crowd.

"I—It feels like hot metal is—" She violently convulsed. "Hot metal seeping into my bones—I'm on f–f–fire. GAHH," she gasped for air and clawed her fingers into the floor.

Emelie stopped.

Jen peered through hooded lids just as Emelie's eyes flicked to Ronan, and then in an instant, she dashed to Jen and knelt in front of her. She pulled up her eyelids to examine her eyes. Jen watched the wheels spinning in her best friend's head until Emelie choked on a relieved cry.

"It's Obscuro," she breathed. "Water of the cursed cave."

She squeezed Jen's hand before sprinting back to the table.

Jen whimpered as her stomach continued to contort around itself. She scraped through her memories until she found the one she was looking for. A book she came across in Gaiana's library after one of their lessons.

Obscuro, from the cursed caves in the Ardovian realm, was said to contain the breath of ancient demons. Ardovian tyrants used it as a form of torturous execution. The violent stomach pain, the molten fire in her bones, the stinging eyes.

Emelie and Jen locked eyes. They knew what came next.

Oh, fuck.

Jen's body went rigid and gurgling sounds bubbled from her throat before her body seized. The roars of laughter around them erupted into a disturbing frenzy.

"Hang on!" Emelie cried, her face was sweating profusely.

"You're running out of time, healer," Bastien taunted. Mobius jumped up and down and clapped his hands in delight.

She threw in blooms of rue and betony and salt from the Sea of Unsung Tears before transferring it to a glass bottle. She drowned the concoction in whatever alcohol was in the carafe in the corner.

The antidote turned a stunning shade of blue. Healing.

She ran to Jen who was still in the throes of violently seizing, a red rash crawling up her neck. Emelie held her head still and poured some of the liquid into Jen's mouth.

Jen sputtered and choked. The corners of her mouth began to foam, and she fell over onto her maimed back. A pained cry sawed out of her as tears fell from the corner of her eyes.

"No! No! No!" Emelie trembled. "It should have worked!"

Someone lunged forward on the dais.

"Blood! Blood of the victim! You need to bleed her, Emelie!"

Bastien snapped his head. "Ronan," he warned.

Ronan shoved passed Bastien and sped down the stairs. "You can't use her if you *kill her*, you idiot," he barked, his voice dripped with loathing.

Mobius charged for him, but Bastien lifted his hand.

"Give him a moment, my pet."

Emelie ran back to the table and retrieved a knife.

Wildflowers and soil before a storm wafted into Jen's nose as Ronan slid to the ground and took her scalding hot body in his arms. "Goddess, she's fucking boiling," he said as he nestled her in the crook of his shoulder.

Jen weakly opened her bloodshot eyes and saw who was holding her. "I'm…" She took a labored breath "very mad…" Another difficult inhale, "at you."

He held her closer to his chest. "Yeah, yeah. You can yell at me later," he whispered into her knotted hair.

Emelie returned with the small blade and grabbed Jen's finger, but Ronan shook his head.

"You need more than that," he said firmly. He gently held out Jen's forearm. "Make a clean cut down the center, not too deep or she'll bleed out."

She bit her lip as Jen's breathing slowed, coming out in short, sporadic exhales. Emelie's hand shook as she placed the tip of the blade to her arm, her eyes welling with guilty tears.

"I'm sorry," she whispered, and pierced her skin.

Jen wailed, fighting against the knife with the little life she had left.

I'm going to die.

Emelie held her arm still while Ronan tightened his grip, rocking her gently.

"I'm sorry, I'm so sorry," Emelie cried as blood dripped down her arm.

"Shh. Shh," Ronan cooed, placing a gentle kiss on Jen's forehead. "You're okay, Fury, I have you." He glanced at Emelie. "Faster, best friend—she's fading."

Tears fell down Emelie's cheeks as she lifted the knife and threw it as far as she could, the clash of metal on stone ringing out over the hall. Ronan held Jen's arm just over the lip of the glass bottle and let the blood flow into the antidote.

It turned the color of tumultuous storm clouds.

"That's it!" Ronan exhaled. "Go. Go. Go."

Just as Emelie moved the bottle to Jen's bluish lips, Bastien dropped his hand and shouted to the crowd of dhokshas and kashyaks. "GRAB THEM!"

The creatures swarmed them, yanking Emelie away before the antidote could be given.

"NO! JEN!" she screamed, clawing at the dhokshas who pulled her back towards the dungeon stairs.

Ronan snatched the bottle from the ground and emptied the contents down her throat before Mobius leapt from the dais and pulled him back by the hair.

Ronan swung his elbow and a howl of pain exploded from Mobius as he flew back, clutching his face. Ronan dove up the stairs, but Bastien was ready, and drop-kicked him back down to the floor.

A pack of dhokshas jumped him, pushing him to the ground.

He turned on his knees and crawled towards her.

"JENEVIEVE!" he yelled, desperation cracking his voice.

Her vision was fading; Ronan's voice was all that kept her tethered to consciousness as the red rash from her neck wrapped around her cheeks. Blood seeped from the wound on her arm.

I'm going to die.

The dhokshas bound Ronan in chains and yanked him back to the grey stone wall next to the dais. He growled and lunged like a beast as they latched his chains onto hooks in the stone.

"JENEVIEVE! PLEASE!"

Bastien appeared in front of him.

"You can say his words, *old friend,* but you no longer embrace his purpose," he tsked. "You haven't for a long time."

"IS SHE ALIVE?!"

"You had such potential, but you turned your back on who you were born to be, such a legendary line ending with a sad disappointment."

Ronan surged against the iron chains. "I will not be bound to a line of murderous betrayers," he spat. Bastien threw his head back and laughed loudly.

"It's a little late for that, isn't it?" He turned back to face him. "Don't worry Ronan, in a few moments you will be much more...*amenable* to my cause."

Jen's heart slowed, a chilling cold crawled through her fingers and toes.

This is dying.

These were her final moments.

At least the pain will end.

She felt Ronan's eyes watching her. Striking green eyes. Jen silently wished she had the strength to look at them one last time.

His voice broke as he prayed:

"Goddess, protect her.

Bring her to the light.

Guide her soul—"

The antidote swept through her body.
She gasped.

CHAPTER 44

Moonlight shifted through the tall window in her room, casting long shadows that crept across the floor to her tattered cot. Half her face sank into darkness. The silence pressed in around her—but this time, her mind made no attempt to fill the void.

Jen could barely open her eyes, let alone move. Remnants of the poison left a dull ache swimming through her blood. The taste of old alcohol mixed with iron coated her tongue, and when she glanced down, she saw the gash cut down her arm.

Her body rolled as the memories came back: the paralyzing fear and the burn of poison flowing down her throat, her stomach in unbearable knots, Emelie's terror, hot metal in her bones.

Ronan's voice tethering her to this world.

She was so cold, so tired. A voice in her head lulled her towards the soft promise of eternal sleep. For a moment, she let herself drift. But then her body lurched, and Jen forced herself up just in time to wretch onto the stone floor beside the cot.

Her hands dug into the edge of the mattress and her arms trembled under her weight.

A shadow appeared in the doorway.

White hair gleamed in the corner of her eye. Bastien quietly walked to the small wooden table by the window. He put down something heavy and the sound of pouring liquid permeated her ears.

His footsteps grew nearer until his black boots stopped in front of her dirty feet, a silver goblet appearing in front of her face.

"Do you think I'm that stupid?" she rasped, her gaze traveling up to meet him. But gone was the malevolent amber fire, replaced by the look of the man she had known.

Her eyes narrowed.

"It's just water," he said, offering it to her with a small grin. She stared at him and didn't take it.

Bastien grabbed her hand and wrapped her fingers around the cold goblet. "Drink," he ordered softly.

She examined the clear liquid within the goblet before taking a small, tentative sip. When she realized it wasn't a trick, she gulped it down, it cooled her aching throat and washed away the taste of blood.

He chuckled. "You should slow down." He took the goblet from her mouth and walked it back to the table.

Jen's eyes flickered down to his belt while his back was turned.

Her chest tightened.

The tiishara.

Her chance at freedom dangled right in front of her. Kill Bastien. Get her friends. Run. Adrenaline surged as a single, brutal idea cut through the fog of her near-death haze.

"I won't turn, Bastien," she said. "Whatever you're doing here is pointless."

He leaned into the window, the moonlight contouring his jagged cheekbones. "Reconvening the *Council of Suran* is pointless, Jen." He crossed his arms, a pensive look on his face. "You think a group of descendants who haven't worked for a common purpose in over a thousand years will be any match for what's coming?"

She slowly rose to her feet.

I just have to keep him talking.

"What exactly is coming?" Jen slowly padded towards him, the lashes on her back stretching painfully with every step. She leaned in the window opposite him.

He looked out into the darkness beyond the fortress.

"A reckoning."

Jen folded her arms and leaned her head on the wall.

"I don't want to be part of any reckoning."

Bastien tilted his head towards her. "The fates sung their song long ago, Jenevieve. Darkness will come like waves of eternal night; it will drown all those who dare to sail through." His eyes softened.

"You are an *iejja;* rare and powerful magic flows through you. Imagine what you could do if you simply allowed that power to meld with the stunning darkness that lurks behind those hazel eyes."

He tentatively took her hand and placed it on his chest, his thumb lightly caressing her knuckles as if they were lovers. Bile rose in the back of her throat.

If I could only reach for his belt—

"I really did care for Fjora, in the ways I knew how. I'm not a mindless animal," he murmured, his face strained with regret.

"You betrayed her," she said quietly, her voice filled with hurt. "You betrayed *me*."

"I've only tried to steer you onto the right path, Jen."

"What is the right path?" she asked, looking down at her feet.

Bastien raised a gentle hand to her cheek. "Join me." He ran his thumb along her bottom lip. "Wield your power on behalf of the righteous, and we can protect those you love *together*." His eyes flickered down to her breasts as they moved up and down with her breath.

Jen tracked his gaze.

"I can feel that ancient magic, even with those cuffs nullifying it." He dipped his head to her neck and inhaled deeply. "I can smell the darkness purring under your skin, begging to be unleashed."

Jen lifted her cuffed wrists, the chain clinking between them. "Such seductive words from an unbound captor," she whispered.

Bastien's breath grew shallow as he wrapped his fingers around the chain to pull her flush against him.

Disgust rumbled through her, but she pushed it away, exposing her neck to him. "I'm so tired, Bas."

He ran his lips up her neck and breathed into her ear. "I will keep you safe, Jenevieve." He nipped her earlobe before he returned to her gaze, his pupils dilating. "You can trust me."

"How?" she asked, her eyes flickered down to his lips.

His brow arched subtly. "I will let them all go."

Her breath caught in her throat. A feline smile pulled at the corner of his mouth.

"Accompany me to Vondur, and I will let your friends leave. I am not the villain here," he purred, his hand finding the nape of her neck.

Jen pressed her body to his, her hand lowering to his hip——closer to his belt. "They're all afraid of me," she said through a sigh as she clutched his tunic. "But you're not."

Bastien licked his lips, his eyes hazy with the lust that grows from power. "I am not."

He pulled her even closer, bringing his face within an inch of hers. "Durche yahvak," he breathed into her parted lips.

"What does that mean?" Jen whispered, her fingers grazing the hilt of the dagger.

Just a little closer.

His eyes locked on hers as he bit her lip.

"Thief."

He wrapped his fingers around her neck and bashed her into the wall, her head cracking against the stone. He unsheathed the dagger and pressed it to her neck.

"You don't think I knew what you were doing?" he seethed, his hot breath making her stomach recoil.

Jen clawed at his hand, her head throbbing. "You think you're not the villain?" she spat through shallow breaths. "You think—you think I would let you anywhere near me? You disgust me."

Bastien squeezed her windpipe. "You're making a grave mistake." He shoved her towards the window, and she choked as air flooded her lungs, fighting the white-hot pain and the revulsion from his touch.

"No," Jen coughed. "I don't think I am." She held her head and stepped away from the window. "My standards aren't *that* low."

Bastien growled and charged at her, smashing his mouth to hers. She pushed him off with every bit of strength she had and smacked him across the face.

He snarled and grabbed hold of her forearm, pressing his thumb roughly into her open wound. Stars plagued her vision. She released a guttural scream and tried to wrench her arm free. He held firm.

"Vondurian steel cuts deep, Jenevieve," his voice was sinister. "It will never fully heal."

He yanked on her hand and wrapped his arm around her, clawing into her back. She cried out, her jaw locked in a voiceless wail. "These won't either. I have marked you. I live in your skin. *Darkness* lives in your skin."

He pushed her to the ground, dusting off his tunic and lacing his hands behind his back as if this ordeal was just a minor inconvenience.

Jen gasped for air, whimpering in pain.

"The next task is to break your heart," he said, looming over her. "And you know who is left."

She groaned from the floor. Eyes the color of a winter sky, and a laugh—deep, explosive—echoed within her memory.

Damien.

Bastien retrieved a small bottle from his pocket and poured a small amount of the silver dust into his hand.

"I have to say, I'll enjoy this task a bit more than the others."

Her eyes narrowed at his open palm.

"I am perfectly capable of walking to my own demise."

Bastien released a bitter laugh.

"But that would be no fun for me."

He crouched in front of her and blew the dust into her face.

CHAPTER 45

"*TAG!*" *Jen giggled as she ducked behind a large oak tree.*

Damien laughed, darting around the other oak beside it. He ran up behind her, grasping her waist and lifting her into the air. She squealed, filling the skies above the meadow with the sounds of two young lovers.

They fell to the ground, and he rolled her onto her back, his elbow resting in the grass beside her head, his other hand rising to meet her cheek. Jen smiled, leaning into his touch with a contented sigh.

He gazed into her eyes and smiled back at her with one of those rare ones that consumed his whole face.

"I love your eyes," he breathed.

"I love your eyes," she sighed.

They stared at each other for a long while, taking in every inch of each other's faces as though trying to memorize every freckle, every contour. Jen looked away, her thoughts dipping into the deep recesses of her mind.

"What are you thinking about, Bug?" Damien asked gently, his fingers idly running through her hair as he searched her face.

Jen slowly pushed herself up and draped her legs over his. She looked out into the meadow from the hilltop on which they sat, the vast landscape extending over the rolling hills in the far-off distance.

"Where do you think we go at the end of this life?" she asked quietly. Damien tilted his head, considering his answer before peering up at the oak trees shading them from the afternoon sun.

He grinned.

"I think we end up here," he said. "I think we meet here, between these trees," he continued, keeping his eyes raised to the treetops. Jenevieve followed his gaze, a small smile blooming over her lips.

Together they listened to the peaceful sounds coming from the meadow; the wind rustling through the tall grasses, the birds chirping along the tree branches.

"Do you think we'll find it one day?" Jen asked.

Damien looked at her. "Find what?"

A moment passed.

"Happiness," Jen said, her focus fixed far away in the meadow. Damien hooked his finger beneath her chin and turned her to meet the winter-sky of his eyes.

"I think we'll find more than that, Bug," he said, bringing her lips to his in a sweet kiss. "I think we'll find peace."

Jenevieve kissed him back, pouring every bit of her heart into the man she loved. "Promise me we'll meet here, between the trees," she whispered.

She could feel the smile forming on his lips.

"I promise," he whispered back.

Jen's eyes blinked open, and smoke flooded her lungs, choking her as the memory faded. She tried desperately to cling to that moment beneath the trees, but it slipped away like sand between her fingers.

She peered down through tear-filled eyes and realized, to her horror, that she was strung up in the air, hanging precariously over a flaming trench by the chain of her cuffs. They dangled from an iron hook attached to a long, thick rope held taunt at the bottom of the stone wall to her left.

Her shoulders ached in their unnatural position, and a thin trail of blood flowed from the long slash carved into her arm. Every time her body swayed, she groaned as the wounds on her back reopened.

You're not in a fortress, you're in a meadow—think of the meadow, of the trees—

Movement drew her focus to her right, and her stomach dropped like a lead brick.

Oh, no.

She wasn't the only one hanging above the fire.

Long, honey-brown hair hung in the woman's face, her head lolling from side to side as consciousness slowly returned to her body.

Lyla.

Her eyes fluttered open and immediately filled with terror. She started thrashing against her restraints, swaying dangerously over the flames.

"HELP! HELP PLEASE!" she screamed, but the maniacal audience surrounding the trench only laughed at her pleas.

"Lyla—Lyla!" Jen shouted.

Lyla's head swung over to her. "JEN? What's going on? Where are we?" she yelled, fear pitching her voice abnormally high.

She shouldn't be here. She isn't a part of any of this.

But then it dawned on her. Damien was about to be dragged out here, and Bastien had been watching them since they arrived in Sachandes, looking for any weaknesses to exploit—

Fuck.

"This can't be happening," she murmured to herself.

"What?!" Lyla shouted.

Jen craned her neck to look at her. "It's going to be okay," she said, trying to sound as calm as possible. "We're going to be fine." She glanced up at the rope Lyla hung from. "Try not to move too much."

Lyla's terrified gaze locked onto the deep gash in Jen's arm. "What happened? I don't understand—"

Jen released a stiff laugh. "It's been a *very* long night."

"And we've only just begun," a menacing voice called from below.

Bastien stood across the trench, the flames painting his face in warped gold and shadow, each flare twisting his expression into something almost inhuman; tighter, sharper—like a marionette carved by madness.

Lyla gasped, shock momentarily silencing her panic.

Surprise, Bastien is a murderous psychopath.

"Let her go!" Jen yelled, her chin jerking towards Lyla. "She isn't a part of this!"

Bastien raised a brow, turning to Mobius beside him and baring his teeth in a crooked grin. He flicked his wrist—and Lyla dropped.

She screamed.

"NO!" Jen bellowed.

Bastien flicked his wrist again and Lyla jerked to a stop, her restraints pulling harshly on her wrists. She whimpered as the hook pulled her back up to her starting place.

"That was a rather poor choice of words, don't you think?"

He looked out towards the dungeon stairs.

"Bring him."

Curses and sounds of a furious struggle echoed across the hall. Jen clamped her eyes shut, her heart already cracking as Damien was roughly yanked through the crowd.

He spat at them, lunged at them. He greeted every jeer with one of his own, looking almost as insane as Bastien.

Jen's gaze shifted behind him, to the person pulling him around the trench—and the crack in her heart grew deeper.

Ronan, only it wasn't him—not really. His body was rigid, like invisible puppet strings controlled his movements, and his eyes were filled with a dark, swirling mist that hid the verdant beauty she had grown to admire.

He said nothing as Damien fought against him.

Bastien caught Jen staring. "I see you've noticed the amenable shift in our dear Ronan. Couldn't have any more spontaneous interruptions now, could we?"

Damien's eyes snapped up to Jenevieve, and he choked on a sob at the sight of her.

"JEN! WHAT HAVE YOU DONE TO HER?!"

He thrashed as hard as he could, but Ronan dug his fingers into his arms, easily overpowering him.

His eyes jumped over to Lyla and his mouth dropped open.

"Wha—Why—Why is she here?!" he asked.

Bastien meandered around the small, wooden table next to them, like he had all the time in the world. "It will be clear in a moment, my friend."

He snapped his fingers and a dhoksha approached with a glass jar. Jen squinted, trying to make out what was inside it, and her breath stuttered just as Damien stilled, his eyes widening.

A black serpent.

"What the fuck is that?" Damien murmured quietly, as if trying not to draw the snake's attention.

Bastien seemed to ignore him as he took the jar and placed his hand inside, the snake coiling around his wrist as he pulled it out.

"The Drakora viper has been used for centuries as a method of—" He ran a finger along the serpent's body. "Truth seeking."

Damien remained motionless, watching the snake intently.

"When the viper bites its victim, it releases a veracity inducing toxin into the bloodstream. Any lie told under its influence becomes... *painfully* obvious."

Damien shook his head. "I'm not letting that thing bite me."

Bastien looked at him with an expression that almost appeared to be disappointment. He shrugged.

"As you wish."

He flicked his wrist and both women cried out as they plunged towards the fire below. Damien tried to lung forward.

"NO! STOP!"

Bastien waved his hand twice more, bringing the women to a screeching halt and then immediately yanking them back up. Jen hissed and fought the stinging in her eyes as the alloy cuffs cut into her wrists.

Ronan released Damien from his grip, allowing him to take a tentative step towards the table.

"You don't have to do this!" Jen yelled.

He peered up at her, and for a moment, all she could see was the boy in the meadow. "When will you accept that I would do anything for you?"

Not this. Please.

Damien splayed his hand on the table as Bastien lowered his own, the serpent uncoiling itself from his wrist to slither across the weathered wood. Damien clamped his eyes shut, turning away as the snake reared—and struck.

He winced, its fangs sinking in just above his thumb. His face contorted with pain as the venom rushed into his arm, his veins branching out like black webs beneath his fair skin before fading away.

Mobius retrieved the snake, giggling like a child as he returned it to the glass jar.

"So dramatic," Bastien tsked. He perched on the edge of the table, his tone unnervingly casual. "Here is what will happen now." He ran a hand through his white hair.

"I will ask you a series of yes or no questions." He pointed his chin at the white orb sitting on the corner of the table. "If you are truthful, the orb will glow—the girls will be safe. If you lie, well." He looked down at the fang marks.

Damien glanced up, and Jen saw it—felt it; all the things he couldn't say held within the winter-sky of his eyes. But then, his focus shifted to Lyla, and she felt something else teetering along the crack in her heart.

He turned back to Bastien and nodded.

"Excellent."

He pulled Damien with him as he strode to the edge of the trench, Ronan following behind with the orb. "We'll start with a nice baseline," Bastien mused.

He pointed to Jen. "Is that Jenevieve?"

"Yes," Damien murmured.

The orb glowed in Ronan's hand.

Bastien pointed to Lyla. "Is that Lyla?" He let the 'l' linger on his tongue.

"Yes."

The orb glowed brighter. Bastien brazenly rested his elbow on Damien's shoulder. "Do you think Lyla is beautiful?"

Damien snapped his head towards him. "I—what—"

Bastien tilted his head. "It's a simple question. Do you think Lyla is *beautiful?*"

Damien's eyes darted to Jen, and when she met them, she pulled on a whisper of memory, clinging to the image of his gaze finding hers across the bonfire at her sister's wedding; no panic, no terror—just him, a boy in a meadow.

"It's okay, Sparky," she said.

He swallowed, his eyes bouncing between hers briefly before answering. "Yes."

The glow of the orb pulsated.

"You've watched our precious *iejja* come into a lot of power. Some of which has been highly—*flammable*," Bastien chuckled at his own joke. Mobius cackled from behind them.

"Are you *afraid* of her?"

A wave of unease seized in Jen's chest when Damien failed to answer the question immediately. He squeezed his eyes closed and mumbled a strangled reply. "N—n—no."

Jen reached for another memory to keep her steady; the feel of his hand lacing with hers on a path of marked trees.

But her thought was cut short as the glow of the orb was wrapped in a ribbon of shadow. Damien keeled over and groaned, his veins turning insidiously dark, his breath growing shallow, as if the venom was suffocating him from the inside.

"What are you doing to him?!" Jen yelled. The crack splintered along her heart, the sight of Damien's pain surpassing that of her own.

Bastien pressed a hand to his chest. "I'm not doing anything. *He* is the one being deceitful." He flicked his wrist and Jen's stomach shot into her throat, stifling her scream as she dropped towards the flames. The crowd of dark creatures roared around her.

Damien jerked up and panic flooded his face. "YES! My answer is yes!"

Jen lurched to a stop, but this time she wasn't lifted back up, leaving her twenty feet below Lyla, and closer to the flames. Heat radiated through her feet, beads of sweat forming on her brow.

Bastien leaned in close to Damien.

"Do you seek Lyla's company?" he leered.

The crack in her heart widened as Damien trembled under the constriction of the venom, and Jen realized then that it wasn't the line of questioning, but seeing the man she loved in pain, that was breaking her heart—breaking *her*.

He struggled to find her gaze, and when he did—she nodded, knowing the only way he would survive this was with the truth.

I need him to stay alive. I need him safe.

"Yes," he choked. "But—"

"Ah." Bastien lifted a finger. "Explanations are not part of the game." He walked toward the wall, the flames casting a sinister shadow that stretched up the grey stone. "Does your heart skip a beat when Lyla enters a room?"

Damien clenched his fists. "Fuck you," he growled.

Bastien chuckled. "That's not an answer."

He flicked his wrist and Lyla plummeted down with a piercing scream. Damien reached out and shouted. "YES!"

Blood trickled from Lyla's delicate wrists as she openly wept. Bastien's sneer shifted back to Jen.

Her blood ran cold, though the flames flicked heat across her skin. Something shifted in his face—cruelty igniting behind his eyes, sharp and unrestrained.

Bastien stared right at her as he asked Damien the next question. "Do you have feelings for her?"

The crack splintered into a canyon of pain, her eyes welling with tears as she watched the conflict contort Damien's beautiful face.

"I—"

Bastien lifted his hand, but Damien stopped him with his desolate response. "Yes."

The orb glowed brightly, and the crowd snickered around them as he looked up at Jen, his eyes filling with broken tears. "I'm sorry. I'm so sorry." His voice broke. "I love you, Bug. I love you so much."

Several memories rushed forward, one right after the other; a dance in a field, a stolen moment in a barn, a waltz on a marble floor, a kiss and a confession whispered under the moonlight.

Jen held on to each of them and spoke through her own quiet tears. "I know, Sparky."

Bastien's tone turned into mock sympathy. "Speaking of *Bug*, have you ever betrayed her?"

Damien's gaze remained fixed on Jen, despite his clear shame. She already knew the answer—that was a tragic time far in their past, but still, it was unbearable to watch as guilt reclaimed him.

"Yes."

Bastien laced his hands behind his back.

"Have you ever…abandoned her?"

Damien dropped his head, his shoulders slumping.

"Yes."

The canyon broke open, and Jen's heart struggled to keep itself intact. She shook against the iron hook, fighting against the alloy around her wrists; she'd had enough of this.

"Stop this!" She pinned Damien with her fierce stare. "I love you, Damien. Do you hear me—"

The air left her lungs as she dropped further toward the raging flames. She jerked to a heavy stop mere feet above the pit. The gashes on her back ripped open, blood pouring down her back as an agonizing cry splitting from her throat.

Damien charged at Bastien, his face in rough lines of raw fury.

"YOU ALMOST KILLED HER!"

The orb shattered upon the stone floor. Mobius and Ronan were on him before he could strike. They shoved him to the ground and pummeled him, blow after blow. Damien thrashed, arms flailing, but they were too quick—too brutal.

Jen sobbed at each sickening thud echoed with his fractured groans. "LEAVE HIM ALONE!" she cried over the frenzied crowd as trails of blood ran down the backs of her legs.

"STOP! PLEASE!" Lyla yelled.

Bastien yanked Damien up by the collar. His lip was split, and his cheek was turning a dark purple. He spat blood on the ground, holding his side and breathing in sharply at the harsh movements.

"Look what you made me do, Jenevieve," Bastien boomed, shaking Damien even harder.

"ENOUGH!" she screamed, expecting to feel her rage crashing against the restraint of the cuffs, but her mind was barely hanging on, and her body was depleted—her magic nowhere to be found.

"*You* did this." He squeezed Damien's jaw. "You allowed the people you love to be hurt tonight. You are dangerous. You are a monster. You are a filthy *bloodliner.*"

Jen shook violently against the chains, using every drop of energy she had left, her legs swinging dangerously close to the fire. "I will never turn. I refuse to be used as *anyone's* weapon. Run back to your *master* and tell him you failed!"

Bastien paused for a moment, his silence even more terrifying than his words. His eyes turned to slits as a cruel smile curled in the corner of his lips.

"If you won't turn willingly..." he said, caressing Damien's cheek with his long, pale finger, "then you leave me no choice."

Ronan grabbed Damien by the arms, his eyes still filled with dark mist. Damien tried to fight but his body was so weak from the beating that he collapsed against Ronan's chest.

Bastien reached for his belt, unsheathing the tiishara and flipping it over in his hand before handing it to Mobius.

Oh, gods. No. NO.

Mobius stalked menacingly towards Damien.

"PLEASE! PLEASE STOP! LET HIM GO! DAMIEN!" Jen screamed until her throat was raw and her voice was hoarse. From somewhere above her, Lyla bawled.

Bastien leaned on the table and looked up at Jen like she was an errant child. "Just remember, Jenevieve. This was *your* doing."

Damien turned weakly to her. "I love you," he said, a resigned tear falling down his cheek. "I'll meet you between the trees."

He turned back to meet his fate.

"NOOOOOO!" Jen shrieked through unhinged sobs.

Mobius raised his arm to strike.

A whistle of wind flew past her ear.

She heard a swift *'thunk.'*

And then another whistle.

A second *'thunk.'*

Jen choked on her tears when she realized who was shot.

Mobius stood stock still. An arrow protruding from his throat, another one between his deranged eyes. A disturbing gurgle fell from his gaping mouth.

The tiishara dropped from his hand, and with a thud, Mobius hit the stone floor.

Dead.

CHAPTER 46

Bastien howled as the room erupted into a cacophony of deranged shrieking.

"WHO'S THERE?" he bellowed into the fortress.

"Always such a charmer, Bas," a voice rang out.

Bastien's wild eyes darted up to the opening in the crumbling tower by the dais.

Samara stood with her bow knocked right at him.

"BASTIEN!" another voice boomed.

Jen let out a ragged sob. Haythem and Fjora barreled into the hall, Gaiana and Rieshi at their sides. The crowd of barbaric creatures grew frantic at the sight of them.

"Haythem, what a lovely surprise," Bastien drawled.

"Why, Bastien?" Haythem demanded, his great sword drawn at his side. Bastien merely pointed up to Jen. Fjora covered her mouth to stifle a horrified gasp.

"Imagine if not only a powerful iejja, but a child of the blood, fought for the righteous side when the great war arrives." He clasped his hands behind his back. "My master could march in tomorrow and take Etheria without lifting a finger."

"We have very different ideas of what it means to be righteous." Haythem seethed.

Bastien laughed, the chilling sound crawling along Jen's skin as he stepped away from the trench. "Ah, you believe that to be you?" he jeered. "The absent King Haythem is also a hypocrite of the highest order."

Fjora stepped forward. "Did you hate us the entire time? Hate me?" she asked, her eyes brimming with tears. "You were my brother, Bastien. I loved you."

But her words fell on deaf ears, his expression fixed with indifference. "I suppose you can consider me the black sheep of the family then," Bastien mused.

Haythem marched further into the fortress, his eyes fixing on Jen hanging from the rafters. "Give us the girl, Bastien. I won't ask twice."

"Did you think you would just walk in here and ask for her back, and I would happily oblige?" His army of dark minions heckled, echoing off the fortress walls.

"You don't want to do this, Bastien," Fjora warned. Her tears gone. Her daggers lifted.

Bastien cackled. "What are you going to do, princess?" His hands rose beside him. "The five of you against my army? How incredibly arrogant of you to come here alone."

Fjora raised a brow.

The air rippled beside Bastien.

Nelysar stepped out. "Who said they were alone?"

He slammed his fist into Bastien's face.

Explosions of power tore through the fortress, unleashed from within the crowd, obliterating every dhoksha and kashyak in their wake. Twenty-four Etherian soldiers lunged out of ripples in the air, swords drawn and magic coursing through them.

Not soldiers.

Warriors of Kiara.

Their ivory fighting leathers flashed through the horde of darkness around them. Their magic crackled in the air and their swords found their homes in the bones of their enemies.

Bastien crashed to the floor, and the magic holding Lyla and Jen released. They screamed as they fell towards the fire.

Damien fumbled to his feet and bolted for them, his legs pumping beneath him as he rounded the trench. Nelysar flung out his hands, power bursting forward to push their fall away from the flames.

Jen closed her eyes and braced herself as the ground came hurtling towards her. She collided with something, but it wasn't the ground. Her eyes cracked open to find Lyla crumpled in Damien's arms.

Who caught me?

"I've got you, my darling."

Jen peered up and her breath faltered.

Fjora's arms were wrapped around her. The dull sting of betrayal faded, replaced by the trembling need of a small child in a thunderstorm—longing for nothing more than to disappear into her mother's arms.

Jen jolted. "The others—the others are in the dungeon." She pointed sharply at the stairway. "Get them out—get them out *now*," she pleaded.

Fjora's head snapped into the onslaught and found Naezara leading the attack.

"Did you hear that?" she murmured to her friend.

Naezara nodded and made a break for the stairs, signaling Samara from her post in the crumbled tower. She climbed down the stone wall with impressive speed and followed after her.

Within the mayhem, Gaiana tore the water from within the old stones and sent it spiraling up the legs of the kashyaks charging toward her. It plunged into their noses and mouths and drowned them where they stood.

Rieshi trailed just behind her mother, blasting columns of raging wind towards the morai in the rafters.

Bastien's army of miscreants attempted to flee from the unbridled magic surrounding them.

"ARGHHHHHH!" Bastien hollered, unleashing a surge of dark magic over the fortress. The room was enveloped in thick smoke.

Jen cried out, the taste of metal careening into her mouth, invading her senses. A hand appeared out of the plumes, thrusting into her hair. Sharp nails scraped against her scalp as Bastien dragged her towards the dais.

Fjora growled, digging her heels in and clinging to the hem of Jen's tattered dress, but she was yanked away by two kashyaks. "JENEVIEVE!" she cried.

Damien shielded Lyla under his arm, pulling her through the chaos. "JEN! JEN!" he shouted, choking on smoke.

Bastien threw her on the ground and waved his arm in a grand flourish, a ring of fire igniting around her. He bounded up the platform's steps as the smoke cleared and cast a protective shield over himself.

"Look familiar, Jenevieve?" His face was pure madness now.

Jen flipped onto her elbows. Her eyes grew round, her heart pounding as realization came over her.

The curse.

Bastien's low laugh made her cringe. "You're missing something, aren't you?" He chucked the tiishara into the ring with her, the metal blade singing as it hit the stone floor.

Fjora and Damien ran for her, but the flames flashed higher, threatening to engulf anyone who came near.

I'm trapped. I'm trapped. I'm trapped.

Bastien threw his head back and laughed.

"I may have used Damien to break your heart," he taunted. "But we both know you were broken *long* before that."

The flames parted and a figure entered the ring.

Jen's face went pale, her body going completely still as the same worn boots from the curse came traipsing towards her.

The source of her nightmares.

The trigger of her rage.

Her gaze traveled up slowly as the figure drew closer, her body began to tremble as his face came into focus.

The man leered down at her, a Vondurian blade in his hand.

"Papa," she breathed.

The battle raged around her, but all she could see was the twisted face of the man who raised her.

She was reduced to a young girl once more. Childlike fear gripped her like a vice.

"You fucking bitch," he snapped.

She winced at his grating, familiar tone.

No, this can't be real, it's a trick.

Jen backed up on the ground, the stone floor scraping against her open wounds. "AHHH," she cried.

Her father heckled, continuing his advance. He dragged the dark metal blade against the stone, his boots landing heavily on the ground, sending tremors through her body.

"Papa, please—" she begged.

This must be a dhoksha—he's not really here.

Jen's eyes darted around; muffled clashes of swords sounded through the air, and shadows of massive wings streaked overhead as the morai shot through the shattered fortress ceiling.

She spotted Fjora through the flames, staring into the ring like she was seeing a specter from her past. Her father followed her gaze and fixed his sights on his wife, a cruel smile turning on his mouth.

Let the darkness in Jenevieve. You could stop him.

She blinked the voice away, and when she opened her eyes, the blade of the tiishara gleamed in the light of the menacing fire.

You should have protected them.

Jen rolled towards the dagger and grabbed it off the ground, that familiar guilt thrumming in her bones, pushing her to move. She tightened her grip on the hilt and struggled to her feet, shuddering as her wounds bled down her back, her dress now more crimson than cream.

She bent low in her thighs and angled her feet.

You failed them.

Familiar anger coursed through her veins. She looked at the vicious man in front of her—the man who broke her so long ago.

He laughed. "Are you going to kill me, daughter?"

But an answer didn't reach her lips. She could no longer distinguish between where the heat of the flames ended and where her blazing fury began, her words lost in the chaos within and around her.

Her father panted like a rabid hound, more animal than human.

"I never loved you," her father spat.

Her hand faltered on the hilt.

He didn't say that last time.

Her eyes darted to Bastien, who looked on with a venomous sneer, giving nothing away.

"You were never enough." Her father lifted his sword and Jen watched as he began a predatory circle around her, her dagger never leaving its pose to strike.

"Papa—" she warned, but her voice lacked the cold, indifferent quality she was hoping for.

He released another maniacal laugh. "I was never your father. Your blood is *dirty*." He took a menacing step towards her. "Your blood is *dark*."

"You're wrong," she bit back. "You don't know me, anymore."

"I know you are *weak*." Another heavy step towards her. "You are *dangerous*." Jen backed away but the burning flames forced her to stop. "You are *unlovable*."

She rolled her shoulders, letting his words fall off her skin.

"And *you* are a pathetic old man," she seethed. He snarled like a wild animal.

This is not him. His words mean nothing.

Within her fragile mind, cracks formed along the white stone, branching out as jagged scars as if to match the ones marring her body.

I have been to the brink of death too many times tonight.

"You will never hurt my family again." She leaned forward on the balls of her feet. "I couldn't protect them then—"

She lifted her dagger.

This thing will not be the end of me.

"But I will defend them now."

Her father lifted his sword above his head and bellowed as he charged at her, and Jen's rage vaulted her forward as she countered him.

He swung at her, but his bulky frame made him sluggish. She ducked under his arm and kicked him away. He rounded on her and swung his blade once more—but she was ready.

Her dagger surged forward.

She let out a rageful cry.

The sound of crunching bone and ripping flesh rang in her ears as the tiishara pierced through the middle of his chest.

Jen let go of the hilt and fumbled back, expecting the thing to shift to its true form.

His sword fell with a clang and his eyes widened in shock, as if he had just snapped out of some kind of trance. He looked down at the dagger protruding from his chest and staggered, his breath coming out in short, unfilled gasps.

"Jenny?" he said, his brown eyes filled with confusion.

She stopped breathing.

What did he just call me?

Shock and fear left her paralyzed.

No one would know to call me that, not even a dhoksha.

That name was barely a wisp of memory.

Suddenly she was a child, asleep in her father's arms as he carried her inside their cottage.

Jenny, wake up sweetheart. We're home.

She pretended to stay asleep so she could spend another moment with him. He had always played along, carrying her to bed and tucking her in like he didn't know she was awake.

I love you, he whispered against her forehead.

Jen peered up at the thing in front of her.

It wasn't shifting back.

Oh gods. Oh gods no. No. No. No. No.

He crumpled to the ground, his arm reaching for her.

She couldn't help the sob that bubbled out of her throat as she ran to him, dropping to her knees beside him. Blood poured from the corner of his mouth as he whispered. "Why, Jenny, why?"

He mumbled incoherently as his eyes began to lose their dark brown warmth.

"What have I done?" she whispered as her trembling hands hovered over him. "Wha—what have I *done*?!"

She had thought she could force the shift if she struck it, like Samara's arrow in the valley. In the back of her mind, she clung to the hope that it wasn't really her father.

How had Bastien managed to bring him here? He lived somewhere in Nimea, Jen didn't even know where.

She whimpered.

My blood is dirty. My blood is dark. And now—I'm a murderer.

Within her fragile mind, cracks formed along the white stone, branching out as jagged scars as if to match the ones marring her body.

Her father's dull eyes found hers. His mouth opened, but no words came.

"I'm sorry, Papa," she cried. "I'm so sorry."

His chest spasmed.

No. This isn't happening.

It rose and fell one last time—and the life left his eyes.

I killed my father.

I killed my father.

I killed my father.

A single moment stretched into an eternity as Jen stared at his vacant eyes, unable to process what had just happened. She fumbled to her feet and stepped back from his body, her hands violently shaking by her sides.

She turned and found Nelysar holding Fjora beyond the flames, her hands over her mouth as tears streamed down her face. Damien still had Lyla tucked under his arm, shock parting his lips.

She whirled around at Bastien.

Anguish scraped at her voice.

"WHAT DID YOU MAKE ME DO?!"

"I didn't make you do anything," he retorted. "His blood is on *your* hands, Jenevieve." He clapped his own together. "What will Rhea think? Darya? Poor Jamie still clings to the naive hope that papa will return."

I murdered their father.

Jen fell to her knees and heaved beside her father's body, gasping through fractured breaths.

"You are a *monster*," Bastien said.

Overwhelming guilt pulled a groan from her throat as her nails clawed against the stone floor.

Something in Bastien's voice shifted. "Speaking of monsters."

He nodded to something outside the ring of fire.

Jen snapped her hands over her ears as a demented chorus of shrill whistles reverberated off the walls.

The kashyaks were calling for their mounts.

Panic turned to stone in her stomach as the monstrous salyaats crashed through what remained of the fortress ceiling, their shrieks spearing through the night sky.

"SHIELDS!" Nelysar commanded. The Warriors waved their hands and conjured golden barriers of protective light around them as the rubble came hurtling down from the roof.

The salyaats slithered through the air and landed hard on the ground, the entire fortress shaking in their wake.

"AIM FOR THE WING JOINTS!" Naezara ordered as the Warriors bellowed a battle cry and charged the beasts. Samara climbed back up to her perch in the tower and shot a slew of arrows into their inky-black feathers.

Nelysar and Fjora joined the fray along with the king and the room erupted into a surge of magic and clashing swords battling against the foreboding darkness.

Jen snatched the Vondurian blade from the ground and ran towards the edge of the ring, but the fire exploded brightly and slammed her against the ground.

Excruciating pain sliced up her back. She screamed.

Bastien seemed to revel in the sound.

"You have your own battle to wage, my dear," he jeered.

He waved his hand, and, to her shock, the cuffs fell to the ground with a *clank.*

She expected her magic to flood into her veins like a broken dam, but instead, it barely trickled—a tiny stream obstructed by dozens of rocks.

Her mind was shredded.

Her body a bloody ruin.

Her heart shattered.

There was nothing left.

Bastien chuckled. "Something wrong, dear?"

She tried to conjure anything. A flame. A gust of wind. A flower blossom, but her magic just sputtered and sizzled.

"I know what will help," he said, his gaze shifting as a malicious grin spread across his face, locking onto a shadow just beyond the fire.

It stepped through the flames, the fire almost trembling in fear around it.

Jen stood perfectly still as the man who saved her only recently became her new opponent.

Ronan.

CHAPTER 47

"**R**onan," Jen said firmly, but her voice cracked. "He can't hear you, but I will say, he fought admirably against the mind bogging."

Jen ignored him, her eyes narrowing on Ronan's black eyes as he stalked towards her.

"I know you're in there."

He snarled at her.

Bastien snickered. "Let us see what your power can do." He raised his hand and Ronan stopped; his sword poised at his side.

"Kill him."

Her head snapped to Bastien.

He lowered his voice so only she could hear. "Or you can join me, Jenevieve. This is your last chance."

Dark magic is fucking festering in every corner of this place—I can feel it…the pull to use that side of the bloodline. I'm too vulnerable here.

She spat blood on the ground. "Fuck you."

Bastien sighed like he was disappointed. "Suit yourself."

He snapped his fingers and Ronan charged. She lifted her sword just in time to block him.

I won't do it.

"Ronan!" she shouted.

He shoved her back and slammed his blade against the ground. She groaned when her open wounds fell against the stone. Her eyes darted to her father's body beside her.

"Ronan, it's me!" she yelled, pushing to her feet as he stomped towards her. "It's Jenevieve."

She tried to jump back but he was too quick and sliced through her shoulder. Jen cried out. "You *BASTARD*!"

He paused for the briefest of moments when something flickered through the dark mist. Jen desperately searched his face.

He's in there.

An idea struck her as she parried his next thrust.

"You met me in The Lion and Lily!"

He bounded towards her, his pace unrelenting as he slashed his blade at her. She leapt back. "Actually, you *accosted* me at the bar, you arrogant prick."

Ronan's shoulders grew tense, and his head rolled against them.

"Ardovians are shit people," she grinded out. She ducked and rolled across the ring. "But they do have their talents."

Ronan shook his head violently as if he was fighting something off. He lunged at her and grabbed her by the throat, lifting her off the ground. She scraped at his hands.

"You said you have *excellent* hearing," she croaked. "But I think you're full of shit," she spat. He threw her to the ground. Her back exploded with searing pain, blood staining the stone beneath her. "If you did you would fucking *hear me*," she hissed.

She hobbled to her feet and looked across the ring. He paced back and forth like a lion in a cage, hitting his head like he was going mad.

"It's no use, Jenevieve," Bastien called from the dais. "You will not break through."

Sweat ran down her face, her hair caked in blood and dirt, but still, she stood tall. Defiant.

Jen would see the verdant eyes of her friend again, she had to—she wasn't done pissing him off, nor was she done calling him an arrogant bastard.

She dropped into her stance and posed her sword above her shoulder. "You once said I was the kind of monster this world needs," she shouted over the roaring flames.

Ronan bared his teeth, his misty eyes more insidious than before.

Her chest heaved up and down and she braced herself.

Fuck, I hope this works.

"Come on, Ronan," she challenged. "What kind of monster are *you?*"

Jen took a breath and screamed as she charged towards him at full force. He did the same, bellowing a disjointed cry. His face flared with surprise when she lunged for his legs, driving every ounce of strength she had left into his thighs. He flipped over her shoulders and landed with a loud *thud* on his back.

She skidded on her arms and clamored to her knees. She breathed through aching limbs and whirled around.

She knew he was waiting for her.

Her blade crashed into his side, and he jerked to a stop.

His bewitched, mist-filled eyes stared back at her in shock, but it wasn't until she heard Bastien cackling that she bothered to look down.

Shit.

Her sword had found its mark, but so did his. A twin blade now protruded from her side.

The air tumbled from their lungs, and they fell against each other, shuddering as blood gushed around the impaling blades.

Ronan groaned against the mind-bogging. His head pushed heavily against hers and something fell from within his sweat lined shirt.

A medallion that hung from his neck.

She squinted—it wasn't a medallion.

It was a stone.

Through painful breaths she wrapped her hand around it. She never noticed him wearing it before. Her lips parted. It wasn't just a stone, it was obsidian, wrapped in threads of delicate silver.

And she'd seen it before.

She turned the stone over in her hand.

Her lips parted as the pieces fell together.

The dream in the Forest of Bri, the cloaked man on the path. Jen's eyes darted up to see Ronan squeezing his eyes shut, choking against the magic keeping his mind prisoner.

"It was—" Jen cringed through the egregious pain in her side. "It was *you.*"

"Gahhh," Ronan choked, his hand grasping onto the nape of her neck. His stone grew warm in her palm, pulling her thoughts to her own stone—the one she had been carrying with her every day, that calmed her, kept her steady.

Her eyes snapped to his face.

"*You* enchanted my stone," she whispered. "You—you've been protecting me this whole time."

Ronan gritted his teeth and trembled.

"C c come—f ff find—me."

Jen's breathing quickened. Something called to her, like the words of a song just out of reach. It was visceral. Raw. She squeezed her eyes shut, her skin like drops of static on a piece of metal.

The image of violet lightning flashed behind her eyelids.

She exhaled into the calling as the wicked flames around them seemed to fade from the corners of her vision. Jen let the sensations guide her until the world went quiet.

A black abyss.

Endless nothing.

Quiet.

Jen's eyes strained and struggled to adjust to the daunting obscurity that stretched out before her.

Where am I?

She glimpsed down to her feet, her face scrunching with confusion.

Water. She was standing in a few inches of it, not enough to even cover her toes.

"Hello?" Jen called into the void.

Her voice echoed as if in a dome.

Nothing.

"Is anyone here?"

Still nothing.

Jen willed her feet to move through the shallow water, soft lapping accompanying every cautious step.

Am I dead?

Jen kept walking, silently hoping that her fate was not to wander forever in this endless void of oblivion. Minutes felt like an eternity as she inched her way through her surroundings. She stopped.

Tiny specks of iridescent light twinkled in front of her, like far away stars in the night sky.

She tilted her head, and when her eyes focused just so on the miniscule movements, she realized what it was.

A wall.

A great wall of obsidian stone stretched out into the never-ending abyss on either side, and unlike her own wall, there were no deep fissures or dark tendrils leaking from it.

Solid. Impenetrable.

She came up to it, nose almost grazing the cool stone. It seemed to hum and vibrate as if it felt her presence.

Her hand instinctively rose. She pressed her palm against it, and for a moment, nothing happened.

And then the wall shivered.

What was that?

She stepped back, noticing a simple black door had appeared a few feet from her, embedded in the star-kissed wall.

Was that there before?

Curiosity cinched her brows together.

Jen found herself reaching for the handle, and before she realized what she was doing, the door was open, and she was stepping inside.

A dim light was cast over the shallow surface of the water.

She looked across the dimly lit space.

There was someone there.

"Ronan?" she called, but they didn't move.

She walked towards the faint light, and the figure finally came into focus. It was indeed Ronan, but he wasn't alone, he was on his knees holding someone in his arms—a woman.

Jen slowed as she approached him, but he didn't seem to notice her. His desolate gaze was fixed on the body he held.

Jen's eyes widened.

It's me.

She stared at her own body, lifeless and limp. Her neck unnaturally draped over Ronan's arm and her knotted hair dipped in the shallow water beneath them. Her neck and face were covered in a red rash, blood trickling from her nose.

The poison. This is what I looked like before the antidote, what I would've looked like if it hadn't worked.

Ronan cradled her, his head pressed against hers.

"Forgive me, please...please," he implored, holding her closer.

Her heart ached as he rocked slowly back and forth, his fingers running methodically over her hair.

Jen reached for him and gently touched his shoulder.

"Ronan..." she said quietly.

His head jerked towards her, his eyes rimmed with tears. He searched her face like he didn't understand what he was looking at.

"Je—Jenevieve?" he breathed.

"I'm here," she whispered.

He stared at her for a moment before his head dropped back towards the body in his arms. It was no longer Jen he held, but a young girl that lay lifeless in his arms. She had long, dark, curly hair, beautifully thick eyebrows and youthful skin.

Ronan's expression went blank.

Jen squeezed his shoulder. "Who is she?" she asked.

"It's all my fault...all my fault...my fault..." he murmured. He rocked the young girl. "I'm sorry...I'm sorry..."

"Ronan." Jen touched the back of his head and ran her fingers over his brown hair. "Hey."

His gaze returned to her. "H h how...How are you here?" His voice was so small, so...defeated.

Jen bit her lip, hating the sad, lost look that plagued his face. "I don't know where 'here' is."

His gaze drifted down and he groaned; the body had disappeared. His hands fell into the water, and his breathing grew shallow.

"You—you shouldn't be here," he stammered.

She knelt in the water beside him, her hand gliding down to rub his back.

"You told me to come find you."

He turned to look at her, his brows drawing together slightly. Jen placed her hand on his cheek, trying her best to conjure a warm smile, despite how she may feel.

He froze under her touch.

"I found you," she said.

Jen stood up and quietly offered her hand.

Ronan stared at it, suspicion roaming over his face. But then he peered up at her, tilting his head as if he was seeing something he hadn't noticed before.

He slipped his hand into hers.

Jen helped him to his feet. Even slumped over with unsung grief, he towered over her. She lifted her chin to look at him, and they stood in the shadow of the dim light.

"We will go when you're ready," she said.

He glanced back at the light for a moment and then found her waiting gaze.

Jen felt a gentle squeeze against her fingers.

They walked together, back into the abyss and towards the battle that raged beyond.

CHAPTER 48

The world around them reappeared, desolate cries sounding from beyond the fire.

Fjora was on her knees, her heart wrenching cries echoing through the hall. Damien released a visceral scream as he tried to fight through the flames. Bastien boomed over the fortress, but his voice was muffled.

They think I'm dead, that we're both dead.

Her head lay against Ronan's, and when her eyes fluttered open, he was staring back at her, his eyes wide.

His eyes.

No longer misty, mindless orbs, but verdant and clear pools.

"Fury?" he whispered.

She sucked in a breath, the moment of relief fleeting as blinding pain returned. "I'm still *very* mad at you."

The corner of his mouth twitched. "I can live with that."

Jen started to move, but he subtly squeezed the back of her neck.

"Not yet."

"What do we do?"

He paused for a moment. Then he peered into her eyes.

"How is your magic?"

"I can barely feel it," she winced. "I'm so tired."

"I know, Fury," Ronan rubbed his thumb against the back of her neck. "But the fight has just begun."

She looked at the floor. "I'm too broken."

My body. My mind. My heart.

Ronan clenched his teeth, also fighting the blinding pain of the swords in their sides.

"We are all broken, Jenevieve," he said through a wince. "Each of us is an arrangement of shattered pieces bound together in a mosaic of irrevocable pain and loss."

Jen's eyes flickered up.

"But when the sun catches the fragmented pieces." He looked at her. "Overwhelming light shines through the cracks, and hope illuminates even the darkest corners of existence."

He squeezed the back of her neck.

"Strength is found in our darkest moments, when you claw your way out and say—"

"Fuck you," Jen said, her eyes glistening.

The corner of Ronan's mouth pulled up into a smirk.

"There she is."

Something stirred beneath her skin. Despite her mangled state, her magic began to churn like waves against a dam.

Power lives in the broken things.

"I know what I have to do," she said. Anger and rage returned to her, heating her clammy limbs.

Ronan lowered his chin. "Do you remember what I said that day, by the garden?"

Jen arched a brow in question.

A challenging grin appeared on his full lips. "My ear, or my sword?"

She glanced down at the blades still embedded in their sides. "*This* sword is currently in the way."

"Then let's remedy that shall we?"

"I thought we could just leave them there."

Ronan pressed his lips together, frustration crinkling his brow for just a moment before his eyes turned serious. "You show no mercy," he said firmly. "For you will receive none."

He looked down at the swords and back up at her. "Ready?"

"No, but what else is new?"

They both braced themselves.

"Bring the reckoning," he said.

They cried out as they yanked their swords from each other. Blood gushed from their wounds as Ronan dragged her to her feet, and she fell against him.

Bastien's head snapped down at the commotion.

"What's this?" he seethed.

Jen staggered away from Ronan, agony lancing through her shattered body. Her knees buckled, and she nearly crumpled to the ground.

But a familiar thread wrapped itself around her and stopped her fall, and a faint, melodious hum once again branched into cascading harmonies and dissonance and swooshed into her mind.

Still, her body faltered.

And then a familiar breeze picked up. The wind rushed through the crumbling fortress and wrapped its supporting force around her tattered limbs. It pushed her forward and blew around her like an unseen guardian.

Bastien flailed with unhinged rage.

"You will meet your end *bloodliner*. He will hunt you down—" he spat and pointed beyond the fire. "He will kill the ones you hold most dear. Not even the power of the bloodline, of an iejja, is enough to stop what's coming!"

Jen watched him, her face in a fixed expression of indifference, but the ring around her pupils burned brightly.

The battle around them surged. The salyaats shrieked, and the dark army turned into a sea of frenzied chaos as the Warriors unleashed in a final strike, weapons crackling and crashing into the horde.

The fire roared, personifying the rage that boiled under her skin.

"DURCHE YAHVAK!" Bastien shouted as he raised his hand.

Another pair of words floated into Jen's mind on a ray of light, weaving through her weary soul as it illuminated the path forward. Words that were both foreign and familiar. Words that had slipped from meaning, like a song just out of reach.

Until now.

A language long since dead caressed her mind, *Eadriir.*

Jen looked over her shoulder at Ronan.

You're exactly the kind of monster this world needs.

Power vibrated within her bones and the ray of light soared within her, giving her the moment of strength that she needed.

Her eyes met Bastien.

Magic flooded her veins, searing through her, the words coming to her as if she had always known them.

"Ufreijaa nuri," she said.

I release my light.

And she slammed her hand into the ground.

Jenevieve unleashed a blast of power through the fortress, extinguishing the ring of fire and knocking every creature and warrior off their feet. The fortress came crumbling down around them, along with the white stone wall in her mind—now a pile of rubble.

Nelysar and Naezara yelled out for shields.

Jen snapped her hands forward, smashing the protective shield around the dais. She took a predatory step toward Bastien.

He leapt to his feet and sent dark smoke shooting from his hands. Jen slashed her arm through the air, and a gust of wind blew the smoke away as if she were snuffing out a candle.

Jen thrusted her hand towards him, and a torrent of magic bashed him into the stone throne with a loud thud. She came to the bottom of the dais steps and Shyra's voice echoed in her ear.

"Fate comes for us all," she said quietly. "But your destiny lies within the courage of your heart," she squeezed her hand, "and the conviction of your soul."

Her rageful gaze seared into Bastien.

"I am the daughter of Aiyla and Lior."

She took the first step.

He fought violently against the magic holding him down.

"The last of an ancient bloodline." She flicked her wrist and a wild vine of ivy burst through the window beside them. With a flourish of her hand, it wrapped itself around Bastien and the throne he sat on, tethering him to the stone.

She took the next step.

"The power of the Aylaenor runs through my veins." She flicked her other wrist, and a second vine blew through the opposite window, entwining with the first and pinning Bastien down. He roared in anger, his trapped limbs flailing wildly.

She took another step.

"You have no idea what's coming for you! You think Heltior is your greatest threat—" Bastien choked as the vines restricted his airway. "This is just the beginning."

Jen smiled at his pain. Her body grew numb, but still she ascended as the thread gently tugged and the air swirled around her.

She raised her hands beside her and snapped her fingers, igniting the vines in flames that licked towards the throne.

"I will not be made a victim by the likes of a beast that prowls in the shadows. I will not yield to darkness when dawn approaches. I am—"

Bastien shook with deranged laughter.

"You are *no one*," he sneered.

She stood atop the dais as the sun broke on the horizon behind her, a halo of light embraced her as she said:

"I am the Oshara."

Bastien's eyes widened.

"That—that's not possible." He pulled against the vines as the flames grew closer. "The Oshara is a myth, a legend."

Jen's lips curled into a wry smile.

"I am neither," she said. "I am a *bridge*."

Deep loathing contorted his features. His jagged cheekbones were severed icebergs upon a crimson sea. His army dissolved into mayhem and attempted to retreat into the hills around the fortress as the warriors pushed them back.

"Bridges are meant to *burn*," he spat, a last attempt to collect himself.

Jen looked down her nose at him.

"Mine is a bridge of light and shadow," she said, her voice like a song on the wind. "I cannot burn."

The flames on the vines halted. She curled her wrist and a ball of fire appeared in the palm of her hand. Jen brought it before her and fanned the flames, reflecting the ones in her eyes.

She smirked.

"But you can."

"NO—"

She blasted him with her furious fire, expelling every ember of magic she could muster. Every moment of shame and guilt and anger flooded from her veins and fueled her flames. It poured from her until there was nothing left but smoke on her fingertips.

An incinerated corpse sat upon the throne, the tattoos on his arms nothing but charred skin crawling up his bones.

Jen stared at what was left of his body, her own working with all its might to keep her upright. She clutched her bleeding side and turned, limping down the steps of the dais. Every movement grew slower, weaker.

She came to the bottom and stood in the ruins of the fortress. Her gaze moved around the room; anyone left standing was staring at her—but her mind was too far gone to care.

Jen's body grew cold, her injuries finally catching up with her one by one. Her limbs were heavy as stone. She was so, so tired.

Her eyes rolled into the back of her head, and she collapsed to the ground.

Someone ran for her.

And then the world went black.

CHAPTER 49

A cool breeze blew through an open meadow of lush green grass where the radiant sun shone down from a cloudless sky. Birds fluttered above her head and small creatures chirped by her ears.

She sat up and peered down at...an ivory gown; her hand reached for her head and gently traced over a crown of ivy. Jen pushed up to her feet and looked around; it seemed she was the only soul here.

Nimea.

It looked so real. Smoke billowed from the chimney of her mother's cottage, sitting just beyond the dirt road at the meadow's edge. The village awaited quietly in the distance. Jen glanced over her shoulder, her eye catching on the wedding arch a few feet away, before continuing towards the top of a small hill.

The lover's trees.

Jen looked on in confusion. Yet again, she wondered if she was dead or dying. Was this what slipping into the next life felt like?

Voices sounded around her, but they felt far away as if she was listening through a closed window of opaque glass.

"Oh, gods."

"Tell us everything."

"Is she going to be okay?"

Darya. Rhea. Jamie.

She felt something cold pressing against her head.

"We have to get her fever down."

Emelie.

"What about the lashes? She's been butchered for fucks sake. Why is she shivering? Get us more blankets!"

Damien.

Her heart swelled at the sound of his voice.

He was alive. He was safe.

"She's already starting to heal herself, look—" Emelie said.

"H h how is that possible?"

She felt the brush of Damien's hand stroking her cheek. She wanted so badly to lean into him, to let him hold her.

"Because not only does the blood the Aylaenor flow through her veins, but the Regals as well."

Fjora.

"What?"

"This is not the time to discuss this, Damien."

There was a pause, and then a pair of tender lips brushed against her head.

"I love you, Bug," he whispered. "Don't go to the trees just yet. Please."

She had no plans to go to the trees, but they stood in the distance, perhaps as a reminder of how close she in fact was.

"You need to get that bite looked at," Emelie said sternly.

"I'm not going anywhere."

"At least give her some space to work," Fjora implored.

Another brush against her skin.

"Darlings, come with me."

"We don't want to leave her, Mama," Darya said.

A hand slid within hers, holding on tightly.

"There's something I need to tell you. You can come right back."

Jen's chest tightened. "No, please," she tried to call out.

She ran through the pasture towards Fjora's voice, but it lived in the endless sky above her, just out of reach. The voices dissolved into the melodious song of the Nimean countryside.

Jen's hand fell against the grasses as she wandered towards the cottage. Maybe being trapped here wasn't such an awful thing. She didn't feel any pain, her lungs were full of fresh air, and she wasn't endangering anyone with her existence. It felt easy, light even.

Her long hair blew in the calming breeze as she came to the dirt road. She smiled faintly at her mother's cottage, her home.

"You did what?"

A different voice echoed through the sky as if carried by the wistful clouds that broke up the bountiful blue azure.

"We soul walked, Nel."

Jen turned at the sound of Ronan's awestruck voice.

"You're sure that's what it was?"

Nelysar sounded unnerved by what Ronan was saying.

"I felt her through the mind-bogging. I *saw* her," he said like he couldn't believe it himself. "What else could it have been?"

"In the moments before she killed Bastien, her immortality snapped into place—" Nelysar started to explain.

"But this happened *before* that," Ronan said.

"You are speaking of something that no longer exists, and if that is indeed what is happening, no one can know, Ronan," Nelysar said sternly. "Especially when—"

"I know, I know."

The bitterness of his voice chilled her to the bone.

"If they find out—" a different voice spoke up—a woman, the sound both familiar and unfamiliar at the same time.

"They won't."

Jen's eyes darted around when the conversation went silent. She began to step towards the cottage when Fjora's voice sounded once more.

"Where will you go?"

Ronan sighed before he murmured, "I need to see her."

Nelysar's voice raised with surprise.

"You're going to—"

"Yes. It's barely holding as it is."

Relief resonated in Nelysar's tone as he said, "It'll be good to have you back, Ronan."

He grunted in acknowledgement.

Jen felt a shift in the air, and the hair rose on the back of her neck. Fjora spoke.

"We'll keep her safe."

"He will come for her."

"And we will have plans in place for that. Don't worry, her safety is paramount," Nelysar said. "She is the hope of this world."

"She is much more than that," Ronan said, his voice low.

Jen thought she felt a bit of conflict in his inflection, but he cleared his throat and heavy footsteps faded into the distance. The faint sound of a door closing was the last thing she heard.

She stood at the front gate of the cottage, half expecting Fjora to walk out the door to greet her. But she wouldn't be here, no one was. This soothing environment was of her own making—her mind's attempt to distract her while her broken body mended.

Jen lifted the iron hinge and closed it behind her. She removed her crown of ivy and turned it over in her hands as she made her way to the door. She bent over to smell the flowers that lined the walkway. Her lips parted slightly as she cupped one of the dark-orange blossoms.

Fiorellas.

Fjora.

She had just made the connection that her mother planted flowers of her true name around their home. Fjora never let go of her home—never fully hid who she was, Jen just couldn't see until now.

She smiled and plucked one of the blooms, tucking it behind her ear. She continued to the door, and when she opened it to step inside—

Her eyes blinked open.

It took her a moment to realize where she was—no longer in the meadow but laying in her bed in Sachandes.

Jen scrunched her face as she gingerly sat up against the feather pillows, the bandages that covered her wounds rubbing against her skin. She lifted one of the bandages on her arm and two lines formed between her brows.

Aside from a long, pink scar, she was all but fully healed, her body only slightly tender when she moved.

How is that possible?

Her ears perked up as faint snores grabbed her attention. Damien sat slumped over in a chair beside her, his head collapsed in his open palm. She looked to her other side and found Emelie in a similar position, a small pillow cushioning her head against the chair. Across the room, the silhouettes of William and Leeyna appeared in the armchairs by the hearth, also fast asleep.

The first light of dawn spilled onto the veranda, the sky a fading ombre of midnight and deep navy, dusted with stars retreating before the promise of morning.

She very carefully pulled her legs from under the dozens of blankets Damien no doubt buried her under, feeling every soft fiber as she moved. She sat on the edge of the bed, staring at him for a moment—his beautiful thick eyebrows, his messy raven hair. Her hand instinctively reached for him, but she paused.

I shouldn't wake him…he deserves to sleep.

Jen stood slowly so as to not wake anyone, wanting to stay in her peaceful pasture just a bit longer. She walked towards the middle of the room, and her feet became acutely aware of how cold the floors were.

Her chest tightened at the new rug where Shyra's body once lay, and although there was no trace of it—Jen's nostrils flared as a faint, copper odor rose from the thin line of grout between the marble slabs.

She pulled her gaze away, and two lines appeared between her brows when she caught sight of something on the table by the veranda. She padded over, her nightgown brushing the marble floor.

A small bit of parchment accompanied by a velvet pouch sat inconspicuously on the edge of the table.

Jen reached for the pouch, but then her head jerked up.

The hum.

One by one the melodious sounds joined one another until a chorus of harmony filled her ears. And something else beckoned along with it, a calming presence curling its invisible finger in a silent request.

Jen smiled.

She quietly retrieved a small blanket from her closet, grabbed the parchment and the pouch, and slipped out the bedroom door.

She walked through the empty hallways, across the grand hall, her steps the only sound in an otherwise silent palace.

Jen entered the stairwell and climbed up the steps.

Up.

Up.

Up.

Until she came out onto the rooftop training ring, just as the sun peeked out over the horizon. The majestic Etherian landscape stretched out before her, the colors seemed more vibrant than usual as the sunrise doused the earth in stunning shades of burnt orange and magenta.

Jen opened the parchment.

Fury,

I found something of yours. Try not to lose it this time.

-R

She opened the pouch, and something cold fell into her hand.

She blinked.

Her stone, attached to a cord of leather by delicate threads of silver.

Jen's eyes burned as she gazed at it gratefully, and when she looked up, she found her sight fixed upon a small black dot in the awakening valley.

He looked up at her, and she down at him.

The pendant warmed in her hand, pulling her gaze down to it. She felt something along the smooth surface of the stone—

Tap. Tap.

Like someone was gently knocking from the inside, reminiscent of a faint heartbeat. Her eyes shifted back to him—a grin forming on her lips. Her finger ran over the stone, and she sent her own message in return.

Tap. Tap.

Ronan turned Bear towards the horizon, and Jen breathed through the unexpected twinge in her chest as he galloped into the distance, disappearing into the hills.

She pulled her blanket tight as her nightgown billowed in the morning breeze. She looked out past the valley towards the realms of the continent that spoke to her very depths.

Etheria was no longer the legend.

She was.

The fates had sung their song and woven her destiny into a melody only she can hear, an iejja whose well of power was unknown, and the fruition of a prophecy that held the fate of a nation over her head.

She was the last of an ancient bloodline, and although the light of the Aylaenor lived within her, she was more than aware of the other half of her lineage—it pulled at her bones, haunted the corners of her mind.

It was only a matter of time before Heltior found out about her, and when he did, he would come for her, and darkness would follow in a cataclysmic wave of never-ending night.

Bastien was right—this was only the beginning.

War was coming, and she stood at its center, holding the scale.

I am Jenevieve of Nimea.

Jenevieve of Etheria.

The Oshara.

Something caught her eye.

She slowly raised her hand in front of her face.

Jen held her breath as a small serpent of dark shadow slithered between her fingers.

That's new.

EPILOGUE

The salyaat flew over the northern border of the Lutteala Valley, its tattered wings barely keeping itself and its rider in the air. They soared through the mist and the endless array of wards and defensive barriers that guarded the ominous peninsula.

Vondur loomed below them, a land forever shrouded in malignant darkness, dotted with settlements of vile creatures.

The kashyak landed his beast at the foot of a formidable cave, hew within the side of a great, black-stone mountain. It dismounted and limped up the steep, carved stairs into the mouth of the cave towards a set of stone doors, where two dhokshas stood guard in black armor.

The doors creaked open, and it dragged itself through the cavern's center, flanked by towers of dark slate studded with opals that pulsed with streaks of teal, casting eerie shadows across the gleaming walls.

It moved nervously over the narrow walkway that floated over an abyss—where the sounds of horrifying creatures echoed from below. The broken creature fell to its knees at the foot of the massive black marble dais. It bowed its head low and presented something in its gray scaled hands.

The tiishara.

A pair of menacing footsteps scuffed down the cascading stairs and retrieved the dagger from the trembling creature.

"You have done well, my friend," his low voice rumbled.

The kashyak peered up, "Th—thank you… click…click…click…thank you my lord."

"Our master will be most pleased." He flipped the dagger over, his tattoos peeking out under his black tunic. "But you will not live to see his pleasure."

The kashyak screamed out in terror. "PLEASE—" The knight shoved the dagger into the creature's heart. A menacing laugh echoed around the cavern as the kashyak slid slowly off the blade, blood pouring from its body into a stream of wicked death.

The Knight looked at the dead kashyak with mild disdain before making his way back up the stairs. He wiped off the blade and presented the hilt to the owner of the chilling laugh.

Upon the throne of carved black stone, adorned with an iron crown of jagged vines and arched tridents.

The man who sired the bloodline.

The monster who destroyed it.

Heltior.

He held the tiishara in his long fingers, his thumb running callously over the lily. His wicked eyes, ripples of green and brown merging together in a striking hazel hue, held within them a ring of scorched earth as he lifted his brow to his comrade.

A twisted smile consumed his harsh features as his knuckles turned white against the hilt. He stared back towards the open doors.

"Find her."

ACKNOWLEDGMENTS

Holy moly. I'm writing the acknowledgements of my debut novel, and you're *reading* them. You're definitely my favorite kind of weirdo!

This book, this series, was never just about creating a fantasy world and a compelling story. Well, I mean, yes it was, at least in part. This book was conceived to indirectly look at my own reflection. I based the characters on real and complex people in my life and added a touch of magic. I poured my struggles into a world, and gave it a name, Etheria.

This book is for the elder sisters, the big brothers, who spent their lives protecting others, putting everyone in front of themselves, all while not having someone to protect them. It's for my millennials who are floating through life feeling a little lost, and for those who struggle with anxiety and depression. This book, at its core, is a mental health journey. The pages are filled with a soft FMC, trying her best to deal with what's thrown at her, much like each of us.

A year and a half ago, I came home from Asia and immediately went to one of my best friends with the absolutely *insane* idea to write a book. Instead of simply placating me, she returned my enthusiasm in kind, jumping on the crazy train with me along with a list of questions that would result in HUNDREDS of hours of unhinged voice notes. Emily, I love you so much, I can never truly express how much your friendship means to me. I wrote Emelie for you, and I am so freaking blessed to have you. This book truly would not have been written without you. You were my anchor, my reassuring voice, my crazy partner in this. Thank you.

Also, special shout out to Jeremy (Emily's hubby) for answering all my questions (since I still have no idea what I'm doing,) helping me format (because that's the bane of every author's existence,) and for being cool with me taking over your house for a weekend every other month and temporarily stealing your wife.

Neva and Ryan. My rocks, my people. The universe really did me a solid when it brought the two of you to my life. Who would have known that one production of Sweeney Todd would bring me two of my best friends. Thank you for cheering me on, for supporting me. But mostly, thank you for forcing me to expect better. To choose better. To advocate to myself. Because of you, I am brave enough to say, no. I now hold the courage to accept nothing less than what I deserve, and you gave me that. I love you.

Side note—thank you, Neva, for the absolutely unhinged smut I've read this year.

Thank you to Billy, who read my manuscript at LEAST three times, and always approached it with fresh eyes and entertaining commentary. Thank you for being a thoughtful, wonderful friend. You deserve the world, and then some.

And thank you to the rest of my beautiful friends, whether you've traveled the world alongside me, shared the stage with me, attended a holiday party, sang in a chorus with me, concussed yourself at band camp with me, or just shared any moment of life with me—I hold each of those memories close to my heart.

Next, thank you to my mom. I wanted the chance to give you an epic story, for you to see yourself as those around you always have—an incredibly resilient, bad ass woman who sacrificed everything for her family. You are loved, and you are cherished, and your story is just beginning.

Thank you to my siblings; Rachel, Danielle, and Jimmy. I love you weirdos so much, we really are just a motley crew of humans, aren't we? I am so incredibly proud of the people you grew up to be, the beautiful, radiant souls that you each hold within you. You are each kind, decent people, and that is such a rarity in this world.

Thank you to Dana, my INCREDIBLE editor. You saw the vision I had for this book, and your input and suggestions coaxed it into something I am truly proud of. This story would literally not look the same had you not graced me with your skill, and your incredible feedback. I can't wait for the next adventure with book two!

Thank you to Sarah, my STUPID talented artist who hand drew my cover. Like. That's insane. You are also just the sweetest human, and I am so excited to continue our collaboration. You're definitely stuck with me.

Thank you to my ARC readers! You took a chance on a debut writer, and I am so grateful for every single one of you!

And finally, I would like to thank YOU. Whoever you are. My book is in your hands. You invested the time it took to read it—you invested in *me*. It is such a wild thought, to think that you are sitting somewhere, reading words that I strung together, about a world that I made up in my head. How crazy is that? The world really is so big and so small, all at once.

I hope you found a moment to laugh, to tear up, to connect. My true wish is that I created characters that you would want to hang out with. I wanted them to be messy, complex, and for the time you existed alongside them, real.

This is only the beginning, friends.

And as a dear friend once told me:

"The journey is the destination."

Read on for a sneak peek of the next
book from
The Chronicles of Etheria
series:

A

*Dance of
Fate & Flames*

Jen rushed up beside Samara—and her heart dropped to the floor.

"Holy fuck."

Over a thousand Vondurian soldiers stood just outside the palace walls, all wearing the same dark armor. A row of massive, wooden catapults lined the field behind them, flinging huge, flaming boulders at the mountainside.

They're here for me.

Her face drained of color.

Is he here? Did he come for me himself?

She snapped herself out of her doom spiral and stepped forward, clutching onto the golden railing.

"What in hells is going on?" she yelled.

Samara shot an arrow into the sea of dark steel.

"An army of obari," she seethed, knocking another arrow. An odd flush of relief swirled through Jen's veins.

Heltior isn't here.

"How did—"

"They used the fucking new moon as cover and veiled themselves in shadow," Samara fumed.

"Where's Nelysar?" Jen asked quickly, scanning the hall for long auburn hair.

"Called away to the Inbetween."

"Where's the king? Fjora?" Again, Jen searched the hall.

Samara pointed the end of her bow into the valley below. There, in the middle of the battle, a shimmer of ashen hair and the flash of a massive broadsword. Fjora and her father fought alongside their soldiers in a clash of gold and onyx steel.

Jen whipped around at the guttural scream of a soldier in the clutches of a dhoksha.

"No! NO!" the soldier screamed, but the creature held the man's golden gorget until blue veins climbed up the soldier's neck and his eyes turned black. He yanked off his helmet and ripped away from the dhoksha, sprinting towards the railing.

"Wait!" Jen lunged for him, but he flung himself over the edge and plummeted to the ground with a high-pitched scream and a sickening crunch against the mountainside.

"Now you know why we don't fuck with dhokshas," Samara yelled as she shot two more arrows.

Tap. Tap.

Jen snapped her head towards the sky just as three enormous fireballs hurtled towards them

BOOM. BOOM. BOOM.

Samara and Jen slammed to the floor as they crashed through the hall, blasting a hole though the palace and destroying the railing around the veranda. The great hall erupted into a sea of flames.

Jen groaned as she fumbled to her feet.

"Fucking catapults," Samara grumbled as she jumped up and looked back at the wreckage. Her eyes darted to Jen. "You want to handle that?"

Innocent courtiers screamed as the fire spilled across the floors and up the walls, threatening to burn anyone in its wake.

Jen's lips parted. "I don't know—"

Samara grabbed her arm. "Then fucking figure it out!"

Jen bounded towards the onslaught just as William tore out of the training ring with an axe in hand. He looked around frantically until he found her and ran towards her.

She jabbed a finger towards Samara.

"Stay with Samara and protect my family," she ordered.

She didn't wait for a reply and leapt into the fray.

*Okay, collect the flames…absorb them? Fuck. No pressure, Jen. Not like this is a life-or-*death *situation or anything.*

She had never tried to absorb fire; it had only ever manifested in a fit of rage. Jen surveyed the room, and breathed deeply, focusing on the pull of the earth, the sensation of twisting and shaping a vine.

Like trapping Bastien against a stone throne.

She closed her eyes. The rage was still there, pecking under her skin, but she exhaled slowly, willing it to a manageable level. She reached her arms out and turned her elbows inward, curling her fingers as if conducting a musical interlude of scorching melodies.

Sweat dripped down her face as Jen coaxed the flames towards her, molding them into fiery ribbons that flowed through the air and danced away from the terrified people cowering against the walls. The wind picked up around her and blew through her hair, wrapping itself around the ribbons of flame. Together, air and fire melded together, forming a sphere of hellish heat.

She sucked in a breath as the flames wrapped around her arms, but she remained focused on containing the ball of fire, pulling her open palms towards her heart and compelling her magic to control it.

Her hands trembled as she struggled to turn towards Samara.

"Where in *hells* do you want me to put it?" Jen bellowed over the roaring flames.

Samara looked around and threw her hands up in a way that said *I don't know I didn't think it would work.*

An angry cry snapped Jen's attention to the other side of the room where Damien was fighting a dhoksha away from Lyla and Margo. He parried and struck with his sword, but the dhoksha smashed him against the wall.

"DAMIEN!" Jen screamed. His gaze collided with hers just as a piercing screech ripped through her ears. Her head jerked towards the giant opening that used to be the veranda and saw, to her horror, the winged, reptilian beasts that had taken her to the fortress.

Three salyats and their riders soared towards them.

"Jen!" Samara yelled, her finger pointing up at them. "Put it THERE!"

Jen groaned as she used every muscle in her body to turn the fiery sphere towards the salyats. She cried out and flung her hands forward, releasing the fire into the sky.

It crashed into one of the vile creatures, and its sharp outcry scraped down the length of Jen's spine as its onyx wings burst into flames and bashed into the other two, lighting up the night sky and plummeting towards the ground.

A howl broke through the chaos. William stopped dead in his tracks and ran to the jutting cliff where the railing once stood. Jen darted over and came to Samara's side.

The ground beneath the field below trembled and swayed like an ocean wave trapped within earth, knocking both sides of the battle off their feet.

"It's the Order!" a young, blonde courtier yelled from one of the mangled marble columns.

Jen looked out towards Sayllana, where hundreds of wielders appeared over the hills, hollering war cries as they slammed into the left flank of the obari ranks. The wind blew wildly with the air-wielders and the ground morphed and formed with the power of the earth-wielders. Gaiana and Rieshi plowed towards the catapults with the water-wielders.

The call of Zethyna rang out into the valley and a sea of ivory armor rippled out of thin air. Naezara smashed her forces into the right flank in a pincer move with the Order.

"The Warriors!" Margo cried from another destroyed column.

Another howl—and another. A moment later, a pack of wolves came running in from the northern hillside.

Selene led the charge, but she wasn't alone.

William gasped at the flash of crimson curls in a sea of darkness.

Leeyna was mounted atop of her bond, riding her into battle. The wolves snarled and snapped their razor-sharp teeth as they joined the fray alongside the wielders and the Warriors.

The fighting surged in the great hall behind them; the sounds of clattering swords and breaking bones clashed with the horns and howls of the battle raging beyond the palace walls.

"JEN!"

She turned around as Emelie came barreling into the hall with the palace healers. She quickly took in the carnage, shock registering on her face for a moment, but she dropped to the first injured person she saw; a young girl with a long laceration on her arm.

Relief flooded through Jen, but she remembered her siblings were still in the corner behind William. She ran over and peered around the partially shattered planters.

"Everyone still alive?"

They nodded and huddled closer together, watching her warily.

Jen snorted. "Great, stay here."

A horrified scream yanked Jen's attention to the other side of the room. A dagger was protruding from a red-haired courtier's chest. He looked down in shock before his head lolled and he collapsed to the ground. Dead.

What the—

The imprisoned assassins ascended from the dungeons and poured into the great hall as a violent wave, joined by another band of dhokshas at their backs. The palace guards hesitated, fear betraying their schooled expressions, for now they found themselves battling not only dhokshas, but highly trained killers.

Jen's heart rammed against her chest, and it stopped altogether at the sound of Emelie's scream. The assassin who had attacked her on the rooftop had Emelie trapped against him, her hair tangled in his aubergine fingers.

Jen snarled and jumped into the center of the hall, summoning flames with a snap of her wrists. Fire licked the palms of her hands, but the assassin pushed a dagger to Emelie's throat.

"Let her go," Jen's voice pierced through the roar of bloodshed around her. Magic pecked under her skin with a violent need to be unleashed.

Tap. Tap.

The assassin flipped his long, black hair over his shoulder and pressed the dagger down. Emelie whimpered as a thin line of blood ran down her neck. Jen's flames flickered wildly against her skin.

"You came to kill *me*," she seethed.

His cruel chuckle rasped into Emelie's ear. Jen glared with blazing rings of scorched earth in her eyes. Her rage was building in her bones—the pecking beneath her skin was becoming almost unbearable.

"So do it," she dared.

Tap. Tap.

Damien and her siblings shot forward.

"Jen, no!" "Jen!" "No!" "Jen!"

The flames flashed at their objections.

This is my fault. Anyone killed or hurt tonight, their blood is on my hands.

"DO. IT," she yelled. "KILL ME." The fire blazed up her arms—

A wave of thick smoke crashed over the ruined veranda and engulfed the hall, leaving everyone blind. It billowed across the valley and through the raging battle, disorienting everything in its path.

Not smoke.

Storm clouds.

The assassins surged further into the hall, attacking with a deranged violence Jen could only hear through the ominous shroud.

She stumbled forward, her flames dulled by the thick clouds.

"Emelie!" she choked, muffled cries and shattering steel sounded both too close and too far.

Her breathing grew shallow.

"RHEA? DARYA? JAMIE?" she screamed, her voice growing hoarse and fear fanning the flames that traveled up her arms. She had to find them. If anything happened to them—her rage returned, and her vision filled with black splotches.

A figure sprinted towards her from the smog. She lifted her arms to strike when Damien's wide blue eyes stopped a foot away.

"Bug—"

Oh gods, he looks—afraid.

But she couldn't snap a lid on it, it was consuming her. Sadness. Anxiety. Guilt. Rage. It all personified over the skin of her arms and flooded through her veins. Damien's gaze softened for a moment, and he reached for her.

The flame flickered at him.

He winced, yanking his hand back. The flames snuffed out immediately as Jen's eyes filled with horror. "I'm sorry," her voice cracked. "I'm so sorry—"

Damien grabbed her hand, his eyes swimming with an unreadable emotion. A crack of thunder sounded behind her. He looked over her shoulder and his eyes went wide before he said, "Take her."

Jen blanched.

"Take me—" she started to look over her shoulder, but Damien grabbed her chin. He kissed her hard, and when he pulled away, tears rimmed his eyes.

"You have to go, Jen," he said.

Panic seized in her chest. "Go where?"

"Where you'll be safe."

Realization dawned on her and she shook her head wildly.

"No!"

"Please, Jen. They're here for *you,*" he kissed her again, deeper, trying to say all the things he couldn't bring himself to. "I can't let anything happen to you," he implored. "I need you to live."

Two hands grabbed her shoulders. Jen fought against them and latched onto Damien's shirt. "Come with me," she begged.

He clutched her hand and glanced back at the onslaught within the fog. "I can't, Bug. I'm needed here."

"*I* need you—"

He cut her off with one last, searing kiss.

"I love you, so much," he breathed against her lips. "I'm sorry."

He pushed her back into the strong chest behind her.

"NO—" she screamed but her voice was lost as Damien's heartbroken eyes faded from view and the world fell out from under her. Thousands of tiny shocks pricked her limbs and her vision filled with dark storm clouds until she collapsed on her hands and knees.

Her ears rang from the sudden silence that surrounded her. She looked down and realized she was touching grass—grass on a hilltop somewhere. The moonless sky held magnificent stars that shone brightly above her, but all Jen felt was desolate despair as she screamed into the silence sky.

She tried to take deep, slow breathes. She needed to get a grip.

Where am I? How far is Sachandes?

She reached for the stone around her neck.

Tap. Tap.

A throat cleared behind her.

Jen spun back on her elbows, and something between a gasp and a groan crawled from her throat.

Fuck.

He held his own obsidian stone in his fingers, his verdant eyes dancing with amusement as a smirk played along his lips.

"Hey, Fury."

ABOUT THE AUTHOR

Jillian A Wiley is a DMV based author, who strives to create epic stories that encompass messy, complex characters, legends and lore that scratch that fantasy itch, and swoon-worthy romance with plenty of yearning and a bit of spice. When she isn't residing in the world she made up in her head, Jill spends her time teaching music to tiny humans, screaming high notes on stage, traveling the world extensively, gardening, riding horses, and drinking wine while binging LOTR or Harry Potter.

Instagram: @jillybeansings97

TikTok: @jillianalisewiley